THE PARABLE OF THE
IRONMAN

TRANSFORMING YOUR WEAK SPOT TO YOUR SWEET SPOT

a novel by
ROBERT LEATHERWOOD

The Great With God Series

The Parable of the Ironman: Transforming Your Weak Spot to Your Sweet Spot
by Robert Leatherwood

Published by Great with God Ministries
14903 Knotty Pine Place, Tampa, Florida 33625
Copyright © 2018 Robert Leatherwood

Printed in the United States of America. First printing, December 2018.

Visit the author's Website at www.GreatWithGod.com if you are looking to save money and purchase bulk orders. Box and half box pricing is available.

ISBN: 978-1-7325501-0-0

Many of the Scripture quotations are revised into athletic terms and are not literal word-for-word translations but rather given an athletic context with the purpose of rendering a dynamic equivalent with the Holy Bible. The author encourages all readers to compare and contrast all verses with actual English translations.

The source of inspiration for Bible verses as quoted by characters in the story is often personalized from the (KJV) King James Version.

King James Version of the Bible

Holy Bible, New International Version. Copyright 1973, 1978, 1984, International Bible Society.

Holy Bible, New Living Translation, Copyright 1996, 2004, 2007, 2013, 2015 by Tyndale House Foundation

Interior design and typesetting/Formatting by Jodi Giddings

Cover art by Sammie Wheaton, Tampa, Florida

Interior art by: Felice Applauso, Don Smith, Todd Dunkle, Sammie Wheaton, Gwendy Gayle Delos Santos.

Editing consulting Team: Brad and Linda Miller, Sue Forster, Vernetta Williams

Prosthetic consultant: Don Smith

"I've done a lot of life and a lot of ministry with Robert for more than a decade. His heart for training and equipping mentors is unwavering. He is a practitioner of mentoring and the wisdom that he shares in this creative novel is based on personal life experience. Every great coach has a coach. Everyone would do better with a mentor. Robert simply offers the tools to equip anyone who wants to be a better mentor. Enjoy reading *The Parable of the Ironman*."

—*Tom and Pam Wolf, Founders of Identity and Destiny Ministries*

If you're an athlete, you're going to love this book. If you're not an athlete, there are still tons of great principles you can apply to your life. Enjoy *The Parable of the Ironman*.

—*Bob Sjogren, Founder of Unveiling Glory*

Robert Leatherwood is the real deal. He genuinely walks the talk. He is a model of what it means to be humbly mentored, and provide helpful mentoring. This material will give you a roadmap for how to be transformed, as well as become a vehicle of transformation for others in your sphere of influence.

—*Matthew Hartsfield, Lead Pastor of Bay Hope Church, Tampa, Florida*

INTRODUCTION

I WANT TO offer a little background as to how I came to write this book. First, my goal was to bring hope to all who face impossible situations. My experience training mentors has led me to understand that many people are disillusioned about the goodness of God. Some are even bitter at their Heavenly Father. They simply don't understand the purpose of their pain, revealing a flawed view of the character of God. For me, growing in my understanding of the nature of the Almighty literally changed everything. And then, when he revealed his secret, that it is his sovereign choice to use "thorns" in their various forms to showcase his greater glory, my life completely changed. It's my life's message: the power of God manifests through my weakness. I am certain of this; God is sovereign and works all things together for the good of those who love him and are living in harmony with his purpose for them, even the painful stuff.

There are five books that I have greatly enjoyed over the last few years: Pilgrim's Progress, Dream Giver, The Links of Utopia, The Harbinger, and Lead for God's Sake. These are all novels designed to communicate truth. I read these books. I loved these books. Hundreds of other books have come through my hands over the years, most of which I either never started or never finished. I wanted to be true to my personal learning preference, so it was obvious to me that my best option to reveal the secrets I've learned about transforming your weak spot to your sweet spot was to write just such a novel.

And yet this is not your typical novel. It is modeled intentionally after the literary classic, Pilgrim's Progress, an allegory where the characters embody the qualities suggested by their names. For example, in this story, "Buddy" is indeed "a best friend."

From a purely literary angle, this is a classic coming-of-age story. Man against himself. From a mentoring point of view, I am addressing the question, "What is the process that the Almighty uses to make a good man great?" I believe God designs/allows the following four crises to transform him to greatness: The crisis of understanding the purpose of his pain, the crisis of clarifying his personal (spiritual) identity, the crisis of proving the integrity of his character, and finally, the crisis of unconditional surrender to the lordship of Christ. This story is a colorful illustration of our main character, Ace, going through this very process.

The story has some Hallmark movie tendencies, i.e., a classic love story showcased in the arena of triathlons. So the reader gets to learn a lot about what it takes to train to be an Ironman. And to put things in a proper perspective: you get straight shooting, insightful answers to each of the four crises from mentoring coaches.

Finally, the book was designed to cause the reader to reflect deeply about the lessons learned from each chapter. Therefore, be prepared to stop reading from time to time and reflect. Chapter breaks are used to offer a creative summary of the major points, followed by questions for personal reflection and application.

CONCERNING THE GREAT WITH GOD "COMPANION" POCKET GUIDE

As you read *The Parable of the Ironman*, you will hear this little book, *The Great with God Pocket Guide*, referenced to periodically. It's not just part of the novel, but it is an actual book (and an iPhone app). I recommend reading them one after the other. The pocket guide is a fifty-two-week devotional focusing on how the image of God is reflected in both the commands of Christ and the promises of God. Furthermore, the guide offers several creative prayers based upon models listed in the Scriptures. And complementing the various components are weekly mission assignments, Faith in Action Challenges.

TABLE OF CONTENTS

"THE TEASE"
THE PARABLE OF THE BIG RACE

THE KINGDOM OF HEAVEN is like a coach that went out to recruit athletes to join his team to run a race.

Some who heard the invitation didn't see any value in the opportunity and immediately turned away.

Some immediately said yes, but never showed up for practice.

Some said yes, but after the first three days of practice they quit the team, discovering that it was going to take more effort than they first thought.

Some thought it was a good idea but didn't like the coach nor his prescribed method of training, so they joined another team.

Some prepared for the big race by doing as a little as possible, making small compromises of effort and shortening the training distances, so on race day they discovered they were unable to finish the race.

Some prepared well but had a poor race day strategy. Those who failed to regularly hydrate throughout the race also failed to finish the race.

Some joined the team and began to enjoy the accolades associated with the team, lost sight of winning, and though they finished the race they were among those who were last to cross the finish line.

Some joined the team, but their hearts grew hard toward the coach and they stopped listening to his voice and while they stayed on the team, they began to listening to other trendy philosophies. They, too, were met with limited success.

Some joined the team and felt the only way to win was to add an illegal advantage, and so they secretly began to seek performance-enhancement through doping. Once they were discovered, their awards were stripped and they were kicked off the team.

Some joined the team and followed the coach's prescribed training and won gold, silver, and bronze medals.

Concerning the parable dimension: the story was originally intended to be a simple retelling of Jesus' parable of the sower, found in Matthew 13:1-23, rewritten in the context of a race. However, the parable grew into a novel, but the idea for the reader remains the same: namely to look for and identify the different types of racers with their various philosophies of preparation. Later, as the race progresses, we discover the outcome of their often flawed approaches.

Now you're ready to take the journey with "Ace" to become an Ironman triathlete. So go for it. Dive in and discover, through a colorful cast of mentors, that the Scriptures are rich in the imagery of sports and watch the spiritual athletic metaphor unfold with the turn of every page.

So enjoy *The Parable of the Ironman*, for it is true, the kingdom of heaven is like an athlete who runs a race....

1

THE LOSS OF A DREAM

EVERYTHING WAS GOING according to plan. Ace was quite pleased with himself, evidenced by the smile and scrunched chin, his signature expression when everything was going his way. One glance at Ace revealed a perfect specimen of a military-fit body. His trim, muscular frame was crowned with a thin, handsome face highlighted by deep brown eyes, and distinguished by an exquisitely chiseled chin with a dimple carved neatly in the center.

Ace was the kind of guy who had a plan for everything. His personal motto was, "Failing to plan was planning to fail." He was a man of action, but he liked to thoroughly think things through to their logical conclusion before he committed to anything. So it was that three months ago, after Ace was honorably discharged from the military, he was pursuing what had become a pressing dream: capturing the love of his life.

Tonight, he was certain, would be a pleasant surprise to Mara. Ace had been working on "this little plan" for several weeks now and tonight he would carefully execute the perfect romantic evening.

Now Ace and Mara sat on the terrace of the Rusty Pelican, a casual dining environment where blue jeans were the preferred attire.

This roofless restaurant adorned the top of the highest building on the beach. Designed for dinner, dancing and parties, it was uniquely situated for the execution of the perfect night. He planned the evening to include an ocean-view sunset followed by a full moon rising from the other direction shortly thereafter. Mother Nature did her part—not a cloud in the sky. Dinner was served, then dessert. Everything was going according to schedule. The band had been tipped to play his songs on cue. So it was they began to dance under the stars to an old classic, "Dancing in the Moonlight." The song came to an end; Ace dropped to one knee and as he pulled out a diamond ring, the band began to play "My Girl."

"Yes, a thousand times, yes!" Mara excitedly agreed. She wasn't completely surprised. It was part of "the grand plan:" first settle into civilian life, then marriage, Ace would finish his college degree, become a teacher and a coach, have three kids, and live happily ever after.

After dinner, the two walked the sandy beach until midnight, dreaming about their future together. Then Ace and Mara mounted his Harley Davidson motorcycle and went home to her apartment. He walked her to the door and as he'd done a hundred times before, kissed her good night and returned to his Harley.

Ace lived only fourteen minutes away if he stayed on the main roads, but he could make it in eleven by taking a shortcut through a downtown neighborhood. He was riding casually along, savoring the feelings of contentment and satisfaction that come when everything in life is going your way. Perhaps that's why he wasn't as alert as he otherwise might have been when the sports car blew through the intersection without stopping. It collided with full force into his motorcycle. Ace's head slammed into the pavement, splitting his helmet.

Ace had no memory of the flashing red lights and sirens of the ambulance. He was knocked unconscious and only came to as they were unloading him from the ambulance into the emergency room.

Ace's life had changed forever, measured now by a new timeline: B.C.—Before Collision and A.D.—After Debilitated.

ꙮ

The Fresh Start meeting at Grace Baptist Church was about to begin. Grace was one of the largest churches in town, big enough to offer every kind of program to reach the disadvantaged and the "lost."

Ace despised the idea that he needed this group. These weren't his type of people, and he definitely wasn't one of the broken individuals needing a recovery program. Ace didn't want sympathy, and he didn't need somebody to listen to his sob story.

Agustin Christopher Eastwood, best known by his initials "A.C.E.," was a young, single man who hadn't lived at home for more than fifteen years. Yet, for the last month he had attended these meetings as a favor to his mother, who had insistently pleaded with Ace to just "please give it a try." So he had, but the one-month trial was coming to an end, and he was running thin on patience.

The meeting format was familiar: singing, announcements, a short devotional Bible lesson, and small-group breakout sessions. Small groups were preparing to begin; they offered labels for everyone. All one had to do was pick a type of brokenness and join the appropriate small group.

"Grief Care" was in the classroom at the end of the hall. A core of five to seven regulars were in this group therapy session. Ace sensed this group had bonded together over years of commiseration. This core still seemed to come weekly after years of attendance. Ace was beginning to wonder what was wrong with the program because broken people were supposed to get well and move on with life.

Ace had the impression these people were lost in recovery. He had no intention of making this "Grief Care" group a regular part of his life. If he was broken on the inside (and he wasn't convinced he was) then he would get in, get perspective, get out, and get on with life. Ace's irritation came from the fact that he felt he already was moving on with his life. He had formulated a new plan, recovery had already been maximized and life was coming together well enough.

The meetings were predictable: Felicia Taylor welcomed everybody, making a special effort to recognize first-timers. Tonight, all fifteen seats were occupied. Each stage of grief recovery was posted, and Felicia directed everyone to read the two charts on the back wall. The group read out loud in unison, "Christ came to preach the acceptable year of the Lord, to heal the broken-hearted, to set at liberty those who are bruised, for the recovery of sight to the blind, and that the poor should have the good news preached to them."

Felicia continued, "Now the next chart." The group continued in unison to read the stages for grief recovery from the second chart:

Stage 1: Denial
Stage 2: Anger
Stage 3: Bargaining
Stage 4: Depression
Stage 5: Acceptance

After the introduction, Felicia took control of the meeting. "For those attending for the first time, we take a group therapy approach. I'm not the expert; I'm your guide. I know how and where to steer conversations but, ultimately, whether you get help or not depends on you. We encourage you to get real with where you're at and tell your story. We encourage class members to share what was helpful for them through their time of loss. In a sense, we all coach one another.

"Folks, I'm telling you, it works because it's truth. The apostle Paul writes that we are to comfort one another with the comfort we have received. That's what makes this group different. You have a chance for someone else to really understand you. There's nothing like when somebody else 'gets' your pain, to have someone listen who has walked in your shoes, someone who found a point of breakthrough.

"Most of all, we have found that many people get some measure of breakthrough just by sharing their story. There is often a cathartic healing that takes place when someone simply shares their grief with an understanding person. So, does anybody have a burning desire to talk?"

After a pause, Felicia looked around and said, "How about you, Ace? I believe this is your fourth week, and you haven't said a word. Is there anything you'd like to share?"

Ace had a cocky attitude this night that was obvious in the tone of his voice, "OK! Today is my day. I've been thinking about it all weekend. It's only been four weeks, but I'm already tired of coming to these meetings. I hate to join in the whining, but you encourage transparency," Ace said as he looked Felicia in the eyes for permission to vent.

"It's OK. Let it out. Speak the truth. Tell us how you feel."

Ace released his pent-up emotions. "Let me tell you, I come here each week, not really knowing why. OK, it's obvious: I lost a foot and part of a leg, but that's been well over three years ago. I've already been through all these steps, whether I wanted to or not. So, I get it. Work the steps. Being here is a lot like AA; been there, done that. I drank to cope for a few months, but I'm not an alcoholic. I don't belong there. I don't drink. I don't have a problem with alcohol. So, I lost a leg. Guess what? Insurance gave me a new one." Ace pointed to his leg as he lifted it up in pride "Look at that! I'm the bionic man! I realize there is some credence to these steps, but I feel like I've gone through them. I'm better, I've reached acceptance."

Ace's attitude changed noticeably. His voice sharpened, and his tone had a bit of disgust mixed with sarcasm. "I'm having a hard time with this 'Fresh Start' recovery brand of therapy. Why are some of you people still here? I don't intend to celebrate recovery by telling my sob stories to someone each week. I'm getting the feeling this whole organization is a bunch of whiners: alcoholic whiners, divorced whiners, grief whiners, ad nauseam. Get over it already! It's time to start living life again. I'm not dead yet! You're not dead yet!"

Ace got louder as he continued. "I've given it a lot of thought this past week, so what am I doing here?" Ace paused to emphasize his point: "Oh! And I'm crystal clear on this now," Ace's voice rose in anger and frustration, "I've got to ask the question nobody here seems to want to talk about, but deep down inside everyone is asking: 'WHY?!' So there it is, out on the table. This is supposed to be a Christian place, so answer that for me: Why?! Why me? I mean if God is all-powerful and God is so good, why did He let it happen? I mean me and the world. All the suffering, all the evil, all the injustice. Where is God in all this?"

Chaplain, who was confined to a wheelchair, said, "That's a big question. In fact, that is two questions: 'Why?' And, 'Why me?' There are reasonable answers to both, but there is no way we can even pretend to answer them without knowing your story. Do you mind telling us what happened to you?"

Ace was ready to reply. "Well, Chaplain, I'm not a wounded war veteran like you. Maybe that would have some honor to it. My story is different, although I did spend three years in the service. I did my time and served my country. It turns out living in America is more dangerous than fighting in the Middle East."

Ace was in rare form. "You want to know how it happened? Almost three and half years ago, I was riding my Harley. Mind you, I wasn't acting foolish like some bikers do. I was riding home from a date one night and got plowed into by a guy in his little sports car. We found out later he was texting and driving and didn't see the stop sign!"

Ace was on a roll, his anger building. "Oh, it doesn't stop there. You're probably thinking, 'Wow, he must have had his leg snapped right off, riding his motorcycle and all.' Nooooo! My leg had multiple fractures, but it wasn't beyond repair. They put more titanium screws and plates in my foot, ankle, and femur than you need to hold a roof down for a hurricane. Nobody promised it would ever work the same again. As a matter of fact, they pretty much promised it wouldn't. There was too much nerve damage. It was going to be a heck of a lot of rehab, but it was my leg and I wanted to keep it.

"Fine! Except did I mention the part where the infection set in?! Yeah, just when I was starting to make some serious progress, they decided if I was going to live, they were going to have to amputate." Ace paused; he was pretty much done with his story but the hurt, anger, and sarcasm were still evident. "So there you have it! Sorry to have made you wait four weeks. Now you have my sob story, but I'm not one of you. I don't need to tell my story to feel better, and I don't need your sympathy. I don't need any of this!"

"Just the answer to your question," Chaplain stated.

"Yeah!" Ace's reply betrayed his doubt as he continued, "But I don't think anybody in this circle has the answer to my question, so no, I don't need this group either."

"Hey, man, give us a chance. Now we know what happened to you on the outside, but what I want to know is what it all means to you?" asked Watson.

Ace paused, then answered sharply, "It means it sucks to be me! It means I deal with it! It means what I already said, I keep on living."

"Yeah, that's what I want to ask you. What do you keep living for?" probed Felicia.

"I don't have that figured out yet. I wake up, I breathe, I don't whine! I don't…" Ace lifted his hands upward. He was empty and out of answers, but he finished his thought: "Whatever!"

"So, what dreams did you lose when you lost your leg?" Felicia asked. "You see, when we talk about grieving, it's not just the loss of a limb; it's what that loss means to you. That's often what we have to deal with. So I ask again: What dream died when you lost your leg?"

Ace gave a long pause and sighed before answering, "Nothing! Losing this leg didn't change a thing!"

"Whooooa," exclaimed Watson, who was listening intently, trying to read between the lines. Watson was a burn victim from a house fire that left scarring from his right hand along his arm up to the right side of his face. The incident had left him with no eyelashes or eyebrows on the right side of his face. Watson was a regular part of this group; he felt his mission was to discern the hidden roots of others' hurts.

Sometimes, the others affectionately called him Sherlock, after Sherlock Holmes, whose partner's name was Watson, because he had an uncanny ability to read people. Watson smiled as he challenged Ace. "Man, you hesitated. There's something there. Don't say there's nothing. A dream died inside of you. Now come on, man!"

Ace's face betrayed that he was miffed this guy had discovered the one thing he didn't want to talk about, the one thing he didn't want anybody to ask. "Are you seriously going to make us guess?" Watson continued. "Did you lose a girl? 'Cause I know what that's all about. Mine ain't exactly the most attractive face anymore. Come on, man, tell us what dream died, 'cause there's something there."

Ace stood shaking his head, contemplating the risk. Nobody said anything for what seemed like a long time, so the question hung in the air, suspended in time. Ace was embarrassed by the thought; his was not the dream of a thirty-three-year-old. He had been shamed before when he'd shared his dream because it was viewed as childish.

Dreams are personal and very intimate. Some men will never be able to articulate their dreams while others will never dare to voice them. Ace shook his head and insisted, "Listen, man, there's nothing there. I get where you're going, but you're barking up the wrong tree." Still Watson pressed, "Come on, man, get real with us, get real with yourself, and tell us what you lost. It's the beginning of healing."

Ace felt this man was pleading with him and wouldn't let it go, so he figured he would throw him a bone, misdirect Watson to get him off the trail. So Ace continued. "Yeah, I lost a girl. Shortly after the leg was gone, she was gone. I haven't had a date since. Now, every girl just wants to be friends. Nobody wants to be in love with a freak."

"Hey, man, I know your pain because I feel the same way," Watson commented. "It gets lonely at times. I wish I could tell you it's going to get better, but I know that pain is real. Do you ever think of your loss as a dream crusher?"

Ace responded with a sigh of resignation. "My dream died long before I lost my leg. So that's got nothing to do with it." He said it with an edge of finality; he wanted this conversation to end.

Felicia wasn't ready to let it go just yet, so she asked, "OK, so you feel you've lost your chance for love. I get it; that's real. I think we can all identify with that. But I want to ask another question which sometimes triggers the reality of one's loss: 'Where are you supposed to be right now that you're not?'"

"It's just stupid childhood fantasies, nothing more," Ace replied sarcastically.

"So what did you always want to be when you were a kid?" asked Watson.

Ace felt like the whole group was ganging up on him. These guys had found his weakness and, like a pack of wolves who smelled blood they were going in for the kill. To be honest, Ace was embarrassed to share his childhood dream because it was too classic, predictable, foolish, and naïve. He felt certain he would be laughed at if the others knew how serious he was.

Finally Ace said it. "I wanted to play in the NBA when I was a kid, and it's a dream I never gave up on. That's where I'm supposed to be right now." Ace's words were laced with hurt, and he responded defensively, "But it turns out five-feet-eight-inches isn't tall enough to get anyone's attention no matter how good you are." Ace's disappointment and bitterness were obvious.

His secret was out, yet no one laughed. Ace continued. "I never even made it to the true collegiate level. You may not believe it, but back in the day, I was team captain, elected to the all-state basketball team. I was the leading scorer on the team. I was the point guard who always brought the ball down court. I could drive and draw the foul. I made every free throw my senior year and could light up threes when my game was on. I led my team all the way to the state championship, and we won. I was named the MVP of the game.

"We were seriously good. Two guys from my team were offered NCAA scholarships, but not me, not the MVP, not the captain of the state champs. I know I sound like an egomaniac, but it wasn't just what I thought about myself. I was voted captain by my teammates, and statistics don't lie. I had more points and assists than any other point guard in the state that year.

"A couple of big schools offered me scholarships to their feeder junior colleges, but they weren't waiting for me to get better. They were hoping I'd have a college growth spurt, but I never got any taller. They eventually gave me my chance, a little practice with the dog-meat practice squad. I started to shine, but a big kid swatted a few of my balls away in one practice, and a week later I was gone. The difference is six inches. If I were six-foot-two, I would be playing in the NBA right now.

ODDS OF MAKING IT TO THE NBA

GOAL	ODDS	PLAYERS
NCAA	1 of 3	112TH grade players
NBA	1 of 365	NCAA players
NBA	1 of 3,249	12TH grade players

About 48 out of 155,955 = 3 in 10,000 or 0.03 percent of high school players join NBA each year.[1]

ODDS OF MAKING IT TO THE NFL

- Approximately 1,100,000 high school students play tackle football each year (1,500 are female).

- Approximately 310,465 play at 12TH grade (senior level).

- Only 6,000 of those seniors will get the opportunity to play college football, including both Division 1 and 2.

- 3,500 college players will declare themselves eligible for the NFL draft each year.

- From them, 256 will be drafted each year. Many won't make the final cut.

256 out of 310,465 = 8 out of 10,000 (0.08 percent) high school senior players will get drafted into the NFL each year.[2]

---

1   What Are Your Odds of Making the Pros? <www.norwichcsd.org/Downloads/ProSportsOdds.doc>

2   What Are the Odds of a High School Football Player Reaching the NFL? <tinyurl.com/y7bL76at>

"You wanna talk about the loss of a dream, there you have it. That's the only dream I ever had. That's all I ever wanted to do. Being five-foot-eight brings a harsh reality! I was lost for a few years and then I joined the military. And at the first, I kinda hoped if I were lucky that I might die in battle. Eventually, things got a little better. But then more dreams were shattered with the loss of this leg.

Which brings us to your question," said Chaplain, as if finishing Ace's thought. "If God is so good and all powerful, why does He allow for such injustice, loss and pain? Has it ever occurred to you that God is trying to get your attention to get you to put your trust in Jesus instead of yourself?"

Chaplain meant well, but his response didn't sit well with Ace. In fact, he was insulted by it. The fury in Ace's next words was palpable: "Are you really going to try and put this on my lack of faith? No way! You're not going to tell me about trusting in Jesus like I don't know Him! Listen! I raised my hand when I was twelve, I prayed the prayer, I got saved, I was baptized, and confirmed! Heck, I was the president of the Fellowship of Christian Athletes at my school. God didn't do this to me because of a lack of faith or some great sin in my life! Listen, I did everything right. I never did harm to anybody. I didn't drink, didn't do drugs, I kept my zipper up, honored my parents. What do I get for being good?!"

Ace had had all he could take, so he headed for the door and hollered as he walked out, "Why? If God is good! Why did He make me this way? Why did HE let it happen? That's it. All I want is an intelligent answer to a reasonable question!" The door swung closed behind Ace, and he never looked back.

QUESTIONS FOR SELF-REFLECTION

- What do I think is God's purpose for the pain in my life?
- Have I suffered a major loss? What dream of mine died at that time? Can any good come of it?

- Can I describe a time in my life when I went through the stages of grief?
- Have I ever experienced inner healing after experiencing a major loss. What was it that helped?
- What should a good man expect to receive from God for being good?

2

BIG CITY–BIG RACE

THREE WEEKS AFTER his Grief Care implosion, Ace felt alive. He'd been looking forward to volunteering at the Big Race for several months.

The Big Race was the world's most prestigious triathlon, the ultra-endurance race with iron distances of a 2.4-mile swim, 112-mile bike race and 26.2-mile marathon run. It was three races wrapped into one with seventeen hours to finish. All who did were crowned with the title "Ironman." Anyone who arrived at the finish line after 17:01 was awarded the title "DNF" (did not finish).

Big City was proud to sponsor the Big Race. Many citizens set their calendar by this annual event. Each year the whole town stopped to observe race day. Over the years, the Big Race in Big City came to stand as a beacon of athletic prowess. The contestants were thought of as nobility. Ace dreamed of being part of this distinguished group—simply being at the race gave him a sense of importance.

Ace had attended the Big Race in one way or another since he was a boy. The course was laid out so that the marathon portion had contestants literally run on the street in front of Ace's parents' house.

VARIOUS TRIATHLON DISTANCE RACES

TYPE	SWIM	BIKE	RUN	TOTAL DISTANCE
Sprint	¼-½ mile	12-15 miles	3.1 miles (5K)	15+ miles
Olympic	1 mile (1500M)	24.85 miles (40K)	6.2 miles (10K)	32 miles
Half Ironman	1.2 miles	56 miles	13.1 miles	70.3 miles
Ironman	2.4 miles	112 miles	26.2 miles (marathon)	140.6 miles
Double Ironman	4.8 miles	224 miles	52.4 miles	281.2 miles

Sometimes his family placed a water hose close to the curb with a sprinkler attached at the end, so competitors could catch a splash to cool off from the heat.

Today he was volunteering as part of the pre-race set-up team and overheard conversations about the prep work associated with the different stages of the race: swim, bike, run. The word "stages" stuck in his mind.

Although Ace had left the Grief Care class, the mantra he'd been indoctrinated with still rumbled around in his brain. The thought of stages had been awakened in him. He thought What were they again? Denial, anger, bartering, depression, and acceptance. To Ace, it was just a lot psychobabble.

The idea of stages also described his involvement with the Big Race over the years. First he had been a spectator, next a fan, sometimes a dreamer, but lately a volunteer. Since Ace had stopped feeling sorry for himself, he was beginning to think (for the first time in years) that someday soon he would become a competitor.

When Ace had attended the race as a boy, the thought that he could win the Big Race was planted deep inside his heart. His childhood dream slowly dwindled when he began to pursue his love affair with basketball. After the motorcycle accident, the thought of competing had completely evaporated.

However, last year, Ace witnessed an amputee compete in the Big Race. At that moment, a new seed was planted. Being an athlete was in Ace's blood—he lettered in the big three sports in high school: football, basketball and baseball. He excelled at them all and had what it took to be great: speed, quickness, and a consuming intensity to win.

Life had changed so much for Ace since his glory days in high school. He was the big man on campus then. Fifteen years later, Ace felt like a nobody—his self-esteem destroyed and his confidence shaken. He was crippled. He hated when others treated him differently because he felt the "handicapped" label did not fit him at all. He wouldn't accept it, and it angered him when others pitied him. Since he had been outfitted with an amazing, 21st century, high-tech (bionic) prosthetic, Ace had learned to move very comfortably with almost no limp in his walk. When he wore pants, no one even noticed. And today he was wearing pants.

The Big Race had a large and active set of volunteers. Though not everyone could race, anyone who wanted to help could do so. Hundreds of locals found ways to get involved and support the race. The most committed served on the Vantex, or the advance team. These individuals ran committees and task forces and spent all their time planning the event, from grunt work to administration. From the very moment the race ended, the Vantex members started planning next year's Big City Big Race.

Many of the thousands of Big Race fans dreamed of being in the race, but while race day always provided lots of inspiration to join the nobility, few fans ever committed to the proper training to be in the Big Race. Such was the case with Ace.

Ace spoke about what was bouncing around in his heart to

Buddy Bonanno, his best friend and teammate from his high school basketball days. The two worked side by side, emptying boxes of supplies as they got things situated for the pre-race activities. Ace asked, "Buddy, how about we actually run the Big Race next year, instead of just volunteering and thinking about it?"

Buddy paused, then replied, "I kinda thought we were getting all the exercise we needed by playing basketball on Saturdays. You know basketball is our thing. Besides, I'm a big guy and don't have the right body type. I'm big and thick. You don't see a lot of six foot, seven inch, 250-pound racers around here. On top of that, I'm completely slammed until after the New Year. But you! You go for it!"

Buddy's comments got Ace thinking about the excuses for why he wasn't participating in this year's race. At the end of last year, he had thought maybe next year…certainly next year. Somehow he let the opportunity pass by. Unfortunately, Ace was clearly seeing a pattern: "next year" would never come.

Inspiration to train never lacked the day of the race, but the timing was never quite right. Ace was as busy as anybody, and as the Big Race came two weeks before the holiday season, Ace rationalized the best time to train would be after the holidays.

After the holidays, it was too cold, so it seemed prudent to wait for warmer spring weather. Surely seven months of training would be enough time to get in shape. However, once spring arrived, basketball took up his time. Ace figured basketball was a type of training.

Summer brought a hodgepodge of interruptions: family vacations, visiting friends, spending time with his nieces and nephews. And once fall arrived, Ace's work picked up the pace. His boss was certain that the last quarter would be the "make or break" season for the company. Everyone was expected to work harder to accommodate additional projects to ensure the company stayed in the black. The workload left little time to get ready for the Big Race. By that point, it didn't seem reasonable to begin training for the Big Race with only a few weeks remaining before the event.

Was Ace going to participate in the race next year, or would this become another year on the merry-go-round? Ace wasn't ready to commit. So he let out a deep sigh and thought, *Let's think about this thing a little longer, nothing rash, but rather intelligently count the cost.*

Last year, Ace's V.P. from work, Jake Reed, nicknamed Mr. Reasonable, had invited him to join the Vantex. It was truly a thrill to be a part of the Big Race's working committee and a step in the right direction. This year, Ace invited Buddy to volunteer. At the moment, Ace felt the thrill of the energy in the air. All the preparation for the event, especially the athlete check-in, was an adrenaline rush.

All that day, Ace dreamed about the proposition of racing as he helped set up for tomorrow's pre-race breakfast event. Buddy reminded him of the basketball game they would play once set-up was done. "When we're done, that's when the fun starts. I got a few guys to join us."

Ace and Buddy's volunteer assignment was to set up a tent, chairs, podium, microphone-PA system, tables, screen, projector, etc., and then power it all up and give it a test. Ace finally read the marquee he set in place on the easel revealing what all this preparation was for. The sign read, "FCA: Fellowship of Christian Athletes breakfast." Although Ace was assigned to run the audio-visuals at this event, he began to look forward to being there the next morning.

Both Ace and Buddy were looking forward to their four o'clock date with destiny, a three-on-three pick-up basketball game with a select few other volunteers on the outdoor courts across the way from the Big Race expo. The Big Race was strategically hosted on the campus of Big City University, a great venue with plenty of space. BCU was an amazing campus with a huge beachfront property that made a great starting point for the race, and the stadium nestled close by provided the finish line.

CR

Titan and Shoveele were a little shocked when they saw Ace's mechanical leg in his basketball shorts. Ace sometimes chose to hide it to avoid the awkward response he often received. When it couldn't be avoided, as in sports, he braced himself for the initial reaction and then tried to set everyone at ease with a bit of good-natured trash talk.

Titan was a big man. Shoveele was an Italian who was small compared to Titan, but evenly paired with Ace. "Are you guys ready to get a beat-down from a poor crippled boy?" Ace asked with a cocky attitude. Titan wasn't backing down. "Yeah, we'll see about that." It was going to be a good match-up. Titan was taller than Buddy, but Buddy knew something the others did not: Ace was the best basketball player he'd ever played with or against, even with his mechanical leg. Most of all, Buddy knew Ace possessed an obsession to win and a three-point shot that couldn't be stopped.

The game began with the teams swapping baskets. It didn't take long for Ace to figure out Shoveele's method. Ace began playing defense a little more fiercely by stealing the ball, blocking, and deflecting passes. It was infuriating for Shoveele because Ace was too quick, spare leg and all. Shoveele was getting exasperated. Ace drove toward the basket, maneuvering past Shoveele, who wasn't going to get beat again. He gave a little shove to Ace as he went by to prevent the basket. Ace slid hard into the ground.

Sometimes a basketball player will hit the pavement elegantly. Part of the game is knowing how to fall and roll so as not to absorb the impact. Except this wasn't a moment of grace. It looked awkward, and Ace wasn't getting up quickly, which is a sign a guy is hurt.

The game came to a stop. The guys gathered around Ace like a flock of vultures.

Titan scolded Shoveele. "What are you doing?? Take it easy! Can't you see this guy is a cripple? What were you thinking?" Ace's face contorted, but not from the pain of the fall. Titan's words and the sentiment behind them brought the pain Ace dreaded most. Ace slowly rose from the ground and looked Shoveele right in the eyes. He said sharply and emphatically, "I don't need any special treatment! I play to win, and I expect you to do the same."

Ace's rebuke hit home, especially since Shoveele was guilty of dirty play. Then, so everyone could hear, Ace said loudly, "I come from the military and we had a saying that applies here: 'No mercy! Expect none! Give none!' Don't let up on me, none of you, not even for a minute! You see this leg?" as he pointed at it. "Forget about it. I'm not in any pain. In fact, you should all be glad that it slows me down a millisecond—otherwise, I'd really kick your butts. Buuuuut," Ace drew the word out for emphasis, "that was a foul, so give me the ball at the line, and let's get on with it. I'm fine!"

"Don't Pity me"

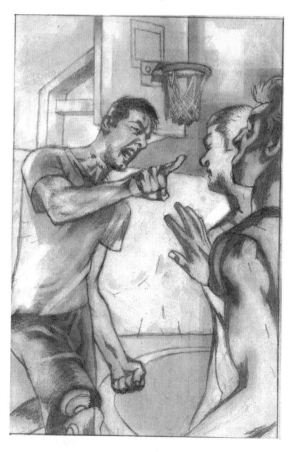

"No mercy! Expect none! Give none!"

The game continued until they ran out of time. The men parted with an agreement to see each other in two days at the race. As they separated, Ace got in the last verbal jab. "Better luck next time, boys!" Buddy sighed as he testified, "You always have to rub it in, don't you?" Ace grinned wryly as he walked to his car.

℘

At home that evening, Ace continued to ponder the possibility of becoming a Big Race competitor. He opened his laptop and decided to blog the journey of his Ironman quest.

Then he thought, *What if I post saying I'm exploring doing the Big Race?* Ace decided to invite his friends to vote: race versus no race. He'd let his friends make suggestions. He would record what he was learning, feeling, what it all meant, and whether it was a good idea or a waste of time.

He blogged:

Hello, world:

I'm considering competing in the Big Race next year. All right, anybody who knows anything about this race knows you don't just sign up and race. You have to qualify for it. So maybe it's better if I say I want to start training and doing triathlons so I can qualify to compete in the Big Race next year. There, I think that is better said publicly.

This year's upcoming race (two days away) has me inspired. I see a natural progression of growth in my life: spectator to fan, fan to volunteer, volunteer to dreamer. Now, it's time to move from dreaming to training. During this time of year, for as long as I can remember, I think to myself, I want to do this race next year. And then in less than a week after the race, I get distracted. So what's the real hold up? Deep down, I believe part of the problem is I'm not certain if it's a worthy pursuit. I'm trying to decide if this race is worth my time. I thought I'd ask my friends for some advice. Please weigh in with your wisdom. List a few reasons (pros and cons) in your reply with things to consider to help me decide. Thanks, Ace.

QUESTIONS FOR SELF-REFLECTION

- What's my plan to move from dreaming into action?
- Can I describe the different stages of growth in my life?

3

BREAKFAST OF CHAMPIONS

ARLY THE NEXT morning Ace was on site making sure everything was set for the pre-race FCA breakfast. His responsibilities were simple: turn the systems on, test everything, play background music while people arrived, adjust sound levels, and advance the slide projection.

These duties were second nature for Ace because of his position as special event operator at Big City Sound and Lights where he'd proved himself over the last fourteen months.

Ace's boss, "Mr. Reasonable," or just plain "Reasonable" to those who knew him well, had recruited Ace to help at the Big Race. Mr. Reasonable was the volunteer coordinator for all the audio-visual needs associated with the Big Race, and he had recommended that Ace be assigned to this breakfast outpost.

As breakfast started, James Champion was called to the podium by Marshall, the race director. "I am proud to introduce all of you to a man who is arguably the greatest endurance athlete of our time. When you think of endurance races, you probably think of a marathon or something like what you will do tomorrow at the Big Race Triathlon.

"Champion has completed a dozen 200-mile runs and is the only man to have ever completed six Double Ironmans before the turn of the millennium. Most of you don't even know such a race existed. To be clear, it is a nonstop race consisting of a 4.8 mile swim, a 224 mile bike ride, followed by a 52.4 mile run. Our speaker, James Champion, the poster child for all Ironmen, finished in just twenty-six hours at the ripe age of sixty. So, I suppose he knows a few things now that he has grown up. Today, he is only ninety-seven years young. Please help me welcome him with a warm round of applause for Champion."

Champion walked to the podium, no limp, no cane, no hunched back. He simply had none of the usual signs of age, other than his thin gray hair. His mind was razor sharp, perhaps even more so now than when he was sixty-five. His raspy voice was the leading indicator of his age. People were drawn to this man by his amazing poise, a true Southern gentleman. He exuded confidence and humility, a man marked by his pursuit of a mission.

"Good morning. I want to start by asking if the Bible has anything to say to athletes?" Champion paused to let the question sink in, then continued. "It seems to me the apostle Paul, who wrote several letters in the New Testament, had a good understanding of the sacrifices athletes often make, for he referred to them often in his writings.

"Let me read the comparison Paul makes in his letter to the Corinthian church. 'Don't you realize that in a race everyone runs, but only one person gets the prize? So run to win! All athletes are disciplined in their training. They do it to win a prize that will fade away, but we do it for

> **It is always worth your time to seek God.**
>
> *There is a reward, a crown that will never perish. He who comes to God must first believe that He is a rewarder of those who diligently seek Him.*

THE SPIRITUAL ATHLETIC METAPHOR

The dynamic equivalent discovered by Christian athletes when comparing any aspect of a sporting experience to the nature of the Kingdom of Heaven. Most commonly comparing the physical rigors of habitual training with the self-discipline, and self denial required for disciples of Christ.

(LUKE 9:23)

an eternal prize. So I run with purpose in every step. I am not just shadowboxing. I discipline my body like an athlete, training it to do what it should. Otherwise, I fear that after preaching to others I myself might be disqualified."

"Paul makes a beautiful analogy. If you will allow me, I would like to encourage you by sharing what I call the principles of the spiritual athletic metaphor. The apostle Paul draws a spiritual metaphor between what happens in the life of an athlete to the spiritual growth of a Christian. I want to suggest this morning that the athlete has a tremendous advantage in understanding the spiritual nature of God simply by being an athlete. The athletic metaphor helps to make the spiritual realities more easily understood.

"Principle number one of the metaphor is it's always worth your time to seek God. The very first point Paul makes is athletes run to win. Why? So they can receive a prize. Athletes are running and training to receive a crown, a wreath that one day will wither and fade.

"Paul makes the connection that we are to sacrificially pursue God with the expectation that we will receive a crown that will **never** perish. It's eternal. The Scriptures say 'Seek first the kingdom of heaven and His right way of living and everything else will be added unto you.' Elsewhere, the Scriptures say that he who comes to God must be convinced that God is a rewarder of those who diligently seek him. Be convinced of this: The pursuit of God is why you were made. It is the only thing worthy of your time."

Ace was warming up to this guy. He'd regularly attended church with his family when he lived at home, then quit attending in junior college. During his time in the military he had attended chapel services, and since returning from the military, Ace went to his hometown congregation from time to time and joined with his parents on holidays and special occasions.

Ace had nothing against church; he just didn't fit in well being 33, single, and handicapped. His church didn't have a singles ministry. People his age were married, and he wasn't a college kid. He felt like a misfit. And then there was the issue he had with God. Ace couldn't help but blame God for losing his leg. *If HE was a good God and all powerful, why did He let it happen?* He believed in God, but needed help with his unbelief. There were so many questions Ace didn't have answers to, but listening to this man speak about the athletic/spiritual metaphor made sense. This was the kind of God talk he could receive.

Champion continued. "The second principle of the metaphor is focusing and setting priorities. Some people think athletes have more dedication than others. This is not true; we all have the same amount of dedication. The only real question is what we are dedicated **to**. Most people are simply spread too thin: they are dedicated a little bit to everything—causing them to be a mile wide and an inch deep, and good for nothing.

"Paul is clear when he says everyone who enters this race is self-controlled in every area of life. A runner focuses his attention on the goal line. He's not running aimlessly. How about you? Are you running through life aimlessly? The true disciple doesn't train his body like a boxer who beats the air. He is dead serious about the training he does. He's bringing his entire body, mind, soul, and spirit into self-discipline. He trains his body to do what he wants it to do. He is not a slave to the passions of his body.

"Many people have asked me how I accomplished so many ultra-endurance races. Here is what I tell them: I don't listen to my myself but rather I talk to myself. I take every thought captive. Discard the bad ones and replace them with good ones. I choose what I allow myself to think about. I memorize Scripture and I choose to rehearse it as I run."

"Stop listening to so many voices. Stop allowing yourself to get over-involved by saying yes to every good idea. Focus inevitably means saying no to a lot of good ideas. The trick to saying no is having a bigger yes. Figure out what will last for eternity and pursue that.

Ace felt convicted because this was the story of his life: He seemed to say yes to a lot of opportunities over the early part of his life, and even now he had a tendency to get over-involved but never focusing on one thing. He prided himself in trying to live a very active, balanced life. Now he was hearing this could be a fault. His athletic prowess and competitive spirit led him to attempt to conquer everything. And he wanted to encourage others in their pursuits, which is why he was here today. He was volunteering mostly because Reasonable said that he could use his help.

Focus and purpose had been lost in Ace's life. Since his amputation, he felt like a ship without a rudder, floating and bouncing through life, always reacting but never driving anywhere with any strong sense of purpose. Ace thought this guy was really challenging him to commit to something. He began to feel really good about feeling really bad about his aimless approach to life of late. Now seemed to be a right time to get a new plan.

Champion continued. "The third principle of the metaphor is get a coach. You cannot do this race by yourself. After talking to hundreds of athletes, I have come to the conclusion that while the Big Race is all about individual accomplishment, it is not accomplished individually. The vast majority of people who will race tomorrow have a training partner to encourage, inspire and hold them accountable. The Christian faith is not meant to be lived alone. God created us for community.

"Every champion, every Olympic champion, every Ironman champion, did not get there by himself, but has a team of coaches who got him there. It's probably safe to say that in this generation there aren't any Olympic champions who don't have at least one coach. Most of them have multiple coaches telling them all the time how to perform, what to eat, read, think, and when to rest.

"Coaches offer insight, experience, encouragement, and accountability. In short, coaches help you go further, faster. They help you reach greater levels of excellence by pushing you to do greater things than you could ever do by yourself.

"When I was a freshman in college, my cross-country coach gave me four binders and said, 'I have a workout plan for you that accounts for every day for the next four years.' Coaches have a plan, a road map filled with little steps to get you from point A to point B.

"Know this: Many would make the case that accountability is the main power of coaching. The statistical research summarized in the chart on this screen documents the incredible value of having a coach. "Coaches help you do what you do not want to do. It is a strange paradox. There are things we want to do, but can't get our act together to get it done. We want to do them, but we don't want to pay the price associated to have them. When you want to change strongly enough, a coach will most likely be the catalyst of change. I love the old proverb that when the student is ready the teacher will appear.

"Jesus once lamented that lost people were like sheep without a shepherd. Sheep need shepherds, and people need mentors. Otherwise, both seem to get lost.

"For me, mentoring's impact on the lives of others was verified by the data from the chart. I must admit the desire to do something great for God is deep inside of me. I want to leave my mark for the kingdom and add value to as many lives as I possibly can. Mentoring is the key, because life change rarely happens from lectures. Life change happens best one-on-one, particularly students with coaches."

Ace listened intently. His eyes were riveted on the chart displayed

STATISTICAL EVIDENCE FOR THE VALUE OF COACHING

STAGE OF INVOLVEMENT	PROBABILITY OF COMPLETION
1. Hear idea	10%
2. Consciously decide to adopt idea	25%
3. Decide when to act on idea	40%
4. Design a plan to act on idea	50%
5. Commit to another person to implement the idea	65%
6. Have a specific accountability appointment with another person related to implementing a plan	95%[3]

on the screen. The message was simple: to do the impossible, to do the thing you can't do on your own, recruit the help of a coach. Ace was absolutely inspired.

Champion brought his talk to a close with these words: "You'll need a coach to reach your athletic potential, and you'll need a mentor to reach your spiritual capacity.

"Today, I wanted to make it easy for you to respond—no excuses. So I invited a team of the best coaches I know in the area. If you are one of the life coach trainers that I invited here, please stand." Everyone took notice as twelve people stood. "Since this is the Fellowship of Christian Athletes' breakfast, these coaches also understand the spiritual metaphor of the race. They will help you grow in your athletic ability and your faith.

"So I close with this: If you're interested in life change, I encourage you to find one of these coaches, shake their hand and begin the journey to life change. Or perhaps you'll pursue a mentor already

---

3   AACC/ICCA data published through Light University, 2012. Credit to Professional Life Coaching, Light University Online.

present in your sphere of influence. Whatever you do, don't be passive about this. Don't spend your lifetime waiting for someone to come mentor you. Take responsibility for recruiting mentors into your life. Go and get one! Listen, if you want to succeed in sports you'll need a coach to reach your highest potential. If you want to be great for God, you're going to need a spiritual mentor, someone skilled who can assist you to first become great with God. Folks, that's it. That's the metaphor of the coach. Thank you for your attention. And God bless you!"

The place exploded with a standing ovation. Champion pointed to the sky. For Ace, the opportunity had just presented itself. There was a coach positioned at the table in front of Ace's operation station close to the back of the tent. He looked to be an average-framed man in his mid-sixties with dark hair blended with a few gray strands. Ace had taken notice of him earlier when the man had taken his seat. To Ace, he looked like a healthy human being with a weathered face and personable smile. What amazing poise. He looked like a man's man, yet there was a gentleness about him. Ace touched him on the shoulder to get his attention, and after he turned, shook his hand firmly. They looked at each other intently, a deep look as into the soul. This coach had piercing blue eyes, and there was a depth evident in him, a hint of some intangible virtue. The two felt an instant connection. Ace introduced himself and the man replied, "Nice to meet you. I'm Doc Mentor."

Ace simply asked, "I could use a coach. Do you think you can work with me?" The two exchanged business cards and scheduled a follow-up consultation. Ace could sense that his life was about to change.

The next night, after the race was over, Ace wrote in his blog.

Hey, friends! I'd appreciate your input. I'm still considering chasing after this race. A lot has happened since I last wrote. For one, the Big Race happened. I met an amputee who, to me, is a trailblazer. He is similar to me, but he has two prosthetic legs. He inspires me. I know if he can do it, then I can do it.

Second, I heard the most amazing man, Champion, give an inspirational speech the day before the Big Race. I'll share with you the wisdom I learned from him below. But suffice it to say, he was persuasive in recruiting racers.

Next, Thank you to my friends for weighing in. Many are advising me to use extreme caution, to count the true cost before committing. I want to say thanks to all of you for your comments. Keep praying for me and keep writing in with your ideas.

I've decided to include the lessons I'm learning along my journey. I call these lessons **Wisbits:** *Little bits of wisdom, bullet points of truth. So here's what I have for you today—these are mostly my notes from listening to Champion. But enjoy the bullet point recap.*

Wisbit tip: *There is a spiritual athletic metaphor found when athletic competition is compared to the kingdom of heaven. Growing with God is a lot like what an athlete experiences.*

Wisbit tip: *Pursuing God is worth my time. It's why I was created. God rewards those who seek Him first.*

Wisbit tip: *Focus and set priorities! This means saying "No" to the good things in life to obtain the best.*

Wisbit tip: *Statistics show that coaches often make the difference between success and failure.*

Wisbit tip: *Coaches help you go further, faster.*

QUESTIONS FOR SELF-REFLECTION

- Do I have a mentor? Try to describe what that relationship looks like.
- What do I admire most about my mentor?
- Who am I mentoring? Am I intentional or passive in this pursuit?
- Am I willing and ready to accept responsibility to do whatever it takes to get a mentor?

4

GET REASONABLE

WHEN ACE ARRIVED at the office the day after Sunday's Big Race, he couldn't wait to tell his friend and boss, Reasonable, what he was considering and how excited he was about Champion's speech. He was certain his friend would be encouraged by this pursuit. After all, Reasonable helped plant the seed by recruiting him to volunteer for the Big Race.

To Ace's surprise, Reasonable was a little reluctant to endorse his new adventure. Reasonable had seen Ace's blog posts over the last few days but thought Ace's enthusiasm needed tempering. Reasonable warned him that people who attempted such things were often left disillusioned, unfulfilled, and unrewarded. He also cautioned that the race wouldn't change anything significant in Ace's life. In fact, Reasonable concluded, it had the potential to do harm. Many who had tried this route ended up changing every part of their lives. And for what? A few went to elite status, but the average person went through the phase and returned to normal.

Reasonable tried to give Ace a dose of reality by explaining that some people lost everything trying to be something they were not. He strongly argued the race was a waste of precious time. He explained, "The race promises much, but delivers little. When it's all over, what do you get? One day of glory and a medal. Not much of a trade for all the training. I'm just trying to say it's a lot of time spent training that would be better invested elsewhere. Don't get your hopes up. Don't get too invested. Your life is safe here."

Ace thought it unbelievable that his friend, who had recruited him to volunteer for this very race, would question his desire to participate and try to dissuade him. Ace thought maybe he offended Reasonable by not including him in the adventure, so he extended the invitation. "Hey, listen. Let's do this together. You up for it? Come on, if a cripple can do it, you can do it!" Reasonable declined. "Thanks, but I don't have time for that. You just make sure it doesn't take over your life."

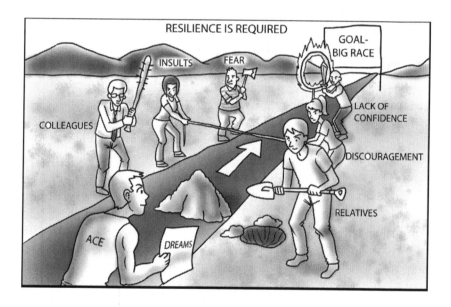

Ace began processing Reasonable's arguments. *Could it be Reasonable was discouraging him intentionally because he believed it was impossible for someone in Ace's condition to endure such a race? If that was the case, it was a form of pity.* Ace couldn't stand that thought, but maybe that wasn't it at all. Maybe Reasonable really thought it was a waste of time. The encounter left Ace realizing he would have to investigate more before he committed to it.

Now more than ever, Ace looked forward to Thursday morning's appointment with Doc Mentor. Perhaps he could help Ace find some perspective. It was all Ace could think about for the next few days.

ത

Doc Mentor was not an athletic trainer by trade. He was an eye surgeon, a cataract removal specialist. His reputation was the eye doctor who specialized in bringing spiritual sight. He spent a lifetime investing his talent, and treasure doing all he could to bring healing to troubled eyes, a real man of faith, a philanthropist for the kingdom of God. As much as he removed cataracts, Doc aimed even harder to remove the clouds of hurt, doubt, and disillusionment from troubled souls.

As Ace entered the lobby of the St. Luke's Eye Clinic, a bronze statue of Christ washing the disciples' feet captured his attention. The message engraved at the base read, "I came to serve, not be served." Behind the desk were a few friendly assistants. Ace was asked to take a seat in the waiting room with the patients until he was called. As he walked toward a lounge chair, Ace was amazed at what he saw: giant pictures of Christ healing the blind lined the walls of the foyer and client waiting room. Evidently, Doc was unashamed to let anyone know where he stood with God.

In many ways, Doc Mentor epitomized the Ironman triathlete. The statistics proved that those who participated and finished this event were mostly entrepreneurial types, business owners, and high-powered executives. Doc Mentor was all that and, as Champion put it, he was in touch with the spiritual athletic metaphor, making him unique among triathletes.

Ace felt overwhelmed by his own sense of insignificance. It was clear this man was important, professional, knowledgeable, educated, busy, productive, and filled with business savvy. Ace didn't feel he had any of those qualities. In fact, he was intimidated, because the only thing Ace had ever excelled at was sports, which didn't count for much in the real business world. Since he'd lost his leg, he felt less than adequate. Feelings of incompetence were there deep beneath his confident demeanor.

When Ace had met Doc on Saturday at the pre-race breakfast, he had been friendly, approachable. Today, in Doc's professional environment, Ace felt intimidated and almost embarrassed. Why should he interrupt this medical doctor from his serious work schedule? Ace didn't even know what he was going to say when they met. Ace wandered around the lobby, looking at everything and occupying himself trying to get calm for his turn.

Ace's name was finally called and he was led to a patient room to wait for Doc Mentor. He didn't wait long. Doc appeared at the door with the same smile, weathered face, and disarming demeanor he'd had Saturday as he said, "Ace, I'm so glad you made it over here today. Hey, did you stay for the finish of the race on Sunday?"

"I was volunteering the first twelve hours. Eventually I was part of the finish line crew. My assignment was to make sure the sound system worked, and then I assisted the finish line DJ. That's also my real job. It's what I do for Big City Sound and Lighting. I'm an audio visual technician."

"Well, then you must have seen the finish. What you don't know is that Brian Fieri is one of the young men I've trained and discipled. I got him started with triathlons years ago. Anyway," Doc brought his hands up as if to stop that rabbit trail and head another direction. He often got animated when he was excited about his subject. Talking with his hands was one of Doc's traits. He liked to use them to help express his thoughts. Now he continued. "It's quite rare for this distance race to be decided by a sprint in the last sixty yards.

"Chet Wildman was just too quick at the end. That's how he earned the name Cheetah. I hated to see Fieri lose, especially after such an exceptional run. You know, Fieri started his run twenty-six minutes behind Cheetah, which means he had to run every mile one minute faster than Cheetah. That's a lot to ask of any man. I thought for certain he was going to get by him. But they say Cheetah is the fastest sprinter in the competition; he runs a 4.5 forty-yard dash. He's a tough competitor who can sprint and go the distance. Fieri lost this race on the bike. Anyway, what a finish!" Doc got carried away telling the story and was now lifting his hands up above his head as a racer often does when he crosses a finish line.

Ace agreed. "Oh yeah! I've been to a lot of these races, and I have to say that's the closest finish I've ever seen."

PROFILE OF AN AVERAGE IRONMAN

COMMON ATTRIBUTES OF ATHLETES IN ALL AGE GROUPS THAT QUALIFIED FOR THE IRONMAN WORLD CHAMPIONSHIPS:

1. Commitment: They plan their work and social schedule with training the number one goal.

2. Positive mental attitude: They visualize themselves succeeding.

3. Patience: Getting to the starting line healthy and strong requires all the building blocks along the way set in place properly and in the correct order. This process takes years, not months or weeks.

4. Confidence: They run their own race, performing on race day to the best of their abilities. They don't get distracted with what others are doing. They are methodical in nutrition, training, equipment prep, and pre-planning.

5. Toughness: Normally considered tough in the face of adversity. The will to finish will not be extinguished.[4]

Other common traits include being highly competitive, persistent, strong-willed, self-motivated, passionate, driven, and goal-oriented.

---

4   Contribution from Lifesport Senior Coach Dan Smith, Training Peaks, Oct. 2015

Doc was now ready to move on to business, "Well, Ace, I'm glad you're here. What can I help you with?"

"When we spoke Saturday morning, you suggested I come in for an initial consultation to help me get started. So I'm still trying to decide if this race is for me. I'm here today because I've mostly decided to do it. But my reasons aren't strong enough yet. I need some clear thinking. When Champion spoke, I felt pretty motivated, and when I asked my friends what they thought I received some great feedback. One of my good friends though, Reasonable, advised me against it and I trust him the most. I spend more time in conversation with him than anyone else."

Ace continued. "I need something more than to just finish the Big Race. A few friends, whom I'd best describe as Shallow, Egotistical, and Optimistic all said to go for it. But to be honest, I trust Reasonable's judgment more than the rest, because he is usually the most objective. He said what I believe, which is a balanced life is the noble life, the life most desirable, and it would be a waste of a lot of time in training, which counts for almost nothing."

Ace went on. "I mean, there's no money in it, and no promotion coming to me because of it. He pointed out that I'd be missing out on a lot of reading time, personal education and social gatherings— including my community service, all for the sake of my ego. And what do I get in the end? A T-shirt worth fifteen hours a week for fifty-two weeks. That's 600 hours of my life spent just to say I did it.

"Big deal," Ace added with a scoff of sarcasm. After a short awkward moment, Ace apologized, thinking perhaps that he may have insulted the man. "No disrespect is meant. I know you've done one, and it is a big deal. I just need to be convinced somewhere deep down it's for me."

Doc responded. "First, let me say it's going to cost you a lot more than you expect. So you are right; you'd better have your reasons squared away in your head. But I hear where you're going with this line of reasoning."

Ace replied thoughtfully, "Listen, I'm looking for a challenge, but I need a little help making sure this is the right one."

"Fair enough. I heard several concerns and objections. Let's talk them through, one by one. First, to be clear, this race is not reasonable. I appreciate your friend. I have a man in my life who has similar inclinations. He is filled with reasonable excuses. Let me say that Reasonable's voice is not the best deciding factor for many of life's decisions.

> *Great things were never accomplished by measuring their reasonableness.*

"I think it is often the reasonable people who are selfish and self-centered. I assure you they are only interested in safety and comfort. Sometimes, I think they are cowards. Think about what I am saying. Reasonable and anyone like him has never done anything great in this world. They play it too safe. Think about love, for example." Now Doc put both of his hands over his heart as he continued. "Is there anything about being head-over-heels in love that's reasonable? Crazy-in-love people constantly do unreasonable things." Now Doc slowed his cadence, "Love is not reasonable—it is extravagant.

"And perhaps the greatest mystery of all is sacrifice and denial of self. I assure you Reasonable has no place for these pursuits, yet extravagant sacrifice is the pathway to true greatness. Great things are accomplished when unreasonably great sacrifices have been made.

"Think about Christ dying for others, in place of others." Doc couldn't help himself; now his hands were outstretched as if to demonstrate Jesus on the cross. "Do you think it's reasonable for an innocent man to suffer for guilty people? Think about what Christ taught: If your enemy strikes you on the right cheek, turn the left to him also. If your enemy sues you for your jacket, give your coat as well. If your enemy compels you to go with him one mile, go with him two. Give to those who ask of you. If anyone would borrow from you, don't turn them away. Christ said to love your enemies, bless those who curse you, do good to those who hate you, and pray for those who spitefully use you. Does any of that sound reasonable?

"Paul used the word reasonable in Romans 12 when he wrote, 'I beg you, brethren, to present your bodies as a living sacrifice to the Lord; this is your reasonable service to the Lord.' Are you following the train of thought? Because he was saying live your life for someone besides yourself. Namely, live your life for God instead of living life with your own ambition. Does that sound reasonable? Paul says it is reasonable, but I bet your friend wouldn't think so. Reasonable is selfish. If all you do is listen to yourself with all your reasonable philosophy, you will never do anything great for God."

Ace sat as if mesmerized. He felt stuck in the middle of two opposing powers and two opposing voices: reasonableness and sacrifice. He was persuaded to follow sacrifice to achieve greatness, but to do so would be to forsake his friend's advice. So he asked, "What do I do with my good friend Reasonable?"

"There was a time when his father was a good friend of mine. As much as he kept me out of some big trouble over the years, I finally had to minimize his involvement in my decision-making concerning my ambitions for greatness. We are no longer close friends. I keep him around as a consultant when I need him from time to time. Let's say I sort of keep him on the board, but he's not the chairman anymore."

Just then, one of the medical assistants came to the door and indicated that Doc was needed. Doc offered a solution to Ace's dilemma. "Listen, I don't feel like I've answered your question fully. I'd like to continue this conversation. If you can stay, I have a lunch break in thirty minutes. Can you meet me in the break room?"

Ace said he could. Without knowing it, Ace was successfully following the golden rule of mentoring. The student was chasing after the teacher. Ace was teachable. His listening eyes and eager spirit lit a fire in Doc, who felt he was discussing important issues with someone who seemed genuinely interested. Doc left the room to see another patient while Ace made his way to the break room.

He was motivated by this conversation. He had thirty minutes to kill and didn't want to forget a single thing. He wanted to capture his thoughts with more Wisbits. Now Ace felt he had something else worthy of sharing, so he opened his cell phone and made a blog post from the break room.

Hello, world:

I'm at the eye clinic with some insight from the doctor to share with you. Now more Wisbits to guide the soul:

Wisbit tip: *Great things are accomplished by great sacrifice.*

Wisbit tip: *What is reasonable is not always the best course of action.*

Wisbit tip: *Being reasonable at times can be a code word for being a selfish coward.*

Wisbit tip: *Expressing true love is extravagant, lavish and completely unreasonable.*

5

THE MYTH OF A
BALANCED LIFE

Doc arrived in the break room promptly at 11:30, carrying a book in one hand and a small plate of vegetables with dip and a cluster of grapes in the other one. He set them both on the table. To Ace, it looked more like a snack for a rabbit than lunch for a grown man. Doc offered Ace a bottle of water, the two exchanged a few pleasantries, then Doc picked up the conversation where they left off.

"Before we got interrupted, we were sizing up the balanced life approach to living." Doc continued. "I realize this is one of Reasonable's concerns, and it warrants a discussion. I call it 'the myth of the balanced life.' It sounds noble and reasonable, but it's an insidious philosophy that often results in mediocrity, infecting its victims without ever being detected.

"Balanced people become the 'Jack of all trades' and master of none, so they leave no mark on the world. Balance is not even a worthy goal. In some sense, it's not even a godly goal. When God made the church, think about how he did it. He arranged the body with different parts to it. Let me apply the athletic spiritual metaphor to help you understand what Paul writes in 1 Corinthians 12, the football revised version of the Bible.

"'A football team has many positions, but all the parts comprise one whole team. So it is with the body of Christ. Some of us come from a family heritage of faith and some come from families that had no regard for God. Some are smart, some skilled, and some come from wealth while some from poverty. Yet we have all been baptized into one body by one Spirit, and we all share the same Spirit.

The football team has many different positions, not just one. If the offensive lineman says, 'I am not a part of the team because I am not a wide receiver,' that does not make him any less a part of the team. If the defensive cornerback says, 'I am not part of the squad because I am not a middle linebacker,' would that make him any less a part of the team? If the whole team were made of wide receivers, who would stop the pass rush? Or if the team were made of kickers, how would a touchdown pass ever get thrown? Our team has many positions, and God has gifted each player to fulfill a particular assignment and role. The quarterback can never say to the offensive line, 'I don't need you.' The offense can't say to the defense, 'I don't need you.' In fact, some positions on the team, like the punter, that seem weakest and least important are actually the most necessary. The positions, like the field goal kicker, that we regard as less honorable, are the ones who often get carried off the field after winning the game on the final play.

"So we carefully provide the kicking game to assist the kickers with a formidable blocking scheme and special rules to protect them so that they don't get unnecessarily hurt. One example is the specialized rule for the punters: no running into the kicker, while all the starters on offense and defense do not require this special care.'

"This is a metaphor of how God arranges Christians. He put church members together with different roles to play. Every role is vital, which creates harmony among the members, so that all members care for each other. If one part suffers, all the parts suffer with it; and if one part is honored, all the parts are blessed.

"If balance means you are trying to be all parts and play all positions, you are mistaken. Discern your place, your gift and your role to play. If you're a quarterback, don't spend all your time and energy trying to be the kicker. Pursue being great at what God has uniquely equipped *you* to do and build your life around playing to *your* spiritual giftedness.

"Spiritual Gifts"

"Which part of the body of Christ are you?"

"All people of great impact excel at something they were designed to do. Play to your strengths and delegate your weaknesses. Allow others to use their gifts to supplement your inadequacies. You will find your greatest joy when you are using your spiritual gifts and others will be lifted up, edified, and blessed. In a sense, you will have maximum impact for the kingdom of God by doing your role and doing it well! It may sound like I've focused on self discovery a lot. But the purpose of all this is to help others. If your life is not lived for others it's not worth living. You're most helpful to others when you're giving from your sweet spot."

Ace was tracking along with Doc but had to interject one all- important question: "So how do I know my position on the team and my role in the church? How do I know my spiritual gift?"

Doc reached for the book he brought and handed it to Ace as he said, "That's a great question. I want you to take this workbook home. It's called *Finding Your God-Given Sweet Spot*. It's filled with different assessment tools to help you discover all the dimensions of your God-tailored identity. One quick exercise to help you gain clarity about your spiritual gift is to find your holy discontent. Take a look at this." Doc opened the book and let Ace look at it.

YOUR HOLY DISCONTENT MAY REVEAL YOUR SPIRITUAL GIFT.

When something really bothers you, it may be that it flies in the face of how you're wired. Your answer to the following question will be greatly influenced by your spiritual gift.

WHAT ONE THING IRRITATES YOU MOST IN OTHER CHRISTIANS? EXPLAIN.

Advanced Seminar Textbook Copyright 1986[5]

---

5   Found in the Advanced Seminar Textbook, IBLP, *How to Understand Spiritual Gifts*.

After a pause, Doc asked Ace, "So what is it about Christians that disappoints you?"

"Failure to grow…when Christians don't mature and grow up!"

"That means you're most likely an Exhorter! One of your main functions in life is to help people grow up spiritually."

"That sounds about right to me, but what does that have to do with racing?"

"Ace, you're running ahead of me, but your question is a good tie-in to your original question, which is whether the race is worth your time. I guarantee you won't get a better place in heaven if you do this race. So what is the value? There are dozens of great reasons. Let's talk about it."

Doc continued. "We've talked about sacrifice, so let's talk about self-discipline. It's the last of the fruits of the Spirit. It's like a muscle: use it or lose it. Exercise it often, and you will have it at the time of need. Neglect it, and it will atrophy. The Scriptures agree: 'He who controls himself is mightier than he who conquers a city,' which is countercultural to everything we hear in the news and TV.

"The philosophy of the day is 'If it feels good do it, and do it a lot.' Nobody wants to work, nobody wants to sacrifice, nobody wants to pay a high price, and everybody's looking for the easy way. This philosophy simply is not going to serve anyone well in the end. Shortcuts are never going to lead to any great accomplishments. Excellence takes effort."

Ace unknowingly kept asking for more with his attentive eyes and interjections of approval and affirmation. The truth was, Ace was starving for a "man's man" type of role model in his life. It wasn't often he sensed that someone who seemed to really have it together had an interest in him. The best way to describe what was happening was chemistry. The mentor-apprentice relationship was blossoming. Doc was full of the spiritual metaphor, and seemed to be starving for someone truly interested to share it with. For such a time as this, God had brought them together. They seemed to be kindred spirits.

Doc summed it up for Ace: "My final reason why the race is worth it is simply what I call 'temple maintenance.' My body is the temple of the Holy Spirit, which means God lives inside of me and expresses his life through mine." Doc was using both hands to point to his chest indicating God was inside of him and then his hands touched his head before he brushed them down his body illustrating that his whole body belonged to God. "Paul said, 'I am crucified with Christ; nevertheless I live, yet not I, but Christ lives in me: and the life I now live in the flesh I live by faith in the Son of God, who loved me and gave himself for me. And you should know that your body is no longer your own, for you have been bought with a price; therefore, glorify Christ through your body.'"

Doc explained. "That's a mouthful of Scripture, but the idea is simple enough. I try to have my body in great shape so I can easily do any assignment HE asks me to do. Staying healthy means He will be able to use my body for a long time. In a sense, you choose the quality of your life in your seventies and eighties while you're in your forties and fifties. The three types of elderly people in the world are the no-goes, the slow-goes, and the go-goes. Why not adopt a lifestyle that will ensure you can be most fruitful in the mature years of your life? Believe it or not, I'm seventy-seven, with no retirement in sight. I rode my bike to work this morning, so I'm practicing what I'm preaching. I don't aim for a balanced life but I do aim for an integrated life; developing body, mind and spirit. Those are a few reasons why it's worthwhile. So what do you think? Does this sound like something for you?"

Ace was trying to process all of it. Mostly, he was stuck on the last thing the man had said: *Doc Mentor was seventy-seven. Impossible, because he only looked sixty-five. And rode his bike to work today!*

Ace finally uttered what he was thinking: "You gotta be patient with me. I get it and I am convinced. This is a great thing. I see now I could get a lot of benefit from it, but you said earlier that we all are part of the body of Christ and everybody has a different part. I still need to know what position I'm supposed to play. Doesn't that figure into this equation? You don't literally think everybody should do this race, do you? This race is not for everybody. How do I know if this is God's will for *me*?"

"No, it's not for everybody. Do you consider yourself an athlete?"

"I was before I lost my leg." Ace pointed down, lifting his pants to reveal the prosthetic limb. "And in many ways, I still am. But you should know that back in the day, I made the all-state basketball team!"

"Hmmm…" was all Doc replied as he thought, *Ace had hidden it well. He even figured out to walk without a limp.*

Looking at the prosthetic leg triggered another thought in Doc's mind and he reassessed his next move. "Listen, I'd like to refer you to a specialist I know. I said we would circle back around to helping you answer your question of which position has God assigned to you, but I'd like you to meet my friend and mentor. He has helped me and dozens of others over the years to discover the answer to your question. His name is Sage Woodward. There was a time when he was uncertain of his purpose. He says lacking clarity of purpose made him a mile wide and an inch deep until God stepped in and changed the equation of his life. Now he's four feet wide and as deep as the Lord wants to take him. Please talk to my assistant to help you make the arrangements. Then plan to see me again in three weeks. Ace, it's been a joy to get to know you. Thanks for stopping by, but I gotta get back to work"

With that, Ace was at the front desk making the arrangements.

⚥

That night, Ace couldn't stop thinking about all Doc Mentor had said. He added so much perspective and insight. He didn't want to forget any of it, so he went to his blog and made a post featuring more Wisbit tips.

Wisbit tip: Seeking a balanced life is a myth. It's much better to be great at something than average at everything.

Wisbit tip: Everybody's got a role to play. God designed it that way. Accept it and play your role with excellence.

Wisbit tip: Self-control is like a muscle—use it or lose it. If I train myself to use it daily, I will have it when I really need it.

Wisbit tip: By taking care of my physical health, I increase the likelihood that I'll be able to do any assignment God asks of me.

For all you friends following my journey, I met with Doc Mentor, my coach, for my initial consultation. He's a brilliant man—all my tips this week were inspired by him. He's a doctor, and like all good doctors, he referred me to a specialist, some guru named Sage Woodward. Hey, when Tarzan got in trouble, he called for his elephant. So when Doc needs a little help, he calls on Sage. Doc is seventy-seven years old (and still rides his bike to work every day like a kid), so I'm guessing Sage must be as old as Methuselah!

Hold on tight for what happens next.

QUESTIONS FOR SELF-REFLECTION

- How would I know if I possess great self-control?
- What great sacrifices am I willing to make to be great for God?
- Am I trying to be a "Jack of all Trades" and live a balanced life?

6

IDENTITY DETERMINES DESTINY

ACE FELT AWKWARD knocking at the door of the simple, one-story house at the end of the cul-de-sac. He shivered a bit, wondering if it was because of the cold weather or his nervousness at meeting Sage Woodward. Ace was prepared to meet somebody very old—since this was Doc Mentor's mentor, he must be in his eighties, maybe even nineties.

A radiant woman with a sweet smile and welcoming eyes opened the door and asked, "How can I help you?" Ace replied, "I'm a friend of Doc Mentor. He sent me to meet with Sage Woodward."

"You must be Ace," said the woman. "Yes, ma'am," Ace answered like a true gentlemen. "The good doctor let us know you'd be by. Allow me to introduce myself; I'm Lauwiel, but the young people around here just call me 'Peaches.' Won't you please come on in? It's a little chilly out there. Can I get you anything? Something to drink, maybe some warm tea?" They moved together through the foyer into the living room.

Sage was lying in a bed with his head turned to the side, facing a chair. The rest of his body was under the covers. He was propped up on his side with pillows and all that was visible besides his head was one arm laying lifelessly across his chest. This position somehow made him look more human than the motionless quadriplegic that he was.

Peaches gave a brief introduction. "Sage, you have a guest today. The good doctor sent Ace to meet with you." She motioned for Ace to sit in the chair across from Sage, who welcomed Ace and thanked him for visiting.

"Thanks for seeing me," Ace replied. "I appreciate your time." Ace felt completely awkward. The good doctor had failed to mention that Sage was a complete invalid. So it was that Ace found himself staring at a round-faced old man whose forehead would wrinkle up when he was astonished. He had a full head of snow white hair, parted neatly to one side. His eyebrows were bushy white and seemed to sprout out in every direction as if escaping from under his black-framed glasses. His countenance radiated wisdom. Crow's feet wrinkles adorned the corner of his eyes when he smiled. So he appeared at that moment as his face lit up at the sight of Ace. Strangely, Sage didn't seem broken, but rather like an angel, as an air of contentment dominated his radiant spirit and beamed right through his face.

He spoke slowly with a calm raspy voice. "Well, what brings you here today?"

"To make a long story short, I met with Doc Mentor last week. He is trying to help me discern my path. I'm trying to discover God's will for my life in one simple area, really—to do the Big Race or not? He gave me a convincing rationale of all the benefits of getting involved. And if you know anything about Doc Mentor, he turned the whole thing into a sports analogy, which I appreciate, but that still didn't answer my question."

Sage wanted to clarify. "Let me see if I have this right. You're asking the classic question of how to know God's will for your life?"

"Yes, sir, you got that right. Doc thought you might be able to help."

"First, let me say that while it is a valid question, I find it to be the wrong question, especially to launch into discovering your purpose in life. A little groundwork can make a big difference in discerning God's will. The better question is, 'Who are you? Who has God made you to be?' Mark my words, Ace, identity always predicts destiny. Once you discover the nature of something, it is much easier to determine how it should be used. Most people simply don't know who they are. Let me illustrate. Can you please hold up that pen sitting on the coffee table?"

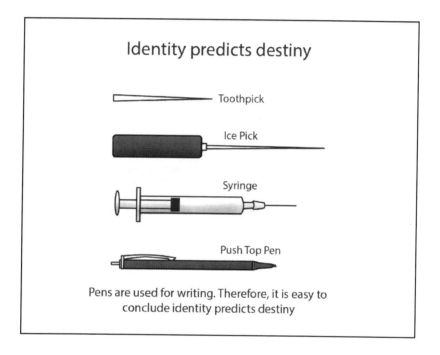

Ace found the pen and held it between them so they could both see it. Sage began, "Now I ask you, what is it? And you say…" He paused to let Ace answer. "It's a pen." Sage continued. "Well, we are clear that it's not an ice pick, though it sort of looks like one. It's not a syringe, although it kind of functions like one. With both pens and syringes you squeeze the top and something comes out on the bottom. But we're clear. It's a pen! So what are pens for? The simple answer is pens are used to write. So the next time you're caught in the conundrum of what God wants you to do, ask yourself, 'Who has God made me to be?' Focus on your identity.

"Follow my logic: if an object's identity can be defined as a pen, you can predict its destiny. In other words, a pen is made to write!! So tell me: Who is Ace?"

Ace replied, "I thought that's why I came here—for you to tell me who Ace is." They shared a little laugh and Ace continued, "That's a tough question. I don't know where to start. I love playing basketball and I'm a war veteran. I'm also a sound and light technician and I grew up going to church."

Before Ace could say another word, Sage butted in. "You are missing the point. Those are all things that you *do*. They come out of who you *are*. Who are you?? Think harder! What's behind the activities you do? Who are you? If I asked your friends, who would they say you are? What three words best describe you?"

"My friends would say I'm good at sports."

"Go on," Sage encouraged him.

"I can encourage and inspire a team. I'm competitive to a fault. I play to win. I like people, but I'm not big on the social media stuff. I like to see people face-to-face. My friends would say I'm an extrovert and optimistic. They would say I'm transparent.

"I like living a planned-out life. I like to think things through to their logical conclusions before I get involved. When it comes to other people, I can usually visualize what others can be, but have trouble seeing what I can be."

Sage complimented Ace on his great start and asked if he had a cause that lit his passion. Ace couldn't think of one. Then Sage asked Ace if there was some injustice he would want to resolve if he could.

"Yeah, I'd stop war. It's just so useless. I find it pointless and nothing is ever permanently resolved."

Sage probed Ace for a group of people he liked working with, and offered a few options, such as kids, college students, the elderly, rehabbers, men, monkeys, elephants, giraffes... Ace chuckled at

Sage's humor. Ace knew he'd be bitter if he were Sage. He wondered how this guy could even enjoy life and smile! He was certainly an anomaly.

"Yeah, thanks for the prompt. When it comes to groups of people, I suppose I like young athletes. And now that I think about it, sports are my passion. I'm processing as I go, and I could just as easily say rehabbers because it takes one to know one. When I came back from the war, I sort of got lost. I turned to alcohol—the classic story, but I didn't stay down long. Once I got my..."

Ace stopped himself because he didn't want to reveal he had a prosthetic leg to a man who was confined to a bed. How could he even compare his loss to this man's? For some reason, Ace didn't want to try to explain how his pain amounted to anything compared to this man, so he redirected and started again.

"...Once I got my own job and my own place, I broke free. There is a road to rehab, and I traveled it. I opened the big book and worked the twelve steps, one after another until I was well. Now I don't even touch the stuff anymore. I don't go to group anymore, either, but I can identify with anyone using alcohol to escape, because they eventually find themselves in a trap. And I'm lucky I was able to get out."

"Sounds like you have a strong foundation of an identity to me," offered Sage. "You are an athlete, a man of action, and a visionary planner. You see what people could be, and you'd like to bring hope to broken lives through practical steps—particularly to young athletes and quite possibly to rehabbers."

His comments resonated in Ace's heart. As he slowly repeated it to himself, the hair on the back of his neck stood up. Sage had done it. He had captured Ace's identity statement in no time at all. Ace was bewildered at how concisely and accurately Sage had discerned who he was. This old, crippled quadriplegic really was a guru of sorts. Sage's facial expressions and voice were so captivating that Ace soon forgot he was talking to a limp body on a bed. He was talking to a spirit, full of life, though his body had all but perished.

Sage continued. "Before we move forward, let me say that destiny is shaped by the unique combination of both identity and character. Let me pause to ask you a question: Do you think a person can change his own destiny?"

Ace replied, "I'm not certain…it seems to me that we are the result of a cross between being victims of fate and somewhat the result of our own decisions."

"You are spot on! It's the old nature versus nurture debate. In other words, you can only change so much. In my illustration with the pen, I believe once a pen, always a pen. With people, it basically means your personality, spiritual gifts, propensities, aptitudes, family of origin, stature, and mental processing abilities all combine to make a unique mosaic which comprises your identity.

"For the most part, those things are set in stone. God is not going to remake that. In a sense, God has already prescribed them to you as your custom identity so you can fulfill your destiny. Those things are unchangeable. Let me give you another illustration. Do you happen to have a Swiss army knife in your pocket?"

Ace had a knife, so he reached into his pocket and brought out a nice-looking flip blade.

"Perfect! You would agree there are various types of knives: butter knives, steak knives, buck knives—a chef has a chop blade—all the way up to various types of swords. In a sense, they all have been created to cut.

"My point is if God makes a person a knife, they will always be a knife. However, I might suggest they can graduate to bigger, more significant uses. Still a knife in essence, but set aside for better use. Back to the pen illustration: Think about the various pens we use. Some of them are everyday, cheap, throw-away pens. However, some people have a personal special pen they use just for signing their signature. Others are used for highlighting and others for markers. Some are made for common use, others for an exclusive use.

CHANGE YOUR DESTINY BY GROWING YOUR CHARACTER

TYPE OF KNIFE	APPLICATION	CHARACTER TRAIT
Butter knife	Common; limited effectiveness	Inconsistent habits
Steak knife	Specific	Dependable habits
Carving knife	Unique	Specific areas of strength
Cutlass	Ultra effective	Convictions tested in various ways
Mameluke Sword	A Marine's prized possession	Convictions proven & trusted

Convictions are the stuff that character is made of: Convictions: A) principles for which a man will die for; b) a refusal to compromise on a given matter; c) marked with unyieldingly good character. Convictions often require the holder to forfeit momentary pleasure for the sake of a perceived greater value that will come in another season of life.

"However, a man can change his destiny by developing his character. Listen to what the Scriptures say about this idea of changing your destiny: 'Let everyone that names the name of Christ depart from iniquity. For in a great house there are not only vessels of gold and of silver, but also of wood and of earth; and some to honor, and some to dishonor. If a man therefore purges himself from these, he shall be a vessel unto honor, sanctified, and meet for the master's use, and prepared unto every good work.'

"It just doesn't get more simple than that. Did you get that thought? 'If a man therefore purges himself from these (unholy activities), he shall be a vessel unto honor.' The Scriptures are clear about this: A man can change his destiny. A man can change his usefulness to God. He can be transformed from a pen of ordinary use to a pen of noble use—from a butter knife to a Samurai sword.

"It's simple: We make decisions to live holy lives or selfish lives. Great works require great men, and men of great character are the ones chosen to do God's greatest works. We are not pens or knives; we are people, and God has predestined us to be conformed to the likeness of His Son in our character.

CHARACTER DETERMINES DESTINY

Butter Knife

Steak Knife

Carving Knife

Cleaver

Cutlass

Larger Sword

Purifying ourselves makes us ready and eligible for greater works.
We don't morph into something completely different
but rather we graduate into a better version of ourselves

"How do you build good character? Simple. Renew your mind. It all starts with good thinking. Stinky thinking leads to stinky living."

Ace objected. "You keep saying it's simple. Doing the right thing is *not* simple. It may be simple in theory. And maybe it's simple intellectually, but good character is a rare thing and very difficult to achieve."

Sage continued. "Look at it this way—I call it the destiny chart. Look behind you on the wall."

Ace turned and saw a framed poster. Sage asked Ace to read it aloud, so Ace began reading the proverb.[6]

Sage concluded. "And that, my friend, is how it's done. The battle is first fought in the mind. It's establishing the right habits in our lives. If you want to have a godly life, you will need to have godly habits. And, as you realized, it's not easily achieved. It will most likely take some accountability from others to build those destiny-forming habits.

---

6   Samuel Smiles Quotes <GoodReads.com>

THE DESTINY CHART

Sow a thought,
You reap an act.
Sow an act,
You reap a habit.
Sow a habit,
You reap a character.
Sow a character,
You reap a destiny.

Samuel Smiles

"So take your identity and decide if you want to be of noble use. If so, then work on the habits of greatness: your character, your decisions, and your daily habits. They shape your usefulness, which in turn shape your destiny. Do you get it?"

"Yes, all that makes good sense to me. Let me try and process all this. You say my identity is like this: I am an athlete; I am a man of action, a visionary planner, who wants to help broken lives through practical steps, even from my personal example, particularly to young athletes and rehabbers. I like that statement. It agrees with me. So if I reset my priorities, I might move from being like a person in rehab to a sponsor of a person in rehab, and then maybe a small group leader or class leader influencing dozens at a time. Is that what this is all about?" Sage gave an affirming nod of his head. "Because this has been a big help."

"I don't know if I did anything. Look at me, I'm just lying here. I asked a few questions, and talked about pens and knives. I'm glad it helped."

Ace queried, "One more thing: We did everything but answer the question I came here for. How do I know if I'm supposed to do the Big Race?"

"OK, let's use what you just learned and see if you can discern an answer. There are basically two components to your destiny: identity and character. So which component does the Big Race fall into for you? Both, neither, or one?"

"My identity statement is definitely wrapped up in being an athlete, so that fact alone is a good match for my pursuit of the Big Race."

Sage asked about the other component to destiny. Ace replied that it was character. But he still didn't know what it had to do with the Big Race. Then he realized, as he said, "Yes, as much as I hate to admit it, training for the Big Race would require continuous implementation of self-control. But with that definition, anybody can do the race. Shoot, everybody should do the race. It's a character builder, right?"

Sage replied, "Everybody should build character. Some can use the race to do so, and others may access other tools to develop character."

"So should I?"

"Are you an athlete?"

"Yes! I am!"

"Then it sounds like it's in harmony with your identity statement, and identity always predicts destiny. Ace, I have an idea that might help. Why don't you sweeten the equation—is there any way you can link your cause to this race?"

Ace sat intrigued by the thought, then said, "I don't mean to look so perplexed. It's a great idea. I'm just sitting here asking myself 'What's my cause again?' I need to do some work on this, but it's worth looking into. Let me think about that."

Then they were done. Ace left the house, but his mind kept revolving the things they had discussed. Later that night, Ace knew it was time to blog again.

He reasoned blogging would keep him accountable because once he posted, he would have to do it or else he would feel foolish and lose credibility among his friends. Once it was posted, there was no turning back. Ace sat in front of his computer just counting the cost one last time. This was a plan, a well-thought-out plan indeed.

ANATOMY OF ACE: SPIRITUAL, PHYSICAL AND MENTAL MOSAIC

Gender: Male   **Age:** 33

Height: 5'8"   **Weight:** 171 lbs. (starting point)   Race day goal: 165 lbs.

40-yard dash: 4.55 seconds (before amputation)   (Avg. NFL defensive back 4.45 seconds)

Vertical leap: 27" (before amputation)   (Avg. NBA vertical 28")

Max Bench Press: 225 lbs. 13 reps (Stephen Paea, world's strongest NFL player, bench pressed 225 lbs. 49 times at the NFL combine)

Spiritual gift: Exhorter

Personality (people versus projects): Extrovert, a people person

Core values: Winning and Wisdom

Passion: Sports

Life Experience (where he's been): Christian, military, athletics, rehabber, sound and lighting specialist

Who you want to help: Youth and rehabbers

Natural Aptitudes and Skills From Six Unchangeables of Your Life

Parents: Integrity and Christian value system

Birth order: Last of three

Nationality: American

Ethnicity: Caucasian

Aptitudes: Street smart, reads people well, AA degree

Physically: Superior athleticism, quick reflexes

Anatomy of Ace

Street Smart Extrovert

Resilience E.Q.

Personality & I.Q.

Spiritual Gift

Strong Will

Who do you want to help

Visionary Exhorter

Passion

Sports God

Young Christian Athletes

Rehabilitation Victims

Competition Wisdom

Adult Triathlete

Basketball

Life Experience

Core Values

Military

F.C.A. Youth Athletes

Weakness

Audio Visual Tech

Ace's Identity & Destiny: I am an athlete, a man of action, and a visionary planner. I see what people could be, I want to see people grow to spiritual maturity. I like working with young athletes.

Illustration created with inspiration from the
Mosaic of Finding Your God-Given Sweet Spot[7]

7   Tom and Pam Wolf.

Ace began his post:

I appreciate everyone's input. I considered all of it. I finally made the decision. I'm going to compete in the Big Race next year. That is a statement of faith, as I wrote in my first post. I have to qualify first, so I guess I'm trying to say I signed up for the qualifying race. I even paid my money and registered for it. It's done...I'm locked in. A date with destiny is set.

Now I need your help again—this time helping me to find a cause to run for. So send me your ideas. Here's what I have so far: Almost nothing. On my first pass, I couldn't even get beyond the Miss America pageant answer "World Peace." HELP! Send me some ideas. I've got to research this and get back to you.

But today was a great day. I met with Sage. He is your Master Yoda type. You know what I mean—the really, really wise guy cloaked in an unassuming package. Literally—the guy I met today was a quadriplegic.

But from his shriveled-up body came the most profound wisdom I have ever heard. He flooded me with so much wise counsel today, so I thought I would pass it along. Get ready for this week's Wisbit tips...

Wisbit tip: *Identity always predicts your destiny. Discover who you are and you will soon know what to do.*

Wisbit tip: *Destiny is the combination of a person's identity and character.*

Wisbit tip: *God prescribes each of us certain unchangeable gifts.*

Wisbit tip: *Character is created by establishing noble habits.*

Wisbit tip: *By eliminating worthless behavior and replacing it with good habits, I will change my usefulness to God.*

QUESTIONS FOR SELF-REFLECTION

- Do I know my God-given sweet spot? Do I have a personal identity statement?
- What habits make someone great for God?
- What other factors determine destiny, beyond identity and character?

7

COACHING: THE DIFFERENCE MAKER

ACE WAS EAGER to get started, so early Saturday morning he made his way to the neighborhood YMCA to obtain a membership. He brought along the free first month's membership coupon which every Big Race participant and volunteer received in their registration swag bag. Along with the Big Race, Ace loved a good deal.

Membership payment would be another source of accountability. As Ace entered the facility he was greeted by a friendly receptionist standing behind the counter. She was an athletic-looking young lady with crystal blue eyes, sandy blonde hair in a magnificent "up do" and a contented smile. She wore a black skirt and blouse. She almost looked overdressed for the job. This was a gym on Saturday morning, yet she looked almost business-professional.

She graciously asked Ace how she might help him. Ace explained he wanted a membership. In the moments that followed she dialed a number and the YMCA director, Remnant Ben Yahuda, appeared. He was a slender, olive-skinned, middle-aged man with a thinly trimmed beard and a big smile. Ace shook his hand and the two men exchanged greetings as they made their way to his back office. The receptionist gave a quick shout out to remind him she was leaving for an appointment and would see him again on Wednesday. Remnant replied, "Thanks for your help today, and good luck."

Once in his office, Remnant didn't have to sell Ace and didn't try. He'd seen this type before—the highly-motivated newcomer. Ace informed him he was planning to compete in the Big Race, so he really only had one question that mattered: "Do you have a program to train triathletes?" Remnant was quick to say yes, explaining they had a rather large group of very competitive triathletes who trained regularly for the Big Race.

Ace was sold, but asked a few more questions. "Do you have a pool? Do you have a spin room? Do you have instructional training classes? Is that part of the membership, or extra? Where do I sign up? What are your hours?" Ace was satisfied and signed the contract before the tour. Now he had a lot of skin in the game. As he handed his check to Remnant, Ace thought, *There's no turning back now.*

Though Ace was sold, Remnant was committed to giving Ace a tour. Ace had been to this particular "Y" as a youth a few times. Remnant was proud of the facilities and the many improvements and additions made over the years, and hoped Ace would share his enthusiasm. While they walked, Remnant asked his favorite question, "So, why did you chose the 'Y?' There are lots of options out there."

Ace was quick to reply. "I hope the YMCA will put me in an environment where I can meet like-minded people and find fellowship to help me grow in my faith."

Remnant was smiling. "I love it when I hear an answer like that. You were very articulate, but I'm sorry to say I only hear the faith motivation from about one in four members who join. We are trying hard to put the 'C' back in the YMCA. Unfortunately, most people don't even know what those initials stand for, and often just call us the 'Y.' But the original intent was to help young men grow spiritually through physical engagement. YMCA stands for Young Men's

Christian Association, a gym for Christian young men to grow in spirit, mind, and body.

"Ace, We're glad to have you here, but don't get disillusioned because everybody here is not Christian. Being Christian is not required for membership, and those who are Christians are each on their own journey of faith; some are still immature, not seasoned saints. So don't expect everyone to be on the same page, but I assure you we have an excellent staff and membership I think you will like."

Remnant and Ace walked alongside the weight room. The gym had a large open-air feel to it. It was filled with people this morning. Just then they turned a corner and went up the stairs to a room filled with stationary bikes and next to that on the right was a door marked "Staff Offices."

Remnant opened the door and began his introductions. "Ace, you asked about our triathlon training program. I want you to meet Spinsey, Domestique, and Bruiser Le Truce. Together, they operate the classes for triathletes." Remnant continued as he addressed the coaches: "Ace signed up for the Rocky Pointe Half Iron, which is eight months from today. He hopes to qualify for the Big Race next year, and wants some help training."

Domestique said, "Well, mate, nice to know ya. Have you ever done a triathlon before?" Ace replied, "I've seen the Big Race live for as long as I can remember. I've volunteered twice, but no more watching for me. This year I race. To answer your question, no, I've never done a triathlon as a race. But I was jumping off the high dive into the pool at age four, riding my bike without training wheels since I was three, and was running before I could crawl, so you might say I have a triathlete orientation. Not to mention I played sports in high school and served in the military. And just to keep things interesting, I have my friend coming along with me." Ace pointed to his prosthetic leg.

"OK, that's interesting. You got a blade, or do you run with that?" asked Domestique. Ace replied that he ran with his leg. Domestique added some humor: "So are you the Terminator, Anakin Skywalker, or the six-million-dollar man?"[8]

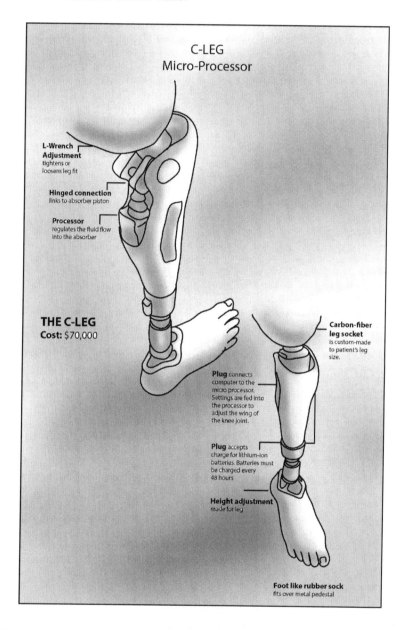

C-LEG
Micro-Processor

L-Wrench Adjustment
tightens or loosens leg fit

Hinged connection
links to absorber piston

Processor
regulates the fluid flow into the absorber

THE C-LEG
Cost: $70,000

Carbon-fiber leg socket
is custom-made to patient's leg size.

Plug connects computer to the micro processor. Settings are fed into the processor to adjust the wing of the knee joint.

Plug accepts charge for lithium-ion batteries. Batteries must be charged every 48 hours

Height adjustment
made for leg

Foot like rubber sock
fits over metal pedestal

---

8   The C-leg is a product of OttoBock, Mfr.

Ace quipped, "Yep, they rebuilt me. American tax dollars going to good use."

"Whoa. I don't even know what to say to that. Let me at least say thanks for serving our country and sorry for your loss," commented Bruiser.

"Hey, thanks, but I didn't lose this while I was enlisted. The best thing to do is forget about it and treat me like everyone else. I don't need anybody's sympathy, and I don't require special treatment!" Ace replied emphatically.

Spinsey was the spin class instructor and now took her turn with the orientation process. She asked, "So being physically challenged gives you several options on the bike portion of the course. What's your approach? Do you use a racing wheel chair, a recumbent bike, or a classic road bike with some type of special attachment to the pedals?"

Ace replied respectfully, but once again with a hint of defensiveness. His tone was emphatic. "Good question! I'll ride the same as everyone else! I'll be using a standard road bike with nothing more than a shoe harness attached to the pedal."

The chip on Ace's shoulder was obvious. Everyone listening heard his attitude, but no one reacted to it. No sympathy was wanted, so no sympathy would be given. These were coaches who understood dignity.

Domestique, the swim coach, was originally from England and spoke with a British accent. He interjected, "All right mate, the Big Race is a great goal, and I like your spirit. Glad you've got a little bit going for you because you're going to need it. You're going from zero to sixty miles-per-hour in the equivalent of 4.2 seconds. Normal training time for an iron distance race is two-and-a-half years. I'm not saying you can't do it, but you have to get cracking. If you're ready to work, we're ready to help."

Remnant seized the moment, "Bruiser, will you meet with Ace?" Bruiser was willing. "Ace, I have thirty minutes right now—or shall we set something up later next week?" Ace quickly responded. "I'm here—let's do this thing." Remnant announced the tour was over, so Ace joined Bruiser at his desk.

The Big Race had quite a history of amazing winners—their stories were memorialized, and each year several of the past winners were honored. It was good publicity and served as encouragement for future participants. While many had won the honor of wearing a green wreath on their head in the ancient Greek tradition, few were as notable as "Bruiser" Le Truce. He had become an iconic symbol of everything the race stood for. Bruiser was a homegrown champion who had defied all odds to make it to the top over two decades ago.

Bruiser was a world-class athlete with an indomitable spirit. At fifty-eight, he was still impressively strong. He was five feet, ten inches and 165 pounds, muscular, and lean. His face was marked by the kind of wrinkles that accompany a serious outdoors athlete. When he smiled, crow's feet appeared from the corners of his eyes and his forehead crinkled with line upon line. He had a rugged square chin, amplified by his flat-top hair, which was thin with hints of gray. His bottom lip was permanently scarred, with a little welt to one side, busted in his youth. Thin eyebrows adorned his brown eyes. And the eyesacks under his eyes framed his face in such away that it reminded one of a bulldog. In short, he looked like he had earned his nickname, Bruiser.

He looked tough; he was tough. A serious guy with a demeanor that communicated he cared greatly for those he coached. He believed in his students and expected much from them. He had a direct manner and a reputation for pushing his clients to new levels of accountability. He found faith in God about the same time he started running competitively. Now mature in years, he was interested in developing men, specifically challenging young males to become godly men.

Bruiser Le Truce had earned his nickname playing defense during a high school football practice. Guidry, the big, fast fullback, blasted through the line of scrimmage. Le Truce did his part and put his shoulder pad right in the mid-section of Guidry. In what should have been a textbook tackle, Le Truce instead landed on his back and was knocked unconscious.

Apart from being knocked out, Le Truce suffered a bruised rib cage from Guidry's knee slamming through his torso. He was "the bruised one." After that, the coaches called him "Bruiser." The name stuck, partly because the coaches never let it go. And partly because he was just a tough kid.

Later in life, Bruiser found his inspiration in triathlons. He was a marvel of endurance—he rewrote the books on age level performance. It was commonly believed that endurance racing belonged to the youthful. However, Bruiser got a late start and didn't run his first triathlon until he was thirty-three, and finally won the Big Race at thirty-seven. It wasn't supposed to happen that way, but Bruiser was different. He defied all the odds and remained the biggest inspiration for all the Big Race participants.

SPEED AND ENDURANCE WORLD RECORDS

Olympic Triathlon Record: Because courses vary, official records are not kept. However, Simon Whitfield holds the unofficial Olympic record for this distance {1 mile (1,500m) swim, 24.85 miles (40k) bike, 6.2 miles (10k) run} at 1 hour, 48 minutes, and 24 seconds.

Ironman World Records: Swim 2.4 miles; Bike 112 miles; Run 26.2 miles = total 140.6 miles
- Craig Alexander set the Hawaii course record in 2011 at 8 hours, 3 minutes and 56 seconds.
- Miranda Carfrae set the women's course record in 2013 with 8 hours, 52 minutes and 14 seconds.

Greatest Endurance Athletes of Our Time:
- James Lawrence completed 50 iron-distance triathlons in all 50 states over 50 consecutive days. He averaged 15 hours of movement per day as he swam a total of 120 miles, biked 5,600, and ran almost 1,300 miles, all with an average of four hours of sleep per night.

(*continued*)

+ Dr. James P. Gills is the only man who completed six double-ironman triathlons before the turn of the millennium. His last one at age 60—26 hours of continuous competition each.

Swimming:
Ultra-distance swimmer Diana Nyad swam continuously from Cuba to Florida in 2013 unassisted—a distance of 110 miles in 52 hours and 54 minutes at age 64.

Speed and Ultra-Distance Bikers:
+ The Hour Record: Sir Bradley Wiggins in 2015 rode 33.881 miles in one hour.
+ World's Fastest Bike Speed: Todd Reichert in 2015 rode 86.65 m.p.h. flat surface, unpaced.
+ Tour de France: 23 days of biking covering 2,200 miles.

Running:
Marathon 26.2 miles: Eliud Kipchoge of Kenya holds the current world record 2:00:25 seconds done on May 6, 2017 at 32 years of age.

Bruiser pulled out a three-ring binder and handed it to Ace. "If you want to be ready for this race next year, all you have to do is follow this schedule every day for the next 350 days, till the next race. It's pretty simple, really. Like a doctor makes a prescription, take your training from this book every day and you'll be ready. You're a man of faith, right?" Ace answered positively, so Bruiser continued. "Think of it as your Bible; your daily guide. A map. Consult it every day—it will keep you on your way."

"Every day accounted for—for 350 days," Ace said incredulously. "No rest!"

Bruiser assured him that rest was accounted for. "It's an important part of the regimen. The five disciplines of a triathlete are prescribed with balance."

Confused, Ace said, "Five? What do you mean? I counted three: swimming, biking and running.

"Yes, now add weightlifting and the final discipline of rest. Honor the Sabbath every week and give your body a chance to recover, refresh, and replenish. It's God's way designed right into the very fabric of creation—six days of work and one day of rest. Triathletes must practice rest to achieve maximum results."

ARE THESE PLANS FOR YOU?

Are you physically prepared to begin the Ironman training Bible regimen? To start these training plans, you should already be able to:

- Ride your bike for at least two hours and 30 minutes (nonstop)
- Run at least 60 minutes (nonstop)
- Swim 400M (nonstop)

*If you do not meet these fitness levels, you need to train to get **ready** to train. In such cases, following the plan below is not advised and could cause injury or death.

This is the simple and critical criteria to begin the Iron Distance training program. This is a program for competitors preparing to do their first Ironman. Example:

WEEK 8	Iron Distance Suggested Training Schedule
Monday	Swim 3,000M
Tuesday	Run one hour
Wednesday	Brick: Bike 4 hours, 15 minutes; followed by a 15-minute Run
Thursday	Bike one hour
Friday	Swim 2,000M
Saturday	Brick: A.M., Run 2 hours; P.M., Swim 25 minutes
Sunday	Rest Day

*Brick is the term for training in two of three disciplines.

This plan modified and adopted from various online training programs. Represents an actual schedule.

"I think I get it," Ace said out loud, but whispered "spiritual metaphor" under his breath. As their time came to an end, Bruiser told Ace it was great meeting him and instructed him to view the swimming and biking class schedules before leaving. He warned him to register in advance for spin class due to limited space. Then, Bruiser told him, as he was about to depart, "I look forward to seeing you around," and left on an errand. Later that day, Ace joined Buddy for some Saturday afternoon basketball.

Ace and Buddy tried to play basketball weekly. Unless life interfered (which it often did), it was a standing appointment. After the game, Ace was pleased to inform Buddy that they had a new basketball location option because he had joined the YMCA as part of his pursuit of competing in the Big Race. Ace said there would be some fresh competition to play against in the coming weeks.

Buddy answered, full of sarcasm, "Fresh meat! Is that what I'm supposed to be excited about? Maybe I could be excited if the fresh meat was some new girls." He paused before continuing. "You know, we're pathetic! We spend our spare time chasing this orange ball. That's what happens when you don't have a girl in your life—you sign up for more sports! I'll have you know that when I find a girl, I'm gonna drop you like a hot potato."

Finding a woman was the subject these best friends always seemed to kid each other about. Why was finding the right girl so elusive? They had no answer.

Later that night, Ace made his blog entry:

I joined the "Y" today. I also found out what the initials YMCA stand for. Trivia question for the day: Tell me what YMCA stands for and their mission. If you get it right, I'll send you an "Atta boy" or an "Atta girl." All joking aside, I joined, I'm committed. I whispered to myself as I gave the man my check, "No turning back." I'm in, and in some ways, I've already started, but training begins Monday morning.

I met Bruiser Le Truce today. No kidding. He was my consultant. How cool was that? He gave me an incredibly thorough plan to follow. It's an intimidating book, and I'm not much of a reader. This thing is as big as a doorstop. It's a training plan for every day for an entire year. I'm tired just thinking about opening it. But it's good to know I don't have to invent it. Listen now to these latest Wisbits.

Wisbit tip: *Resolve without planning, preparation, and accountability still equals failure. These four together equal success.*

Wisbit tip: *Preparation is ninety-five percent of every job. I've been preparing to prepare. It sounds weak but it's necessary.*

Wisbit tip: *Get your reasons, your resources, and a few coaches. Put yourself in a place that allows you to succeed.*

Wisbit tip: *Training schedules are a lot like Bible lessons; refer to them daily for guidance and you will succeed.*

Wisbit tip: *Honor the Sabbath and remember to keep it holy. Winners honor the discipline of rest.*

QUESTIONS FOR SELF-REFLECTION

- What do I do to honor the Sabbath and keep it holy?
- How am I currently preparing for greatness? How much energy am I ready to expend to prepare for my next achievement?
- What is the difference between a coach and a mentor? Who am I accountable to in order to maximize my life impact?

8

NO PAIN, NO GAIN

ACE HAD REGISTERED for Spinsey's Monday 6:00 A.M. stationary bike training class. Now as he entered the class he thought, *Incredible, twenty stationary bikes squeezed into this tight space.* One bike rose above the others front and center on a platform. There she was: Spinsey on deck pulling off her pink warm-up suit to reveal an all-black racing suit.

Wow! Ace thought, recognizing the contrast. *Spinsey is the real PBJ* (Pink and Black Jewel)—*the ultimate definition of a woman: both feminine and strong.* Pink for charm and gentleness, but underneath was an athlete and trainer. She was striking: high cheekbones, blue eyes, and blonde hair pulled back in a ponytail. Spinsey had the perfect body of a full-time fitness instructor. Her face was determined and focused. She was all business and took her craft seriously. She had to—because she was leading strong, accomplished athletes.

In Spinsey's case, her reputation, along with Bruiser's, had built the strength of the credibility of the triathlon team at this YMCA. Her clothing was modest for a form-fitting body suit. The other women seemed to be trying harder to look good with more frills and outfits revealing lots of skin.

Ace wondered who the women in the spin class were showing off for, the other girls or the few guys? The place was filled with plenty of young women, most in their young twenties and thirties. Some were single while others were moms, with a few in their forties battling to maintain their fitness.

There were only six men enrolled. Every bike was taken. There was also a waiting list. He overheard someone say, "Where's Maudrey?"

"Yeah, and where is Gladice?" Ace wondered if he had taken someone's spot. He sensed that some regular cyclist may have been bumped by his addition.

Ace reminded himself he shouldn't feel guilty for doing the right thing by being diligent. He seemed to be welcomed. Spinsey remembered him and introduced him to the rest of the class. "Everybody, welcome Ace, a first-timer."

"Awesome."

"Congratulations; glad you're here," commented the other bikers. Then, Ace heard a soft, flirtatious voice beside him say, "Nice to have another man in the lioness den."

Ace turned to behold Tanga. *Oh my*, he thought at first glance. *This was actually Tanga, the sports model superstar!* He'd seen her picture on the cover of Tri-Mag and he had seen her at the finish line of the Big Race—fourth place among all the pro women.

Tanga Bravo was one of the few world-class athletes with sponsor endorsements who had yet to win a race. She only had several finishes in the top five. So why all the endorsements? Simple: she was sexy and a serious competitor. At twenty-seven, this up-and-coming phenom was a good risk. Her beauty alone attracted the publicity of a rock star. Along with her long legs and olive skin, Tanga's body had curves in all the right places. Her long, dark, wavy hair was pulled back with a burgundy scarf, which accentuated her sensuous brown eyes. She spoke with a sweet demeanor. And whenever she wanted, Tanga could communicate to any man, *"Hey, look at me!"*

Tanga gazed at Ace, looked him over, and stopped with an eye-to-eye gaze—more precisely an eye-to-chin gaze as she said "Hey, big boy! Or should we call you Kirk Douglas? Look at the dimple in that chin!" Ace smiled and replied, "You can call me anything you want!"

Ace was handsome. His body was also athletic—lean and muscular. He had a military appearance and wore his short brown hair parted on the side.

Just then, Spinsey pumped up the music and barked out her first command: "I want you to imagine we are biking up the mountains today. Our first slope is only a slight incline. So put some medium tension on your resistance and get out of your seats. Your pace should be about eighty RPM."

An hour later, they imagined descending the hill at 110 RPM. At the end, Ace had a puddle of sweat beneath his bike. Spinsey conducted a cool-down stretching routine to help the body release lactic acid built up in the muscles. Finally, the lights were back on and the music silenced. Everyone gathered their belongings and headed for the door.

Ace didn't know what to say to Tanga, but wanted to say something to continue their conversation. So he blurted out his feelings in her general direction. "This is it. I found the insane asylum. We did the Tour de France and never traveled an inch."

Tanga took the bait and bantered back, "Yes, we did! And Spinsey always does it with such class. She's the best instructor there is, and I've heard them all. Spinsey can get your mind into Neverland, and she's got that mesmerizing soft voice, classy, and strong. Wait until she takes you through the desert." Ace said he would return for that experience. Tanga winked at him and was gone.

The others filed past Ace, but the last one out dropped her towel. Ace picked it up and returned it to her. "Hold up a minute, ma'am; you dropped this," he said as he reached out his hand with her towel.

"Thank you, but did you really just call me 'ma'am?' You make me feel like an old lady! Please, call me Charity." She was so sensible in her demeanor she was easy to overlook. Ace hadn't really noticed her until now. She was not loud or dressed to get attention. There was humility and a warmth about her that made Ace take notice. Her reply was filled with kindness.

Then Ace recognized her—it was the receptionist—with her hair in a ponytail! She was dressed like an athlete, the skirt and blouse gone... but the contented smile and crystal blue eyes were recognizable.

"I think I met you before. Were you working at the office here Saturday morning?"

"Yep, that was me."

"Nice to meet you again. I'm the rookie for the day."

"Yes, I'm glad you're making use of your new membership. Thanks again, and have a nice day." Then she was gone.

The moment Ace had been waiting for was before him; he was alone with Spinsey. Though there were plenty of pretty women, coach was most impressive. Tanga was beautiful, but Ace didn't pretend that he had a chance with her. To be honest, he wasn't certain he could be loved at all. His leg had ruined his love life. He often thought, *Who would want to marry someone who was half man and half machine?*

Soon after the motorcycle accident, Ace's fiancée gave a dozen reasons why they couldn't stay together. But he knew the leg was the real reason she dumped him. Since then, each girl he had shown interest in had only wanted to be friends. Besides the missing leg, Ace felt he was missing other things women were attracted to: wealth, a prominent degree, or an envious job. Ace was an audio/visual specialist, which would never translate into a lot of money. He only had an AA degree and was disabled. It was a battle to find self-worth.

Though Ace's confidence was shaken, he longed to get married and have a family. He was beginning to believe it may never happen. But today, he was around a whole new group of eligible women. *Maybe*...he had let his mind consider the possibility as he rode through the mountains during class.

Spinsey made her way to the door and asked Ace, "So, how do you feel?"

"Tired but great. That was interesting. Do you always do the imagination thing?"

"Every time. You gotta work with me here; we're all sitting and spinning. Try that for an hour with no enhancements. Music, lights, a good attitude, and imagination are the only tools I have."

"I liked it, I'm just trying to see where you're coming from. I'll be back."

Spinsey had a commanding demeanor about her and she kept her distance with her male students. And yet it seemed to her that Ace was inviting a declaration of her qualifications and so she respectfully obliged with a powerful tone. "Well, I'll tell you my spin on things. Hard work, diligence, self-discipline, being a self-starter, taking control, assuming responsibility for your life...you shape your future. You are the sum total of all your decisions. You are not a victim of circumstance. Everyone gets a choice. Day after day, you get to choose. When was the last time anyone made you do anything? When was the last time God made you do anything? We are made to be productive. I believe in living every minute to the fullest. I live to serve, I love to serve, and when I'm not productive, I feel guilty. My students know they can count on me to push them. I try to model what I want. I assure you, I work harder than anyone in class, including Tanga the pro." A possible twinge of envy was showing.

She continued. "Unfortunately, hard work is no match for talent when talent like Tanga's is willing to work hard. Sometimes I wonder if she is going to get comfortable with all the toys she's accumulating. They gave her a convertible BMW. She lives in Frostwood Estates and she's not even thirty. Not that I wouldn't do the same, but it's like winning the lottery. It ruins the life of almost everyone who wins. She's the best student I have. I push her, and she loves me for it.

"Stick around here, and I'll push you too. Excellence is what a good coach expects from their students. Practice does not make perfect. Perfect practice makes perfect. So that's what you can count on from me. So get ready to spin your legs off. No pain, no gain."

> *Great sacrifice is the basis of exceptional accomplishment.*

Ace heard something in her voice about the coach-student relationship that made him wonder, *Was this a boundary or an invitation to something beyond student coach?* For now, he was connected to her way of thinking. Hard work was one thing he understood. They had that much in common. The imagination thing was a little out there, but at least the rationale made sense; creativity versus boredom.

Ace closed their meeting with, "I got it, you're the real tormentor type. One thing I'm not afraid of is hard work, so I'm certain we'll get along fine. Thanks for everything. See you again next week." The two hiked down the stairs and into the lobby. Ace thought, *The journey begun is half done.* There was no stopping him now. He showered and made his way into his office.

That night, Ace felt tired. His morning trip to the gym had taken the gas out of him early, so he didn't feel like posting to his blog.

But the night was too young to turn in, so he scarfed down some macaroni and cheese (the dinner of college students and single men). Afterwards, he was rested enough to sit in front of his computer as he thought about what to write.

Today I really began the journey. Everything else—YMCA membership, consultations, registering for everything—was all preparation for the preparation to begin. I've been preparing to prepare, and now I'm finally preparing. I attended my first spin class today. For those who don't know what that is, it's a stationary bike class with a mind-blowing tour of the imagination. A bunch of crazies there, and some beautiful crazies to boot.

I met a celebrity—Tanga, the star from the cover of Tri-Mag. We sat together; now we're pals.

So I've been thinking about what I learned. I've been fishing for some juicy tidbits...I mean Wisbits to share, so here we go:

Wisbit tip: *Showing up is half the battle.*

Wisbit tip: *Coaches exist to push you beyond your self-contained limits, to hold you accountable, and call you to levels of excellence you couldn't achieve on your own.*

Wisbit tip: *Chase your dream. The energy spent chasing it has as much value as achieving the dream.*

Wisbit tip: *Determination = Striving to accomplish predetermined goals regardless of the opposition. Even if the opposition is from yourself.*

Life isn't always easy. Getting started in the face of uncertain success can be a major barrier. I found a poem quoted by Matthew Kelly[9] called "Anyway." It has given me hope to start with the promise of finishing this journey to become an Ironman. I believe it will encourage you as much as it encouraged me.

> People are unreasonable, illogical, and self-
> centered. Love them anyway.

---

9 Matthew Kelly, "The Rhythm of Life, The Need for Courage."

If you do good, people will accuse you of
having selfish ulterior motives; do good anyway.

If you are successful, you will win false friends
and true enemies. Succeed anyway.

The good you do today will be
forgotten tomorrow; do good anyway.

Honesty and frankness make you vulnerable;
be honest and frank anyway.

Big people with even bigger ideas will be shot
down by small people with even smaller lives;
think big anyway.

People favor underdogs but follow only top
dogs; be the underdog anyway.

What you spend years building may be
destroyed overnight; build anyway.

People really need help but may attack you if
you try to help them; help them anyway.

Give the world the best you have and you may
get kicked in the teeth. Give the world the best
you have anyway.[10]

Matthew Kelly then comments on this poem:

"Everything in life requires courage. Life takes courage. Courage is essential to the human experience. And yet it is the rarest quality in the human person. The most dominant emotion in our modern society is fear. Fear paralyzes the human spirit. Courage is not the absence of fear,

---

10   Paradoxical Commandments <www.paradoxicalcommandments.com>

but the acquired ability to move beyond fear. You weren't born with it. Courage is an acquired virtue."

QUESTIONS FOR SELF-REFLECTION

- What is my greatest fear? How can it be overcome?
- How willing am I to try something new?
- How do I determine if a pursuit is worthy of my effort?
- Have I ever quit anything? Did I make the right decision, or do I regret it?

9

ACE MEETS THE POSERS

THE NEXT MORNING, Ace woke up sore all over. His legs felt tight and ached with every step. He was fortunate to be motivated by his determined attitude. As a one-and-a-half legged man, he was surprised how much his thigh and hamstring were knotted up on his mechanical side. Eventually he made his way out of his house.

At the door of the YMCA was a friendly man, who looked to be in his late sixties and healthy. He was wearing a Tommy Bahama brand outfit, a casual island style shirt, designed to be worn untucked with a matching white wicker hat. To top it all off he sported a thick brown and graying mustache. If his goal was to look like Jimmy Buffet in concert at Margaritaville, he had nailed it. Now, he was acting as a self-appointed welcoming committee. He held the door open for Ace.

"Come on in, glad you're here this morning. I don't think I've seen you before. Welcome. I'm E.Z. Parker."

"You say that like you own this place."

"Yep, you could call me a shareholder for all the years I've been a member here. Is this your first time?"

"Yesterday was my first day; spin class with Spinsey…I'm back for more punishment."

"Well that's a heck of a way to get started your first day. You really *are* tough if you've come back."

"Well, not as tough as you think! I'm sore all over."

"Yeah, I bet! What are you trying to do, join the Tour de France?"

"Nope, been there, done that. All in the imagination of Coach Spinsey. They're all crazy." Ace's comment brought a smile to E.Z.'s face.

"Yes, I have to agree with you; those spin instructors are a unique breed. Bizarro, if you ask me!"

They walked into the locker room and then bumped into each other again as they exited into the weight/exercise room. Ace stopped and winced from discomfort as he stretched.

E.Z. was now wearing a T-shirt with a parrot on it and a pair of tan hemp woven shoes that might rather be worn at a country club than something you'd wear in a gym.

"Hey, if you're going to hang around here this morning, you may as well meet the gang." E.Z. hollered, "Hey, fellas, come over and meet…." He paused as he looked back. "I don't think I got your name." Ace introduced himself.

"Well, Ace, meet the 6:30 A.M. gang. This is a reliable group of friends that are here most mornings."

Ace extended his hand and shook each one with a quick exchange of names. "Shorty Cuttler," "Walkie Talkie," and "Sloppy Joe."

E.Z. inquired, "So what got you motivated to join the 'Y'?"

When Ace explained his plans to do the Big Race, Sloppy Joe replied, "Mercy me! We've got another racer."

"What do you mean; are you a racer?" replied Ace with astonishment. Sloppy Joe carried a few extra pounds on his frame. To be honest, Sloppy Joe didn't look out of shape; he just didn't look *in* shape. He looked like a little league umpire. He had a barrel of a chest and gut to boot.

"Oh, yeah; every year. Maybe not the big one, but every Thanksgiving we all race."

The guys kept talking with Ace for thirty minutes. He got the feeling they would never finish! Finally, Ace told the guys he needed to start working out.

E.Z. piped in. "The way to do this thing is little by little. You want to ease into things. Otherwise you could hurt yourself. Don't do this all at once, but gradually. Make sure you pace yourself. Spinsey yesterday, and a light workout with the weights today, and that should set you on the right path. Shorty knows every machine and station in this place. Let him help get you started."

"Well thanks, I could use some help."

Ace and Shorty Cuttler began stretching, then picked up a few dumbbells and went for the incline bench.

"Since you're just getting started, let's keep it simple—light weights and a few repetitions and we'll hit a few stations. When do you have to leave?"

"I've got about twenty minutes."

"Perfect! That's all I had on my schedule."

They did one set of eight reps on the incline bench. Then Shorty suggested due to the short time remaining that they do one set at each station, so he could show Ace all the major equipment.

It sounded like a good plan, so they did just that. While they made the rounds, Shorty shared his philosophy on life and working out. "Be yourself, guide yourself, follow yourself. Do what feels comfortable for you. Don't let somebody else tell you how to run your life. You know what's right for you. Let that guide your workouts."

When it was time to go, Ace was encouraged that he found a few friends, some real racers to help him on his way. Ace made his way to the gym each morning that week. He was in with the 6:30 A.M. gang.

On Wednesday, Walkie Talkie showed Ace how to program the treadmills to get the most comfortable workout. Then they walked side by side for almost the full hour. Ace was glad to be moving and not just talking. He felt like he'd wasted most of Tuesday. But Wednesday was nonstop motion. At the end of his workout, he felt little need for a shower, but he repeated E.Z.'s line: *Gradually*, he thought to himself, *gradually*.

Thursday, Sloppy Joe showed Ace several stationary bikes in the exercise room, so there was no need to go to the spin classes. Sloppy Joe explained that the stationary bikes in the grand room allowed them to ride at their own pace, increasing gradually as they felt ready. The two chewed the fat, took their hands off the handle bars, and cruised for about thirty-five minutes until Sloppy Joe was just plain pooped.

"When I get to this point, I like to move over here where I can lay down on the floor. Then I do a little routine with the bouncy ball to see if I can knock the gut off of this stomach. Six pack here we come...one, two, three..."

Ace was feeling the glory of being in the gym routine and mixing it up a little. He began to look forward to meeting with the guys. They took an interest in him and his mechanical leg seemed invisible to them. He received unconditional acceptance.

On Friday, E.Z. was proud to show Ace the lap pool. E.Z. loved to use the pool on Fridays because there were no swim classes scheduled at that time during this season. Besides, the other gang members liked to go to the coffee shop on Fridays. It was their way to start a grand weekend. E.Z. was hitting it off with this young man and wanted to teach him his easy way of swimming. It was a technique used by many distance swimmers to survive when their strength was exhausted. The crawl was performed while swimming on the back with the face toward the sky.

E.Z. preached on longevity. "If you want to go the distance, sometimes you have to crawl." It was a bad joke, but E.Z. was serious about his method. "Better to live to swim again than drown by overexertion," he warned Ace. "It's easy," as E.Z. demonstrated the technique.

But for Ace, it wasn't easy. The swim was his greatest fear in the competition. He'd done so little of it in his life. When he was a boy he'd spent some summer fun at the community pool but little more than that. And the missing leg was going to be a major challenge in the water. Ace didn't know how his body would respond to swimming. Everything he tried was ineffective, awkward and off-balance: crooked, zigzagging, sinking, crawling, or freestyling. A wave of fear seized Ace. *What if I can't do it?* he thought. He had been mentally preparing for this single moment since he said yes to the idea of triathlons. One of the hidden reasons why he never pursued triathlons in his younger years was simply a lack of confidence to swim well. And today was a horrible reminder that his missing leg was making a tentative situation worse. E.Z. saw him struggling, called practice off early, and suggested they make their way to the Jacuzzi.

Just then, Bruiser took a dive into the pool to cool down. He recognized both of them and greeted E.Z.

"So, you decided to get your toes wet this morning. How have you been, old man?" asked Bruiser.

"Old man yourself! You're no spring chicken anymore!" replied E.Z. It was a little playful bantering between long term friends.

"True, I'm no spring chicken, but I can still outwork all these young 'bucks' here! Someone's got to show the young men how to work. So, Ace, it looks like you've met 'old faithful' here. How's the training going?"

"Great week! I've done a little bit of everything. And E.Z. can testify I've been here every morning. So how about you—what brings you here this early?"

"Well, while you slackers were sleeping in, I was leading boot camp from 5:30-6:30 this fine morning."

"I've been in the military, but what's boot camp like here?" asked Ace.

"Not so different...we'll work you till you drop. We do strength and conditioning old-style. I mean some serious jaw-breaking stuff. We run suicides, transitioning every stage with push-ups, sit-ups, or squat thrusts. Then step masters on the picnic tables, jump rope, obstacle courses, and more pain than the body can endure." Bruiser was on a roll. He continued as he eyed E.Z., "Sorry, old buddy, but there's nothing *easy* about my class, pun intended."

E.Z. chuckled. "That's why you won't see me there."

"My class is just stopping by at the end to cool off. Ace, you ought to consider joining the 7:00 A.M. run group tomorrow. I'll introduce you to everybody. I just want you to know there are several groups traveling different speeds and distances. Come by if you can."

"I suppose I could—where do we meet?"

"The back door…7:00 sharp."

The conversation ended. Then Ace and E.Z. went to the Jacuzzi to find Tanga pleasantly lounging with two other men who were members of Bruiser's boot camp. It wasn't a pretty sight. Ace was not wearing his mechanical leg in the pool, so he hopped over to the Jacuzzi on one leg. His nub had been seen in all of its gruesome deformity. Ace couldn't sit in the Jacuzzi fast enough to get some sense of normalcy.

Almost simultaneously, Tanga quickly made her move to leave, but recognized Ace. She said to him as she stepped out, "Well now, Kirk Douglas is a swimmer too?!"

Strange feelings inside Ace warped this moment. Tanga remembered him, which made him feel good. However when she and her friends made a quick exit, it made Ace feel self-conscious that perhaps he was making others feel uncomfortable. But Tanga winked at him as she left and said, "Gotta run, see you around," and she was gone.

Perhaps she was just busy today, Ace thought, and let it go. He had no chance with this woman anyway. *Let it go,* he reminded himself. If he didn't get emotionally involved, Ace could keep an even keel about the others' reactions to him. He knew the more comfortable he was with his handicap, the more others would be comfortable around him.

℘

Saturday morning was a blur. Ace showed up at the last possible minute. Because Ace was late, Bruiser had no time to assign him a running group and told him, "Just stay with my group. I got the newbies today; 5K in thirty minutes." Then he gave directions to the group. "Everybody meet Ace. Now the time has arrived, so get ready and let's go!"

After they arrived back at the "Y," Ace didn't feel well. It was the banana he'd crammed down on his way over earlier that morning. He had felt queasy at the second mile, but wasn't going to quit—not with one mile to go. When he stopped, Ace took a big gulp from the water fountain. For some reason, that made things worse. He found himself retching under a tree.

Bruiser saw the whole thing, and now waited for a discreet moment to re-engage Ace. In a situation like that, he felt it best to give a man some space to let him keep his dignity. Now the time seemed right, so he called out, "Hey, you gonna be OK?" Ace was making his way back to the small gathering of runners.

"Geez, I hope so!"

"It can happen to anybody. Good job for your first day! It may seem like a reasonable pace, but if you haven't run for a while, it can wipe you out. It was strong for a first run. Anyone who's a little out of shape probably would not be able to keep up today. Based on what you said last Saturday, it's a testimony to your determination. Nevertheless, there's a price to pay for the years of coasting like a civilian. So, how did your first week of training go?"

Ace answered with some enthusiasm, "It was awesome. I was at the gym every morning. I felt sore after I jump-started the week Monday with Spinsey's bike class. Then I met with E.Z. and the 6:30 gang. I totally cross-trained all week. I practiced four of the five disciplines you taught me: a little running, a little biking, a little swimming and some moderate lifting."

Bruiser felt compelled to share his observation, "Sounds like a proverb I know—a *little* sleep, a *little* slumber, a *little* folding of the hands and a man shall come to ruin. A modern translation might say something like this: Sleep in till the last possible moment, and when you show up to the gym, don't break a sweat. Talk a lot, keep your repetitions moderate, follow that plan, and you will atrophy to the point of becoming unfit for racing, and into the grandstands you go."

"Sounds to me like the spiritual metaphor for athletes."

"I was there," said Bruiser, catching the hint and the allusion to the breakfast message.

"No kidding! Was that great or what? Champion rocked my world with that message. Wow! But I don't remember seeing you there."

"Well, it was a really big crowd, but I was there. I've heard him speak before. He's the real deal. He is resetting the finish line for retirement for me. I wanna be like him when I grow up." Ace and Bruiser both chuckled.

"Yeah, well, you guys speak the same lingo: 'spiritual metaphor.'"

"Making the spiritual connection to athletics has made a huge difference for me personally. So I get it and try to make my own para-phrased translations to help make better application of it in my life."

"Well, I'm starting to get it myself. That's why I'm here."

"Back to my question. Sounds like you got a great start—congrat-ulations! You're on your way. I'm just not sure where you're going. I saw you with E.Z. and his friends this week. So I'm curious about the workout plan I gave you…did you find it helpful?"

Ace was embarrassed and hesitant to reply. "Well…" he confessed, "I'm embarrassed to tell you I haven't had time to open it yet."

"Ace, there are lots of plans out there. Not all of them will get you ready for the Big Race. It's going to take a full year of training to get ready—you don't have time to waste. I've got to warn you, in some ways you're already off track. Get back to the book and follow the plan. I realize you already signed up. You're making some progress, but you cannot follow E.Z.'s plan of action. It will not get you across the finish line, because E.Z. doesn't know the way. He's never paid the price. He isn't willing to pay the price. He wants things easy. He likes to do as little as possible. He thinks like this: What is the least I can do and still be part of the YMCA workout team?

"Think of the Big Race triathletes as the special ops team. E.Z. and his men are posers. They are little better than the fans who sit in the seats. They have never done the Big City Big Race. In fact, E.Z. and his friends may boast to you that they have done a race, but the truth is they do a 5K, 'The Turkey Trot,' every year—a Thanksgiving Day slacker special. They look for the easiest race of the year and the shortest distance of the year. Then they take a 5K, which is a twenty-five-minute run, and turn it into a fifty-minute marathon, stopping at every Gatorade station along the way. And then they get a T-shirt to wear all year.

"Listen to me; you can't follow the E.Z. way to get to the finish line. 'Strive to enter in at the straight gate, because wide is the gate and broad is the way that leads to destruction. And many enter there. Because straight is the gate and narrow is the way that leads to life and few there be that find it.' You need to get the book open and follow the narrow way. You can do it, but you must remain focused. You're physically challenged, not a geriatric case. Be careful or you will inevitably become like the people you spend time with and call your friends. Wrong friends corrupt right living. But among good men, iron sharpens iron. Are you getting the spiritual metaphor, young man?"

Ace felt like he had been rebuked, but Bruiser did it with class and strength. Like velvet-covered vise grips, Bruiser put the squeeze on him. Ace liked direct talk; his military background helped him respect leaders. He replied, "OK, that's fair enough. I signed up, I took the book from you. I apologize. I didn't mean to waste your time. I give you my word. I'll open the book and get on it."

Bruiser Replied, "Nice. You'll thank me for it later. Ace, I know you've got what it takes to compete and finish this race. You showed me that today. That kind of resolve, mixed with the right preparation and planning, and you'll definitely make it." At that the two shook hands and departed each their own way.

As Ace walked to his car, the next group of runners arrived. He looked up in time to see Charity near the end of the trail. Their eyes met and they waved. Ace shouted, "Hey ma'am!" Charity smiled in return. Then Ace got into his car and was gone.

Later that afternoon, Ace met Buddy for a little Saturday afternoon basketball game with a few friends. And then, in the early evening just after supper, Ace opened his Triathlon Training Binder, read through the schedule for the coming week, and took a good look at what was involved. It was clear his workout time with the 6:30 gang was far below what the regimen called for in the training guide, "Bruiser's Bible."

Later that night, Ace blogged his week in review.

The spiritual metaphor continues. Hardly a day goes by without a chance to expand the spiritual metaphor of being an athlete and being a Christian. I met a coach today who had the courage to shoot straight with me. A little direct message to keep me focused. Mostly he won me over because he spoke a good destiny over me. He believes in me: in that sense he helps me believe in myself. Thx, coach.

I have fears—this swimming challenge is in my head, and I almost drowned the other day. OK, I didn't almost drown; I simply stood up in five feet of pool water. But I was sinking more than swimming. I don't have it solved yet. But where there's a will, there's a way. So God, help me figure this thing out. I am resolved, now I need a swim plan. I hope you enjoy this week's wisdom. Here's what I'm learning.

Wisbit tip: *Keep an eye on who you choose for your friends. They will inevitably shape your destiny.*

Wisbit tip: *Not all training programs are created equal, nor do they all prepare you for the same destination. Choose wisely. Training determines outcome.*

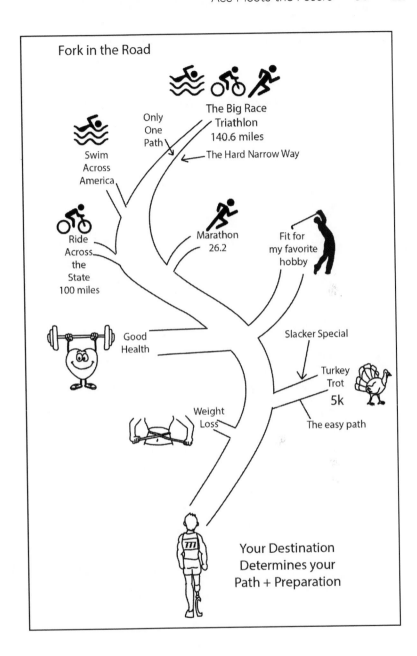

Fork in the Road

The Big Race
Triathlon
140.6 miles

Only One Path

The Hard Narrow Way

Swim Across America

Marathon 26.2

Fit for my favorite hobby

Ride Across the State 100 miles

Good Health

Slacker Special

Turkey Trot 5k

Weight Loss

The easy path

Your Destination
Determines your
Path + Preparation

Wisbit tip: *No pain, no gain. There are no shortcuts to greatness.*

Wisbit tip: *Everyone seems to ask, "What is the least I can do to get by?" How about asking, "What is the most I can do?"*

Wisbit tip: *Better to try and fail, than to never have tried.*

QUESTIONS FOR SELF-REFLECTION

- Do I often find myself making small compromises to my values, goals, and dreams?
- Who are my friends? What are they like?
- How do I respond to high levels of accountability?

10

THE SPIRITUAL METAPHOR: FOOD FOR THE SOUL

A LOT HAD HAPPENED in three weeks. Time was flying by, and today Ace was excited to return to Doc Mentor's office. He had fulfilled his assignment and already learned so much. He wasn't sure what they would talk about and so didn't know how to prepare.

Ace walked around in the waiting room where he stopped to look in one glass case where he saw a photograph of Doc as a boy, accompanied by his bike and his dog. The thought occurred to Ace that Doc must have been an athlete himself in his earlier years. Now he began to think about all he had been through and asked himself: *What's the purpose of our meeting? I don't want to waste this man's precious time. I can tell him I decided to pursue the race. I can tell him everything, but why am I here? This man is important. At first it was to help me evaluate if I should run. But I'm decided now, so what else?* The uncertainty made his heart beat fast. Ace thought and pondered. And then it finally dawned on him, the perfect question to ask and then his heart settled.

Finally, Ace was called into the same room as before and told to wait for the doctor. Like clockwork, the smiling, weathered face appeared shortly thereafter. "Ace, thanks for coming by. Glad to see you. I've been praying for God to give you wisdom to help you decide. We covered a lot last time, didn't we? We finished by listing several good reasons to race, but the discovery of your identity was the issue, I believe. So tell me how things went when you met with Sage?"

"His name says it all. Very impressive insight. But at first I was a little shocked by his appearance, but then it seemed like he had more life than most healthy, able-bodied people I meet. Thanks for allowing me the privilege of meeting with him."

"You're very welcome. So what did the two of you discover?"

"He helped me formulate my identity statement in no time. Give me a second and I can tell you." Ace thought hard, and it slowly returned to his mind. "I am an athlete...I am a man of action...I am a visionary planner...I bring hope to broken lives through practical steps from my personal example...particularly to young athletes and rehabbers. Hey, that's me! I also learned that identity predicts destiny. So I am happy to report I've decided to do the race. It fits my identity and it certainly is worth it for all the reasons you mentioned on our last visit: temple maintenance and the pursuit of the spiritual metaphor. In keeping with my identity, Sage challenged me to see if I could even run for a cause. I am still looking for a noble way to satisfy that. But that hasn't stopped me from starting; I'll figure that out later. I want to report that I joined the local YMCA and spent all last week there. And I've even registered for the qualifying event, the Rocky Pointe Half Iron so I already began, and I must say a great big thanks to you. Your words keep echoing in my head. I'm finding the spiritual metaphor as I train almost daily. I can't say thank you enough."

Doc replied, "It sounds like you two really hit it off. You know, I don't think there has ever been a person stand before him whom he hasn't asked his favorite question: 'Who are you?'"

"Yeah, that's how we got started, and then on to pens and knives."

"Knives? That's new, but the pen illustration is his favorite. He shared that with me twenty years ago, and it really stuck with me too. So you've decided to join the triathletes and become nobility. Congratulations. Great decision—what can I help you with today?"

Ace posed his question. "I was hoping you might give me a few pointers on how to prepare for this race...what to do and what not to do?"

"Now that's a loaded question and it's the right question. I've got more to share than you can imagine. Thanks for asking. But before we get started, let me give you a pop quiz and we'll see how much you learned from Sage. See if you can answer my riddle by filling in the blank: A dog barks because....??"

"He feels threatened?" Doc shook his head. Ace tried again. "He's hungry?"

"No, a dog barks because a dog is a dog! Dogs do what dogs do; essence has its expression in behavior and thus is easily able to forecast outcome. Essence produces after its own likeness"

"Right on; that was the lesson. It makes perfect sense to me."

Doc began once again to talk with his hands. "Essence"—he held his left hand up with his palm facing the ceiling with his fingers bent as if he were holding an imaginary hand full of essence—"and outcome"—now Doc held up his right hand with the same gesture—"are inseparable;" then he joined his hands together with woven fingers as if to pray. So now that we are clear on that, let's ask the question, What is the essence of God? And what therefore is our ultimate Christian outcome?"

Ace sat there, uncertain if he was supposed to try to answer. This was getting deep—fast. He finally blurted out, "I don't know, what?"

"Follow my train of thinking here. Essence determines outcome. So the next logical step is that we need to attempt to define essence: namely, the essence of God and how that impacts you. This is extremely important, because you can't achieve what you cannot define. So when we clearly define the nature of something—voila! Behavior, destiny, and outcome can easily be predicted.

"God's essence never changes, but ours should be continuously transformed more and more into His likeness. The Scriptures are clear on this. Paul writes that we are to be conformed to the image of Christ, to be made after His likeness. That doesn't mean to wear Jesus sandals, a robe, and a beard. I'm not talking about outward appearance, but the inward character. That's what a disciple is: someone who follows after, imitates, lives with the same values, attitudes, purpose, and goals of the leader. We need to press in to the essence of Jesus to more clearly define the nature of God. When we do, we can become like Him in our essence and behavior.'"We call this the Imago Dei, which is Latin for 'the image of God.' And Christ is the expressed image of God, Imago Dei.

"Let's explore this further. For example, we know that God is love. If you aim to grow in love, how will you ever know if you are acting lovingly unless you can clearly define what love is? By the way, it was so important to God to define love that He took a whole chapter of the Bible to add clarity. Why? Because that's His essence. Clarity of God's essence, matched with the power of the Holy Spirit, make attaining Christ-likeness possible. So if you want to measure your lovingness quotient, open up I Corinthians 13 and start to compare and contrast your life against this standard.

"God is love, so how do you think He's going to act?"

Ace simply replied, "In love."

"Now you're getting it: understanding the image of God is fundamental. And believe it or not this is exactly what God says is truly worth bragging about. Here is what God says about the matter in an athlete's paraphrase of Jeremiah: 'Let not the educated man boast about his fine diplomas from an Ivy League college, nor should the Ironman boast about his strength, speed and endurance. Do not let the rich man boast about his possessions, his stocks, his investments and big growth plans. But let him who boasts, boast that he understands me with his mind and knows me in his heart. I am the Lord God Almighty and the essence of my being is expressed and understood on earth, through things like my unfailing love, justice and righteousness, for these things give you clues to what I'm really like. I love to be known in this way, these qualities highlight my essence.'

"God's essence is love, justice and righteousness; we train by making personal life application according to this revelation. *Act loving* by defining God's version of love! *Render justice* by applying the right mixture of God's mercy and truth! *Behave righteously* by coming to understand God's right way of living as revealed in the Scriptures! That's the spiritual dimension of this metaphor.

"Now I want you to think of the physical dimension of the Big Race preparation. To finish the race, you are going to have to train hard to transform your body through strength and conditioning. That's how you'll get your cardiovascular system renewed. You will need a training program that allows you to participate in every phase by training with each element no less than twice a week. Swim twice, bike twice, and run twice. Little by little is the rule. Don't increase your workout more than ten percent a week at a time. Start small and gradually build.

"If you are planning on doing the Big Race eleven months from now, you'll want to build up to it by first doing an Olympic triathlon in about four months, and then do the Rocky Pointe Half Iron qualifier eight months from now. You are ambitious to try to conquer this in just one year. Something more realistic would have been two or three years. But since you've already registered and paid, I'm not going to talk you out of it. Don't think you're going to set any records. If you finish before the cutoff time of seventeen hours, count yourself a winner."

"OK, so I was a bit optimistic on the time frame, but they have my money, so there's no turning back. Tell me again you believe it can be done. Tell me it's possible."

"You've got guts and I sense you've got the discipline to prepare, and a starting platform of athletic engagement. One year is ambitious, but yes, you can do it."

"OK, I needed to hear that," Ace said, feeling the gravity of his choice for the first time.

"I know you've counted the cost. There are so many hidden variables that will knock you out if you don't prepare. Seven percent of all athletes who start the race don't finish. That's a staggeringly high number, considering those who show up have prepared extensively to finish.

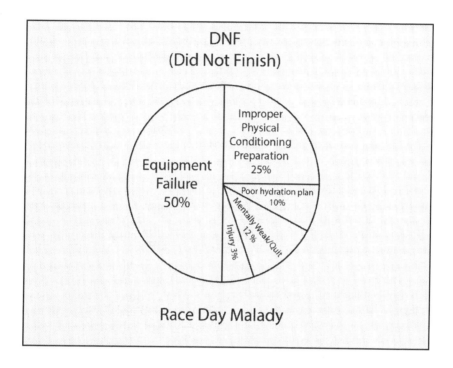

"The body is depleted after three to four hours of intense exercising. Think of professional athletes in other disciplines: football, basketball, and soccer. These games are played for one to three hours, and most of these world-class athletes are totally spent. You're going to be going pretty much nonstop for fifteen to seventeen hours, and that's just to finish. The guys who win these things train for years to run it in nine hours or less. The average newbies like you are going to be pushing themselves to the limits just to cross before the time expires at midnight. After that, you just become a pumpkin, another statistic going into the DNF file. You know what that means: 'Did Not Finish.'

"The spiritual metaphor is unmistakable. If you want to be like Christ, spend lots of time with Him. He actually created you with the goal of being best friends with you. I like to say it this way: I was created **by** God, I was created *for* God, and my life's highest ambition is to be best friends **with** God. Start by attending church regularly and allow your time with Him to grow each day. You will find being in His presence has a transforming effect. You'll find peace as you learn to rest in his redemption. His essence rubs off onto you. And, in due season, behavior follows essence. Then you'll be known as a disciple of Christ because you resemble Him with your genuine expression of love for others.

"In short, you become what you consistently look at and think about. To morph into Christ's image, stay focused on His character and his essence, and try to imitate it. Little by little, transformation happens. The popular saying is you are what you eat and more recently people are saying you are what you drive, but the truth is you are what you think.

"The physical preparations for a race are the same: intense focus is required. You need a plan to follow routinely, even daily. Get around a great team of coaches with whom you have continuous contact and eventually, you will morph into a great triathlete.

"Those, my friend, are my tips for the race," Doc said with a wink and a smile. "Here's a recap: get yourself signed up to race in an Olympic distance triathlon in about four months, and then train, train, train if you want a chance to qualify for the Big Race at the Rocky Pointe Half Iron. That is the path you need to take to get ready. After you have finished the Olympic distance race, why don't you pay me another visit?"

Moments later, Ace was out the door. Later that night, he wrote in his blog about his encounter.

Today I met with Doc Mentor again and took the love survey. I discovered that I have been selfish in my living. No one probably ever mistook me as being a disciple of Christ because my love has been so weak. *The expression of Christianity is to love like Christ, but behavior follows essence, so in order for me to love like Christ, I've got to enjoy the pleasure of His company and let him transform me. It's an inside out job. It is overwhelming to think of, but my mentor says we make changes little by little—purposefully living, bit by bit. Here's what I learned:*

Wisbit tip: *Be transformed in your essence by being with God; spend enough time with him and his essence will rub off on you.*

Wisbit tip: *Repetition in lifting weights transforms the body. It takes mental repetition to transform the soul. Rehearse the Scriptures to transform the mind.*

Wisbit tip: *God likes to be known for love, justice and righteousness. That's my target.*

Wisbit tip: *Imago Dei = the Image of God. Christ is the image of God on earth.*

QUESTIONS FOR SELF-REFLECTION

- Am I spending enough time with God each day to be transformed in my character, attitudes, and actions?
- How does my life compare to the definition of love found in 1 Corinthian 13? What can I do to improve my ability to act lovingly?
- Am I daily seeking first to advance God's kingdom and His right way of living?
- What is my basis for justice? Does it match God's nature?

11

SHAPE UP OR SHIP OUT

Late Sunday night, Ace once again picked up the triathlon training binder to get a sense of where it was going. He skimmed the pages, pausing long enough to digest the overall objectives and flow of growing intensity. He studied his next week's assignments to understand what Monday's workout should be.

Monday morning Ace attended Spinsey's class. Then on Tuesday he continued to modify his interaction with E.Z. He'd simply greet them warmly, spend a few minutes with them, and quickly move on. But the intensity, duration, and choice of activity would be determined by the training regimen needed to prepare for his race. Ace would set the agenda, not the other way around. He simply had to do things differently to get ready for the Big Race.

In the two weeks that followed, Ace's growing intensity naturally separated him from the "E.Z. Gang."

After another two weeks, Ace met another man in the gym closer to his age. Bobo was in his mid thirties, married, and a father of three young daughters. He'd been a triathlete for many years. Training was a part of his life. Like Ace, Bobo had been a high school athlete, but his life proved to be filled with distractions, so his training had been sporadic.

Bobo had a hard time staying focused because everything had something important to offer him. Football season meant watching games, and the internet begged to be researched. His daughters often needed to be dropped off or picked up somewhere. He also needed and wanted to take his wife out. Over the last few years, Bobo's training was a "blink on/blink off" type of affair. Recently, he had recommitted himself to competing in the Big Race.

Ace found Bobo to be both a friend and accountability partner in his training. The two had plenty in common, so when Bobo showed up, they challenged each other. Bobo became the 6:30 gang alternative. Ace was glad to have Bobo at Spinsey's class, which was always sparse on males.

With the emergence of Bobo as a training partner, Ace's workout intensity went up. They were pushing each other to greatness. That's when Ace started to feel a growing discomfort in his prosthetic. There was a stinging irritation where his flesh and harness met. Ace was tough, so he never complained to anyone about his discomfort. That was one excuse he'd never allow himself to use. He wanted to be treated like everyone else, so he taught himself to ignore what he considered trivial pain. But this sting hadn't dissipated over the last few days. And so he knew it was time to schedule another appointment with "The Great Oz," the prosthetic engineer who had fitted him from the beginning.

☙

Don Osbourne was a consummate craftsman. A lifetime of service to handicapped amputees had gained him the reputation of being a bit of a wizard, hence the nickname "The Great Oz," or more commonly, just "The Wiz." He was a matchmaker. Everything about prosthetic fit was always custom, because every amputee was unique. Ace was very active and his insistence on playing basketball made his need for adjustment from "The Great Oz" more frequent than most.

Ace entered the Veterans' Affairs, or va, hospital through a side door and checked in at the receptionist window. He took a seat in the waiting room. Ace noticed a younger man sitting across from him with a similar amputation—right leg at the knee—no prosthetic in sight, only crutches leaning against the wall. The man had let his hair grow out quite a bit beyond military regulation and he sported a scruffy beard. Ace sized the situation up quickly and asked, "Is this your first time here?" The young man was busy filling out a form and replied in a hushed tone, without looking up. "Yeah, I just had my initial consultation." His tone made it obvious he was feeling dejected. "They say I have to fill out this paperwork for insurance, then fill out more paperwork to apply to a foundation to help fund the equipment." Ace could hear the resignation in his voice. He responded with empathy and introduced himself. "I'm Ace, good to meet you." The young man looked up for the first time and introduced himself like someone on the verge of depression. "Dan Strubie, but everyone just calls me Scoob. I kind of look like Shaggy and I once had a Great Dane, and now people just call me Scoob."

The office assistant called for Ace to come in for his consultation. Ace reassured Scoob as the two parted. "I feel your pain, but I need you to know it gets better. I know the paperwork is a hassle, but you'll get through it. Then 'The Great Oz' will have you walking again in no time at all. Hang in there."

A few moments later, Ace was seated in what looked more like a workshop than a patient consultation room. After all, this wasn't medicine in the traditional sense. Oz was like a refined modern-day blacksmith. He wore a dark leather apron which hung around his neck and also tied around the waist. He was built like an anvil. His biceps could not be contained in his short-sleeved shirt. His compassionate brown eyes were framed by a reddish orange head of hair and a neatly trimmed thick beard. Oz was personable and disarming. He extended his hand to Ace as he asked, "How are you doing? Is that new leg of yours continuing to give you the responsiveness you were looking for on the basketball court?" Then he looked at his notepad. "You wrote on your questionnaire that you're experiencing a hot spot on the crown of your knee. Ace, you've had that leg for some time now. What do you think is going on? Are you doing anything differently?"

"I think it's pretty simple. Since I last saw you, I've become a tri-athlete. Right now, I'm training for the Big Race, and I've discovered when I'm running longer distances, I seem to be working my hip a lot harder to compensate. To tell you the truth, there is a lot of soreness in the muscles that operate this hip joint. And I'm wearing down my gel liner and that's causing problems as well. So I'm ending up with some blisters and a little bit of bleeding, accompanied by a lot of pain."

Oz made his conclusion. "Well, that makes perfect sense to me. You have the wrong tool for the job. You're probably thinking you've got a $70,000 'bionic leg,' so that's all you need. But when it comes to running long distances, you're going to need a blade. How is your other leg feeling?"

Ace replied, " I feel like it's responding with strength. My pants don't fit like they used to. I seem to be bulking up on the thigh and the calf muscle."

"More specifically, what about your knee?" asked Oz.

Ace said, "Well, I am feeling some strain in two places." Ace pointed at his knee as he talked. "On the outer edge I'm experiencing what I'd describe as tendon aggravation. And there's a sharp pain under my kneecap, especially after spin class."

Oz was putting the pieces together. "That's just what I suspected, Ace; one of the hidden variables for the handicapped athlete is the law of compensation. It's as real as the law of gravity. Your body is trying to adapt. The other parts of your body are compensating for the missing leg, which translates to greater stress in the ligaments of your good leg and hip. I know we've talked about this kinda thing before, but as your specialist, I've got to warn you: training for the Big Race is going to wear your body out twice as fast. The research has validated that the average handicapped athlete's body is working forty percent harder through the law of compensation. So while every able-bodied athlete is doing 140.6 miles of iron distance racing with the energy split between two legs, you have one working leg. That exacerbates your energy output, impacting your body more like 200 miles. And nobody knows for sure how that's going to affect your good leg. There is a lot of research indicating endurance racing among the handicapped will take its toll over time. I can't tell you what to do, but I'd be irresponsible if I didn't tell you the likely effects in the later years of your life."

"I hear you, boss. It could cost me everything. Doing the Big Race might not be reasonable, but nothing great was ever accomplished by its measure of reasonableness. Sorry, Oz, it's too late! I've already decided I am going to do this race regardless. God made me to be an athlete, and I feel His pleasure when I race."

"Well, if that's the case, my job is to help you succeed. So let's at least get you outfitted correctly. If you're going to do this race, you're gonna need the right equipment. First, the bike. I think I can help there with a modification of your 'Total Knee 2000,' but if you're going to be running marathons, the wise thing to do is get fitted with a blade and a Cheetah Knee. You know the drill—we need to write a compelling case for another grant. These blades aren't cheap."

The agreement was made and now the dreaded paperwork was started for Ace to procure this luxury specialty item. Eventually they got it done and now began the waiting game.

ACE'S PROSTHETIC PRESCRIPTION AND HISTORY

Ace's first leg: Total Knee 2000 with a Vari-Flex Foot (Ossur, mfr. for both). He gets a suction socket with a cushion liner that incorporates a ring to seal to the inner socket wall. Ace's leg amputation is called AK meaning Above the Knee (technically transfemoral).

After a few months of rehab and getting used to wearing the leg he starts playing basketball with the Total Knee prosthesis. This startles the VA because so many amputees say they are going to play ball again but don't. Ace actually does!

After eight months, he goes in for a follow-up evaluation. VA prescribes a new socket because the first socket is loose causing suction loss and irritation that accompanies an insecure fit. The C-Leg 4 Microprocessor Knee with TaiLor Made Foot (both OttoBock, mfr.) is prescribed. This is a great above knee prosthesis for a very active person. The C-Leg 4 is very responsive at any instant no matter what walking speed he has. This is what Ace refers to as his "Bionic Leg." The foot is shock absorbing and conforms well to uneven terrain outdoors and gives a good energy return through his step on the prosthesis.

However, Ace, without asking, begins playing basketball again in this new computerized bionic leg more and more but it becomes a problem with friction heat. The knee sometimes seizes up when hot after running the court. Also the pounding on the hip on his amputated side is getting worse over time.

Several months ago, the VA ordered an AllPro Foot to fit on the old Total Knee 2000 specifically for basketball. The AllPro Foot (Fillauer, mfr.) is a super shock absorbing blade-like running foot but with a heel for a basketball sneaker to fit on the blade. The first of its kind. It's awesome for quick-cutting, side-to-side moves, and shock absorption for his hip on the jumps when landing.

At this point, Ace has written a lot of grants and received a lot of specialized prosthetics for his active lifestyle.

Today, The Great Oz prescribes Ace for a Cheetah Knee and Flex Run Foot (Ossur mfr. for both) to run the long distance triathlons. Ace will have to apply for a special VA grant to get this new prosthetic combo. This Cheetah knee is perfect for running with hydraulic knee swing control and is very light and inherently stable (meaning the knee will not buckle) due to its polycentric joint design. The Flex Run Foot is a blade foot without a heel. It has a Nike made sole attached on the bottom of the toe which bounces on the pavement every step. Again, the blade foot really saves the hip joint from the constant pounding onto the ground.

Oz modifies Ace's Total Knee 2000 with a "Ferrier Coupler" enabling a quick interchange between biking and running with a modified Vari-Flex Flex Foot with attached pedal cleat. This is a very light knee, and this specialized foot lends itself to being easily modified for resting on the bike pedal and attaching to the cleat bracket.

His sockets are fit with a suction valve that suspends the prosthesis on the residual limb. The socket materials provide a flexible inner socket brim for pelvic comfort.

For his triathlons, Ace wears one socket using a gel liner with a sealing rubber ring. The gel liner is rolled on very carefully directly on the limb. The socket goes on over the liner precisely in alignment with his limb anatomy. Once it is on, he doesn't want to have to take it off in the race. At the end of his socket is the top half of the ferrier coupler. The two different knee and foot systems have the bottom half of the ferrier coupler, which allows him to switch his knee and foot systems quickly, shortening his transition times.

Such is the condition of Ace, "The Bionic Man."

Total Knee 2000 and Vari-Flex Foot Px = $14K including socket
C-Leg 4 with TaiLor Made Foot Px = $70K including socket
AllPro Foot = $6K including attachment adapter
Cheetah Knee and FlexRun Foot Px = $25K including socket
Total Knee 2000 and modified Vari-Flex Foot with cleat = $15K[11]

In the meantime, week after week, Ace attended Spinsey's class; eleven weeks to be exact. He was faithfully there imagining mountains, beaches, plains, deserts, wind, and more. The rest of his imagination was mostly devoted to whether he could get a few words with Spinsey before or after class. He thought he was making relational progress; the chemistry was growing.

ଔ

After many weeks, it happened! He received the invite he wanted. By faithfully attending and paying attention to what others said, Ace became aware of a group of real riders—riders with real bikes in the

---

11   Don Smith, Consultant.

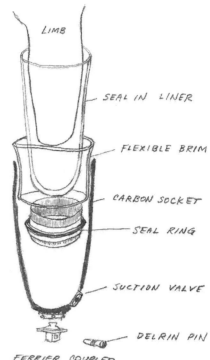

LIMB

SEAL IN LINER

FLEXIBLE BRIM

CARBON SOCKET

SEAL RING

SUCTION VALVE

DELRIN PIN

FERRIER COUPLER

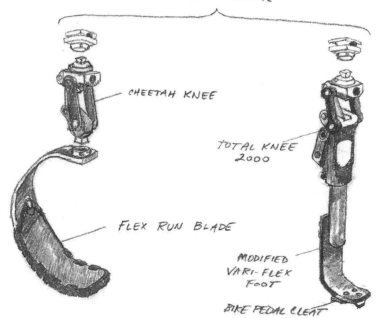

CHEETAH KNEE

TOTAL KNEE 2000

FLEX RUN BLADE

MODIFIED VARI-FLEX FOOT

BIKE PEDAL CLEAT

real world; a group led by Spinsey. It seemed to be an unpublicized, closed group of Spinsey's friends. Today was Ace's lucky day. After class, he hung around to engage Spinsey in conversation when she extended the offer.

"You know, there's a group of us who ride Saturday mornings up on Sky Way trail. You should consider joining us; but I gotta tell you in advance—we ride fast, and we will drop you if you can't keep up, so don't take it personally. These are the best of the best and they take training seriously. So it's probably not fair to ask you, but I've watched you in class and you're looking good."

Ace was amazed she watched him and thought he looked good! He quickly answered. "Sure! I'd love to; what time do you start?"

"Wheels down 7:00 A.M., so plan to get there before that."

"Well, thanks for the invitation. I'll be there." Ace smiled as he walked away. *Maybe there could be something brewing,* he thought. *No doubt this was a good sign. They were comfortable enough for a group date. OK, maybe it wasn't a date, but it was* **something.**

☙

Saturday at Sky Way trail, the parking lot filled up quickly with bike racks attached to every vehicle. Ace had a truck, and easily pulled out his ten-speed Schwinn. He had put air in the tires before leaving the house since it had been several months since he rode it last. Spin class had been his "bike time."

As he walked his bike toward the trailhead, Ace noticed that many of the bikers checked and added air on site. Then it hit him like a ton of bricks. His bike was not like the others. This was his old high school 10-speed bike, electric blue, black-wrapped handle bars, pretty nice in that respect. *Whoa!* he thought, *there was some money in the bikes he passed.* His bike resembled a child's toy compared to the others. Every bike he saw had some exclusive name written on the side. The designs were novel and aerodynamic.

At least he had a helmet, he thought. Then it occurred to him that his helmet was not like the others, either. In high school, he thought those bike helmets looked squirrelly, so in the past he would use his skateboard helmet, if any at all. Suddenly he felt awkward and out of place, embarrassed to meet Spinsey's gang. He thought about turning around and offering some excuse on Monday, but backing out was off the table when he heard a loud voice calling him.

"Kirk Douglas, over here!" It was Tanga. He also saw the rest of the quickly-assembling group. Ace sensed they were almost ready to roll. He checked his watch; it was 6:55. Ace had cut it close, but he was on time. Spinsey, as usual, was about to assume her leadership role and gave Ace an enthusiastic shout-out as he came closer.

"You made it! Glad you're here." Then Spinsey started to give directions. "OK, everybody, we're all here. I think most of you know Ace from spin class, but the rest of you say hello to Ace—it's his first time riding with us."

"Hey, Ace, I'm Jack Rabbit." Someone else said, "I'm Ray Boltz," and another said, "Glad you're here. Nice to meet you; they call me Wendy."

Nobody poked fun at Ace or made snide remarks about his helmet or bike. This was one of those times he felt maybe it was a sympathy gesture. People tended to treat him with sympathy because he was crippled, and Ace hated that the most; all he wanted was to be treated normally. However, it may have helped today, because it was apparent Ace hadn't dressed appropriately either. He wore gym shorts with a T-shirt.

It never occurred to Ace that there might be a dress code. The guys in spin class somewhat dressed as he had today, but apparently it made a difference on the trail. The other men looked like the professionals on the Tour de France. He felt vulnerable, yet everyone treated him with dignity.

Spinsey piped up. "Look, everybody—we'll be doing the usual. We're going thirty-five miles today in an hour and forty-five minutes. That includes the pit stop at the water station at mile fourteen on the return trip. Do the math: We're going to average twenty-three miles an hour. Coasting steady at twenty-one and pushing twenty-six a few times…let's keep the rotation going at five minutes a clip. Everybody take your turn cutting the headwind. Hold it as long as you can and then rotate to the back. If you need to drop for any reason, we'll catch you on the way back. Saddle up and get ready to roll!"

Spinsey scooted herself over to Ace before mounting her bike to give him a few additional personalized tips. "Ace, the idea here is called a peloton. It's all about drafting and sharing the load. We go faster and further together. It's like geese flying in 'V' formation and rotating the lead position. You'll want to follow closely behind me. Get your front wheel two feet behind my back wheel and let me pull you. When I rotate back, you lead. It's a lot harder, so hold it as long as you can and then rotate back." Then Spinsey mounted her bike as did the other riders. Spinsey shouted out, "OK, let's go!"

Ace was second seed in a two-abreast peloton. Ray Boltz had the other lead position. Beside him was Wendy, with five more behind him and five more behind her. Fourteen was not so small a group. Ace felt they were off to a speedy start, but it was just the first mile to warm up. The pace increased when Spinsey was satisfied with the warm-up. This was how she did it in class: five minutes to get loose and comfortable, then imagination into the never-lands began. No imagination today. Spinsey dropped a gear or two. Ace followed her cue and dropped to tenth gear.

Though the pace was fast, Ace didn't know how fast because his bike had no speedometer, which was standard equipment for triathlete bikes. His muscles began to burn. Ace was glad he was drafting because he could barely keep up. He struggled and they were only 10 minutes in…this was **not** spin class!

Spinsey and Ray Boltz rotated back, which left Ace leading the peloton with Wendy. The additional load of breaking the wind was too much, so Ace only lasted a minute and had to drop to the back. He tried to fall in behind the peloton and enjoy the drafting position

again, but it was too late. His legs were gassed, his breathing was too heavy, and his heart rate was too high. The group had moved on; Ace could see them quickly distancing themselves from him as he rolled to a coasting cruise. He needed to recover.

The group was out of Ace's sight when he began to seriously pedal again. He had been warned. Now, he was his own coach. *Push yourself*, he thought. He made the most of it, riding free and furious at times. Ace felt stupid and beat himself up mentally for the next fifty minutes. Eventually, he stopped at the water station when he saw the peloton coming toward him on the return path.

The group was coming to a stop; now he was reunited with the team. Perhaps Ace would be able to rejoin them. They knew they had dropped him and had discussed what to do. They would stop and help Ace rejoin when they found him. The water station was an easy meeting point because the peloton had planned this break for water and to stretch out a moment. Spinsey came over to Ace and said, "Come on and join us again. Hop in at the back, enjoy the draft."

"I'd love to, but I don't think I can keep up your pace even if I draft."

"You're right. You won't be able to stay with us long, but the way to grow is to stay with us as long as you can. We want you. You coming or not?" Spinsey prodded him. "Come and ride as long as you can."

Ace incredulously agreed. "You've made an offer I can't refuse; gimme a second." Ace drafted at the back and greeted the rider next to him. His name was Resilience.

Ace peddled too hard to talk much, but Resilience blurted out phrases of encouragement every fifteen seconds or so.

"Hangeth thou in there, buddy.

"It takes courage not to give up.

"Never, never, never give up.

"The race is not given to the swift or the strong, but to those who endure.

"Bounce back; you ain't going out like that!

"Live to fight again.

"Fall forward, fail forward.

"It's not that you fall; it's the getting back up that matters.

"What doesn't kill you only makes you stronger.

"The only losers are the quitters."

Ace stayed longer this time than before, but fifteen minutes was all he could stand. He had to quit because his muscles couldn't take any more. He was left with the haunting words from Resilience, "The only losers are the quitters." Ace was quitting, or at least dropping off again, gassed and out of breath.

> I will not quit.
> I will never give up.
> I do not listen to
> myself; I talk
> to myself.

Ace felt like he was quitting but made himself put it in context. "I'm not quitting!" he finally blurted out, mostly to himself, God, and whoever else might be listening. "I won't quit, at least not altogether. I'll live to fight another day. I'll fail forward. Who am I kidding? These are the best of the best, seasoned bikers, years of training. I haven't even trained three months. Give yourself a break." Then Ace encouraged himself with these words: "I'll get there in due season."

As Ace was cruising on the way back, he saw a familiar face riding towards him in the outbound direction. It was Charity, along with a friend.

"Hey!" Ace said as he slowed his bike to a stop. Charity was becoming more than an acquaintance. He entertained the thought, *Am I even allowed to like two women at once?* He'd spoken to Charity regularly after class each week, and she'd even gone out of her way to say hello to him a few times. Ace thought, *Charity is so pleasant, friendly, and conversational. Too easy to talk to; more like the girl who's your friend, but not your girlfriend. Girlfriends were hard to get along with and difficult to understand—friends who were girls were friends.* The two stopped their bikes as well.

Ace asked, "Nice to ride in the real world, eh?"

Charity agreed. "I love to feel the sun on my back. It's a beautiful day."

"Yep, sure beats the sweat house."

"Ace, let me introduce you to my friend Faith."

"Hello," Faith said as Ace extended his hand and said, "Nice to meet you."

"So you're the Lone Ranger today, huh?" asked Charity.

"Not really. I was riding with a peloton for a while, but I couldn't keep up."

"Yeah, I saw Spinsey's gang in the parking lot a few minutes ago."

Ace commented, "They ride really fast; it's nothing like class."

"Tough crowd; no mercy there. Speed of the leader, speed of the pack. Keep up or bow out."

"Sounds like you know this gang. Have you ever ridden with them?" asked Ace.

"I know them," Charity said, "however, I take a different approach: no man left behind, bringing assistance and mercy to the weakest link. We go together or we don't go at all. These two philosophies are not good versus evil, not wrong versus right, just different."

Faith had the appearance of a seasoned biker. She looked the part— not only with the way she dressed, but the expression on her face conveyed poise with calm confidence. She had a deep look in her sparkling, powder-blue eyes, and her jet-black hair was pulled back in a ponytail. Faith looked older than Ace and Charity. Her eyes were captivating; framed by a deepened brow, like an eagle's, they hinted at strength, boldness, and wisdom…yet mysterious. Faith and Charity were quite the pair. Stunning! Ace couldn't help but think he was the luckiest guy in the world. These two winsome women were actually showing interest in him. Ace felt energized and affirmed by their company.

Ace wanted to engage Faith in conversation, so he asked, "Faith, that's a nice bike. This is my first time out since high school, but… you look like an experienced biker. Are you a regular out here?"

"You got that right. Journeys are my joy. I've done a few 100-mile trips, 200-mile racing, and crossed the country with various rides traveling for a day, all the way up to a month. Well, I've said too much. But I find that… reflecting on accomplishments and victories of the past give me the courage to do greater things in the future. I've ridden with Spinsey's gang. They are tough, and those athletes are some of the very best in the city. Rome wasn't built in a day. Don't get too discouraged with your slow progress. In due season, you'll be able to keep up with them. You're on the right path. Stay at it. Ride, ride, ride, believing your body is in-perceptively responding with strength, and one day you'll discover you have it. Listen, I'm sorry you got dropped today. But trust me, there will be a day when you will be able to keep up with Spinsey's flash mob, and even more than that if you're inclined to do so. Nothing is impossible, for with God all things are possible to them that believe. Faith is simple enough. It's discerning what God wants to do in and through your life and moving courageously in that direction, regardless of the opposition. Racing is no different than anything else. We race by faith and we live by faith, for it is written: the just shall live by faith."

Ace was stunned! Faith spoke right into his life; he didn't even know her, but she was spot on. Somehow, Ace stood a little taller as he said, "I'm glad you brought up the subject of racing. I'm looking for an Olympic triathlon to do within the next two to three months. Do y'all know of any races in the area?"

Charity had the answer. "There is only one Olympic distance triathlon in the area at that time of the year. It's St. Anthony's Triathlon in April. It's kinda the kick-off event for the triathlon season. Athletes from around the world will participate. I'm registered. This will be my fourth year in a row. You should sign up now before the end of the month because they always seem to sell out."

Faith added, "It's a nice distance race. It'll push you, but not break you: one-mile swim, twenty-five-mile bike, and 6.2 miles for the run."

"OK, then that's my race. I'll get registered right away. Thanks for stopping. I don't want to hold you up any more. Have a good ride. See you on Monday!" Ace said, looking to Charity.

"See ya around!" Charity and Faith both said as they began to roll apart in opposite directions.

Ace was elated by the time he got to the parking lot. He had been embarrassed, subsequently dropped, then dropped again, so he should have been depressed. Yet Charity and Faith had revitalized him. *Girls, girls, and more girls...* Ace let his mind wander through the choices. Girls were all around him. Several seemed available and Ace was beginning to think he had a chance of catching one. *Maybe this time would be different, something more than friends,* Ace thought. *Maybe....*

♋

Ace looked forward to the Saturday afternoon basketball game with Buddy. The two hadn't played together in a few weeks; triathlon training had put a damper on the basketball fun in Ace's life. Today Ace felt he needed to play hard, somewhat to make up for the humiliation he experienced during the morning ride. Basketball was his source of affirmation, and today Ace was fiercely determined, so he played with intensity with a mission to dominate.

Afterwards, Ace shared his girl dilemma with Buddy. Buddy then sarcastically summed up what he'd just heard. "So let me see if I got this right: now you have four girls—Spinsey, Charity, Tanga, and Faith—to choose from and that somehow makes life hard for you?! Let me solve this for you. Why don't you set me up with one of them? Just choose the tallest girl for me and that will make things easier for you. I don't want you to suffer trying to work through so many options. Besides, it's not fair. You need to share; it's just the right thing to do. Ya know what I mean?"

Ace gave Buddy a wry grin, magnifying the dimple in his chin and then said, "Let me get this sorted out and I'll see what I can do."

That night, Ace reflected on his day and decided to make a new blog post.

What a day. Highs and lows. I rode on the trail today with the area's best athletes. I got smoked and left for dead. I got a strong dose of humble pie. I really thought I was something special—training hard these last eleven weeks, but now I realize I've only just begun and have a long way to go. World-class athletes pay a high price to perform at those levels. I have a new respect for triathletes today. It's not a walk in the park. Anyway, I have to get a real bike if I'm going to ride with this crowd. Hey, I know it's not the bike, it's the engine, so I'm not blaming it all on the bike. But really, it's the bike! These guys are paying for speed. Some guy had a bike that was light as a feather, and another guy got his wheels with ball bearings made in Germany—frictionless action, coast for eternity. It's all about the bike. If you only had a bike like Lance Armstrong, you would also win the Tour de France. It's the bike, I tell you.

On another note, while I was licking my wounds from getting blown off the road by the pros, I met some friends along the way to lead me back to a vision of what things can be. Thanks, Charity and Faith. Because of you, I clearly see the reality of where I am, and you filled me with a vision for the future.

Wisbit tip: *Synergy: We go further faster when we go together, like geese flying in formation.*

Wisbit tip: *The speed of the leader determines the speed of the followers.*

Wisbit tip: *Share the burden, take your turn, and do your part.*

Wisbit tip: *No man left behind. Care for the weakest among us, and carry them along with you. We go together or we don't go at all.*

Wisbit tip: *The Law of Compensation: The body will adapt, adjust and compensate for any weakness with greater strength elsewhere.*

QUESTIONS FOR SELF-REFLECTION

- Have I ever experienced the power of synergy. If so, when and where?
- What do I consider my greatest failure? What great lesson did I learn through it?
- What is my definition of faith? Is my life marked by living in faith?
- What do I think is the spiritual metaphor of the law of compensation?

12

THE MAIDEN VOYAGE

ACE HAD WRITTEN a compelling story and submitted his application to the foundation for a prosthetic run blade. The only problem was that time was running out. Race day was less than a month away. Already many weeks had passed with no word from the foundation. That's when the Great Oz got on the phone to see if he could move the process along. His investigation solved the riddle, but the "unfunded" answer was discouraging.

Ace had a long history with this foundation; a few years ago he was awarded the deluxe, bionic C-leg. Shortly thereafter, he'd been awarded an AllPro Foot to pair with his Total Knee 2000 specifically for basketball. The foundation had limits to their distribution, and thus tried to make decisions based upon urgency of needs. The consensus was that either of these prosthetic legs ought to be sufficient for athletic running. So this blade was deemed a convenience item and was therefore moved to low priority, with an invitation to reapply next year. Ace was not completely dejected; he had been training with his C-leg since the beginning. He was familiar with it, and the irritation he had experienced earlier had been minimized with a new gel sleeve prescribed by Oz. And so it was that Ace would have to race as he had prepared. No upgrade.

*THE OLYMPIC GAMES OF ANTIQUITY

History: The Olympic Games as we know them today have a long history. According to existing historic manuscripts, the first Olympic Games were celebrated in 776 BC in the city of Olympia. These games were dedicated to the Greek god Zeus and took place in the same place every four years. This four-year period became known as an "Olympiad."

The games endured for over 1,000 years. In 393 AD, Emperor Theodosius I, who converted to Christianity, decided to abolish all pagan cults and centers, and thus the Olympic games were abolished.

Tradition of the "Olympic Truce:" Messengers went from city to city announcing the date of the competitions. They demanded a halt to fighting before, during, and after the games. The Truce was agreed to and athletes and spectators traveled to and from the games in safety.

Award Ceremony: At the conclusion of the games, the winning athletes stood upon a raised platform, where a crown made of an olive branch was placed upon the winner's head.

ATHLETIC EVENTS OF ORIGINAL GAMES

- **Running**
    1. The Stade: One length of the stadium—modern day equivalent of the 100-meter dash.
    2. The Diaulos: Two lengths of the stadium—modern day equivalent of the 200-meter dash.
    3. The Dolichos: Twenty lengths of the stadium—modern day equivalent of the one-mile run.

- **Wrestling**
- **Boxing**
- **Pankration**—Equivalent to martial arts.
- **The Equestrian Competitions**—Chariot and horse races.
- **The Pentathlon**—Comprised of five events: Running, long jump, discus, javelin, and wrestling.

ANCIENT WORLD RECORDS

Milon of Kroton: Six-time consecutive wrestling champion, a record unmatched even in the modern arena.

Leonidas of Rhodes: One of the most famous runners of antiquity. For four consecutive Olympiads, he won three races for a total of twelve Olympic victory wreaths.

*Taken from the International Olympic Committee publication, "The Olympic Games of Antiquity."[12]

BUZZ BUZZ BUZZ! It was 4:30 A.M. and Ace's alarm was going off.

The greatly-anticipated day was getting off to an early start. It was not The Big Race, but it was to be Ace's first—St. Anthony's Olympic-distance triathlon: swim a mile (1,500M), bike twenty-five miles (40K), and run 6.2 miles (10K).

While the length was roughly a fourth of an iron distance race, it would still be intense. Ace's body was about to be pushed to compete, as he figured, for at least three continuous hours. There was some uncertainty, and Ace wasn't sure how it would all end.

The triathlon debuted at the 2000 Summer Olympic Games in Sydney.

Today, Ace felt like the Lone Ranger; he'd spent the last four months training mostly side by side with Bobo. Last night, and early this morning, Bobo got blindsided as his eldest daughter had come down with a high fever. Bobo gave his apology and offered this sentiment: that he had participated in this race before, and promised he'd definitely be at the Big Race qualifier in four months. And then he reassured Ace that he'd do fine.

Despite the fact that Bobo wasn't there, the truth was, Ace would

---

12 Adapted from the Olympic publications, History of the Olympic Games. <www.olympic.org/ancient-olympic-games>

not be alone. More than a half dozen racers from the YMCA were competing. Not to mention that several of his coaches were coming to assist and inspire their racers.

Ace was racing today for two reasons: First, to learn by experience the reality of the race. Second, he was here to finish no matter what the cost. It was a race to get ready for the qualifying race. *Nice plan,* Ace thought as he contemplated the wisdom of Doc Mentor.

CR

At the race site, the entire triathlon experience was exciting; a buzz was in the air as people arrived. Though there were lines, plenty of Vantex team members handled registration efficiently. Ace was signed in and given his bib, number 1480. He figured correctly that it meant no fewer than 1,480 people were racing.

The transition area and registration was like a bee hive; people were literally everywhere. However, the transition zone was on lockdown—only participants could enter. Gatekeepers checked to ensure everyone's "act" was together, including those who marked the racer's bodies. These volunteers used a black marker to write Ace's number on both shoulders, his thighs, and his age on the back of his calf muscle—thirty-three. That's when Ace first laid his eyes on Titan, who guarded the entrance to transition as a gatekeeper. His sheer size was intimidating. The two greeted one another.

Titan spoke first. "Look at you, basketball-star-turned-triathlete. How ya doin', man?"

"Well, I got tired of dreaming about it and decided to get my mojo into the triathlon world. So today is my maiden voyage. It's no iron distance, but I'm here using my training wheels."

"Well, you're the man! Dude, you look totally legit! Go for it!"

Ace was prepared and proud of his new bike, new helmet, new shoes, and new race suit that doubled as his swimsuit. He also had the "Big Race" backpack specifically designed for triathletes. He had gotten it for volunteering at the Big Race last year.

Ace had mixed feelings about carrying it. He didn't see anybody else toting a Big Race bag, but he saw a racer with an Ironman tattoo on the back of his calf and another wearing an Ironman T-shirt. Ace felt cool, even like he belonged. He still hoped no one would ask him about the Big Race bag. He saw a few familiar faces—some he had seen competing in the Big Race; others had volunteered with him.

Now, as he finally passed the gate into transition, Ace found his space among rack after rack of bikes. Although he was a rookie, he felt ready. He had thought through everything, made his list, played it through in his mind, and placed all his equipment out sequentially for transition. Ace removed his mechanical leg and headed for the beach where the race would start with the aid of his crutches.

Once he reached the swim starting gate, Ace was looking everywhere for someone in particular when his gaze fell upon a man he recognized from volunteering at the Big Race a few months earlier. Slider was in his late fifties, a heavyset, big man, with jumbo-sized tummy, legs, and arms. They shook hands and shared greetings.

"How have you been?" asked Slider.

"Well, take a look at me—today is my first triathlon. Out of the stands and onto the field."

"Sweet. I remember my first race, same race, right here, twenty-nine years ago, at age twenty-nine." Ace must have let his face show what he was thinking because Slider called him on it. "Don't look at me like that! I know what you're thinking!" Slider said with a laughing smile. "Me, a triathlete? Hey! There was a time when I was a slim, handsome young man, and I'd have kicked your #*€%# in this race today! No kidding!"

Ace was thankful that Slider made fun of himself; it made it easier to talk about it. The man was self-aware and in no shape to do a triathlon.

"Well, you're one up on me. So, Mr. Veteran Triathlete, you got any advice for me today?"

"Yep! Don't get yourself killed. First, don't drown. Second, don't get run over by a car. Seriously, watch out for cars. It's not like riding on the trail today. I'll tell you, some of these idiots don't deserve a driver's license. And don't run so hard that your heart stops. I'd stop eating all those hot fudge sundaes. Stay away from the brownies too, and you'll be fine."

USA TRIATHLON COMPETITION

Commonly Violated Rules and Penalties

Helmets: Helmets must be worn at all times while on your bike.

Chin Straps: Buckle your chin strap unless you are off your bicycle. **Penalty:** disqualification.

Outside assistance: No assistance other than that offered by race and medical officials may be used. Triathlons are individual tests of fitness. **Penalty:** time penalty.

*All Physically-Challenged Racers may both give and receive help as needed from other racers and designated volunteers.

Drafting:
- **Drafting:** Keep at least three bike lengths of clear space between you and the cyclist in front. If you move into this zone, you must pass within 15 seconds.
- **Position:** Keep to the right-hand side of the lane of travel unless passing.
- **Illegal Pass:** Cyclist must pass on the left, not on the right.
- **Blocking:** Riding on the left side of the lane without passing anyone and impeding other cyclists attempting to pass.
- **Overtaken:** Once past, you must immediately exit the draft zone from the rear before attempting to pass again. **Penalty:** time penalty.

The Course: All competitors are required to follow the prescribed course and stay within all coned lanes; cutting the course is an obvious violation, and going outside the course is a safety issue. Cyclists shall not cross a solid yellow centerline for any reason. Cyclists must obey all applicable traffic laws at all times. Runners, swimmers, and bikers must navigate around all coned markers. **Penalty:** Referees discretion; time penalty or disqualification.

Unsportsmanlike Conduct: Foul, harsh, argumentative, or abusive language or other unsportsmanlike conduct directed at race officials, USA triathlon officials, volunteers, or fellow athletes is forbidden. **Penalty:** Disqualification.

Headphones: Headphones, headsets, Walkman, iPods, MP3 players or personal audio devices, etc. are not to be carried or worn at any time during the race. **Penalty:** Time penalty.

Race Numbers: All athletes are required to wear a race number at all times during the race. Numbers must be clearly visible at all times. Numbers may not be altered in any way that prevents a clear identification. Do not transfer your number to any other athlete or take a number from an athlete that is not competing. **Penalty:** Time penalty for missing or altered numbers. Disqualification and one-year suspension for membership in the USA for transferring a number without race director's permission.

Time Penalties: Two minutes per offense

*Other exceptions may apply to physically-challenged racers.
Consult a Course Marshal for details.[13]

"Sounds like a reasonable plan. I'll see if I can follow through on that for you."

"You'd better follow through on that. Seriously, you don't get like this overnight. It happens little by little. I ran this race on a big frame—Clydesdale (special designation for the heavyset racers). Hey, I'm a big man any way you slice it—six feet four inches, 245 pounds—when there was nothing but muscle on these bones. Add five to six pounds a year for twenty years and bingo—360 pounds! But let me congratulate you for training to come out here. You'll do fine today. You look great."

"Thanks for the encouragement."

---

13   Copied & adapted (to fit story purposes) from USA Triathlon Competitive Rules: Commonly Violated Rules & Penalties <www.teamusa.org/usa-triathlon>

Ace looked around again, trying to find her. Where was she? *It was not like her to be late*, Ace thought. They had agreed to meet at the swim start gate. Where was she? This was an important component to his race preparation and plan. Finally, after what seemed a lifetime of waiting, Ace saw in the distance the form of a tall blonde in a pink warm-up suit walking toward him. Their eyes met; then they exchanged smiles.

"Hey, thanks for coming by."

"Sure, my pleasure. Anything to help one of my rising star athletes."

Ace smirked and squenched up his chin. Spinsey wasn't racing, but came to encourage her athletes. Since she had planned to be there, Ace had recruited her to help with the transitional moment, namely, to take his crutches from the swim start to the swim out and make sure he got the crutches again to help enter to transition for his bike encounter. Ace had some unfinished business he wanted to discuss with her. Over the last several weeks, he had refused the invitation to ride with the Saturday peloton, citing he wasn't ready, but would join once he had a proper bike. In the meantime, he had been faithful to attend her spin class.

"Listen, I wanted to tell you I got my new bike yesterday. I assure you I'm ready to ride like the wind. I am so pumped. Hey, if I survive this, you have to give me another chance with the peloton."

Spinsey inquired, "So, what kind of bike did you get?"

"I got the Jabez, jumbo touring edition, cobalt blue and black with gold lettering and white pinstripes. The design is definitely cutting edge. Same bike that won this year's Tour de France; an all carbon fiber bad boy."

Spinsey recognized the bike. "Well, with a bike like that we'll have to put you up front and let you pull the whole peloton. Nice bike. Congratulations! So, we know where your leg went. Those things are expensive. At least they let you keep your arms, because you're going to need 'em for the swim." Spinsey had a lot of pep and enthusiasm in her voice. She tried to inject a little humor, and Ace appreciated it.

Marshall began to review the rules over the PA: "We will have a staggered start, wave after wave, every three minutes. Release from the start line when you hear the horn. Pay attention to color groups distinguished by your swim caps." Ace's group was orange for men, thirty to thirty-four. Marshall continued. "Swim out to the first buoy; swim to the left of the buoy. Turn right and you'll see the next big, yellow buoy. Stay to the left, and then turn back to the beach. You can see the water exit just down the beach from here. You must go through the channel if you want your time to count. On the bike, remember to keep at least three bike lengths between you and the rider ahead of you. Do not ride side by side except to pass, and always pass on the left. We have field marshals along the way, so if you commit a violation, you will be assessed a two-minute penalty.

"We have water stations at every mile during the run. When you're finished, we have a lunch bar waiting for you. Good luck. Now please stand for the singing of our national anthem."

As Ace stood there with Spinsey, he saw the unmistakable form of none other than Cheetah, current world champion and winner of the Big Race, walking right toward him, or rather, toward Spinsey. The two old friends embraced. Then he gave her a quick peck on the cheek. Ace was stunned. He was trying to figure out what the relationship was between these two? Spinsey was part celebrity herself. Somehow she seemed to know everybody.

Cheetah asked, "How you doing, girl? Long time, no see."

"Training the next set of world champions, I suppose. I'm here to encourage some of my students. Let me introduce you to Ace. This is his first race."

"Hey, Ace! I'm Chet, but just call me Cheetah—everyone else does. Nice to meet you. You've got a great instructor here," he said while looking a Spinsey with a smile. "She taught me everything I know about cycling." Then he addressed her with a nod of his head. "World champ because of you, baby."

Spinsey was quick to reply. "That's right, and don't you forget it! So, have you got a girl in your life yet? Please tell me you do. I'm praying for someone to come along and spare me the pain of having to marry you at forty."

"Of all people, you should know that a serious romantic commitment and pro sports don't go together."

"Well, don't bank on waiting for me. You know the deal is only a deal if you can beat me when you're forty, and that will never happen," Spinsey said. She looked at Ace as she told on Cheetah to embarrass him. "This guy has a donut for breakfast and Mickey D's for lunch; not exactly the choice of champions."

Cheetah was rolling with the punches. "Hey, it works for me. You ought to give it a try."

Spinsey unleashed another volley of verbal jabs, hooks, and body blows, sarcasm behind every word. "You are a mystery, an enigma, and a bad role model! While it may work for you now, at forty when it counts, you're going to be a miniature of Slider over there," as she pointed in Slider's direction. "I assure you I'm safe. I'm not marrying a slacker like you!"

Cheetah looked at Ace and said, "I win the Big Race, and she treats me like this. Women! Can't live with 'em, can't live without 'em." The pleasantries and sarcasm were coming to an end.

Spinsey changed the subject. "So, what are you doing here? This is like the peewee league for you!"

"I thought I'd stop by for a little workout and fun. Besides, my sponsor insisted. Endorsements pay the bills these days. They're hoping to make a fuss over me, so I thought I'd give them something to talk about."

Later, Ace got the inside story on these two. Cheetah had been a foreign exchange student from Australia his junior year of high school and ended up in Spinsey's class. They joined a local YMCA tri-team together since there were no such teams in high schools. The two became best friends as they rode together and did triathlons.

Cheetah returned to the States after college to work and compete in triathlons. The two renewed their friendship, trained together, but no romance resulted. When they were twenty-seven, they watched a movie together about two high school friends who pledged to marry each other at thirty if neither found love by then. Age thirty seemed ridiculous to both of them, so they jokingly changed the age to forty. It was a joke, mostly, that they would marry at forty if neither had found love by then, with one caveat: Cheetah would have to beat Spinsey in a tri-race at age forty, mostly because there was a time when she was faster than him, especially on the bike. That fact changed when Cheetah went pro. In Spinsey's mind, his success was temporary; he would lose his edge by forty.

Spinsey sounded the alert. "Look! The race is about to start. You'd better quit talking and get over there."

"It's OK. I'm not racing with the pro-flight today. I'm going by age group." Cheetah looked in an obvious manner at the thirty-three written on Ace's calf. "His age group, to be exact," as he showed the thirty written on his calf.

"Yeah, right! You're not thirty! At least not yet—your birthday isn't until January."

"True, but here's the plan: by joining and starting up an age group, I give everybody a fifteen-minute head start. You see, it's more fun for me that way. When I won this race two years ago, I won by ten minutes. I'm a little faster now, so it should make for an interesting finish. Look, I'm the fastest swimmer here, I'm the fastest biker here, and in some regards, I'm the fastest runner here. OK, a few guys can outpace me; but in a sprint, no one in this field is going to touch me.

"So, let me tell you how that plays out for me: I would be the first one out of the water, and I would not see another competitor until well after I cross the finish line. I may as well train by myself today if I were racing pro. Now I've got something of a challenge. I reckon from my starting flight, that'll give me 350 people to catch. Spinsey, you know how it goes—first wave is the pros, then the boys, then the girls." Then, putting his arm around Ace to show solidarity, he continued with a cocky attitude, "And then the men."

Spinsey rolled her eyes, acknowledging that Cheetah was the consummate egomaniac that he was claiming to be. "Get outta here!"

she said as she motioned them with a sweeping of her hand toward the starting line as if to push them away.

Ace asked Cheetah, "Could I borrow your shoulder to help me get in place?"

"Sure, glad to help."

It didn't take much; the paparazzi were already next to the start gate. Ace hopped into place with one hand on Cheetah's shoulder, and it was a perfect picture moment. The paparazzi had their eye on this icon's every move. The cameras snapped fast and furiously; all the two could do was smile, and then it was over. The piranhas had their prey and then left him alone.

Ace could not resist asking, "So, you got any advice on how to navigate this race? This is my first time out today."

"Sure! You see that first buoy up there, and that far buoy down there?" Cheetah said as he pointed them out to Ace. "There's going to be a log jam at both spots—imagine forty to fifty swimmers all in the bottleneck. It's dangerous. Prepare to get kicked and hit, or you can just do what I'm going to do, which might not be a bad idea for you." Cheetah said it in such a way as to hint that a one-legged man could use any break he could get.

"What's that?"

"Well…today I'm going to do an underwater swim just inside that buoy and avoid the whole thing altogether, or I'm never going to catch the leaders. Going through that mess would cost me at least two minutes each getting beyond each buoy."

"Yeah, but you'll be disqualified."

"True. However, it doesn't matter because I'm already ineligible. I'm not registered for this race today as a pro, so I can't win that. Because I'm a pro, I'm ineligible to win the age group. Just practice, my friend. Here's something else you might try: After you get out of the water and onto the bike, start counting and keep track of all the people you pass. It gives the mind something to do and keeps the competitor in you motivated."

"OK, thanks." Ace was satisfied.

13

THE RULES WERE MADE FOR BENDING

EVERYONE WEARING AN orange cap raced into the water as soon as they heard the horn sound. Ace purposely waited for a moment so he would not interrupt the crowd of swimmers, then hopped anxiously into the water a few seconds behind.

Whoa! This is so different than swimming in the pool, was his first thought. It was Ace's first open water swim, and it wasn't a pool or a lake. The ocean waves were tame today, but Ace kept getting water in his mouth. When he turned his head to breathe, a few waves slapped Ace in the face. He almost choked, but managed to recover.

Ace faced another problem: his goggles fogged up, so he had trouble looking for the buoy he needed to swim to. Ace switched to the breast stroke to regain his composure and get his bearings. Once he regained his line of sight, Ace put his head down and swam at least 300 yards. *Come on! Where was that buoy?* He thought, *I've got to be getting close.*

Ace stopped the freestyle and returned to the breast stroke to regain his bearings. Somehow he had lost his aim. He swam a little crooked for more than 300 yards, so he was fifty yards off to the inside of the path. Now he had to swim back to get around the buoy to be fair, or he could cut the corner. He assessed the situation. *No way am I going to cut the course. This was not the short cut Cheetah was talking about. I am definitely going around that buoy.*

Ace changed his pace and swam twenty-five meters at a time, throwing his head up to check his bearings. The group behind had now caught up to him, and the turn around the buoy began to pile up like a traffic jam. It was difficult to navigate. Ace was simply treading water among a mob. Once around the corner, it loosened up again. Ace thought he would put his head down and get after it again. But 200 yards later he paused to get his bearings and it happened again. He was off course. He became furious as he discovered he was all alone about fifty yards outside the designated swim channel. It was just too irritating—the volcano inside of him erupted. He cursed and then he cursed his leg.

After treading water for another ten seconds, Ace rolled on his back and did the crawl E.Z. had taught him. It gave him a chance to regain his composure and catch his breath. He rolled back and resumed freestyle swimming for twenty-five meters. Then he switched to the breast stroke to get his head up and help stay focused.

With each twenty-five meters, Ace realigned himself to the buoy. Unfortunately, the next group converged at the turn around the buoy. Traffic jam again. After he navigated himself through the turn it was another 300 meters to return to the beach. All Ace had to do was swim straight ahead, no buoy. *Just aim for the exit gate*, Ace thought. But he didn't trust himself to swim straight. His goggles were fogged and he was already drained. Ace tried to get out of the way of the others and rolled on his back to once again begin the crawl stroke, swimming on his back for a second time to catch his breath. E.Z. would be proud.

Ace wasn't panicked, but there seemed only two ways off this course: swim it or notify a kayak patrol. Ace felt more exhausted than when he swam his laps in the pool because of the adrenalin of treading water, redirecting, and not being able to touch the edge of the pool. *Sink or swim—so different than the pool,* he thought. Ace caught his breath and swam at a much more relaxed pace. "Keep it steady," he whispered to himself.

Ace finally arrived to the shore, only to discover that his head was spinning with dizziness. Hopping on one leg, he tripped and stumbled, catching himself with his arms and hands. As soon as he got to the water's edge, Spinsey was waiting for him. He reached for her shoulder. Together they hopped to dry land.

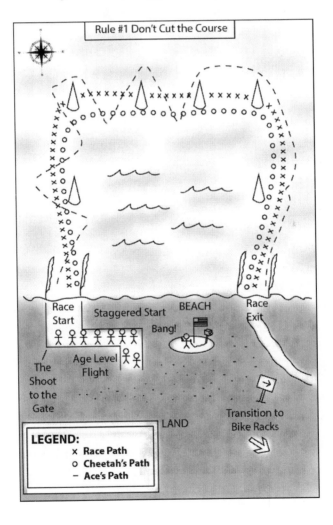

Spinsey handed Ace the crutches and tried to encourage him, "Listen to me; you're a third of the way done. Now you're going to be moving to your strength—take that new bike and make up some time. You got this thing. Go on!" she shouted as Ace hobbled into the transition zone. Ace was lightheaded, and the sand was difficult to maneuver. He tried to hurry, but others passed him each second.

Ace had prepared appropriately for transition, although he took a little longer than most racers as he had the additional time to fit his prosthetic leg into place. Overall, he was off again in a hurry, but then the official flagged him down before he could get started. He had forgotten to fasten the strap on his helmet. He was asked to stop and adjust before continuing.

When Ace started riding, he could tell how fast he was going because his new bike had a speedometer. He found a nice pace; his new bike felt fast. He rode at twenty-one miles per hour and experienced the thrill of passing people. The race had 2,000 athletes, so there were lots of people to pass. Ace got a little shot of adrenaline each time he passed up another opponent. They dropped like flies. He kept count: twenty in the first three miles. But about nine people passed him.

After several miles, Ace realized he could not keep up the pace. He dropped to nineteen miles per hour after the adrenaline rush passed. He was cruising. However, he was being passed. Some racers really flew by him, including some girls. He saw a kid pass by with the number thirteen written on the back of his calf. Ace wondered how that was possible.

As the next guy eased by, Ace saw seventy-two written on his calf. His name, Vintage, was written on the back of his jersey and his race bib was number 144. Ace thought, *That's just not right.* Ace's competitive nature surfaced, and he was determined not to let this guy pass him without doing something. Ace pulled close to this competitor's back wheel, which provided relief because the draft made it easier for Ace to keep the faster pace. *I'm not letting you go, buddy!*

Ace thought. *Vintage, you don't even know it, but you just became my source of inspiration. You're pushing me to give my best. I'm sticking with you. I'm not letting you outta my sight.*

Ace held this position throughout the rest of the biking section: twenty miles per hour, which was a good average. Ace felt proud. His new bike was awesome. He was definitely faster; money bought speed, but not comfort. Ace experienced saddle soreness. While the seat was light, it was very thin. Italian-style leather with no cush for the tush. Ace's old ten-speed was more comfortable than this seat. Nevertheless, Ace counted the whole way; he passed forty-five riders and was passed by twenty. In his mind, he was winning.

They dismounted their bikes and Ace transitioned for the second time. It was a quicker turnaround, much faster than when he adjusted his mechanical leg into position after the swim. He was in and out in a jiffy. After 100 yards or so, Vintage, the seventy-two-year-old Ace had followed on the bike, passed by and commented with a little irritation, "You were following a little close on the bike, don't you think?! Three lengths, buddy, I don't care who you are."

Ace's conscience was pricked; he knew the rule and consciously ignored it. Going fast and winning had dominated his decision against his better judgment. Ace even thought he had gotten away with it, but the man's comment was a rebuke. Ace knew he was wrong. His mind was distracted, and he had to recover and move on. *Forget about it; you've got a race to finish,* Ace thought. *Deal with the guilt later.* Ace encouraged himself to refocus.

Ace had estimated it would take him an hour to complete the remaining 10K. He was two-thirds done. He mentally prepared for what was ahead. *One step at a time; hang in there,* he thought. *The only losers are the quitters.* Resilience's words bounced around his head as Ace filled his mind with positive "self-talk."

Ace ran slower than he thought he would. He wasn't passing anybody, yet he was being passed. Biking was his strength so keeping score was fun, but the first three miles of running was a different story. He lost ground. The score he kept in his head shifted; he passed forty-seven people, and forty-five people passed him. It seemed to have leveled off. Very few racers were doing any passing. Now it was just racers following in a long line with various gaps between them.

Ace was passed by a beautiful woman in a cobalt blue and black outfit, with gold pinstripes and white lettering. He remembered when he passed her on the bike portion—it was like a bottle of sweet perfume passing by. Her outfit even matched her bike, perfectly color coordinated.

Instead of looking tacky, she was elegantly sexy. She wore top flight elite racers, the only easily-recognizable, pure white shoe with a gold lightning logo on each side. The top shoe in the industry with a top price to match. Ace knew the price and story because he had done plenty of research in preparation for this race. Purchasing the right shoe was important. Ace wanted to project the right image. He wasn't going to be embarrassed by sloppy appearance or noticeably cheap shoes like the first day he had ridden with the peloton. He noticed her shoes because he was wearing the same pair, and her bike was the same model as his.

She wore a gold necklace, gold bracelets, and a few rings with big diamonds. One looked like an engagement ring. *What a diamond!* Ace thought. Most people chose to run without jewelry. She was the most dolled-up triathlete Ace had seen all day, and very attractive. Now he ran behind her enjoying that refreshing smell. She was running his speed, so he used her as a pace guide. Ace thought again, *I'm not letting her go.*

At the next water station, Ace thought he would talk to her, so he ran beside her and asked, "So, have you ever done one of these before?"

"About eighteen times."

"Wow, that's amazing! You don't look old enough for that many races. Did you start when you were ten?" This was the compliment she wanted.

"Trying to stay young."

"So how do you feel?"

"It doesn't matter how I feel; it only matters how I look. The crowd I run with is a tough crowd. All these men want the younger women, so shape up or ship out. And the older women who manage to keep their men, now that's a crowd that's hard to impress. I do what I can to keep up. I'd love to have that kind of money, and I will soon enough. I just gotta keep this body going."

"So, you run to stay fit?"

"Yep, and I stay fit to stay desirable. Everybody wants to be liked. Remember when we were kids and we got lectured about not caving into peer pressure? It never goes away. Now we're just keeping up with the Joneses. Still looking for acceptance among our peers. It's true; racing is my way of fighting back. My way of earning acceptance."

"Well, if it makes any difference to you, I want you to know you set the bar high today on being well put together. You look like you're in great physical condition, and you obviously have an eye for fashion. I couldn't help but notice your taste in shoes." Ace looked down as he spoke until she noticed that their shoes matched.

"You have such a handsome face and good taste in shoes. And so fashionable and well put together yourself."

"Well, I don't even know your name, but I assure you, I'm nothing but a poser today. This is my first race ever."

"You could have fooled me! I saw your bike—that's no toy. It's big league equipment. You're looking awfully good there...what's your name? I'm Vanna Teia Fair. And I'm called by my first and middle name, southern, like Mary Sue or Betty Joe...Vanna Teia."

"Well, Miss Vanna Teia, I'm Ace. It's been a pleasure meeting you. Please go on. I need to slow down for a moment," Ace said as he slowed to a walk.

"OK, nice day to you."

Just like that, the meeting was over. This was the mode of operation in a race: lots of short conversations, talking for the rare moments when side-by-side, but no one stopped for another.

This was a solo race at its core. It was respected as such and courtesy was not shown by stopping or slowing because a nearby competitor did. The competition was against the field and yourself. Unless something tragic happened, a racer with a flat tire or a runner stretching out a cramp was passed. Every person ran his or her own race.

In short, respect for the race meant respect for the preparation of others who sacrificed to achieve their personal best. So Ace wasn't surprised when Vanna Teia kept going. He wasn't tired at the moment. He had another problem: during the last mile, Ace started to feel major discomfort in the ball of his left foot. He hadn't stopped sooner because he enjoyed the company of Vanna Teia. Now, however, his pain grew more intense, so he had to stop.

Ace realized it was the new shoes. He had not worn them before, practiced in them, or broken them in. They were a little rigid compared to his old shoes, and he was paying the price. Ace sat on the side of the road and removed his shoe and sock, revealing a nasty blister. Looking at it did not make things better. Ace recognized his folly. Putting the sock and shoe back on only made the blister more tender.

No quitting, Ace thought. *I'm not going to quit. I won't. OK, get a hold of yourself. You have a little more than a mile to go.* Ace could see the five-mile water station ahead. When he arrived there, he asked for and received a Band-aid. It helped some, but was too late. Ace was one awkward-looking, limping, one-legged guy. He wasn't limping on his mechanical leg but tenderly favoring the left.

Ace toughed it out and hobbled along the last mile. Lots of people passed him. The counting game was over. He thought, *Let them all pass me; I don't care. I am going to finish even if I'm the last one.*

Ace saw the finish line and, to his great pleasure, he also saw Charity, who had already finished. They had played a little yo-yo game during the race. Unknowingly, she had passed him in the water. Then he passed her on the bike. Finally, she passed him again on the first part of the run. After she finished, Charity circled back around to cheer him across, but because of his blister, Ace was twenty minutes behind, not just the few minutes as she had originally thought.

Ace smiled at the sight of Charity as she stood about fifty yards in front of the finish line, which was jammed with people. Ace wobbled along and winced in pain. Charity's heart broke at the sight. Watching Ace hobble and grimace was more than she could bear. Tears welled up in her eyes. She tried to cheer, but her emotions wouldn't let her. She could only whisper, "Come on Ace! You're almost there."

The large crowd gathered around the finish line was inspired and wildly cheered Ace on. He raised his hands in triumph as he crossed the finish line. A team of volunteers greeted him with a bottle of cold water, a wet towel, and a St. Anthony's T-shirt. At the moment, there were overwhelming crowds all around the finish line.

Ace looked for Spinsey and Charity, but there was too much congestion. He didn't see either one and decided to follow the flow of racers which was leading him towards the snack hut. He hobbled over, grabbed an energy bar and some Gatorade and, most importantly, found a place to sit. He didn't wonder that much where everybody was. He knew he'd been slow to finish, and his coaches had plenty of athletes to look out for. *But where was Charity?* Ace thought. *I just saw her. But the crowd at the finish line was too great; it was bedlam.* Ace sat exhausted, content and in a lot of pain. His bionic leg had manifested another problem. Not only did he have a blister on his good foot, but the pain at the end of the nub knee he knew all too well. It meant there would be blood. What was going on inside his prosthetic socket was beyond a blister. This race had pushed his pain threshold to a new level. But for Ace, quiting was never an option.

Now, as he sat there, a deep satisfaction filled his soul. He smiled his wiry smile and scrunched up his chin. He was experiencing an affirmation of his existence. Today he was among the elite. He'd finished a triathlon.

Shortly thereafter, he heard someone making announcements. It was time for the awards ceremony. Ace could see the platform from where he sat. The MC mentioned none other than Cheetah. A new course record was set today.

The MC proudly acknowledged, "Folks, before we get started with the awards ceremony, I have an unusual announcement to make: this year's winner is not the winner at all. Cheetah, this year's Big Race World Champion, did not register as a pro and ran at the age level where he is not eligible to win because he is a pro. It's a conundrum—I've never seen it before. Cheetah, who lives right here, is ineligible to receive any of our prizes, but the new course record will stand. One hour, forty-six minutes, forty-six seconds, smashing the previous record held by former champion Bruiser Le Truce by nearly two minutes. Cheetah, congratulations! It was a privilege to have you at our race today. Everyone join in a round of applause for Cheetah."

Everyone clapped and the awards continued, but Ace was distracted. He saw a crowd gathered around a results board that listed the actual time, placement, and standings of all the athletes.

ELITE GROUP OF ATHLETES

KUDOS TO THE TRIATHLETE

- One in 10,000 people worldwide complete an iron distance race.

- Only six in 1,000 Americans compete in any type of triathlon.

- Popularity continues to grow with an average of more than two million triathletes competing annually.[14]

---

14   Huffington Post: "Triathlons Grow In Popularity; Participation Reaches All-Time High."

His time was 3:32:02; his place was 1,795. Ace had beaten only 205 people and finished in the bottom ten percent. However, there was something interesting about the data listed for Ace's race: swim time, bike time, run time, *penalty* time, six minutes. He looked up and down the list to see if there were penalties applied to anyone else. A few other penalties were assigned. He was not alone, but only he had six minutes. *What did this mean?* Ace wasn't sure, so he asked a friendly-looking man. The reply was a simple, respectful explanation. "Probably happened on the bike portion. That's where most penalties are assessed. If you rode too close to another biker and failed to pass, then those motorcyclists driving around, up and down the course, ding you two minutes each time they see you."

"OK, that explains it, thanks." Ace wasn't in the mood to challenge or discuss it any further. He only walked away with his head hanging low, accepting that he hadn't gotten away with anything. His conscience burned. His face reddened with shame and he cringed. *Why had I been such an idiot?* Ace was disappointed with himself and wondered if anyone else he knew saw his penalties. Ace comforted himself by thinking, *Probably not; all the fast ones had certainly already left the premises.*

	MALE AGE GROUP 30-34									
PLACE	NAME	AGE	CITY	TIME	SWIM	TRAN 1	BIKE	TRAN 2	RUN	PENALTY
1793	Maverick	32	Boulder	3:30:23	34:44	3:54	1:24:51	3:11	1:16:53	
1794	Braveheart	34	Bath, GBR	3:31:07	35:09	3:37	1:32:21	3:31	1:12:37	
1795	Ace	33	Big City	3:32:02	38:03	4:37	1:16:24	3:01	1:24:37	6:00

Then Spinsey found Ace. She had not been at the finish line due to another athlete of hers crossing the line two minutes before Ace. The moment was lost, missed by his coach. She felt terrible about it, but when she had found Ace, *she hugged him* and apologized. "Hey, sorry I missed you at the finish line, but congratulations! You did it!"

Wow! Ace thought, *that was the first time they had hugged and it felt good.* Everything was made better by that moment. Ace's mind raced. *This could mean she likes me!* Ace also wondered if she had seen his time and penalty marks. For now, it was all encouragement.

Late that night, Ace sat down to write his blog post.

In the words of Julius Caesar: I came, I saw, I conquered. That's right baby. Today, I finished my first triathlon. And I beat 200 people. OK, that's a little misleading. I finished behind nearly 1,800 racers. But I finished! Dozens of lessons learned today. I can't wait to share them with you.

The scary part of what happened today is this: I was spent when I crossed the finish line. I mean I was done, sore all over, fatigued. And then I was reminded that the race today was only one quarter of the time and distance of the Big Race. My time today was 3:32:02. Projected finish of the Big Race for me would be 15:00 to 16:00 hours at today's pace, if I could even finish it.

I am seriously concerned about being able to qualify for the Big Race. I have just four more months before I run the prequalifying Half-Iron. And they only take the first forty from every age division. I'm going to have to turn up my intensity and consult my coaches.

To tell you the truth, it's too late to turn back now. I went out and bought the proper gear and all. You should have seen me—I looked like the real deal; I could have passed for a Tour de France competitor. I had the proper uniform head to toe. I spared no expense on looking the part. I even matched my uniform to my new bike and new shoes.

*It wasn't until I met Vanna Teia Fair on the run that I realized what had happened to me. It was kind of like buying a new car and suddenly recognizing how many other cars are just like yours. Vanna Teia and I could have been twins: she was the female counterpart of looking good at the race. Same bike, same color coordination. I'm afraid I placed a little too much emphasis on **looking** the part instead of **playing** the part. You know, fake it till you make it. Well, I may have looked like I knew what I was doing, but it's a shame my game wasn't as good as my gear. So here we go on lessons learned.*

Wisbit tip: *It's what is on the inside that counts; not what's on the outside.*

Wisbit tip: *Quitters never win. Winston Churchill said, "Never, never, never give up."*

Wisbit tip: *Practice like you intend to play, for you will eventually play like you've practiced. Practice does not make perfect but rather perfect practice makes perfect.*

Wisbit tip: *Little by little. Small compromises routinely made make a huge impact over time. He who is faithful with little will eventually be trusted with much.*

QUESTIONS FOR SELF-REFLECTION

- Which character do I identify with in this story? How have I been like them?
- God does not look at men the way we do. Men look at the outward appearance, but God looks at the heart. What does it mean to see the heart of someone?
- Do my outward appearance and my heart match?
- Does my appearance reveal what's in my heart?

14

THE ESSENCE BEHIND
THE RED LETTERS

THE MONDAY AFTER the race, Ace was in no shape to attend Spinsey's class. He needed another day or two to physically recover and more time to heal the scabs on his foot and nub knee. So Ace spent his spare moments setting up appointments. Doc Mentor was available Friday. Bobo would ride early Saturday morning. The Great Oz would see him Saturday at noon. And, as usual, Buddy agreed to a late afternoon basketball game.

The week sped by, and Friday morning arrived in no time at all. The scene repeated itself at St. Luke's eye clinic: waiting room, followed by a private room. The door opened and Doc Mentor greeted Ace.

"Ace, how in the world are you? Tell me what you've been up to!"

"I finished my first triathlon—St. Anthony's Olympic distance, a few days ago."

"So how'd you do and what did you learn?" Ace thought *This guy is such a pro. He couldn't just ask how I did, but also asked what I learned. Other people wouldn't think to ask.*

"OK, if you really must know, I tanked it. I finished in the bottom ten percent. I got penalized for following too close to another rider. I swam in perfect "z" formation. I swear I swam twice as far as everybody else. On the bike, I rode on a brand new leather Italian saddle, which may sound impressive, but I got soreness and chafing in places it's not reasonable to talk about. Then, on the run, I blew out my one good tire," as Ace pointed to the ball of his foot before continuing.

"Major blister, thanks to my new shoes. And my spare leg was screaming at me from inside the harness. I hobbled across the finish line with grandma and grandpa, except grandpa was in front of me! So what did I learn? I don't know. All I could hear in my mind were the words of a biking friend—the only losers are quitters and never, never, never give up. What did I learn? Race day is not a good day to introduce new equipment to your game. I learned that looking good on the outside is not as important as *being* good on the *inside*. You gotta do it to know it; experience is the great teacher."

Doc replied, "Well, that's a lot of learning, and you're right: personal experience is the master teacher. Sometimes we call that the University of Hard Knocks. Experience is the most convincing teacher, but not the only teacher. You can learn some of life's lessons from the mistakes of others. And yet some lessons, as you have suggested, have to be learned through experience. So you are off and on your way. No place to go but up."

"I'll agree with that."

"So tell me about some of the people you've met through this race."

Ace thought it through before answering. "I met some interesting people, that's for sure. To start with, my bike coach is Spinsey…"

Doc Mentor interrupted before he could go on. "Hey, I know Spinsey. You've got the best bike coach—sharp young lady with a strong work ethic."

"Well, it turns out she knows about everybody who's anybody. She introduced me to world champion Cheetah, fastest man on the planet. He gave me a good suggestion to mentally keep score of those I passed to keep me motivated and give my mind something to do while I race. I also met triathlon pageant queen Vanna Teia Fair, who was all about looking glamorous and dressed to impress—only to discover I was guilty of feeling inadequate and seeking approval through the same method. And then there was a volunteer I'd met before named Slider, who gave me good advice on how not to get off track and unfit to race. He said the road to destruction is achieved little by little. Poor decisions repeated over and over will do you in—like don't eat extra brownies, lay off the Twinkies, and don't get second and third helpings of desserts. Yep, that about sums it up."

"Excellent recap. Thanks for paying attention to everything going on around you. Alertness plays a big part of learning and spiritual growth. And then taking those observations and making the metaphor come alive with spiritual application, and voila! Growth happens! Now I want to focus on two comments I heard you make. You know you set me up. What Slider said about watching your diet is truly essential, and I mean physically and spiritually. Let me share a few thoughts about each.

"Ace, sliding into compromise happens little by little. You neglect your spiritual life a little and your heart grows cold. You cheat on your diet a little bit at a time and eventually you'll find yourself unfit to race.

"I realize you aren't that overweight. You could probably lose six to eight pounds and tighten up a bit. You're probably sitting at seventeen

> ### BODY FAT: LEADING INDICATOR
>
> *Did you know that the leading indicator of people who finish iron distance races is this one factor: they have 15% body fat or less. Any more than that and statistics show fewer of these people make it.*

to eighteen percent body fat. Did you know the leading indicator of people who finish the Ironman is this one factor? They have fifteen percent body fat or less; sixteen percent or more and statistics show fewer of these people make it.

"Fuel—the right fuel—is essential for race day and all the training leading up to that day. An athlete's body will exhaust its metabolic resources in just three hours. After that, you're either running on storage supplies or your fuel intake replenishment. You must have a well thought-out plan or the body starts to react and even shuts down; muscles begin to cramp. When that happens, it's almost too late to replenish. You must stay on top of it from the beginning.

"Here are simple rules: Try to eliminate as much processed food as possible. If it comes in a box, can, bag, or jar, it's most likely processed. Eat real food, lots of fruits and vegetables, and minimize all candy. When I say that, realize that ice cream is not candy, so eat that when you can," Doc said, smiling. Ace appreciated the humor and realized even this tower of power made room for a little pleasure in his life.

"Don't take yourself too seriously! I love ice cream, so I don't eliminate everything, so don't make a ridiculous commitment. Yes, I still eat meat. I'm not a vegetarian. Concerning drinks: simply eliminate all soda and other sugary fruit drinks altogether."

"So, what's the spiritual metaphor here?" Ace asked.

"You've got to give careful attention to your spiritual intake; you need to eat, as it were, the words of God. It's the word, the word, the word of God! The whole dynamic of the spiritual life begins there. Christ said that man does not live by bread alone, but by every word that proceeds from the mouth of God. So get a steady, even daily, intake of the Bible. I want to suggest something different than what Cheetah suggested to entertain your mind. As you race and work out, make your mental time meaningful. Rather than counting the people you pass, spend your time meditating on God's Word, rehearsing Scripture in your mind as you run and bike. I've run the Big Race and I attribute my success to rehearsing and meditating on the word of God the whole way. That'll get your mind off the pain in your body and onto the things of God. This is exactly what I do every morning. I do my physical workout with my body while engaging my mind with the word of God. That's the spiritual metaphor of the diet of food for body and food for the soul.

"Ace, like a workout schedule increases slowly, growing spiritual maturity takes time. We start with little by little and we add to it. For example, don't expect that you're going to read the Bible every day for an hour when you aren't reading it at all right now. Aim for 10 minutes every day and increase a little at a time, when you are ready. Remember the Bible is not to be conquered, although it is a worthy goal to read the entire Bible. I have found it more productive to take small portions and reread them over and over for a week or two until I really get it.

Ace, I'm a slow learner. I can read an entire chapter of any book, including the Bible, and too often I wouldn't be able to tell you what I just read. So I learned to slow down instead of plowing on to the next chapter. I now read the same two chapters every day for a week or so, until I start to get it into my soul. Sometimes I might read a book of the Bible over and over for a few weeks, or even months. It's better to go slow and get something out of it rather than conquer it solely for the sake of progress.

Ace replied in hearty agreement, "I know exactly what you mean. That's my problem too. I don't even like to read and, when I do, I often don't remember a single word. Doc, thanks for being transparent with me. I need the slow approach. Maybe I can grind a little bit into my soul."

"Exactly. So let me recap: you're going to transform your body by adhering to a healthy diet and training through repetition." Doc started using his hands to make his point. He was standing now with imaginary dumbbells gripped in each of his fists. He was doing alternating arm curls, slow, dramatic, and repetitive as he talked. "This is how it's done. The body is transformed through repetition. The soul is also transformed by repetition. It's the renewing of your mind, which is accomplished through repetition." Doc finally stopped with the arm curling. "Do you get the point?!"

Doc handed Ace a small book. "Here's your assignment: I want you to start each day with a ten-minute study, before you work out, by reading this little book *Great with God*. It's a pocket guide so it's easy to keep with you. Read the same three pages every day for a week before you move on. Focus and memorize the key verse highlighted in bold. It's important to put these Scriptures to memory. In short, what you don't memorize you won't utilize. And repetition is how we learn. This book is filled with verses that reveal the essence of God and the teachings of Christ that emanate out of that essence. You'll find Bible promises and questions for life application. It closes with some prayer suggestions. In short, it's like taking a multivitamin for the soul.

"Let me give you another illustration of why I am so excited about this little book, Ace.

SOUL FOOD: THE SPIRITUAL METAPHOR OF THE DIET

PHYSICAL FOOD FOR THE BODY	SPIRITUAL FOOD FOR THE MIND
Fruits, vegetables, nuts	Specific Scriptures that address specific needs
Protein, as in meat	Study the Sermon on the Mount. Matt. 5-7
Hydrated, lots of water	The Essence of God: The Commands of Christ

ELIMINATE	ELIMINATE
Candy	Worthless TV time and video games
Processed food	Blasphemous Movies
If it's in a box or a can, it's processed	Frivolous social media
Soda, fruit drinks, and alcohol	Excessive Cell phone gaming time
Fast-food restaurants	Worthless entertainment, books, magazines
Donuts, cookies, and desserts	Worthless recreation and free time usage

WHAT IS WORTHLESS? LET YOUR CONSCIENCE AND THE WORD OF GOD BE YOUR GUIDE.

Garbage in equals garbage out.

Putting garbage in your body diminishes your performance.

Putting garbage in your mind affects the outcome of your words and behavior.

Guarding your heart and mind is something that requires daily vigilance.

Think of a dart board with numbers one to twenty scattered throughout, outer ring triple, inner ring double. At the center, the outer bullseye is black, the inner bullseye is red. It's like the Bible, with sixty-six books making up the whole. Every book has value. Some help me more than others at various times of my life. But at the center is the essence of God which we discussed during our last visit. Out of that comes the Commands of Christ. These are His teachings, often called the red letters of the Bible. There is nothing more important than to learn and apply these to your life. So what does it mean to be a disciple of Christ? Simply put, to follow in His footsteps, live life from His point of view and according to His values.

"Ace, this little book will help you adopt His values as your own. This tool has simply taken the red letters (the words of Jesus) and organized them as expressions of God's nature taken from the various names of God, the example of Christ, the fruits of the Spirit, and the beatitudes. It's like having the best of the best at your fingertips.

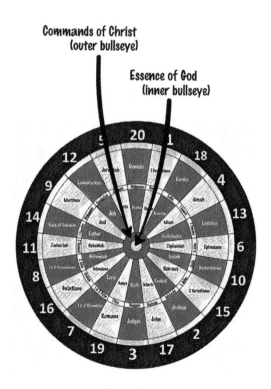

I want you to think of this tool as the Cliffs Notes of the Bible. I have found that studying one dimension of the image of God per week, over and over each day, has made a huge difference in my understanding. Remember: you are what you think. So I can't recommend this book strongly enough. It's what I use.

"Furthermore, I want you to remember: we tend to become like our friends. They rub off on us. So choose them wisely. Wrong friends corrupt right living, but he who walks among the wise will himself become wise. So there you have it. That's today's lesson, the diet of champions. What's next for you?"

Ace was pleased to reiterate that he had registered for the Rocky Pointe Half-Iron (The Big Race pre-qualifier) scheduled a little less than four months away.

"Well then, Ace, put some of these thoughts into action. Then come see me after you've finished that race."

"You got it, Doc. Thanks for the input. I'll see you again before you know it."

℘

The next day Ace spent the morning riding with Bobo on the trail with his new bike and equipment. He rehashed the entire race, including his surprise meeting with Cheetah and visit with Doc Mentor. Bobo was all ears and shared his own penalty story; he had gotten one on his first race for drafting as well. So Doc was right. There was definitely a bond between people who could commiserate.

Ace shared that he intended to rejoin Spinsey's Saturday morning peloton next week and asked Bobo if he wanted to join him. They'd at least have each other to fall back on if they couldn't keep up. It sounded like a good idea and Bobo agreed conditionally. Next Saturday was open, but the following Saturday he had a schedule conflict. So his answer was, "I'll join you when I can." Bobo was on his game and had become a Monday-Friday mornings training machine, at least for the time being, but his weekends belonged to his family.

Later that day, Ace entered the VA through the side door to see the Great Oz. He welcomed Ace with a big, toothy smile. " I've got good news!" Then he hesitated and winced as he shrugged his shoulders. "Well, bad news to some…an amputee recently died who was a marathon runner. His family donated his prosthetic limbs back to this office, which included two running blades and two knees. I told my boss your story and we agreed that one set of them is yours."

The two spent the remaining time getting Ace properly adjusted to this retooled prosthetic blade. Oz began working his magic, creating a custom fit, so their conversation took place in the moments between fine tunings. Ace recounted his first triathlon from the vantage point of the performance and pain associated with his prosthetic leg. It was the kind of unique conversation you only have with your prosthetist.

"Ace, you are definitely a multifaceted man with multiple legs. Here is the new plan: I want you to keep using your bionic leg for your everyday activity. But for all your various athletic activities you get the benefit of having one socket, which you can now interchange by way of the Ferrier coupler. Keep using the AllPro Foot I fit to your Total Knee 2000 to play basketball. And you can connect it to the Vari-Flex Foot with attached pedal cleat for biking, but from now on for all your long-distance running, training and racing, use this Cheetah Knee and flex run foot. Amazingly, this carbon blade is really going to prove very forgiving and should give you some spring in your step. The end result is you'll be more comfortable and faster."

As Ace was exiting the workroom, he saw Scoob sitting in the lobby. It was a coincidence indeed, a repeat encounter. Scoob was waiting to see Oz next. Ace stopped to exchange greetings and discovered today was also Scoob's delivery day. Before Scoob would leave the workshop of the Great Oz, he'd exchange his crutches for a comfortably-fitted new leg. Scoob was in a different mood this afternoon. Last time he had been depressed and detached. Today he was engaged, but skeptical. Ace tried to reassure him there'd be better days ahead before they parted ways.

CR

Later that afternoon, Ace met Buddy at the YMCA for a pick-up game of basketball. The competition was soft because no serious players were in the gym. On those days, the two liked to add a little style to their game, which meant Ace served up slam-dunks to make Buddy look like he belonged in the NBA all-star game.

Ace had to let up on his game to keep the opponents interested. Otherwise, he would steal and block passes and literally knock the spirit out of them. So he bragged to make it fair he'd play with only one arm to even things up. Regardless, the game was short and fun, just another under-challenged day at the courts. Rare was the occasion when Ace and Buddy had any real competition.

After the game, Ace had a classified girl report for Buddy. "You know, joining the YMCA is the best thing I ever did. I'm telling you, attending spin class is the highlight of my week. There's a lot of good-looking women in there, and I'm making some serious headway with coach Spinsey. You know, at the race, she was my personal assistant, and I even got a serious 'congratulations for finishing' squeeze from her."

"Yeah, but when we spoke on the phone, you mentioned this Cheetah guy she's involved with. How are you getting around that?"

"It turns out they're just old high school friends. I don't think there is anything romantic between them. She is definitely available. And the chemistry is building. Next Saturday, I'm rejoining her peloton ride. So I'm probably going to be too exhausted for any basketball next week. How about you? You see anything interesting out there?"

Buddy's response was deflated, "Nah, not even a nibble. I'm telling you, six feet seven inches is not what every girl is looking for. I've got a diminishing pond to fish in. Dude, if I don't find somebody soon, I'm going to have to join your spin class. And they don't make a bike big enough to fit me."

They chuckled and said goodbye. Buddy got the last word in. "Hey, good luck with the spin instructor. See you in a few weeks."

That night, Ace sat down to blog.

I feel so lucky. I've got the greatest coaches in the world: Swim–Domestique, Biking–Spinsey, Bruiser–running, and spiritual growth–Doc Mentor. If that wasn't enough, I've even got the Wizard of Oz as my equipment manager.

Doc Mentor is tenacious about the spiritual metaphor. This week, we talked about diet, both physical and mental. First, simple stuff like eat real food, eliminate processed food, but the spiritual metaphor was insightful. You gotta feed your soul. And that should be daily as well.

Wisbit tip: *You are what you think, so guard your heart's desires with great diligence, for out of it flows the issues of life.*

Wisbit tip: *Feeding yourself good thoughts requires continuous (even daily) attention.*

Wisbit tip: *The red letters of the Bible are the most important, the bullseye.*

Wisbit tip: *Learning is not about conquering the material, but being conquered by the material.*

Wisbit tip: *When it comes to learning, slow down and realize repetition is king. Take a little info and go deep before moving on.*

QUESTIONS FOR SELF-REFLECTION

- What do my calendar and spending habits reveal about my relationship to God? How much time does God get from my schedule?
- The best word to describe my spiritual diet would be…(nonexistent, junk food, organic, milk, or meat)?
- Do I guard my heart by giving careful consideration to everything I watch and listen to? Is there anything I should eliminate?
- What is the leading indicator of people who will grow to spiritual maturity?

15

GET THE ZIG OUT OF YOUR ZIGZAG

SINCE PURCHASING HIS new bike and completing the race, Ace had the confidence to rejoin Spinsey's peloton on Saturdays. Though they still dropped him, Ace could stay with the peloton for longer periods of time. He could sense that he was growing strong and his endurance was improving. He believed in a few more months he'd be able to stay with them for the duration.

With the Rocky Pointe Half-Iron a little more than three months away, Ace was more focused than ever. He had what they call "tri fever," which translated into "I want to do my best and reach my highest capacity." Ace didn't know what that was; he just knew he wasn't anywhere near what he believed was his personal best, so he trained hard.

Training dominated his life in a good way. The only downside Ace could see was that basketball with Buddy on Saturdays had faded almost into oblivion. They kept in touch, but it seemed to them that training was getting in the way. Ace was chasing a dream and Buddy was still on the hunt for a girlfriend.

Friday mornings were Ace's main focus. He simply had to get

better at swimming. All the wasted effort zigging and zagging back and forth during the race had infuriated Ace. He concentrated extra hard to swim straight each morning. Just now, Ace and Bobo had really been pushing their limits. So it was that after practice, Ace discussed his swimming challenges with Bobo.

Bobo had his own problems and felt apologetic for not being able to show up a little more regularly throughout the week. His schedule had changed, so now he was going to be a three-day per week workout guy: Mondays, Wednesdays, and Fridays. While Ace and Bobo talked, their swim instructor Domestique interrupted with a question, "All right, mate, you had mentioned that you wanted to get chatty after practice—how can I be of service?" Bobo took that as a cue and quickly excused himself.

Ace hadn't taken much time over the last few months to get to know this man well, so today he had planned to stay after practice to see if he could get some help from Domestique to address the issue of his crooked swimming style. Domestique was several years older than Ace. Once a college phenom in the pool, he was tall and trim and kept his sandy blonde hair short, and sported massive, broad shoulders. He was very pleasant in his disposition, a big-time problem solver. He worked more on form and technique for his students than Bruiser or Spinsey. And his British accent made him a bit of a novelty.

The two men considered every possible option, so it wasn't surprising when the idea of a prosthetic swim leg came up, especially since Domestique had been consulted for the film *Dolphin Tale*. He had worked for the Clearsky Marine Aquarium (CMA) while the film was being made and appeared in the movie as the swimming star's competitor. CMA was home to the world famous "Winter" the dolphin and star of the movie. Since Ace was unfamiliar with the movie, Domestique relayed the plot to Ace:

"*Dolphin Tale* is about a baby dolphin who loses her tail when it gets entangled in a crab trap. The movie hinges on the team that creates a special high-tech adhesive material attaching an artificial tail to the dolphin, so the movie is supposed to be inspirational, especially for amputees. Changed my life forever. I'm no bloke anymore! I'm a movie star; fancy that, I was in the movie," Domestique bragged. "Anyway, it made me think there's got to be some kind of prosthetic leg for you to swim with."

Ace put things into perspective for Domestique. "That is an amazing suggestion. I love your thinking, but it's just not realistic. To my knowledge, there is nothing that exists. Even if there was, I assure you it would cost more money than I could afford. My grant application for a blade to run with was recently rejected by the VA because they said it was a needlessly extravagant convenience, especially for someone like me already generously equipped with several prosthetic legs for which I'm truly grateful—but now I just gotta learn how to swim with one leg."

Domestique wasn't ready to surrender. "Rubbish! I don't believe it! Dr. Goodfellow is a personal friend. And I think he'd be excited about solving this challenge."

Ace's mechanical leg came with the warning and instructions not to swim with it or immerse it in water. He didn't think it would be a problem swimming with no attachment, but open water swimming had proved more difficult than he had anticipated. *What to do? Was the answer an artificial leg for the swim?* Ace thought, *I've been called the Bionic Man and the Terminator. Could I be Aqua Man?* His mind raced, fantasizing whether a special prosthetic, a unique fin design, would allow him to blow by Cheetah.

Ace was hesitant, fearing the potential cost of such a prosthetic enhancement. He doubted insurance would cover the creation of another recreational limb. However, before it was over, they agreed that Domestique would talk to Dr. Goodfellow, his friend and prosthetic engineering specialist. Domestique concluded by saying "The whole idea is blooming marvelous! If it's good enough for a dolphin, who knows what it could mean for a man!"

Ace countered, sensing it was a long shot, "First, I want to say thank you for your generous suggestion, but this is the kind of thing that I'm certain is going to take some time. There is no way we're going to get that kind of a solution in time for the Half-Iron race, and maybe it won't happen at all. Is there anything else we could do that's practical right now?"

Domestique did have an idea. He suggested Ace power his stroke with a scissor kick by rolling his hips slightly with each breath. The scissor kick might neutralize the off-balance propulsion of his standard kick. Ace gave it a try. It seemed to work.

Domestique encouraged Ace by commenting on his new technique, "That's the way to go. You'll be cracking if you master it. See if you can swim without the lanes and go straight."

Ace liked this solution, and felt his sense of tempo and stroke would come with time. Domestique was intrigued by Ace's tenacious spirit and asked him more questions about his race day experience. "So other than zigzagging, what else did you discover about open water swimming at the race?"

"Swimming is definitely my biggest challenge. I never really swam much before signing up for this race. I was on a lot of teams in high school, but never the swim team. I've got problems galore. My goggles fogged up, and I got squeezed and batted at the buoy turns."

"At least there are easy solutions to those problems. We'll get you some "no fog" gel for your goggles. And avoid the buoy collision by taking the outer edge."

"But that means I swim farther than everybody else if I do that, right?" objected Ace.

"It is an option, maybe a little more distance but not necessarily more time. How much time did you lose slowing down to go through the funnel? Plus, it's blooming dangerous in that log jam. Just avoid the whole thing. Swim around it."

Ace's mind raced; he could not help but think of Cheetah's suggestion to cut the corner. Ace said nothing, but agreed. "OK, I get it.

It's a trade-off. Go through the funnel slowly, which is the shorter distance, or swim faster by going further around it."

Domestique bolstered his point by adding, "I know it's written in the good book: a wise man sees danger coming and makes adjustments to avoid it."

"The spiritual metaphor continues..."

"What do you mean?"

"Well, a friend of mine is always looking for the spiritual metaphor in athletics, and you quoted a Bible verse, and it triggered the thought. Anyway, what I'm trying to say is that I get it; slow and steady wins over the traffic jam."

"Ace, that's exactly right." Then Domestique looked down at his watch just before he said, "Sorry, mate, but I gotta go now, so give the scissor kick some practice, and I'll see you next week. Cheerio."

ॐ

A few weeks later, as spin class ended, Spinsey indicated to Ace that the Half-Iron bike training on Saturdays had been moved to Sunday mornings. "It's time for the intensity to change. Eleven weeks will pass before you know it. And we all want to be ready. So here's the new plan: Saturdays we run with Bruiser's group and Sundays we ride all the way to the top of Sky Way trail—thirty miles up and 30 miles back. The group wants to really push it. You are doing so well and making excellent progress. The way to get better at biking is to increase distance and then the speed. I hope you can make the change and join us. The gang really likes you."

Ace tried to read between the lines. *Was she really saying that she likes me?* The invitation was accepted.

ॐ

Saturday morning at seven was Bruiser's running club, only this time more people attended than ever. Summer tri-season was approaching, so training was in demand. Ace saw Spinsey talking with Bruiser in the distance. She really knew everybody and was surrounded by the "in crowd." Tanga and a few others from the peloton team were there. They made Ace welcome, but he still didn't feel like one of them. Ace couldn't keep up, so he wasn't one of them yet. But it was nice to be known by them.

The YMCA was family-friendly with lots of regular folks training for one reason or another. As he listened to the crowd, it seemed like everybody was signed up for one race or another: sprint triathlons, 5K's, 10K's, half-marathons, and century bike rides. The people who pushed the limits of endurance were the few, the proud, the Half-Iron pursuers. Ace smiled when he was asked by the circle of people he was standing with what race he was working toward. He replied, "The Rocky Pointe Half-Iron" with a smugness that he couldn't control. He felt good about himself.

One hour later, and the group had run a modest 10K. It was a nice way to start the day. The water hose at the back of the "Y" building was a nice way to cool down. It was also where Bruiser began to re-engage Ace on their previous conversations.

"Hey, Ace, how are you doing? I was beginning to wonder about you. I lost you on Saturdays for a while, but I found out you were biking with Spinsey's crowd, and I knew you must be doing well. Riding with Spinsey the Wonder Woman will make a man out of you, an Ironman at that. She's tough. That's good company. Not quite like the company of E.Z. Good job! You're looking good."

"Well, Doc Mentor says I have to starting watching what I eat. So I've got a few more pounds to shed. And a long way to go. Six months is the countdown for the Big Race. And now just a little over two months until the qualifying event at the Half-Iron."

"How ya doin' with the practice schedule?"

"I am doing well, and this time not just a little, but a lot. I just finished my first tri, got the T-shirt," Ace said as he pointed down at his chest at the St. Anthony's Triathlon logo.

Bruiser offered his approval. "That's a big race. Congratulations! I saw you there. You skipped right over the sprints, eh?"

"No time, no money; I hit it big. I have the Big Race to conquer and a short time to get there."

"Sounds like you're working hard. I'm still curious to know if you're working out by the book. More precisely, how's the guide book schedule going?"

Ace tried to dodge that specific question and thought, *Why must he ask this precise question?* Ace was embarrassed and a little ashamed and tried to defend himself. "Okay, after we talked last I went home and really went through it, page by page, watching the increase of intensity rise with each week. I used it as a directional force, and while I don't open it all the time, I'm using the philosophy behind it."

> ## GENIUS IS MAINTAINING FOCUS
>
> *All it takes is 24 hours to lose vision and unwittingly get off track. Looking daily at the plan will keep you focused to reach your goal.*

"Nice approach. It sounds like you're doing a lot of the right things. However, while I don't mean to bust your chops, the tri-training manual needs referencing daily to stay focused. Ignoring it is like removing the sun from its place in the solar system. Darkness will ensue. Look—you have one shot to be 'Star Racer.' That's an actual title, you know. It's kind of like being named Rookie of the Year. There is only one first year of tri-athlon training. Star Racer would put you among the few and the elite of those who have ever pulled it off. I am proud to say I'm in that group. Qualifying for the Big Race on your first try is like a law student passing the bar exam the very first try. Unusual and rare. Think about it. It's a lot like going to the Super Bowl in your first season in the pros.

"Listen, Ace, in order to make the cut, you have to finish in the top forty of your age group. If you look at the last five years, you'll discover you are going to have to run the Half-Iron in less than five hours. Something like a 4:58 and you're most likely in. No one who finished after 5:01 in your age group has ever qualified for the Big Race. So that's your target. If you're going to hit your target, you'd better follow the guide with a little more precision than just the philosophy behind it. Seriously, it's your only hope.

"Ace, I suppose there are two routes to get ready for the Big Race. You can take your own route or the tri-training guide route, but let me warn you again: strive to enter at the straight gate that leads to life, because wide is the gate and broad is the path that leads to destruction, and many enter there because straight is the gate and narrow is the path that leads to life, and few find it. I'm just saying sometimes the genius is in the details. Listen, I still look at my schedule daily, and I'm a veteran. It helps keep me centered, sensible, and on target."

Ace accepted the rebuke. Twice he'd been admonished by Bruiser for book neglect. *Why was it so hard to open this stupid book?* Ace couldn't tell you why he didn't like reading. He just didn't. He dreaded reading books of any kind. He liked plans; he liked preparation. He liked to learn, he just preferred audio visual learning. All his life he just found it hard to get excited about studying through a book.

Now, the strange thing was he admired Bruiser all the more for having the courage to have this focused conversation with him. Ace appreciated the accountability.

For the next few weeks, Ace opened his tri-training "bible" and began to follow it to the letter. It became his primary focus. He had a willing attitude to do whatever it took to succeed. If following the book was the answer, that's what he would do. Bruiser was emphatic. Ace was a slow learner, but he got it. He would follow this formula and live or die by it. Finally, Bruiser had Ace convinced that the way to succeed was to follow the narrow way and that meant following the training manual in detail.

Ace felt rich in relationships and excellent about his health and conditioning. He rose early each day. He had been careful with his diet. Amazingly, even to him, he had lost a little weight. The tri-training guide prescribed doing bricks, which is triathlete talk for executing two of the big three disciplines in one workout. For example, Ace might ride with Spinsey in the morning and swim immediately after. As Ace started to regularly execute bricks, he began to feel strong. His confidence grew. He really started to feel prepared for the coming qualifying event.

Yet Ace had a growing problem: he liked two women at one time. One seemed hard to get, and he liked the challenge of trying to win her favor. The other seemed too comfortable and easy, a wonderfully good friendship was developing. He was enamored with Spinsey and was making headway with her, as she was slowly letting her guard down. The Sunday rides had turned into Sunday lunch following the ride. The riding group was growing close. Ride together, eat together, and have fun together. Lunch was where the bonding occurred. First they suffered together riding on the trail. Afterwards Ace learned everyone's story as they hung out to refuel. The people who stayed for lunch always varied, depending on schedules. One Sunday recently, it was just Ace and Spinsey who stayed for lunch.

It made Ace wonder if she'd planned it. Maybe she had arranged for the other women to leave them alone together. The peloton shrank in number when they made the Sunday switch. There were only three guys: Ace, Jack Rabbit, and Ray Boltz. The rest were women, eight altogether, including Tanga. Ace felt he was buddies with greatness and beauty.

This Sunday, everybody had somewhere to go except Ace and Spinsey, and that's when the magic happened. Yes, there was chemistry. Yes, it was a date. Spinsey clearly enjoyed Ace's company. They stayed and talked for another hour, discovering they had much in common. Ace had played his hand slow and calculated. He'd spent seven months making sure he didn't scare this fish away. Everything had paid off! Maybe he didn't need to like two girls. Ace carefully had not pursued Charity, who seemed a more obvious catch, to keep the possibility going with Spinsey. Today he believed he was a genius.

Over the past few months, Ace had not kept up with his blog posts. He had lost the initial enthusiasm. The novelty was gone, and there wasn't much new to report. There were a few new insights, training was steady, and his growth was steady. Now, after spending time alone with Spinsey, Ace was in the mood for writing. People needed an update because too much time had passed.

Hello World,

I'm on target to do the Half-Iron 70.3 mid-summer. That's a 1.2-mile swim, fifty-six-mile bike, and half a marathon, 13.1 miles. I am so amped up about this. I've got a team of people helping me. Everybody thinks this is an individual sport, but the more I get engaged, this is definitely a team sport. Coaches, teammates, mentors, and competitors all help bring out the best in me. And that's what I want to say to all of you out there following my story. Stretch yourself to be the very best version of yourself. What I'm learning through all this is that I can do so much more than I ever thought possible with the help of others.

Qualifying for the Big Race has captured almost all of my attention. It would be such a shame to work as hard as I have thus far and not even get to participate in the race. I've got to qualify. I've already made up my mind to pay whatever price it costs. I just don't know if there is enough time. Some of the experts say two or three years is the usual approach for preparation for the Big Race. But others say that a born athlete can make the one year blitz "Star Racer" designation. I've talked to the pros, I've done the research, and I'll have to do a sub five hours in the coming race to be close to getting the last spot. That race is roughly double the distance of my first race. So do the math—that's the equivalent of shaving off one and one-half hours of what my time was last race. Is that even possible? I wonder. I hope so; I think so. I look back at the race and see lots of room for improvement on the swim, bike, and run.

I've got two different coaches; one saying seek creative solutions, the other saying follow the book exactly; so who's right? I suppose both. I'm reminded of the serenity prayer right now as I write: Lord, give me the courage to change the things I can and the grace to accept the things I can't. And the wisdom to know the difference.

Two more weeks and the qualifying race is here.

Here is what I'm learning:

Wisbit tip: *People never do what you expect, only what you inspect.*

Wisbit tip: *Two minds are better than one. In a multitude of counselors, there is safety.*

Wisbit tip: *Asking tough, precise questions is the role of a coach.*

Wisbit tip: *The magic is in the details. Careful, thoughtful planning and precise preparation hold the key to success.*

Wisbit tip: *Daily reviewing of one's goals is the necessary ingredient to maintaining focus.*

QUESTIONS FOR SELF-REFLECTION

- Describe a time in my life when I have not followed the details and it really cost me?
- When have I achieved excellence? What was involved to do so?
- When and under what circumstances do I find myself following the broad path (the easy way)? What will it take for me to live on the narrow path?
- Who in my life have I given permission to ask me tough accountability questions?
- What do my actions reveal about my priorities? If an investigation was made of how I spent my money and my time last month, what would be discovered about my priorities?

16

WHAT YOU DO WHEN NO ONE IS LOOKING

I T WAS 4:30 in the morning. Rocky Pointe Half-Iron race day had finally arrived, and Ace was parked in front of the garage at Bobo's home. Bobo had planned to ride over with Ace, then a little later, his wife and three small girls would come at a more reasonable hour and spend the day watching the race and playing at the beach. For athletes, it was usually nothing less than a ten-hour day that consisted of rising early, driving to the destination, allowing an hour for orientation and race preparation, doing the race, then having lunch and attending the awards ceremony. It was more than the small girls could endure. Bobo's family would show up later, skip the awards ceremony, have a family celebration, and take their daddy home.

Ace had his support team as well. Buddy had agreed to meet Ace at the beach to help navigate through the transitions zone.

On the way over, the two men discussed their hopes and fears. Bobo was doing the race on about half the training that Ace had, but Bobo had a lifetime of being in shape and years of doing triathlons. Although he'd never done the big one or even this one, Bobo had experience. Yet he wasn't sure he had done enough to finish with a qualifying effort. But they were there to find out—it was test day.

After their arrival at the race site, the two men agreed to proceed separately through registration and look for each other at the beach by the starting gate.

This race day simply felt different than the previous one. Ace was more settled, more confident, and more mentally rehearsed. He was in better shape and had made many adjustments to make sure he'd do well. He'd been counseled to stay hydrated throughout the race. This was going to be a five-hour race for Ace. He remembered what Doc said about keeping the body fueled. He had gotten a half dozen gel packets which were quick liquid energy, a time lapse forty-five-minute intake plan, and salt tablets to help prevent cramps. He was ready.

Ace got settled into his transition space—setting up his bike and arranging his belongings into the most logistically efficient sequence for the first and second transitions. For Ace that meant the additional planning of navigating his prosthetic legs. The coupling ferrier designed and installed by the Great Oz was the genius behind his transition plan. He'd spend extra time in transition one getting set, but would sail through transition two with a click and snap installation of his blade for the run. It was here in the transition area during the pre-race set-up that he met Markist, a young man of twenty-four. He fastened a sticker marked 222 to both end posts of the bike rack. Ace was curious. It didn't seem like vandalism because there seemed to be some underlying intentional purpose to what the guy did.

So Ace asked him: "What is this all about?"

Markist was ready to answer. "Take a look around you. There are over 200 bike racks here. It can get confusing trying to locate your bike; it's easy to get lost. By posting my sticker at the ends of my bike row, it helps when I come in from the swim. It makes it easy to find my bike, no delays."

"So what's the meaning of 222? That's not your race number." Markist wore 153 on his bib.

"True. It's a code. I bet you've seen similar stickers on the backs of cars as you drive around town. You see lots of different numbers on bumpers: 13.1, 26.2, 70.3,140.6…they're all codes. This is a code. And, I am the designer. Consider my sticker a gift from Markist! It's my mark!"

Markist held up the sticker and showed the number 222 in a classic oval, black and white design. In small script 2 Timothy 2:2 was printed as an outer pinstripe. It read, "The things you have heard me say in the presence of many witnesses, entrust to reliable men who will also be able to tell others."

"That's cool. I'm Christian also; nice to know you." Ace extended his hand. "My name is Ace."

"Well Ace, this is a simple reminder to share the love. I call it the 222 principle. You know the fish is the symbol of a believer, and 222 is a similar sign. It's a reminder to be a disciple maker. The two kinda go together. Jesus said, 'Follow me and I will make you a fisher of men.' There are two steps the way I see it—first a follower, then a fisher of men. I use this mark as a constant reminder to be about the business of making disciples of Christ who are committed to paying it forward. We are looking for a special type of disciple, someone who is willing to become a channel of His love. Someone willing to make another disciple with that goal in mind.

"Hear me out, Ace! A disciple is a good thing, but the greater goal is to make a disciple who will in due season make a disciple. Do you know what a mule is? A mule is different from a donkey, though most people mistake them as the same. A mule is an excellent servant; it's a work horse with a good demeanor to serve. A mule is what you get when a horse mates with a donkey. The only problem with a mule is that they are incapable of reproducing; they are sterile.

"Too many Christians are like mules: good servants with an excellent disposition, but they are either not interested or ineffective in making more disciples. When that happens, as is well documented in our country, the population of Christians diminishes with each successive generation. I'm trying to inspire every Christian to accept the mantle of the great commission, to accept the command of Christ to be disciple makers.

"I put these stickers anywhere I can. I'm starting a revolution. I want to inspire people of faith by this secret code to remind them to share the love and become disciple makers. Let the light out. Here's what can happen: now that you've seen the 222 sticker, your eye will be trained to see 222 everywhere you go. It's like buying a new car and noticing a day later that everybody is driving the same car as yours. Once 222 is in your soul; the Holy Spirit will help you see it, and it can prod you into action, sharing the love."

Ace was inspired but was also starting to feel restless. In the background over the loudspeaker he could hear the announcement that transition was closing and all racers should head immediately to the swim start .The race was starting soon. Ace brought the conversation to a quick close. "I like what this is all about and I'm glad I met you today. Godspeed to you. But we'd both better get going towards the starting line. We have a race to run."

Markist finished the conversation. "Nice to have met you as

well…keep the faith and finish the race." But before the men separated, Markist gave Ace a sticker. Ace quickly put it in his bag, detached his prosthetic leg, grabbed his crutches and made his way to the beach.

At the beach near the starting gate, a small group of athletes from the YMCA were gathered. Ace was greeted by all his coaches, who were also his competitors in this race. Looking around, he also spotted several friends from the peloton. Bobo gave Ace a high-five. Then Ace saw Buddy and Charity walking his way. She was in her warm-up suit because she wasn't racing today. Buddy didn't even know he walked behind the woman Ace had frequently mentioned in their conversations.

HALF-IRONMAN QUALIFYING FOR THE BIG RACE

ACE'S TARGET TIMES: *1.2 miles swim (40 minutes) ; 56 miles bike (2:21); 13.1 miles run (1:53); Transition (5 minutes)*

ONLY THE TOP 40 PER AGE GROUP QUALIFY.
Average amateur low qualifying time is 4:59—40TH place finisher (average) in his age group—Ace's target goal to qualify for the Big Race.

WORLD RECORD HOLDER FOR HALF-IRONMAN DISTANCE:
Clearwater, Florida: German Michael Raelert, **Ironman 70.3** distance, won the **World Championship, Nov 14, 2009**, with a time of 3 hours, 34 minutes, 4 seconds.

Buddy was quickly introduced to all of Ace's tri-family. He had been called into service since Spinsey was unavailable to assist Ace (she was racing). Buddy would help with his crutches at the takeoff and swim transitions. Charity, on the other hand, was there as a casual friendship to Ace and to support the others who trained at the YMCA. Although Ace felt some attraction to her, he kept his boundaries. He wanted to make sure Spinsey didn't get the impression that he was involved with Charity. It was weird because he liked them both. Under different circumstances, he would have pursued Charity. For now, most of his attraction was locked up with infatuation for Spinsey. Charity seemed happy to play the friend role she was used to.

⁂ ❦

The race began. It was a staggered start. Finally, Ace's flight launched. Ace had a different approach for the swim this time. His goggles were anti-fog ready. His initial approach to swimming was less tentative than the previous race. But he kept popping up his head to make sure he was swimming straight. He took the route for the outer edge around the buoy, which played to his advantage as he missed the congested corner that was sheer pandemonium for the dozens of racers who swam close to the buoy. Ace reasoned *he swam a little farther, and perhaps he'd lost some time with the added distance, but the path was clear.*

Once he'd cleared the corner, Ace felt confident enough to put his head down and give his new scissor kick a serious try. He swam strongly, and the movement of his stroke and legs was well executed. He was moving right along, *The next buoy should be here,* he thought. He stalled into his breast stroke to look up again and gather his bearings. He had aimed and drifted too far out into the ocean, just the opposite of what had happened the race before. When Ace realized what had happened again, he stopped. As he treaded water, he was infuriated beyond belief. He cursed his leg out loud, grimaced, and cursed the situation. He was livid, because he knew he didn't have time to waste. Ace had trained too hard to let this happen.

Mastering his frustration, Ace pulled himself together and adjusted, which meant a hard correction was needed. He turned back toward the beach and buoy for the next turn. He swam straight for the traffic jam. By the time he looked up again, Ace was in the thick

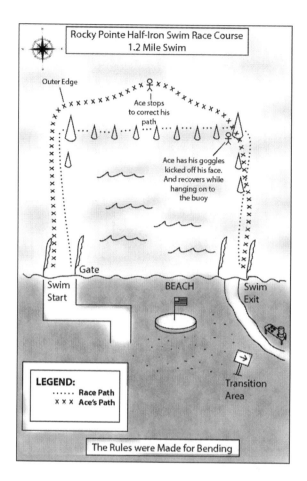

Rocky Pointe Half-Iron Swim Race Course
1.2 Mile Swim

Outer Edge

Ace stops
to correct his
path

Ace has his goggles
kicked off his face.
And recovers while
hanging on to
the buoy

Gate

Swim
Start

BEACH

Swim
Exit

LEGEND:
· · · · · **Race Path**
x x x **Ace's Path**

Transition
Area

The Rules were Made for Bending

of it and too tired to go the long route. He was deeply concerned that he had mismanaged his time. He felt rushed, and there was no time to waste. He decided to navigate the corner as tightly as possible.

Then it happened. Someone kicked Ace in the face, and his goggles were knocked completely over his eyes. The blow to the head stunned him. It wasn't a knockout kick, yet it caused him to stop swimming. He reached for the buoy to steady himself. Ace positioned himself inside the buoy, out of the line of traffic to get his goggles back into place.

Ace had a decision to make because he had not gone around the buoy. Should he re-enter the battle zone and take the chance of getting batted and kicked again for the sake of going round the buoy, or go forward? He remembered his conversation with Cheetah and reasoned it was all about the distance. With the outer edge excursion he took earlier, Ace would easily exceed the 1.2-mile required swim; he decided quickly, because time was ticking and every second counted. Ace needed to qualify, so he moved forward and not around the buoy.

As he arrived at the beach, Buddy was there to assist him as he exited the water. He gave him a shoulder out of the water and quickly handed him the crutches. Same as before, Ace went his way waddling into the transition gate. Buddy only had time to say "nice swim." He had marked his time when he started and announced his progress: "Thirty-four minutes. Great! You are a few minutes ahead of your goal. Keep going!"

The rest of the race was grueling, yet Ace remained focused.

At the finish line, Buddy and Charity stood cheering. He had not only helped with the crutches but also had been his official time-keeper. He knew what was at stake, knew the plan, and shared in the moment of rejoicing. "You did it!" He screamed again, "You did it!"

All the hard work had paid off. Ace met his goals and finished with precision. He hit his benchmark of 4:57:57, which did exactly what was predicted by securing him the fortieth spot in his age group. He had qualified for the Big Race. Once again, he kept score on the bike and run. Ace passed seventy-six people altogether, mostly on the bike, which was his strength (thanks to Spinsey's peloton training). He was only passed by twenty-one riders. Ace was on top of the world.

Buddy was the first person to give Ace a high-five to celebrate, but others were at the finish line to congratulate him as well. Spinsey and Bruiser had each finished their race much earlier but now gave attention to their star runner athlete. It was a big deal because Ace talked so much about qualifying over the last two months that everybody rooted for him. It was the feel-good story of the year for the tri team and trainers at the YMCA. When one of their athletes excelled, it was a feather in their cap as well.

When Spinsey found Ace, she gave him a big hug as she said with a great deal of emotion, "Star Racer! That's you! You're a superstar! Congratulations; you rock!" Ace was barraged with more people to celebrate with. It seemed everyone Ace trained with had qualified for the Big Race and finished before him, except Bobo. Bobo started well with his swim, and even biked to a personal best. But when he started the run, he hadn't finished the first mile when he immediately experienced cramps in his thighs and calf muscles. To his credit, Bobo never quit. He did the cycle of walk, pause to stretch, jog, walk, pause to stretch, and repeat until he crossed the finish line more than a half hour after Ace.

After Ace's finish line celebration, he pillaged his way through the snack pavilion; racing for five hours can make a guy hungry. Then it was finally time to gather his belongings from the transition area. There, Ace met a man whose bike was next to his. He had greeted him briefly with a little conversation earlier as they set up before the race. Now he was less rushed.

Ace noticed something a little unusual about this man that he had not seen earlier: he wore a Christian T-shirt. Ace looked further and noticed a Christian fish symbol stuck onto the bike's center post, and his backpack had a Bible verse embroidered on it.

Ace commented, "Nice shirt—you attend church around here?"

"Yeah, man. Thanks for asking. I'm a deacon over at the First Church of the Angel of Light. But for a living, I'm a personal trainer. I assure all my clients we are practitioners on the leading edge of technology, science, physiology, diet, and innovation.

"That sounds amazing. Nice to know you; I'm Ace."

"And glad to meet you as well, I'm Deuce Aaron—a lot of folks just call me 'Double A.'"

"Double A; that's cool; I get it. So are you the energizer bunny or the copper-top brand?"

"Just power, man, that's all. God's got power, He rules the universe. God is serious, man."

Ace chimed in. "Hey, you don't have to convince me; I'm a man of faith myself."

Deuce spoke with passion and attitude; it was easy to tell he was on a mission of righteousness. He continued as Ace listened intently. "People don't even know the Ten Commandments any more. That's why the world is in such a sorry state. It's simple: don't kill, don't sleep with anybody but your wife, don't steal, don't lie, show up at church on Sunday. You'd think that's reasonable. That's all we gotta do, man. So why can't we teach this to our children? I'll tell you why—it's those bozos up on Capitol Hill, that's why. I hate them with perfect hatred. They are tools of the devil and against everything that is righteous."

Just then, Tanga walked behind Ace. Deuce stopped in mid-sentence and let his head turn and eyes bug out in delight. Ace turned to see who Deuce was gawking at. Tanga waved at Ace, winked and said with a bit of sass, "Congratulations, Star Racer."

Ace waved back and whispered, "Thanks."

Deuce exclaimed, "You know her?!"

"I do," Ace said with a bit of pride.

"Well, it ain't a sin to look, and that girl is too fine." A moment later while they were both putting things away and gathering their belongings, Deuce was again distracted. He saw something on the ground, next to his spot, almost in no-man's land.

"Look at that," said Double A as he held up some goggles. "Strike Deluxe, fog-free guarantee. I always wanted a pair. These are just too expensive, you know what I mean? Finders keepers, losers weepers."

Ace cautioned, "Maybe that belongs to the racer stationed next to you. He just hasn't returned yet."

"Yeah, maybe, but it's right there in no-man's land. It was probably left by accident by someone else." Double A placed the goggles in his backpack. Ace shrugged it off, and they continued their conversation. They walked and arrived together at the gate, but there was a guard stationed there. Ace knew the man—he was the big man Titan, his basketball friend from last year's Big Race. Titan was there to make sure no one left early. No one was allowed to leave with their belongings yet. It was the race director's way of making sure nothing was stolen, as a measure of security.

Ace started a friendly conversation. "Titan, right? Basketball, remember?"

"Yeah, I remember you, man." They shook hands. "The unstoppable machine man, like the Terminator—you just kept coming. So you racing again, huh?"

"I came, I saw, I conquered!" Ace said smugly.

Double A grew impatient, so he spoke to Titan with a sense of urgency. "Listen, I need some help. I have to get out of here now. My wife's been calling me. My girl's at home sick, and I need to leave so I can help her get to the doctor. Can you help me out?"

There was no stopping that story. Titan checked Double A's number against his bike number and granted his exit. Ace would have to wait another ten minutes to leave. Double A shouted back as he left, "Light of the world, man, salt of the earth. Glad to have met you. Ride on, brother!"

Ace was left standing perplexed. *What had just happened?* he thought. *This guy talked with amazing passion for righteousness' sake. He even schmoozed me by the strength of conviction in his voice.* Upon reflection, Ace saw Deuce as truly Double A, for that is who he actually was: "Double in Appearance," the ultimate hypocrite. He looked one way on the outside with his Christian-ese talk, but what about the inside? Jesus clarified the law. Hatred was equal to murder, and lust was equal to adultery. And taking what doesn't belong to you, no matter how you look at it, is stealing. Not to mention stretching the truth. Ace thought, *Double A is the double man.*

While he waited to have his bike released out of transition, a small crowd gathered. Everybody had the same idea: the race was over so they wanted to go and get on with their day.

Domestique saw Ace waiting. He hadn't had the chance to congratulate him just yet, so he was glad to bump into him. "Hey, mate, I hear you're a Star Runner!" The two shared a high-five. "Jolly good news! Sorry I missed you at the finish line, but I did see your posted times. It looks like you had a brilliant swim. So tell me, did the scissor kick work for you? And did you go with the outer edge strategy around the buoys?"

"Yes and no, and yes and no." It was a cryptic answer that Ace was ready to explain. "Yes, the scissor kick is giving me amazing power, and no, it's not completely working for me. Now I'm swimming crooked in the *other* direction. I went 100 yards off track to the outside after the first turn. Out there with the sharks in the middle of the deep-blue ocean—a little scary, but a lot infuriating. For some reason, I keep swimming further than everyone else. Add another seventy meters to my distance, because that's what it felt like. I still got the zigzag path going on.

About the outer edge strategy. I split the difference. Outer edge on the first buoy, but I tried to navigate through the traffic of the second buoy. And I got a major kick in the face. Got my goggles knocked completely off my eyes! It was one heck of a mess, but I got through."

Right then, Ace dropped his head. He said nothing more, but felt like a liar. His conscience burned, and he heard a voice inside his head: *Cheater! Liar!*

"As they say in America, you knocked it out of the ballpark! All that extra swimming and still you beat our projected swim time by over six minutes. Bloody good job! You were cracking, that's for certain. Fancy that, now you've got a title to live up to. Star Racer!"

Ace smiled on the outside, but on the inside he was cringing. But he did manage to say, "Thanks, I couldn't have done it without you."

"Hey, Ace, while we're standing here waiting, let me give you an update on my conversation with Dr. Goodfellow. You were right about one thing—there is nothing speedy about getting this thing appropriated. But what you don't know is that Dr. Goodfellow and Don Osbourne (the Great Oz) know each other in a professional capacity. They've already met a couple of times to discuss your project, and they think it's a creative challenge they'd like to pursue. They even put you on the priority list—they're cracking to get the 'swimfin' done before the Big Race gets here."

Ace was speechless. "Oh, my! That's amazing!" But then he had a second thought. "Can I afford that?"

Domestique was ready to add the cherry on top of the good news. "It's the bees knees! You don't have to. Goodfellow already got a grant approval. They are viewing this project as leading research into aquatic prosthetics. For humans!" It was a simple statement reminding him that Dr. Goodfellow had already pioneered aquatics prosthetics with a dolphin tail. "All we have to do now is wait and pray that they can get this done before the Big Race."

It had been an amazing day. Ace felt pretty good about the race and himself. No penalties on the bike portion, although the run had been bittersweet. He had to stop and hurl not once, but twice on the 13.1 mile trek. He had been so diligent to follow his schedule with his sustaining fuel plan and salt supplements, so he wasn't sure what made him feel sick to his stomach.

Ace didn't figure it out until a few days after the race when he spoke to Bruiser, admitting he'd hurled again. After a little questioning, Bruiser had the answer. Ace had not practiced using salt tablets or gel supplements.

Bruiser exhorted him. "Listen, the key is you have to practice like you play. We don't introduce anything new on race day."

"I thought I learned that lesson last time. But you mean more than equipment, don't you? No new stuff, no new food, no new salt tablets, no new techniques, no new philosophy! OK, I think I got it."

Later that night, after the race, Ace made his blog post.

I did it! I qualified for the Big Race today with a time of 4:57:57. A sub five-hour race with time to spare. My goal was 4:58. That's about as close as you can get to being spot on. And that was indeed good enough to qualify with the last space for my age division. I'm in! I want to thank all of you. I couldn't have done it without you.

I've met a young man at the race that provided the inspiration for these latest Wisbits

Markist: *A young man on a mission. He was creatively looking to share the love of God and make disciples of Christ. He seemed to be very effective in using the platform of a triathlon to do so. Truly inspirational.*

Wisbit tip: *The 222 principle: from 2 Timothy 2:2; Make disciples who make disciples.*

Wisbit tip: *We need to be constantly reminded "to share the love."*

Wisbit tip: *Posting visual reminders all around you will help you find your way. And keep you from getting lost.*

Wisbit tip: *Chase your dreams. They only come true if you pursue them.*

Wisbit tip: *When our inside and outside match, that is sincere and authentic. Very powerful.*

QUESTIONS FOR SELF-REFLECTION

- Which character in this story do I identify with most? Why and how so?
- Think about the spiritual athletic metaphor: How do we "cut the course" spiritually?
- Have I ever cheated? How do I respond when my conscience is violated?
- How can I share the love of God practically today?

- Am I a mule or a donkey? What are the ingredients needed to make a disciple of Christ who could also make a disciple of Christ?

17

HAND MANEUVERS

ONCE AGAIN, ACE was excited to meet with Doc Mentor. A pattern was emerging: Ace would race, then debrief with the wise man's questions concerning the spiritual metaphors of the race.

Then the door opened once again to the waiting room.

"Ace, great to see you today. I hope all is well. What have you been up to?"

"Well, let me remind you where we left off. Last time we spoke about fuel for the body and soul. The challenge was to put it into practice and report back after the Rocky Pointe Half-Iron. So here I am—I qualified for the Big Race. All your advice about fuel supply paid off. I had it all planned out, and the truth of the matter is that it *did* sustain me—no cramps. And I had enough energy to finish well. I finished with a time of 4:57, which meant I qualified to do the Big Race in three-and-a-half months. They only take forty qualifiers from my age division, and I was number forty. So I'm in. I'm a Star Runner. They say that's when you qualify for the Big Race your first season. Not to mention I passed up seventy-six people and was only passed by twenty-one. It was a good day."

"Congratulations, well done! The last time you raced you had a few penalties...no penalties this time?"

Ace thought, *Why did he have to ask that question?* Ace couldn't fudge answers with this man, so the truth came oozing out. Ace hadn't shared it with anyone, but his conscience had bothered him. It was such a little thing, yet he couldn't stop thinking about it.

"No penalties assessed, but I have to admit I've felt a little bit like a cheater—not on the bike this time, but on the swim." Ace recounted the buoy incident to Doc, blow by blow, and said, "No penalty was assessed, but my conscience condemns me, calling me a *'cheater.'* Then I justify myself. And then it starts over again in my mind. Doc, it's nagging me on the inside so I just don't let myself think about it. Heck, I was about over it until you had to bring it up. What do I do?"

"You just did step one: Admit it to another human, confess it to God, bring it under the blood of Christ. Repent which means resolve to get it right next time. And forgive yourself and move on."

"OK, but what about the race I just qualified for? What do I do about that? Should I just forget about it or what? I feel like I'm DQ'd, at least in my own mind. I can't believe I did it! What was I thinking? Stupid, stupid, stupid."

Doc felt Ace's pain and shame. He did not cheapen the moment of conviction. "You're right; sometimes our actions need more than confession to God. Sometimes restitution of some sort needs to be made. Since there was a type of compensation given for your performance, you might consider how to make that right. In this situation, the next step really is a matter between you and God. What do you think you ought to do?"

"I don't know...do you mind if I think about it for a few more days?"

"Sure. Listen, we got off to a pretty heavy start. Let me redirect and lighten up a little by changing the subject. Tell me about the people you're meeting through your training and competition."

Ace was astonished! For some reason, the questions Doc asked always seemed to have so much depth to them. He thought for a moment before answering.

"I suppose the list could be quite lengthy, but let me recall some of the people I work out and train with, and then I'll tell you about a guy I met at the race."

Ace was able to switch gears. Now he spoke with great enthusiasm. "First, I've got the best trainers in the city helping me. I mean it; they are strong. You once said you become like the people you hang around with. Well, I'm with good people. I've been working hard on my swim training with Domestique. We're working on another solution for my swimming nemesis to compensate for this blasted leg."

Ace made a hand gesture and nod of displeasure as his eyes looked on the mechanical prosthetic. "The zigzag path is still a problem. Thank God for Domestique. He is such a blessing. He has taken a lot of initiative on my behalf. He asked his friend to help me; Dr. Goodfellow, who makes prosthetics. I'm not kidding when I tell you it's the same guy from the movie *Dolphin Tale*. Actually, not the guy from the movie but the real guy behind the actor. Anyway, he's cooking something up for me to swim with, like a prosthetic fin of some sort. I know you know Bruiser Le Truce. I'm running with him on Saturday mornings. And you also know Spinsey. You gotta like that girl. I know I do."

Ace tipped his hand as he spoke Spinsey's name. His tone easily indicated he had fallen for her. "I meet with her twice a week— every Wednesday for spin class and Sunday mornings at the Sky Way trail. We have a peloton we ride with. Believe it or not, I stayed with the peloton the entire ride for the last few Sundays. We go between twenty-two and twenty-six miles per hour. They flat out fly. It's taken me months to stay with them and that's only because I never take the lead. At this point as long as I'm in the train and not leading it, I can keep up. You know they drop you when you can't keep up. It's sink or swim with them, or shall we say, ride or roll!

"Now, let me tell you about this guy I met at the last race.

Interesting guy; goes by the nickname Double A. I met him after the race was over in the transition zone, He was a pretty intense Christian, I suppose. The only reason I say it that way is because he talked one way, all about righteousness and the corruption of our country. He barked that big government has kicked God out of our schools and courtrooms by taking the Ten Commandments off the walls of all our buildings. But on the other hand, I think he broke four of the Ten Commandments in the fifteen minutes we were together."

Ace described in further detail what he had witnessed and felt about the situation. "I ended up thinking of him as Double A, the Double in appearance, as in hypocrite."

Doc agreed. "There are true and false believers. Jesus told a story about this—the parable of the wheat and the tares. Only God knows for certain, but don't be fooled. Not all who say 'Lord, Lord' will enter the kingdom of heaven, but only those who truly know Him. Which brings me right along to my next question: How is your devotional life doing? We've talked a lot about feeding the soul in our last few meetings. You know the spiritual metaphor: right diet for the body and right diet for the soul. How have you liked the little book I gave you, *The Great with God Pocket Guide*? Have you been reading it?"

Ace had anticipated that he might be asked this very question. And while he had neglected the book for most of the three months, when he made the appointment to see Doc, he realized he didn't want to look completely foolish at such a moment, so he had read the book a few times in the last few days. He reviewed enough to say, "That's a good little book. I've used it some; not every day, but every now and then."

Doc asked another question. "So, I heard you say you kept count as you raced. I'm wondering if you were able to try rehearsing the Scriptures at all as you competed in the race?"

Ace felt the sting of the question because he had not done it even a little bit. And now he had to admit it. Doc grimaced with disappointment. Ace really did not want to let this man down. Doc sensed Ace's embarrassment, and said, "It's partly my fault. I know better than to tell a man what he ought to do without showing him how. I've got a suggestion to make at the end. But I've got another question. You mentioned riding with Spinsey on Sundays; so when was the last time you were in church?"

Again, Ace felt stung by his conscience. He was feeling convicted but admitted, "A little over three months ago."

"You know we talked about honoring the Sabbath and the physical metaphor of resting the body as well as seeking the Lord on the Sabbath." Ace shook his head meekly in agreement.

Doc had another question. "Have you found a mission to support yet? You know, the cause for your running?" Ace was cornered and could not escape. He was being humbled by the interrogation and had to admit that he hadn't.

Doc continued. "Nine months ago when you started, you were on target and motivated by the thought of helping others, even the thought of running for a God-honoring cause. I haven't heard you say one thing about it since. You know the man you met at the transition, Mr. Double Appearance? Take a look at yourself because you are that man! It seems to me you're listening, but not really applying much of what we're talking about. Ace, you've fallen into a trap, which is easy to do. I've done it myself. You are completely missing the spiritual metaphor. Maybe you're listening, but that's not enough. You aren't applying any effort to developing the spiritual dimensions of your soul. A great tragedy has happened; you've fallen in love with racing and left God on the sidelines. Let me give you an illustration."

Doc held up both of his hands with his palms facing out toward Ace and continued. "These represent the two sources of fulfillment you are finding in life. My left hand represents your relationship with God. My right hand stands for your ability to serve God—in this case, to physically race. When you first started, you didn't have any ability. You were a wounded warrior sitting on the sidelines of life feeling sorry for yourself, feeling like a nobody. Then you decided to chase the spiritual metaphor by training for the Big Race. At that moment, you were all about God."[15]

Doc moved his left hand up and over on top of the right hand and continued. "All you had was God. You had no special ability to serve Him nor talent for the race. It was God first. He was all you had to hold on to. Over time, your skill increased." Doc moved his hands side by side. "At that stage, your competency in serving the Lord by training for the race approximately equaled your fulfillment that you had in your relationship with the Lord."

"Now you've got some skill and it's being recognized by you and others. In some ways, you could justify that this was a great way to serve the Lord: racing. You know, temple maintenance, camaraderie, and the whole ball of wax. You've no doubt been starting to feel really good about yourself. In some ways, you've been more productive

---

15   Verbal illustration of the hands was borrowed and adapted from Secrets of the Vine, Bruce Wilkinson

than ever. You fell in love with racing. Faster and faster you go, trying to find out just how much potential you could really have, becoming the best version of you. It all sounds really good. It's just a little skewed because your walk with God began to suffer.

"Ace, you let your priorities shift. True pursuit of God dropped. And if you look inside, you'll notice true joy has dropped as well. All the evidence is there: You barely read your Bible or devotional guide. You've decided getting faster on the bike is more important than honoring God by showing up for worship on Sundays. You get up early to go to the gym, but can't spare the time at the beginning of your workout to get your thoughts centered on God. You're willing to cheat to improve your time, and you've completely lost sight of the cause to run for. Ace, you are right here right now." He repositioned his hands as his left hand drifted slowly under the right as he continued. "Racing is first in your life and God is somewhere down here in last place."

Ace felt exposed; the big hypocrite he had become was plain to see. Ace was feeling a little desperate and a lot contrite. "Doc, you hung me out to dry. What you said is true. I admit it; guilty as charged. This is embarrassing. Nobody wants to be embarrassed, but I'd rather hear the truth from you—that's what doctors do. You

have exposed the reality of my life. It makes me feel convicted in a shameful way. What can I do to make this right?"

Doc had this direction to give. "Well, we just talked about this: confess it to God, admit it to yourself and someone else, recommit, then execute on a new path, which usually requires heavy accountability. So this time, I'm going to do my part and model it for you. What's a mentor for, if not to walk alongside the apprentice? I've told you about my morning routine. But if you're willing to recommit, then let's add a little strategic planning to the equation. I want you to meet me at my house at 5:30 every morning next week. Come in your workout clothes and running shoes, and we'll seek the Lord together. I'll show you how I enter into the presence of the Lord, which was passed down to me from my mentor. Ace, you've got to make the final transition."

SAYING VS. DOING: THE TALE OF TWO HYPOCRITES

"DEUCE:" – DOUBLE IN APPEARANCE – THE HYPOCRITE

Thou shalt not steal	Taking goggles that don't belong to him
Thou shalt not commit adultery	Lusting after Tanga
Thou shalt not lie	Telling stories to get what he wants
Thou shalt not murder	Condemning others with hatred
Respect authorities	Speaking disdainfully of leaders

"ACE" – DOUBLE IN APPEARANCE – THE HYPOCRITE

Don't judge others	Picks out hypocrisies in "Deuce"
Do not bear false witness	Cuts the race course
Do not steal	Drafts on his bike illegally
Love the Lord with all your heart	Half-hearted attitude about devotions
Honor the Sabbath to keep it holy	Skips church to ride in the peloton

As Doc made his last statement, he held his hands up once again. Moving the left hand to the top, he added, "You've got to rediscover your first love. Make God first. Live the spiritual metaphor, don't just talk about it. Get on God's team, get in His playbook, and get into His practice regimen. Then find a way to stay there." Ace was eager to say yes, but deep down, he was anxious about the early hour. *What a price to pay,* he thought as he departed from the office. Once out the door, Ace gave a deep sigh. It was the kind of sigh that meant, *I'm glad that's over,* and then he gave another deep sigh as he considered the proposal. *We're really going to do this? OMG! What have I gotten myself into now? No turning back. It's probably for the best.* Ace was recommitted.

That night, Ace blogged.

I met with Doc Mentor again today. I don't know how he does it, but he always takes me deep. I say things to him that I would never share with another human being. How does he do that? I just don't know.

Somehow he is able to "hold up a mirror" in front of me so I can see myself, including all the blind spots. It's like going to the barber shop. He puts a mirror in your hands, spins you around, and you see the back of your head. Actually, it's not a pretty sight to see a side of your human soul that's filled with hypocrisy. And yet it seems the price of spiritual growth.

Wisbit tip: *Integrity is what you do when no one else is watching.*

Wisbit tip: *When you're wrong, own it. Then take responsibility, confess it, and forsake it.*

Wisbit tip: *Losing your first love happens by degrees, little by little.*

Wisbit tip: *Mentoring is more about apprenticeship than mere teaching. Model what you are trying to teach.*

Wisbit tip: *On Judgment Day, we will be held accountable for not only every action, but every word and every thought.*

QUESTIONS FOR SELF-REFLECTION

- Have I lost my first love? What evidence is there in my life for or against this?

- Do I need to make any apologies for unresolved disputes?
- Am I willing to do whatever is necessary to clear my conscience with God?
- What does it mean to repent?
- Can there be mentoring without modeling?

18

MORNING MEETINGS WITH THE MAN OF GOD

THE ALARM BUZZED loudly at 5:01 A.M. Ace had moved it across the room so he would have to get out of bed to turn it off. His head was spinning and his adrenaline kicked in. He had left no margin of time. He had to get dressed, out of the bathroom, and in his car if he was going to be at Doc Mentor's home by 5:30 A.M.

Doc Mentor's garage door opened at 5:30, right on time as agreed. There was to be no knocking on the door or coming inside. Doc didn't want any noise that would wake his wife. Doc also did not want to invade his wife's privacy. She was the type who would want to be presentable before seeing visitors.

Doc had a small office in his garage, a custom-designed man cave. He met Ace, who had parked outside the house waiting for the cue of the garage door opening. The two men greeted each other, shook hands, and Doc invited Ace into the man cave.

Just inside, Ace was warmly met by a friendly black lab who nudged up against Ace's good leg eagerly hoping for a little pat on the head. "Ace, meet Kismet; best dog ever. He loves to give kisses." Doc bent over and gave Kismet a big playful hug and let Kismet lick his cheek. Ace responded with a chuckle and a smile.

Now, Ace began to notice the inspirational sayings and family pictures all over the walls. A giant map of the world hung on one wall. A desk faced the other wall. The other end had two chairs facing each other and no TV. The two men sat down, and Doc explained what they would do.

"Thanks for coming over this morning. This is one of my favorite things to do…join with other men to seek the Lord. We didn't come here to talk so much as to meet with God. I don't want you to think anything creepy is going on here, so let me tell you exactly what we're going to do and we'll proceed.

"First, we are literally going to get on our faces and humbly approach the Lord, taking a few minutes to acknowledge His lordship over our lives and our need for Him both to forgive us and reveal himself to us. Then we will return to these chairs and go through the little book I gave you, The *Great with God Pocket Guide*[16] as Doc held a copy up in his hand.

"It's simple: There's a list of five or six Scriptures on this side of the page, which focus on the nature of God and a command of Christ. On the next page, you can find the application evaluation questions

> ### SOUL FOOD
>
> *The fuel of a man doesn't just come from the bread that goes into his mouth; that will only fuel the body. But a man is more than just a body; he needs fuel for the soul and the spirit. That kind of fuel comes from every word that comes out of the mouth of God.*

and a single challenge assignment to put the whole thing into practice. Turn the page and there's a Scripture based prayer. Total time is six to eight minutes. I've got to tell you, I like this model because it is so easily reproduced. Every guy has six minutes a day. But he won't necessarily give you fifteen or thirty. And like I said before,

---

16 *Great with God Pocket Guide* <GreatWithGod.com>.

although there are fifty-two lessons, I turn the heading page once a week. In other words, I learn the material slowly. I'm not trying to conquer this book, I'm trying to *digest* it. So I study these same two pages every day, morning and night. That way I start to understand it through repetition.

"Then we are going to memorize a key verse right out of this book. We will each write it out, right here on a Post-it note. I like writing it out for three reasons: First, the very act of writing it helps me begin to memorize it. Second, I call it the kingly discipline. Did you know that the book of Deuteronomy lists the responsibilities of a king? God required the king to write a copy of the books of Moses—the first five books of the Bible—for himself. So there you have it, the kingly discipline. The third reason is so I can take it with me and refer back to it as I go on this walk we are taking next.

"Ace, it's important that we memorize these verses for two reasons: First, whatever is not memorized will never be utilized. Second, memorization is the foundation of meditation.

"When we leave this office and hit the streets, we will walk about ten minutes. As we walk, we meditate, repeating the verse over and over, each time emphasizing a different word. For example, the LORD is my shepherd. The Lord IS my shepherd, the Lord is MY shepherd, and the Lord is my SHEPHERD. Can you see how that helps me to think more deeply about the verse we are memorizing?" Ace quickly agreed.

"Then, we will be at Shiloh—that's the name of my sacred place to pray to God; ten to twenty minutes; not that God can't hear me anywhere, but it's my Biblical outdoor prayer closet. It's on the nature path in the city park, close enough to walk there. I find privacy there, with just me and the Lord. I spend a lot of time there, almost every morning. Sometimes ten minutes, but most of the time about an hour, and I've been there for three hours sometimes."

Ace interrupted for the first time. "*Three hours??* Now *that's* interesting. I can't even conceive of praying for an hour. What do you say to God for *three* hours? I run out of words after two minutes."

"Most of the time, I'm in conversation and meditation with God. I try and keep it creative, so I do different patterns for my prayer each day. Once again this little book will teach a man how to pray. There are no fewer than seven different index prayers that I've learned from these pages," he said as he lifted the book up to emphasize his point. "These index prayers become my guide when I need a little help to pray. We will make use of some of the tools over the next few days. You'll see. I call the place we're going Shiloh because after the Israelites wandered in the desert

> ### THE LORD'S PRAYER AS AN INDEX PRAYER
>
> *Our Father, who art in heaven,*
>
> - *Thy Name*
> - *Thy Kingdom*
> - *Thy Will*
> - *Give Us*
> - *Forgive Us*
> - *Lead Us*
> - *Deliver Us*
>
> *For thine is the kingdom and the power and glory forever.*

for 40 years, they came into the Promised Land and the tabernacle didn't move around any more. It stayed at one place called Shiloh. That's me, that's us; I am the tabernacle of the Holy Spirit. I am the movable tent of God. He lives inside of me, so wherever I go, He goes. But this is a sacred place for me. It's where I go to meet with God when it hurts and when I'm full of praise. I recommend you find a set place as well. Mine happens to be outside and for a very good reason. I tried for years to have a morning routine. I got up and tried to read the Bible, only to plant my head between the pages as I fell back asleep, or sometimes I would kneel at the sofa where my prayers turned to mush before I conked out. The whole thing was futile, but when I get outside and walk, I feel alive, like I'm giving God my best.

"I go to Shiloh mostly to offer myself in daily surrender." Doc's body was becoming a living illustration. He lifted his hands over his head as he lifted his eyes to heaven. "I present my body to God daily as a living sacrifice. That means I show up and surrender. I transfer all my rights of ownership to God. He owns it all: my house, my wife, my sons, my practice, my schedule, and my dreams. So I show up and die to myself. Because I do so, I find joy and peace as my faith is exercised. So there you have it.

"After we pray, Ace, we will walk back another ten minutes and talk about whatever you want. When we get back to the garage, we will do a weightlifting cycle, fifteen to twenty minutes, except we don't count our repetitions. Instead, we rehearse Bible verses as we lift. So it's not one, two, three...it's counting like this, slowly pronouncing the words." Doc made the movement of a weightlifting curl as he'd done at the office with an imaginary dumbbell. "...The Lord...is...my...shepherd.... Then we'll call it done. You'll be on your way back to your house by 7:00 so you can start your day."

And that is exactly what they did, Monday through Friday. The only variation was the prayer time and the different weightlifting exercises. On Monday, they prayed through the Lord's Prayer as an index prayer. On Tuesday, they gave thanks for everything possible. Wednesday, they prayed through the alphabet to find the names and attributes for God, such as "A" for Almighty, "B" for Bread of Life, "C" for Creator, etc. On Thursday, they used the Tabernacle Furniture as an index prayer.[17] On Friday, they walked through all the streets in Doc's subdivision praying for all his neighbors by name with the assistance of the phone app "Great with God," which partners with Bless Every Home Ministries.[18]

Eventually they made it to Shiloh, but they didn't stay long since most of the praying had already been done in the neighborhood.

However, it was on the walk back from Shiloh on Friday that Ace took his turn to sincerely thank Doc and ask the burning ques-

---

17   Praying the Tabernacle, Prayer Lecture, Paul Youngi Cho.
18   Bless Every Home, from Bless Every Home Ministries <blesseveryhome.com>.

tion that had been lingering in his mind over the days they had spent together: "Doc, I'm wrestling with God more than I thought. Don't get me wrong—this has been the greatest week of my life. Starting my morning this way with you has changed everything for me. But I can't get one thought out of my head. If God is so good and all-powerful, why did He let this happen to me?" Ace looked at his leg so Doc was clear about what he meant.

> **NAMES AND ATTRIBUTES OF GOD FROM A-Z**
>
> *Adonai, Author and Finisher of My Faith*
> *Bread of Life, Beginning and the End*
> *Creator, Christ*
> *Deliverer*
> *Everlasting, Eternal*
> *Father, Faithful*
> *Good, Great*
> *High Priest*
> *I AM, Immortal*
> *Jesus, Jehovah, Jealous God*
> *King of Kings, Kinsman Redeemer*
> *Lord of Lords, Lion of Judah*
> *Messiah, Master*
> *Newness of Life*
> *Omnipotent, Omnipresent*
> *Prince of Peace*
> *Quintessence of all things*
> *Redeemer*
> *Savior, Standard*
> *Triumphant*
> *Undefeated*
> *Valiant*
> *Excellent*
> *Yahweh*
> *Zealous*

"Yeah, I hear what you're saying. However, I'm not going to try and answer that now. I know one thing for certain: you're going to have to abandon yourself to His providence and learn how to rest in His redemption. Furthermore, that seems to be the most pressing question in all of Christiandom. And there isn't anyone on the planet who understands the role of suffering better than Sage. So to get the best answer for that, I think I'll send you back to him. I'll help set it up. And I'll let him know you'll be calling him when I see him tomorrow. You wouldn't know this, but I see him on most Saturday mornings. We have a standing appointment."

"OK, I'll be glad to see him again."

Doc changed the subject with the next question. "Did you decide what you want to do about the buoy incident?"

"Well, I've given it a lot of thought, and I can't make up my mind.

I'm bouncing back and forth. It seems like such a small thing, inconsequential to my skill level. I swam so much more than was required. I could have shaved off another two minutes if I hadn't swum so crooked. I've been contemplating. I've concluded that my options are either resolve not to do it again and let it alone; withdraw and DQ myself; or call the race director and explain my case and let him DQ me officially. It seems a little much for my conscience's sake. He is either going to think the whole thing is silly or simply do what he ought to do. The rules are clear—not following the course as marked means disqualification. He's most certainly going to enforce the rules, and then I'm going to be disqualified on a silly, meaningless technicality. All I've wanted to do for nine months is to compete in the Big Race."

Ace could not hold back; he started to speak with a sense of fervor. His emotions were engaged and he was agitated. Answering this question had hit a nerve deep inside of him.

"Ever since I was a boy, I've wanted to do this race. And yes, there is part of me that wants to show the whole world that I'm normal, so don't feel sorry for me. There is a lot at stake for me. I've invested everything for this goal. This race is expensive—they've got my money, in more ways than one: race registration, equipment, gym

---

TRAINING IS LIKE A PART-TIME JOB, EXCEPT YOU DON'T GET A PAYCHECK.

15-20 hours per week
5½ hours Biking
3½ hours Swimming
6 hours Running
52 weeks x 15 = 780 hours per year. Minimum for
World Championship Ironman Competitors.

THERE ARE INTANGIBLE THINGS DERIVED FROM TRAINING THAT ARE MORE VALUABLE THAN MONEY.

memberships, special diets…I've trained way over the top, over 15 hours a week at least for the last six months. It's like another part-time job on top of my full-time job at Big City Sound and Lights. I've literally sacrificed everything for the privilege of being a part of the nobility. You know—race, live the dream, and yes, chase the spiritual metaphor. And it seems like all that is going to be lost for nothing."

Ace choked on his words as he talked. "Not to mention everybody at the YMCA tri-club. They all believe I qualified for the Big Race. They are all pulling for me."

Ace couldn't hold back the tears. He began to sob. "I don't want to let them down. And my friends who pledged to support my cause. All that would be for nothing. What a waste. I don't know what to do, Doc."

Doc simply reached his arm out, pulled Ace under his shoulder, and let him sob. The tears rolled down both their cheeks. Doc shared Ace's pain, knowing there was no easy way out of this one. Doc offered, "I know you'll do the right thing!"

❧

ACE'S DILEMMA

COUNTING THE COST TO DO THE RIGHT THING

THE RIGHT THING	THE COST
Tell the truth and honor God	*Be seen as a liar*
Clear his conscious	*Be exposed as a cheater*
Play by the rules/turn himself in	*Be disqualified from race*
Admit his fault	*Suffer humiliation*

That night, Ace sat for a while in front of his computer, contemplating his options.

Finally, he entered his blog post.

I've got a mentor who is busting my chops. He is skilled in asking the right questions. The Holy Spirit has used him to awaken the "fear of the Lord" in me. Now is a time when courage is required, because doing the right thing is not always the easy thing to do. I am at a crossroads. I'm sick, because I've done something foolish. I regret it and I hold myself accountable. Let it be documented so I don't chicken out. I'm going to right my wrong. Don't ask me about the details. I don't even know what's going to happen next. But I'll let you know how it eventually turns out.

Wisbit tip: *Doing the right thing is usually not the easy thing.*

Wisbit tip: *What is not memorized, will never be utilized.*

Wisbit tip: *Just because others can, doesn't mean I can, or should.*

Wisbit tip: *Aim to live life with a clear conscience. Do whatever it takes to make things right, no matter what the cost.*

QUESTIONS FOR SELF-REFLECTION

- Do I have a daily morning routine with a designated space where I seek the Lord?
- Have I ever invited someone else to join me in my morning devotional routine?
- Is my morning routine dynamic and filled with diversity? Or you might ask it this way: Do I have a morning routine worth sharing?

19

THE PRICE IS ALWAYS MORE THAN YOU THINK

Ace arrived for his scheduled appointment with Marshall, the area Triathlon Competition Director. The receptionist escorted Ace through the hall to Marshall's office. Ace stepped in, they shook hands, exchanged pleasantries, and then came the moment of truth. Marshall asked him, "What can I help you with?"

Ace had rehearsed the scene in his mind, but his heart still raced, and his words were awkward. "Well, I have a story to tell you. I competed at the Rocky Pointe Half Iron a little over a week ago. I qualified for my age division, thirty to thirty-four, to compete at the Big Race in November. Everything is fine, except my conscience. I've come to admit a foul I committed, but none of the race officials know, including yourself. I suppose I got away with it, except for the problem of personal integrity. In short, I cut the course. I did not go around all the water buoys, and I have heard you state the rules at least twice at different races: 'You must go around the buoys. If you don't follow the course, it is grounds for disqualification.' I don't mean to waste your time, but I needed to let you know to remove my name from the qualifiers' list and let the next eligible competitor on the list know as soon as possible."

Marshall sat for a moment, trying to take it all in. He was stunned and bewildered. "In all my years, this is a first. I've never had anybody turn themselves in. I can admire that. Listen, ultimately the DQ is my decision. Can you tell me a little more about what happened to give me a better frame of reference? Did you show up on race day planning to cut the course? Were you that devious, or was it something else?"

Ace gave the full explanation of his kicked goggles incident, how he ended up inside the buoy, and his conscious decision to proceed forward to improve his chances of qualifying. "So there you have it. It has bothered me incessantly for days now. I'm glad to get it off my chest. Thank you for hearing me out."

"Thanks for sharing the details. I've had my goggles kicked off my face before as well. All things considered, I see no reason for disqualification. Yet I can't ignore what happened. As race marshal, I can disqualify and I can assess penalties. The rule book authorizes me to assess a minimum two-minute penalty in such cases. That seems about right to me. So my ruling is not to disqualify you, but add two minutes to your time. You're free to go."

"I can't thank you enough for your graciousness, but it may not be that easy. Those two minutes may actually alter the outcome of my qualifying."

"What do you mean?"

"Well, there are only forty qualifiers for my age division, and I got spot number forty. I have no idea how far my next competitor was behind me."

"I see...well, let's have a look." Marshall reviewed screen after screen on his computer until he came to the right one. "OK, I found you. You came across the finish line at 4:57:57. That was right in the thick of things. In a forty-minute window from 4:45 to 5:25, almost 500 racers crossed the finish line. That means someone was crossing the finish line every three to four seconds. In the two minutes after you, it looks like forty-three people crossed the finish line; and of those, two were males (thirty to thirty-four)."

"As you suspected, that moves you from position forty to forty-two, and that I can't help you with. I'm sorry. I wish this had a better ending, but I admire your personal integrity. As field judge, I must maintain the race's integrity. You're a good man, Ace; I suppose you've learned your lesson, so I encourage you to try again next year. Thanks for coming by."

PLACE	NAME	AGE	CITY	TIME	SWIM	TRAN 1	BIKE	TRAN 2	RUN	PENALTY
40	Clarke	30	Buckhead	4:58:23	31:44	2:54	2:29:51	2:14	1:51:50	
41	Kirk	32	Wilcreek	4:59:21	33:21	2:37	2:30:37	2:31	1:51:15	
42	Ace	33	Big City	4:59:57	34:03	3:37	2:24:24	2:16	1:53:37	2:00

ADJUSTED MALE AGE GROUP 30-34 FINISH TIME OF HALF-IRON AFTER 2-MINUTE PENALTY

Ace walked to his car. Justice had been served. Ace's mind was rumbling as he thought to himself, *Stupid, stupid, stupid! Why was I so stupid?*

Ace knew the next week would be his most difficult. Trying to explain why he was not doing the Big Race would be humiliating. Ace composed a hundred different ways in his mind to make it more acceptable, but there wasn't much wiggle room. He finally decided to tell the whole story to his coaches, which meant talking to Spinsey after spin class Wednesday morning. He would speak to Domestique on Friday after swim class. And he would tell Bruiser Saturday morning before the training run. He always arrived early to prepare for his run squad.

Loyalty cannot be known without testing

❦

Butterflies filled Ace's stomach as he waited to tell Spinsey. This confession, he knew, would be a major curve away from his careful pursuit of her. He had been seriously ready to move the relationship to a real date and had mentally planned the whole thing. Ace knew Spinsey would be impressed with his qualification, and she was. However, the revelation of his own hypocrisy, along with the mornings of prayer with Doc Mentor had changed everything. His priorities had changed and that meant he would be quitting the Sunday peloton ride so he could regularly attend church.

To Ace it was a sad thought as he knew he was only a month away from completely hanging with the pros (taking his turn as the lead of the peloton). To make matters worse, the lunch that followed Sunday biking was their only "date time." He had made his way into the group, and was accepted during the months between the St. Anthony's Olympic Tri and the Rocky Pointe Half-Iron Tri. Just now, it felt like he had proved he belonged by qualifying, but he was about to throw a wrench into the mix. This could change everything with Spinsey, but he also knew after spending a week of mornings with Doc, God needed to be more important than training. Spinsey would have to accept that and allow it to redefine the relationship. A lot was at stake. Doing the God thing was costing Ace more than he had initially expected. One major decision to put God first, and he felt like he was losing it all, even his dignity.

CR

Spinsey listened intently to all the details of the story of the buoy and the appointment with Marshall before replying, "Wow! That's quite a story. Similar things have happened to me on the swim course. It's understandable. And then your encounter with Marshall; that's admirable and disappointing. You did the right thing. I just wish it had a better ending. Anyway, it usually takes at least two years to get ready for the Big Race. We'll have you ready for next year.

Now came the hard part. Ace shared the rest of the story, his meetings with Doc Mentor, and feelings about God. He shared the new conviction about Sunday worship that was forming in his heart.

He was resolute. He explained that the decision was not just about quitting the peloton because he wasn't training for the Big Race, but he was pursuing God first and racing second, which meant worship and resting to honor the Sabbath.

Spinsey was awkwardly speechless again. Then she put her thoughts together. "I don't know how to feel about this. Listen, I grew up going to church from time to time, especially on holidays and when my grandparents were in town. God is important, but you don't have to go to church every Sunday to be a good Christian. Are you sure this is what you gotta do?"

Ace countered. "Yeah, I really think this is important and it's not just a 'have to' kinda thing. It's a 'want to.' Maybe we could switch the peloton ride back to Saturdays. And come join me at church on Sundays." Ace put it out there; it was a proposition of sorts. In a sense he had just asked her on a date.

Spinsey was silent, thinking. Then she got it out. "That's a very kind offer. You're a great guy, but I'm not ready to make that journey just yet. Sounds like that might be right for you, so I encourage you to go for it. I don't feel like God is more or less pleased with me based on church attendance. For me there are just too many hypocrites in church, including the pastor. It sounds like you've made up your mind. So for me, in race terms, all I can say is I don't know if I can keep pace with where you're going. I can't move the peloton at this time." And with that, Spinsey made it clear she did not want to discuss it any further.

It was clear to Ace that the relationship that hadn't even started was instantly redefined. And then Spinsey's demeanor changed. Suddenly, she was coach again.

"Ace, you're a good man. I hope to still see you at spin class. I respect your decisions, and there is always next year. I hate to cut this short, but I've got an appointment to get to."

"No problem. Thanks for all you've done for me. Thanks for listening. I'm sure you'll still see me in spin classes. See ya."

Spinsey exited the room. Ace was left alone, thinking. *That did not go so well.* What did he expect anyway? There was nothing between them, at least not formally. Ace clenched his teeth and thought, *Good grief, another chance for love—lost; how many girls do you meet that actually have the capacity to be the one?* Ace liked Spinsey on so many levels; they seemed to be a good fit.

Ace thought she had a faith like his, but that belief had been crushed. He thought it through again. He had changed. Maybe Spinsey had faith, but his faith was changing. Ace didn't want to be a casual Christian any more. The spiritual metaphor of "all in" took root in his heart. All in for God! God first! Although he felt perplexed about his feelings for Spinsey, Ace's shoulders felt lighter. Some of the load had been lifted. His remaining two coaches would be easy to tell compared to her.

CR

Thursday, after swim practice, Ace asked if he could talk to Domestique alone. He explained the buoy story and his visit with Marshall just the same as he had shared with Spinsey but with one small caveat. "Domestique, I owe you an apology. In some ways, I was not completely truthful when I shared this story last time. I was misleading when I said, 'I got through it (the buoy incident).' I may have gotten through the incident, but I didn't get through the buoy traffic. So that's why I'm not going to be competing in the Big Race. One stupid decision followed by an overly-sensitive conscience, and a warped sense of integrity. First, I don't do right in the pinch, and then try to make up for it afterwards. Why couldn't I get it right the first time?"

"Listen, I respect you for what you did, and that's not twisted integrity—it IS integrity. We all do things that are stupid, wrong, and just plain sinful, but it takes a real man to own it, admit it, and move to make it right. At least you can live with yourself, and that counts for something."

"Thanks for listening to me. I thought you deserved the truth."

"It's not the end of the world. We'll get you ready for next year."

One last thing, coach. I really need you to tell your friend Dr. Goodfellow to call off his generous offer to create the aqua fin for me. I got the impression when we talked about this last time that it was some kind of priority rush to get it done in time for the Big Race. Now there is absolutely no need to complete the project in any rush since I'm not competing. Thanks for all you've done. I'll keep training and plan to race next year."

❧

On Saturday, Ace was outside the YMCA at 6:30 A.M. He pulled his car into the lot the same time as Bruiser. Then they started talking. Ace told the story again, except Bruiser hinted that he had already heard the story. After all, he shared an office with Domestique and Spinsey, and it seemed they had discussed their star student's turn of events.

Bruiser gave it a lot of thought and had a creative solution to offer. "Ace, have you ever considered racing for a charity? That's another way to compete in the Big Race. I know the Big Race offers forty spots for fundraisers each year. These spots are awarded to triathletes who agree to run for the cause of their choice. Is that something you'd be interested in?"

"Other than hitting me upside the head with a two-by-four, I'll take this as confirmation that I ought to get on the ball and run for a cause. I've thought about doing exactly that, but I just haven't slowed down enough to give the whole thing enough thought."

"I need to caution you; just because you fill out the paperwork doesn't guarantee anything. There are a lot of applications, usually over a hundred that come in, and only forty spots are available, so it's selective. I checked the website and the application is due this Thursday. Check it yourself for the details. The only qualifying condition I could find is the applicant's completion of a Half-Iron. And you've already done that."

"That's the best news I've heard all week—thanks. It's a long shot, but it's something, and I will certainly give it a try. You can count on it. I'll have it done Thursday before 5:00 P.M."

The other YMCA runners were beginning to arrive. Today's run: twelve miles at an 8:45 pace. Ace joined the group. After the run, Bruiser asked, "Hey, Ace, you going to be in church tomorrow?"

"Yep! That's my plan. I've made changes in my priorities. I made a decision to check out of the peloton on Sunday mornings and into the Sabbath rest."

"Awesome. I'm glad to hear that. So where do you go to church?"

"I go to the church I grew up in. My parents still attend Big Rock Methodist."

Bruiser knew the church and commented, "Hey, that's a great church, a pillar of strength in this community for over a hundred years."

"Well, I think most of the members are over a hundred years old as well." They both chuckled.

"So do they have programs for single adults your age?"

"Not so much. I think I'm the only early-to-mid thirty-year-old there who isn't married."

"If you're looking for something a little more contemporary with a strong group of young adults, you're welcome to visit my church."

"What church do you attend?"

"Clearsky House of Prayer. It's not too far from here; fifteen minutes tops. I'm not asking you to change your membership; just visit and enjoy the best of both churches."

"OK, you sold me! I'm in—at least for this Sunday. My folks will just be glad to hear I'm attending somewhere."

"That's great—service starts at 10:30 and I'll save a seat for you. It's located at the corner of Straight Street and Broadway Boulevard."

"OK, I have a pretty good idea where that is."

"It used to be a Safeway grocery store. The church bought it and remodeled it. Now it's really a Safeway, if you know what I mean."

That night, Ace sat down to make a journal entry into his blog.

Dear, friends: I've got some heavy news. I'm sorry but I was misinformed about my qualifying placement. You know that they only take the top forty for each age division. The official final race times and order of placement had me at forty-two, not forty. That's because I was assessed a penalty for failing to round the water buoy and fully complete the course. Nobody noticed. The race officials were not even aware, but last week I turned myself in. In my last blog post, I left you wondering what I was talking about when I said I needed to right a wrong. Well, that's it. I couldn't live with myself. Now my conscience is clear, and I feel a burden has been lifted from my shoulders.

I'm not giving up. So I didn't qualify this year, but I'll make sure to qualify next year.

But all is not lost yet. A ray of hope still exists. I learned today that I have a chance to receive a race-for-charity entry spot for the Big Race. So say a prayer for me, and I'll keep you posted as to what comes of it.

Wisbit tip: *The price of sin is always greater than expected.*

Wisbit tip: *It's always the right time to do the right thing.*

Wisbit tip: *Putting God first starts with honoring the Sabbath. Showing up at God's house is tangible evidence of honoring this commandment.*

Wisbit tip: *When God closes a door, He often opens a window.*

QUESTIONS FOR SELF-REFLECTION

- Am I keeping the command, "Remember to keep the Sabbath day holy"? What is the Lord convicting me about that I should change to better honor the Sabbath?
- Is there anything in my life that is competing with my love for God?
- Is there anyone the Lord is now convicting me to reconcile with?
- When will I go to the person I have offended to make an apology and/or make restitution? Set the date: _____.

20

FINDING A CAUSE
TO LIVE FOR

On Sunday morning, Ace visited the Clearsky House of Prayer. The old Safeway grocery store had had a face lift, including a cross on top. The church was like a beehive, busy with greeters in the parking lot to help visitors get pointed in the right direction. Their presence helped guests like Ace feel welcome.

Ace entered the sanctuary and found Bruiser and his wife holding a spot for him on the right, third row from the front. Anticipation filled the auditorium. Shortly after Ace found his seat, the music started. The music was contemporary, as promised, with a few older hymns mixed in.

Ace had been to church frequently, but this congregation was definitely into the music. Everyone raised their voices in praise, with eyes closed and hands raised. Ace couldn't describe how he felt, but he sensed God's presence.

After the singing, a man walked to center stage and began speaking. "Good morning! Welcome to Clearsky House of Prayer. I'm Chip Heard, Junior. I'm the junior pastor, trying to follow in the footsteps of the chief shepherd. If you're a guest, let me be the first to say we're glad you're here.

"As we get started, I want to ask: Does God have an unchanging purpose? And if He does, do you know it? Is your life aligned with His unchanging purpose? Can you live your life for the wrong cause? Lots of people do, chasing their selfish ambitions. I don't know about you, but when I get to the finish line of this life, I want to hear 'Well done, good and faithful servant.' Remember the servants who heard those words of commendation were busy carrying out the Father's business. So I ask again: Are you certain about the Father's unchanging purpose?

I want to be clear that God has an unchanging purpose, and I look forward to sharing it with you in the coming moments. First, I want you to study your Bibles with this in mind: The Bible is one story, so while it is true that it's made up of sixty-six books, try to read it as it is: one book..." Chip held up his Bible over his head to make his point. "Think of it as sixty-six chapters with one introduction, one story, one conclusion, one major theme, one unchanging plot and one unchanging purpose.

"With that in mind, let's take a look at Hebrews 6:13-17. We read, 'When God made his promise to Abraham, since there was no one greater for him to swear by, he swore by himself, saying, 'I will surely bless you and give you many descendants.' And so after waiting patiently, Abraham received what was promised. People swear by someone greater than themselves, and the oath confirms what is said and puts an end to all argument. **Because God wanted to make the unchanging nature of his purpose very clear to the heirs of** what was promised, He confirmed it with an oath.' Pastor Chip repeated very slowly and deliberately, "'Because God wanted to make the unchanging nature of His purpose very clear **to the heirs**...' I've got to pause for a second, because there is a lot in those few verses, so let me walk you through it a little more slowly. Let me give you some historical context of when this promise was originally given. Genesis chapters one through eleven is the introduction of the Bible. In chapters one and two, God is the Creator, and all is perfect. Chapters three and four is when Adam and Eve eat from the forbidden tree and sin enters the earth. Next, after hundreds of years, the hearts of men were continually bent toward doing evil, so God destroyed the earth with a flood. God saved Noah and his family and two of every kind of animal on the ark. After the water cleared, the people came together with pride and rebellion to build the tower of Babel. God addressed the issue with a 'divide and conquer' strategy. The people of Babel were confounded because their languages were confused. Then the people were scattered over the earth according to their languages, and formed the nations of the world. That's the introduction of the Bible! You could make a case that the story begins in Genesis 12 with God's covenant to Abraham.

"As I mentioned, it was a 'divide and conquer' strategy. After the nations were divided, God chose one nation to be His special people, to be agents of reconciliation to the other nations, a type of missionary nation. They had a cause to live for. According to Moses, they were to be a whole kingdom of priests. So what does a priest do? They stand in between two opposing parties. They are the intercessors and mediators, somewhat like lawyers today. These priests would help sinful people get right with God. They help with the payment of whatever price is necessary to bring reconciliation between two parties.

"So God's unchanging purpose started with this covenant with Abraham. Let's look at it. Genesis 12:1-4 reads: 'The Lord had said to Abram, 'Go from your country, your people and your father's household to the land I will show you. I will make you into a great nation, and I will bless you; I will make your name great, and you will be a blessing. I will bless those who bless you and whoever curses you I will curse; and all peoples on earth will be blessed through you.'

"I want you to notice a few things here. First, there are two parts to this covenant: what I call the top line and the bottom line. Top line: God wants to bless Abraham. Blessed means an amplification of resources, to have God's favor, resources of every kind imaginable. The bottom line is that Abraham is blessed to be a blessing. He is not supposed to hoard all the blessing nor consume it all upon himself.

He is to *become* a blessing. To whom is he to be a blessing? All people(s) on the earth. Some translators say all families, some say all nations.

"The idea is God makes a covenant with Abraham, who will be given the resources to eventually bring the blessing of reconciliation and eternal life to *all* the nations. This is in exact harmony with the last command of Christ: to go into all the world and make disciples of all nations. In fact, one could conclude that the whole

> ### GOD'S UNCHANGING PURPOSE FOR YOU IN THE WORLD
>
> *Top line: God wants to bless you.*
> *Bottom line: You are blessed to be a blessing to all other nations.*
>
> GENESIS 12:2-4

reason for the time between Jesus' first coming and his second coming is the spread of the Gospel. When this Gospel has been preached to all nations, then, said Jesus, the end will come.

"Are you following me, folks? This is one book, one story, one unchanging purpose. Let's go to the end of the story to read the conclusion of the book. Turn to Revelation 5:9. We read that in heaven, a new song is being sung, saying:'You are worthy to take the scroll, and to open its seals; for you were slain, and have redeemed us to God by Your blood out of every tribe and tongue and people and nation.'

"There you have it! The conclusion is what God sets out to do in the beginning of the Bible, He accomplishes at the end of time. I'm telling you, you need to see your Bible this way: one book, one introduction, one story, one conclusion, one mega theme, one unchanging purpose. God recruits, blesses, sends forth, and uses His people to become a channel of God's blessing to those who are not His people, defined as all nations. You can't just be a blessing to everybody in your culture and think you've got the job done. God's unchanging purpose is to reach all nations. Jesus commanded the same. If you're looking for a cause to live for, you would do well to join God and help fulfill His unchanging purpose. Can I hear an Amen?"

Everyone responded with a hearty, "Amen."

HOW TO APPROACH READING YOUR BIBLE

One Book with One Story: 66 smaller books making the different chapters of the Bible.

One Design: Man was made to glorify God by enjoying him forever.

One Introduction: Genesis chapters 1-12. God creates the world and people.

One Major Plot: Man becomes separated from God through his sin. God seeks to remedy the situation.

One Rescue–One Gospel: God plans a substitutionary atonement to be made by the future arrival of Jesus Messiah to reunite man with God. However,

One sin: This eventually leads to major rebellion: Mankind united stands against God. But,

One Strategy: God mercifully designs a divide and conquer strategy at the tower of Babel forming the nations of the world. His plan is to divide the nations so he can win them all back to himself one by one. Why? Because united as one people, they hardened their hearts. Divided into multiple nations, their hearts would be open. Reaching all the nations, which he had formed, was always the plan. It is true God loves everyone.

One Storyline: God chooses one nation to be a type of missionary nation to bring salvation to the other nations: They become the channel through which God executes his rescue plan for all nations. This storyline represents most of the Bible–Genesis chapter 12–Jude.

One Chosen Nation: God makes a covenant promise to Abraham to bring the blessing of salvation to all nations through his heirs. He becomes the founder of the nation of Israel. God then uses this nation (Israel) to reach all other nations.

One Messiah: Jesus arrives and dies as a substitutionary atonement for the sins of all the world. Making reuniting man with God possible to those who believe.

One Great Commission: Jesus then commands his apostles to finish the previously established rescue mission, namely preaching to all nations that people can be reunited to God through the substitutionary atonement of Jesus.

One Conclusion: What God set out to do at the beginning. He pulls off at the end. According to Revelation 5:9, at the throne of heaven are representatives from **every** tribe, people, language, and nation. To reiterate God keeps his promise to Abraham: salvation to all nations. People from every nation are reunited with God through the blood of the lamb.

One Unchanging Destiny: Not until the Gospel has been preached to all nations will Jesus return and the end of the age come. Matthew 24:14.

One Story of the Bible shared through 66 books (chapters).[19]

After the service, many people gathered in the lobby for a chance to connect with their friends. Ace began talking to Bruiser and his wife. Bruiser then waved some friends over to meet Ace. It was an arranged meeting. Two people moved through the crowd in their direction: one a tall, thin male college student wearing khaki pants and a polo shirt. Ace recognized the other face, a radiant young lady who was all "dolled up," wearing a black skirt, matching blouse, and a pink ribbon with a golden pendant around her neck. This sandy blonde with crystal blue eyes wore her hair in an updo— like the first time Ace had met her. Ace's chin buckled as he smiled at her.

Bruiser began the introduction. "Ace, I wanted to introduce you to Charity, but when I spoke to her last night, I discovered the two of you already know each other from the 'Y.' But did you know she is also our new Director of Care Ministries here at the church? We hired her about six months ago, and she's doing a fine job. And because she is not one to flaunt, you may not be aware that Charity has competed in the Big Race for the last three years, raising money for some pretty neat causes. Anyway, I asked her to meet us here, thinking she might be able to give you some tips on how to make your application compelling and give you some suggestions on which charity you might consider running for."

"Good morning, Ace." Charity smiled in return as she continued. "I am excited to see you here. Let me introduce all of you to my little brother, Clay."

---

19   Adapted from Bob Sjogren's books and lectures.

Clay shook hands with everyone as they exchanged names.

"Little brother?" Bruiser asked with a little sarcastic humor in his voice. It was a classic oxymoron. Clay was easily six feet four inches, and his big sister was doing well at five feet nine inches, including high heels. The contrast was clear.

"Yes, little brother! He might be taller, but I've got him by nine years. I have to remind him of that from time to time. He's just started his first year of college, so he's still somewhat new to the area. I told him we've got the best church in town and he should check it out. And he's also interested in competing in triathlons, so I told him about our little holy huddle of triathletes here."

Bruiser knew he had a little celebrity status that accompanied his Big Race win years ago, celebrity at least among triathletes, so he tried to use it to be a positive influence. He chimed in, "Well Clay, please know you are welcome here. I trust we will see you here again soon. Your sister is one of my favorites, and she has rock star status around here. I can't think of anyone who serves this church more. If you're anything like your sister, we'd love to have you here on a regular basis."

"I had a great time," Clay said. "I like your preacher. Chip was bringing it on today. I'm sure you'll see me again."

Ace quizzed Charity, "So you've run for charity three years in a row, but you're not racing for charity this year?"

"I know it sounds a little corny—Charity runs for charity—but I love it. I'm taking the year off. There is a time and season for everything. I felt I needed to give it a rest this year and regroup, reevaluate my priorities, and throw myself into this new job. Don't worry, I haven't given up temple maintenance. I'm certain I'll raise money for charity again."

"I'm told this application thing is really competitive. They only accept forty out of over 100 entries. You have to know something to get it three years in a row."

"Actually, just one year, the first year. You can run the Big Race for charity anytime you want. The last two years I qualified in my age group but still ran for charity."

"OK, so you're both beauty and beast! Very impressive, qualifying on your own merits. I'm impressed."

Charity blushed at the compliment and smiled. She understood that the term "beast," when applied to a woman athlete, is a compliment. It classified her as strong, tough, competitive, and not afraid of serious physical exertion.

"So, I'm curious—what charities have you run for?" Ace asked.

"My first year I ran for the cure for leukemia. It's a great organization and can really help triathletes learn how to train and get started. The second year I ran on behalf of Pink; my mom is a cancer survivor. And last year, because of sermons like we heard today, I wanted to run for a cause a little more kingdom-focused and more international. So I ran and sponsored some orphans through Compassion International in Kenya.

"Those three are some good ones to consider, but now there is an exciting new team on the block: Kingdom Builders Athletic Team—you run a race and build a church in a developing country. Maybe next year for me, but you should take a look at it. Choose what's best for you. Here's what you do: figure out what you're passionate about, do some research online because there are literally hundreds of charities, then choose the one you like. Listen, I'm not running this year, but if you get in, I'll be glad to help you. I can be like a marketing director. You know, help spread the news and round up a cheering squad for you on race day. I realize some people dread raising support, but I have to tell you, I absolutely love it."

"Now that sounds like a heck of a deal. I better get accepted so I can cash in on that. Right now I need a few tips for a great application to get this thing done. You got any suggestions for that?"

"Actually, the application isn't so much about the charity. That's important, but it's more about you. How getting involved in the charity has impacted you, why it's important to you. You need to be thinking why it makes a difference to the world and to you. Both components are vital. Create some sense of urgency; like if this doesn't get funded, the world as we know it will come to an end."

The little circle of friends were listening to Charity's impassioned explanation, and her humor at the end brought a chuckle from everyone.

Ace responded, "OK! This thing is due Thursday by 5:00 P.M. So what if I get a draft prepared to show you on Wednesday night? Can you meet me for coffee and take a look at it?"

"Sure, it's a deal." And just like that, Ace had a date.

Ace didn't wait until evening to write his post because he felt inspired when he came home and didn't want to lose his thoughts.

Hello, world! I realize that you may have lost interest in my pursuit due to the nature of my last post, but the last thread of hope is still dangling out there. And today it was strengthened. The Bible talks about the power of a three-fold cord as being much stronger than a single cord. Well, I got some encouragement from two friends who are trying to help me win a charity entry spot. We'll see what happens next, but the application is due this Thursday. Then I have to wait another two weeks until I hear anything. I'll keep you posted.

I visited a new church today, and the pastor has got it going on! All I can say is my heart was strangely warmed as the Spirit of God was clearly felt among us.

My Wisbits today came from my reflection of a comparison I began to make between the traditional church I grew up in and the contemporary one I visited today.

Wisbit tip: *Traditional church vs. contemporary church. Style is not the issue.*

Wisbit tip: *The church with the band vs. the organ/piano is not the issue.*

Wisbit tip: *The choir vs. select song leaders is still not the issue.*

Wisbit tip: *The impromptu preacher vs. the highly-structured preacher is not the issue.*

What is the real issue? *What's important are three things: finding a like-minded fellowship that will help you maintain a living communion with Christ and help to get His words at home in your heart, and can help you get actively involved in the Great Commission! That's it! That's the issue! Let me phrase it this way. With all that I've learned, the real issue is: Contemporary or traditional, is the church effectively aligned with God's unchanging purpose to make abiding disciples of Jesus Christ in all nations who will make abiding disciples of Jesus Christ unto every nation?*

QUESTIONS FOR SELF-REFLECTION

- Do I have a cause that I'm living for? What is it?
- Is my cause in alignment with God's unchanging purpose?
- Is there a friend or colleague whose cause I can help fulfill?
- Am I a channel of the blessings that God has given me? Or am I guilty of hoarding them to myself?
- What are the consequences of ignoring the responsibility to make disciples of all nations?

21

THE PURPOSE OF PAIN

ACE'S HEAD SPUN as he stood at the door of the house once again on Tuesday morning. His brain was on overload from all the charity websites he'd read over the last two nights. *Why am I here again? What is this meeting supposed to be about anyway?* he thought.

While he was lost in thought, Sage's wife, Lauwiel, came to the door and again escorted him into the living room. "Hello, Ace. I'm glad to see you again," Sage called out.

"I'm the one who needs to thank you for seeing me again," replied Ace.

"Well, did you watch the game last night? That was a good one, some kick, a fifty-seven yarder, last play of the game, no time left on the clock. I absolutely love it when my team wins. Ace, are you a Steelers fan?"

Ace was absolutely blown away. This man was so disarming, so much like a regular guy. He wondered…*How does a guy stuck in a bed even watch a game, let alone talk about life like he's somehow actually a part of society?* Then it hit him—lying in bed and watching the game on TV is all he can do.

Ace followed Sage's eyes as he made his last comment while

looking at a picture on the wall. It was a team photo of the Steelers after they won the Super Bowl a few years ago. It was inscribed to Sage and signed by the head coach. As Ace looked around the room he discovered all kinds of Pittsburgh Steeler paraphernalia: a bobble-head of number fifty-four and a signed football, along with some other items. Ace also noted a collection of eagles scattered throughout the room in various forms: paintings, brass statues, ceramic molds, figurines, and more paintings—eagles galore.

"I hate to tell you I only saw bits and pieces of the game, so I don't even know the final score."

"The Steelers stole the game again, 23-21. That makes two last-minute back-to-back saves. Maybe this year they'll make it back to the big game. Well, enough about that. Ace, what can I help you with today?"

"To tell you the truth, I'm here to talk about one thing, but my mind is preoccupied and troubled with another thing."

"OK, then let's take them one at a time. Tell me what's got your mind racing at the moment."

"It's not a life-or-death matter, so it's not that big of a deal. You may remember the first time I was here, you helped me discover my identity—I'm an all-in athlete who leads teams by visualizing what people could be and offers action steps for achievement, particularly to young athletes and quite possibly to rehabbers. You then suggested I find a noble cause to run for, something in harmony with my identity. Then it would make the race experience more meaningful for me.

"Well, Sage, I got a little off track along the way. I found myself running for the wrong reasons. But I'm back on track and running for a cause—running for God and running to serve. The only problem is I've got to turn in my application for my run for charity by Thursday. I've spent the last thirty-six hours literally poring over charity websites. I'm just overwhelmed. My head's spinning with options and I have no idea what to choose."

HOW AMERICAN CHRISTIAN MONEY IS SPENT

For every $1,000 earned, $42 is given to Christian causes.

Of that $42, $1 goes to foreign missions.

Of that $1 to foreign missions, 97 cents will go to relief work, feeding and clothing the poor, orphans and widows.

Three cents will go to support frontier evangelistic mission work.[20]

Sage's deep, raspy voice and slow tempo seemed to emphasize the depth of his next words. "OK, let's discuss that. Choosing a charity is very important, and I have given this dilemma a lot of thought over the years because not all charities are created equal. It seems everyone could use a little help with this. People who work hard for their money want to make sure they are getting a great return on their investment. When you run for a charity, it means a lot more if you're not only passionate about it, but you know it's an organization with integrity. And, perhaps most importantly for Christians, significant spiritual impact as well. But the starting block is always passion. What motivates you? What makes your heart beat fast?"

Ace had some fresh wind in his sails to answer this question this time around. "I'm not certain how what I am about to tell you aligns with my identity, but I heard a compelling cause to live for during last Sunday's message. It really struck a cord deep inside of me, so here is what I am thinking about: running for worldwide discipleship, namely something to benefit unreached foreign nations. So that narrows it some, but there are still a lot of choices."

Sage affirmed Ace's choice. "That's a noble cause. Now use your identity to narrow the focus and then realize that heart is only half the equation. It is the place to start. But the next step is equally

---

20   Adapted and conjoined from Lecture, State of the World, Bob Sjogren, and dramatic presentation from the Joshua Project at Perspectives On the World Christian Movement Class.

important. The effectiveness of the mission is just as vital. No one wants to give their money to poor stewards. Let me tell you about a tool I've developed to help you with the next step; it's a little acrostic. I call it HELPP for giving. Run any mission or charity through this grid, and it well help you make sense out of your giving cents. Read each question and then write your response to discover each charity's rating. See what scores highest and that should help a lot towards choosing the right charity.

"So, Ace, without taking up too much of your time, let me suggest you take this tool home with you and use it to 'helpp' you evaluate your options and make the best decision."

"That's very helpful. Thank you."

"You said there was another reason why you came here today—are you ready to talk about that now?"

"I suppose so…the last time I was with Doc Mentor, he deferred answering my question to you. My question shouldn't bother me the way it does—God can do whatever he wants—but I find myself kind of blaming God for messing up my life. It's not fair. I lived my life righteous, clean, holy, whatever label you want to put on it. I've been good; I've tried to do the right thing! So here is the puzzle: What's a good guy to expect to receive from God for being good? Because it doesn't add up. I've served God and what do I get? In fact, I kinda feel like I am being punished. If God is so good and all-powerful, why did He let this happen to me?" And with that Ace lifted his leg and pushed up his pant, revealing the bionic prosthetic.

Then Ace continued. "And that's only half the problem and half the question: all my life, the one dream I always wanted has been out of my reach. And I mean 'never going to happen' out of reach. I don't think I told you before, but my one ambition was to play in the NBA, and even before I lost my leg, that dream was crushed. I can't help but think God is responsible. Why would God even bother to put the drive, the talent and the mental toughness into a five-foot eight-inch frame that would never be able to achieve his dream? It just isn't fair and doesn't seem right to me."

HELPP[21]

PLEASE SCORE 0-1-2-3

HUMANITARIAN IMPACT

_____Reaching out to the poor, widows, and orphans

_____Does it distribute food, clothing

_____Does it provide education opportunities

EVANGELISTIC IMPACT

_____Can the evangelistic impact be quantified? How many churches have been planted? How many baptisms? How many laborers sent into the harvest?

_____Is the word of God being enabled into the culture?

_____How many Christians have been in discipleship beyond Sunday service?

_____Is it pioneer church planting?

LEVERAGING OF DOLLARS DONATED

_____What percentage goes to staff salaries and overhead expenses? (how much of every dollar raised actually does the work of the cause?)

_____Are matching monies available to amplify your giving?

POWER FOR RECIPIENTS

_____Does it enable recipients to become part of the solution?

_____Does this charity create dependency or empowerment?

PATRON PASSION

_____Is the cause something the donor is passionate about?

_____Does the project have lifetime donor significance?

_____Does the donor feel emotionally engaged?

_____Can the donor get personally involved?

_____Are there follow up reports on future developments?

Sage replied with empathy, "Ace, I'm sorry for your loss. I realize this is a very important question, and I'm glad you asked it. I assure you I wasn't always in this condition. I used to run marathons and

---

21   Evaluation Tool created by Robert Leatherwood.

pastor a large church. I have a family with grown kids, so I've had to personally wrestle this question to the ground as I lost my health over the years. I even wrote a book called *30 Biblical Reasons Why God's People Suffer*, so maybe Doc had good reason to refer you to me. You can take a copy as you leave, but I want to explore the question while you're here.

"I believe I have some insight into the problem of why God's people suffer. In short, God loves you just the way you are, He accepts you just the way you are, and He loves you too much to leave you just as you are. God is irrevocably committed to the proposition that you are going to mature. And suffering is often the precise tool He uses to cause growth. I have found several people in the Bible who asked some version of the same question you're asking. I think we can learn something from these men. First, Job is easily one of the most popular stories in the Bible. He literally lost everything, and he was a rich man, and also the godliest person on the planet. He lost all his possessions, his children and his health. I observe a few things from his life: First, he was not being punished for some grave sin, although he was being tested for the cause of bringing God greater glory. In a sense, his suffering put his faith on display, a showcase of sorts of his great loyalty to God. With no suffering or trial in Job's life, we would not even be talking about him. Think about it, Ace. Loyalty is the one quality you will never know about another person until it's been tested by trial. Only then can you say if a person is loyal or not.

"In a way, Job was suffering because he was exceptionally good. He had the same question you have: What should I expect to get for being good? God was showing off Job's faith. His display showcase just happened to be suffering, as it often is. Maybe God thought you were capable of handling this. Maybe your tragedy is more about God's glory than your comfort. Don't be selfish, don't ask what do I get, but rather what does God get?"

Ace countered. "Sounds like a raw deal to me. If God blesses like that, who needs enemies?"

Sage pushed back. "There was a happy ending for Job. After he passed the test he was doubly blessed! Let's move along and we will come back to this thought of a proper payoff.

WHY SUFFER?[22]

GOD SOMETIMES PERMITS HIS PEOPLE TO SUFFER BECAUSE:

1. He is fiercely committed to the proposition that His people are going to reach their full maturity in Christ. Suffering is often the catalyst for growth.

2. He wants us to increase our fruitfulness with a cutback that often looks like a setback.

3. He desires to turn the weakness of His people into a showcase of His strength.

4. He wants to teach us to depend on Him; otherwise we tend to forget about Him.

5. He wants his people to forsake their pride and learn humility.

6. This is the way he turns a good man into a great man.

7. His light shines bright to a lost world when His people remain loyal in difficulties.

"My next observation is that suffering is what God uses to make good men great. Think about the times in your life when you have grown the most—was it in good times or troubled times? We don't often grow that much when things are going well. This paraphrase from the letter of James sums up this thought: 'Stop viewing your problems as intruders, but rather welcome them as friends, for they have come to refine your character, so let the trials continue until the character desired is fully formed.' Did you catch that, because

---

22 Excerpt from 30 Biblical Reasons Why God's People Suffer, Dick Woodward.

that was big? I'm talking about a dramatic change in perspective. Most people view their problems as a nuisance and immediately try to eliminate them. Nobody wants to have any problems. But if your gonna go anywhere with God, you have to change your perspective on your troubles. You must welcome them as friends, because they've come into your life as a blessing, not a curse. And I want to talk more in a moment about the benefit of taking this perspective.

"You know, that particular translation always reminds me of making brownies with my mother as a boy. After we mixed the batter and poured it into the pan, we put the pan in the oven and waited. But the problem with baking brownies is that the batter is brown, which is the same color as when they are done. So when the timer went off, we'd take out the brownies and put a toothpick in the middle and quickly remove it. If there was any brownie mix on the toothpick, they weren't done—and back into the oven they'd go.

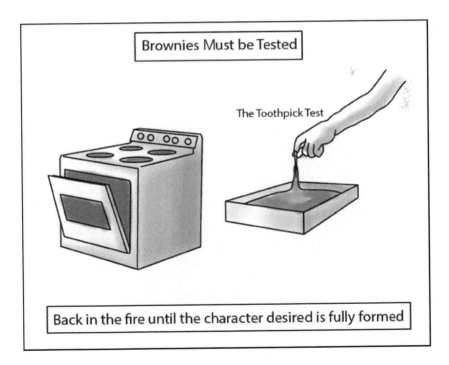

Brownies Must be Tested

The Toothpick Test

Back in the fire until the character desired is fully formed

"In a similar fashion, Ace, God keeps us in the trial and tests us every so often to see if we have matured. In the oven we stay until the character HE desires to be manifest in us is fully formed. The trials help us mature. Otherwise, most of us would never leave our comfort zone to reach greater levels of spiritual maturity. The quickest way out of the fire is to grow up. Give God the response He is looking for—surrender and rejoice—these are both core expressions of faith. You gotta abandon yourself to His providence and learn to rest in his redemption.

"Ace, do you see all the eagles in this room? The eagle is my favorite illustration of how God moves us out of our comfort zones. You see, the golden eagle builds its nest high in the cleft of a mountain. After the young eaglets are born and grow to be juveniles, the mother begins to deconstruct the nest, removing all the creature comforts: down feathers, pelts of small animals, etc. It's like removing the carpet in your house. Then she actually ruffles the sticks in the nest so that the sharp edges point uncomfortably upward, causing the young birds to strengthen their legs as they maneuver around.

"Finally the day comes for flight school. The father takes flight and hovers a few feet over the nest. Then the mother will literally push the young eaglets out of the nest, forcing the juvenile birds to use their wings and attempt to fly. The bird usually plummets downward on the first attempt, so the father swoops down, flies under, and catches the eaglet on his back. Then he returns it to the nest and the mother and father repeat the process until the eaglet succeeds in flying. In short, the parents are irrevocably committed to the fact that their young are going to mature. They are going to learn to fly whether they want to or not. God also is irrevocably committed to the fact that we are going to grow up whether we like it or not, because He loves us. Trials, tests, and suffering are for our good, refining our character into the image of Christ.

"The next person in the Bible we learn about suffering from is the apostle Paul. He had his famous 'thorn in the flesh.' If you're not familiar with it, let me share it with you. It reads something like this: 'In order to keep me from becoming conceited there was given unto me a thorn in my flesh, a messenger from Satan, sent to torment me; this thorn was my gift to keep me from becoming conceited. Concerning this irritating thorn, I pleaded with the Lord three times that it might depart from me. And he said to me, 'My grace is sufficient for you, for my strength is made perfect in weakness. Therefore most gladly I will boast in my infirmities, that the power of Christ may rest upon me.'

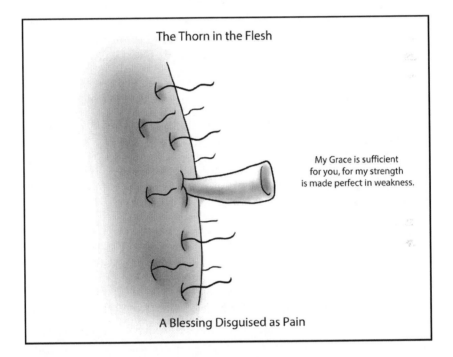

The Thorn in the Flesh

My Grace is sufficient for you, for my strength is made perfect in weakness.

A Blessing Disguised as Pain

"Did you catch that Paul gave two more reasons why God's people suffer? First, to keep us humble! God cannot use proud people. It's almost as if God was saying to him, 'Paul, you're hanging by a thread; you are almost completely unusable. I'm going to give you the gift of a thorn. The Bible does not tell us what the thorn was, I think, on purpose. It's kind of a catch-all: What's your thorn? Fill in the blank. Mine, I'm a quadriplegic. You, I suppose, your leg. A thorn keeps you humble and dependent on God.

"Next, God says the most remarkable thing: *'My strength is made perfect in weakness.'* Can you get your mind around that? Your weakness, your missing leg, is the great opportunity for God's power, His strength, to flow to you and through you. In short, your leg is a source of grace. Maybe you've never thought about it this way, but in some ways, it is your greatest asset. Without it, you'd be quite ordinary. With it, you have a source of God's power in your life. Once Paul fully got this, he never again asked God to fix his thorny problem; instead, he rejoiced. And he was used mightily, probably the greatest Christian who ever lived. Encourage yourself, Ace, remembering that Paul had a thorn in his body. It actually helped him do his work. You'll know you've experienced a breakthrough when you can honestly thank God and even rejoice over the condition of your lost leg."

Ace's suppressed anger and hurt came flooding out; he couldn't help it. It was like gas had been ignited in him and, like a volcano, he began to spew.

"Seriously?! You want me to thank God for this? I'm supposed to rejoice? This thing has wrecked my life! I lost my fiancée because of this. Girls don't allow themselves to get too close to a one-legged oddity."

Ace paused for a moment. His face contorted and his eyes teared up. Ace's next words revealed the depth of his pain. "I feel like a freak! People stare at me; they don't treat me the same." Ace continued, now more ticked off than wounded. "You got any idea what that'll do to your head? I lost my sense of direction, I lost my ambition, I never finished college. I'm a loser. I'm an AV technician. I'm going nowhere in a hurry. Heck, I'm glad I even got a job. Nobody wants to hire a freak. You want me to pretend this is a blessing? I'm sorry; I don't see it that way." His emotions had been raw as he vented. Ace sniffled as he held back the tears.

"It sounds to me like you're right on schedule."

"What do you mean?"

"I also went through the stages of grief: denial, bartering, anger, then acceptance. In a sense, you could see your whole reason for choosing to do this race as fueled by anger and bartering for acceptance and validation. The thinking sounds like this: I race, I compete, I finish, I validate my existence. It's even somewhat powered by a low-grade unidentifiable anger, best summarized by, 'I'll show you'... to the world and everyone in it."

Ace pushed back. "Anyone who knows me will tell you I don't have a problem with anger. I've only gone nuclear a total of three or four times in my whole life. Isn't that normal? Nobody can say they've never gotten angry. I'm not a screamer. I don't throw things, I don't fight; in fact, I'm predisposed to walk away from idiots."

Sage wasn't buying any of it. "That all sounds well, but anger wears many masks. Do you frequently find yourself *just a little* frustrated, impatient, annoyed, upset, and the list goes on?

"That's what we call low-grade anger. It's real, and if you're honest with yourself, you'll see that it's there. It's not evil, not wrong, but it is a symptom and categorically a phase of grief. Sometimes a phase people get stuck in for years. But, Ace, God wants you to fully mature, and yes, I am asking for a radical adjustment to your perspective. The sooner you get to acceptance, marked by thanksgiving and rejoicing, you'll be on your way to inner peace and the fruitfulness of service to Him. In a real sense, I add an

> ### THE DISGUISES OF ANGER
>
> *I'm not angry, maybe just a little...*
>
> Upset
> Irritated
> Frustrated
> Out of Patience
> Agitated
> Provoked
> Disgusted
> Ticked Off
> Shocked
> Tired
> Grouchy
> Bothered

additional stage after acceptance for victorious Christians, and that is to rejoice in your affliction. Realizing that all things are working together for your good. All things! Even the seemingly bad things.

"Paul said he took special delight in weaknesses of every kind for when he was weak, then the power of God made him strong. His perspective was transformed and at that moment he began to experience that his weak spot, this painful thorn in his flesh, was the exact tool to cause him to tap into his sweet spot. Namely, complete dependence on God's power for living. Why all this emphasis on weakness? It's simple. It showcases God's power to a skeptical world. When He works through broken vessels, it becomes clear to everyone that God was the true source.

"Ace, I can honestly tell you that I've never been happier or more fulfilled in my life than I am confined to this bed. God has chosen not to heal me, but I feel so wonderfully used by Him. And there is a spiritual intimacy I share with Christ that simply wasn't there before, even when I was pastoring a church. Now it's just Sage and

Jesus. I'm telling you, abiding in His presence, maintaining a living communion with Him is my greatest joy.

So why aren't more people enjoying spiritual intimacy with God? They are all so wonderfully blessed. Enjoying a problem free life. Nobody wants problems; they aren't welcome; so they don't need God so much and they pursue other things. With no pain to drive them to God, they get busy doing everything but seeking God. It's the great tragedy of our day. People are too busy for God.

"That was me. I used to be six inches deep and a mile wide—now I'm four feet wide, the width of my bed, and a mile deep. I've been slowed down with my infirmity, my thorn, and I'm so glad because life is better."

Ace was dumbfounded. He wasn't fighting it now, but he wasn't completely buying it either. Sage had exposed a deeper motivation for Ace, pointed out the grief journey, and had lived it. It just wasn't that easy to believe. Understanding tragedy as a blessing in disguise was such a stretch he'd have to think about it long and hard.

Ace crossed his arms in front of his chest and could only reply, "I don't know about that…I'm not there yet. You've given me a lot to think about. I don't even know if I can get there like you have. I guess I need more time."

Sage added, "You know, there is a Bible character who God also blessed with a bum leg."

"Yeah? Who?"

"A man named Jacob. He was a real rascal—he was always on the lookout for 'Number One.' He routinely manipulated circumstances for his own benefit, not caring who he hurt in his wake. Well, God got a hold of this rascal. It took an all-night wrestling match with an angel. But at that moment, God forever changed his life. During the wrestling match, the angel did him a favor and touched him so that Jacob's hip socket was out of joint, a condition he lived with the rest of his life. It was God's mark of ownership, kind of a branding. It became a daily reminder to Jacob that he belonged to God, that he needed God instead of relying on his own craftiness. At the same moment, God blessed him, and his name was changed. In a sense, God gave him a new identity. Instead of being known as sly, he would be known as victorious through God. He was then called Israel, the good book says, 'because as a prince, he had power with God and men.'

"Ace, in a sense, you are like Jacob. God is the designer of your weakness, any way you look at it. He allowed this thorn to come to you. In due season you will understand it as the symbol of the victorious one. Strange mark, huh? Jacob's bum leg was his trophy. I call it his 'cripple crown.' It became a constant reminder to him that his victory was through trusting in God and not in himself. His destiny required a thorn, a hobbled leg. The best thing you can do is transform your perspective on your weak spot for it is God's intent to make it your sweet spot. He had to slow Jacob down to give him a crown. He had to make him realize that relying on God was what was most needed for his future success. Change the meaning of your mark. Attach a new meaning to it. Stop thinking of it as a curse and call it—even embrace it—as a blessing, and you too will be the victorious one."

Sage continued. "So, you want to know why? Why, if God is so good and all-powerful, would you have this dream inside you that you can't ever reach? Did it ever occur to you that God has a different dream for you than you currently have for yourself? If you embrace it, a better life story, this leg is your ticket to greater glory. It can be your 'cripple crown' if you'll let it. It's your opportunity to see God's strength made perfect through your weakness. A different destiny; one with eternal substance. A better destiny."

Shortly thereafter, Ace left with a lot to think about. He was experiencing so many emotions he wasn't familiar with. Needless to say, his mind and heart were troubled, but he didn't have time to process yet. He was busy every spare moment, getting his application finalized.

Later that night, Ace sat down to blog.

Hey, everybody! I finally selected my charity! Now I am finalizing my application, just fine-tuning a compelling story. I'll have it finished and turned in by Thursday at 5:00 P.M. I met with the guru of all gurus again today. I'm telling you, this guy Sage is seriously like master Yoda. He opens his mouth and out comes wisdom. Anyway, he helped me clearly see exactly what charity to run for. Sorry to give you a cliff-hanger, but I am going to make you wait until I hear back whether I get accepted to do the big reveal of the charity I've chosen. So let the suspense drive you to prayer. God, help me get accepted. And I've got some amazing tips for living to share. So here we go:

Wisbit tip: *God causes all things to work together for the good of those who love Him and are living according to His purpose. All things! Even the good, the bad, and the ugly.*

Wisbit tip: *There is a purpose to pain. In fact, it is one of God's most misunderstood tools to bring maturity in his children.*

Wisbit tip: *The quickest way out of a trial is to mature. Surrender and rejoice.*

Wisbit tip: *Not all charities are created equal. Do some investigating before you give.*

Wisbit tip: *While you can't take your money with you when you die, you can send it on ahead.*

QUESTIONS FOR SELF-REFLECTION

- Have you been too busy for God? Have you been ignoring his whispers? Is he now using trials to get your attention?
- What response do you think God wants from you when pain is allowed to come your way?
- How many reasons can you think of why God's people suffer?
- Do I thank God and rejoice for the trials He allows in my life?
- Can I see God's greater purpose behind my pain?
- What criteria do I use to help steward my charitable giving?

22

WHEN I SURRENDER IT ALL, I GET IT ALL

WEDNESDAY NIGHT WAS about as close to a real date night as Ace had experienced in some time. The same was true for Charity. But was it a date at all? The local coffee shop was the agreed-upon meeting place. These two had established a friendship, and so the conversation started easily with the discussion of Ace's application.

Charity held the finished application in her hand. She handed it over to Ace with this sentiment: "This is a real heartwarming story you wrote here about your dad. And I love the charity you chose. I'd say it's a slam dunk. You did a good job of writing it. All I did was polish up the grammar a little here and there. But you nailed it. It's ready to send. Just scan it and email it before 5:00 P.M. tomorrow. And then we pray and we wait. It'll be the longest two weeks of your life, but you need to keep training like you've already been approved. Let's just call it training by faith. I really think you've got something here. It's compelling."

Ace's application, which he had passed along to Charity just a day before, had been edited and slightly rearranged by her to get it in final form. He was confident he had picked the right cause to run for. He liked his reasons and felt good about what he had written. After all the research, there had been only one clear choice.

Ace had decided to build a church in Vietnam through a partnership with Kingdom Builders Athletic Team. He used three criteria to select a charity: His identity, Pastor Chip's compelling story of God's unchanging purpose to reach all nations, and the HELPP grid from Sage. It was the perfect trifecta. Kingdom Builders partners with ICM (International Cooperating Ministries), and allows athletes to run a race and build a church in another country. It was simple, but it really resonated with him. It was an A+ through the HELPP grid.

Ace committed to raising $10,000 to build a church for the Dak Ruong congregation in Vietnam. In some ways it was part of his family identity because his dad was a Vietnam War veteran. Ace discovered that many soldiers lived with regrets about their experience in Vietnam. Ace came to believe after talking to his dad that many of them would want to help bring God's peace where they once dropped bombs of destruction. The project had a double dimension to it. Ace could empower Christian war veterans in America, some of whom would fit in the bucket of rehabbers, while empowering the Vietnamese people to build their own church to preach to their own nation. Dak Ruong was the congregation he was assigned specifically for its proximity to the place his father had previously bombed. He enclosed the pastor's photo and congregational picture, as well as the floor plans for the church along with his application.

The business side of their meeting was quickly done, but neither gave any indication that they wanted to leave. Now the conversation kept pouring out. The atmosphere and the quantity of time allowed them to go deep. They had so much in common. Ace shared his water buoy story and his life-changing week with Doc Mentor as well as his new conviction to be in church. Charity was impressed by his resolve. This little coffee meeting turned into two and a half hours of blissful conversation accompanied by a dessert tray.

Ace couldn't put his finger on it, but there seemed to be a moment when the friendship type of conversation morphed into something more substantial. He was almost certain the feelings were mutual. As the evening came to a close Ace wondered, *Where do we go from here?* But Charity was a step ahead. "You oughta come join Faith and me this Saturday at 1:00 at the Sky Way trail. By the time you're done running with Bruiser, I'll be getting off my shift at the 'Y,' and then we will help you get your brick workout in for the week. We don't ride as fast as the peloton, but I assure you we ride fast. We'll make you work, but we won't drop you.

"And then give me a call as soon as you hear from the charity racer committee. If you're going to let me be your promoter, we won't have a moment to spare. Ten grand is a super big goal. You've got more faith than I do. But I love the idea of building that church to honor your dad. If you want my help, you've got me. Just let me know when you hear the word."

Ace picked up the tab as they departed: $22.20. Seeing this number was kinda like a smile from heaven. It served as a little affirmation. He thought to himself, *God you see it all. You're right here, right now. I feel your pleasure.* He gave a wiry smile and scrunched up his chin. He was pleased; everything was going his way.

↺

Now Ace was facing an unavoidable time gap. It would be two weeks before Ace could expect an answer from the Charity Racers Committee. In the meantime, Ace trained and prayed. He was doing it by the books: his two bibles. He opened his tri-training guide every day, following the schedule precisely. He rose early every morning and started every day off right. He opened his *Great with God Pocket Guide*, read the Scriptures, and memorized his weekly verses.

One thought was plaguing Ace's mind: he couldn't stop thinking about Sage's evaluation of him. The incredulous plan to thank God for his missing leg, find some reason to rejoice about it, attach new meaning to this thorn, and embrace it as a blessing in disguise. His thoughts chased each other around inside his head. *They were preacher words, good ideas, just not very practical.* But this wasn't any preacher; he was a quadriplegic saying it with a smile on his face. *Best thing that ever happened to him. Yeah, right!* he thought.

Ace felt double-minded. He spent more time with God, getting closer to God, yet he wasn't talking to God, not quite like Doc Mentor had modeled for him. He spent most of his time thinking in his quiet morning routine. He prayed some, but mostly for his application to get accepted. The second thing on his prayer list was for things to work out between him and Charity. And then, as usual, he asked God to provide, protect, and direct his life. However, he started to feel guilty about his praying. It occurred to him how selfish he was acting. Ace felt like he was treating God like a candy store—always asking for his own pleasure and desires.

Why was prayer so difficult? Eventually it came to him: the disciples must have had the same difficulty, for they asked, "Lord, teach us to pray." In response, Jesus taught them The Lord's Prayer. And Doc had modeled it as an index prayer. Finally, Ace was beginning to see the value of using the prayer as an outline.

☙

Thursday night finally arrived. The Charity Racers Committee was starting their meeting to review the applications. Bruiser was new to this committee and full of excitement as he came. The committee of ten had each been given ten applications to read during the two weeks prior to this official meeting. Bruiser's assignment was to make four selections to recommend to the committee. The chairman called the meeting to order and they began to go around the table and reveal their candidates.

On the other side of town, at the same moment, Ace was pacing back and forth in his apartment. Thursday night was growing intolerably long for Ace. The last two weeks had been the slowest of his life, worse than a child waiting for Christmas. Tomorrow he would get his email from the Charity Runners Committee, in or out.

Ace was restless; his adrenaline was pumping. It was 9:00 P.M. and he was entirely too amped to sleep. He thought to himself, *I may as well go for a run…maybe I can tire myself out so I can finally sleep later. I need to pray. I can't get any rest in my heart or my mind. I've got to find a way to give this to God.* This moment represented another chance to beg and plead with God to answer his prayer favorably.

Ace exited his apartment into the darkness wearing his running apparel. No clouds, no moon…it was pitch black with a starry backdrop. There was very little light, except for the street lamps and the occasional car headlights. He ran along the roads in the nearby neighborhood. Eventually he came to an empty park with a jungle gym, swings, and a basketball court. Ace had not been to this little neighborhood park before. He jogged onto the center of the basketball court, looked up, gazed at the beautiful, starry sky, smiled big and gave one quick satisfying laugh; hah! He knew he had just found his own sacred place, his Shiloh. This was one of his assignments from Doc Mentor. At the moment it provided Ace a great deal of privacy—it was situated far enough off the road so he wouldn't be interrupted by cars. No lights. Ace felt as if he were covered in a cloak of darkness, invisible to the world.

Now began a collision in his soul, an uncharacteristic moment filled with memories, dreams, and feelings. Ace was flooded with emotion. He looked up again and tears filled his eyes as he wept. He was carrying a load too great for any man to bear. Everything was at stake. He had invested so much to participate in this race. He wondered, *What could he possibly do to bargain with God to get his way?* And then he broke. His tears gave way to a sobbing, gut-wrenching prayer.

Ace got on his knees and bowed his head, "God, I am so sorry. I don't even know what to say to you. I can't take it anymore. This thing is out of my control. I know I keep coming to you asking you to give me what I want. My prayers have been the exact opposite of your prayer: 'Hallowed be Thy name, Thy kingdom come, Thy will be done, on earth as it is in heaven.' God, I surrender. I simply give it all to you. I'm so sorry. I've been praying for you to do *my* will. But, Lord, I surrender to *your* will. Let your will be done in my life, whatever it is.

"I don't care anymore, Lord. I want what you want. I'll serve you either way—if I get in or not. I know deep down inside what Sage said about me is true. I've been trying to make my name great. I've been trying to impress people, caring more about what they think of me than what you think of me. God, I want to advance your name, let your name be lifted up, may *you* get the glory."

Now Ace laid himself prostrate with his face on the pavement. He felt convicted. "I know I've cursed you, sometimes with my lips and sometimes in my heart for this leg. I've blamed you. I've been mad at you. And now, the king of cripples tells me I'm supposed to **thank** you for it!" He paused, and returned to his knees. Now all he could do was wimper in a whisper, "OK...thank you. I mean it. I believe that you are big enough and great enough to cause all things to work for good to those who love you and are living according to your purpose. If I haven't been living according to your purpose, I want to now."

Ace stood to his feet, turned his face toward heaven and lifted his hands up. "I give you the rest of my life—do with it whatever you want. From this day forward, Lord, I belong to you, and I accept this crippled leg as your branding. This leg is going to be a daily reminder that I belong to you, that you are Lord and I'm not. I live for your will, not mine. Thank you that this leg has brought me back in touch with you. Thank you that it is your special gift to keep me humble and dependent. Let my weakness be a channel for your strength. And when anything good happens, I'll be careful to give you the credit."

When Ace finished praying, he felt like a thousand pounds had been lifted off his back. He had met with God. He didn't know how, but the experience was real. The Holy Spirit was in his heart, making him know it was real.

On the other side of town, in the board room, after more than two and a half hours, the Charity Runners Committee concluded with their final comments. "That makes forty," said Chairman, who was glad to end the marathon meeting. He continued with his closing remarks. "Let me thank each of you for your hard work again this year. This race is better because of the charity dimension. You are changing the lives of racers and those less fortunate who benefit from these many charities."

Bruiser interjected. "May I interrupt, please? I know we've been here a long time, and I'm the new guy. And what I'm about to say may sound like I came on board to play favorites, but that's not why I'm here. I believe in what we're doing, but the truth is I was hoping to hear the name of a young man I've come to know over the last year who put in an application. This racer is special: an amputee with a serious work ethic and a big heart. Does this committee ever make exceptions? I mean, can I go to bat for him, or maybe switch my number four choice and add him instead?"

Chairman laughed softly to demonstrate he understood the dilemma. "Bruiser, we've crossed this bridge before. The reason we do things exactly this way is so we won't play favorites. These slots are awarded 100 percent on merit only. And we have found by processing them this way, we insure that no one gets an advantage over another. This committee was full of that several years ago, and we finally put an end to it. And now this is what we've got—it's not perfect, but it's been working well. These procedures keep us accountable. I assure you there are a few people sitting in this room who remember the days when we could select our personal favorites. And those people will also remember the lawsuit brought against us for discrimination. I'm not sure exactly what you had in mind, but our bylaws prohibit a substitution at this point. Maybe we can put your friend to be the first alternate on the list, although that's a long shot."

"All right, I get it…but can't we make room for one more? Is there a rule that says we can only have forty and no more?" Bruiser still tried to solve the dilemma.

"Actually, there is. The governing board of worldwide triathlons, for liability reasons, sets the limit to no more than 2,000 racers. It's their version of the fire code, which limits the number of people that can fit safely into a room. As silly as it sounds, 2,001 is deemed an insurance liability and a major risk. If something goes wrong and something always does, the whole race is exposed to lawsuits. I think you get my drift."

"OK, so the issue could be resolved if we had an extra space, like you said, a first alternate?"

"Yeah."

"Then, I surrender my spot. I won't run this year. Let's agree to allow Ace to run in my place. This young man has come to mean a great deal to me. And I know this race means the world to him. I am happy to do it. Are we good with that?"

"That's not exactly what I meant by first alternate. What I meant was first alternate among charity candidates, but I see no reason why we can't accommodate him under these circumstances. All in favor say, 'Aye.'"

The committee chimed "Aye" in unison.

"So let it be written, so let it be done. This meeting is adjourned."

ॐ

Ace slept well after his encounter with God. Now, as the sun began to rise, the anticipated day was finally here. Ace had been checking his computer all morning when his phone finally rang. Ace answered only to discover that it was Chairman, from the Charity Runner's Committee. After they exchanged greetings, Chairman made the reason for his call clear.

"Ace, I am sending an email to all the applicants with the results of the committee meeting today. However, I have two reasons for my call. First, to inform you that you have been accepted to one of our charity racer spots. I wanted to let you know I looked at your application thoroughly. It was exceptional; very well written.

I want you to know that I am also a Christian. This was the first time I'd heard about the Kingdom Builders Athletic Team, but I know International Cooperating Ministries (ICM) very well. It's an efficient and an effective mission, so I'm glad they've now made this new partnership; racing to fund their projects: Run a Race, Build a Church. That's got a little snap to it, I'd say.

"Ace, I noticed you're trying to raise $10,000 to construct a church in Vietnam. Well, it just so happens that I'm a Vietnam vet, and when you said you were building it in honor of your dad who also served there, it touched a chord inside me. So I want to be the first to participate. Count on me for the first $1,000. I'll mail you a check before the race.

"The next reason I called is this: we have a process to select our charity racers. On the first pass, the committee denied your application. But an advocate on your behalf was so inspired by your story he made an appeal. However, there was a stalemate that could not be resolved. I felt you should know that a very extravagant gesture was made on your behalf. The only way this could be resolved was through a substitution. One of our board members literally forfeited his qualified spot so you could race for this cause. I also know this person would like to remain anonymous. But I think it makes a difference that you know a God-inspired sacrifice made this possible. It shouldn't be taken lightly. It was the most noble thing I've seen in twenty years of service to this organization. And I thought you deserved to know. So go run for the glory of God, and let's build a church in Vietnam."

Ace was overwhelmed. "I…I don't know what to say. I guess I need to say thank you, and thank God. I assure you I don't feel worthy to take someone else's spot. I will treasure the opportunity and do all I can to make it worth the sacrifice."

"Have a nice day, son, and I'll get that check to you shortly."

"Thank you, sir. Bye."

Ace was thrilled! He had to call Charity to share the good news.

When he called, he exclaimed, "You've got something to cheer about, and you have a racer to manage. Let's go build this church!" Then he shared the news they were off to a good start with their first thousand.

Later that night, Ace was ready to post his blog.

Hello, world. Hello, friends: I've got good news—I'm in! I found out today I was accepted into one of the charity spots for the Big Race. Yeah, it's a big deal. Thanks for praying with me. So what does all this mean? First, I get to reveal what charity I'm racing for. I know you've been waiting on pins and needles. We are going to be funding the construction of a church building for a congregation in Vietnam with a ministry called ICM *(International Cooperating Ministries). They recently partnered with Kingdom Builders Athletic Team, which is a program where you run a race and build a church in a developing country. Their byline is* Race for the Nations. Run a Race, Build a Church!

Second, please notice I used the word "we" above. I'm trying to raise $10,000. I'm going to be racing (swim, bike, and run) 140.6 miles in one day. It's a noble cause. Would you consider sponsoring me for fifty cents a mile or a one dollar a mile? And if you've got the big bucks—how about ten dollars a mile? I want you to know "we" are off to a good start. "We" already got our first gift of $1,000! It's easy—just $9,000 to go.

Please consider praying for me and supporting me by visiting razoo. com and type in "Kingdom Builders Athletic Team." –Ace.

Below are what lessons I've been learning lately.

Wisbit tip: *Miracles still happen. Don't stop believing.*

Wisbit tip: *With God, nothing is impossible.*

Wisbit tip: *Let go and let God.*

Wisbit tip: *You get more done with God by surrendering and rejoicing than you do by begging and pleading.*

QUESTIONS FOR SELF-REFLECTION

- What is God asking me to surrender right now (personal ambition, money, time, reputation, a cherished possession…)?

- Have you ever presented your body to God as a living sacrifice, pledging to prefer to live for the advancement of His kingdom, rather than your own ambition?
- What have you given to God and what happened when you did?

23

CHARITY IS AT THE CENTER OF IT ALL

THE NEXT THREE months were the best in Ace's life. He lived filled with purpose, intensity and discipline. He lived by the books. In fact, Ace told everyone that he was a man with two bibles. He trained hard and found great success integrating his prayer and meditation time into his workout time. He loved mixing the two together—he figured out that if he started the first ten minutes of his morning in the *Great with God Pocket Guide*, he had something to think about while he exercised. And then praying flowed right out of that meditation.

The weeks went quickly. Ace spent a lot of time with Charity. She really knew what she was doing. Ace was savvy with the digital world, but Charity took everything to a new level. She was a wordsmith who knew how to handle Facebook, Twitter, Snapchat, Instagram, blogging, emails, and text messages. She even sent a few things through the post office. As a result, the money poured in. She posted a thermometer on the Razoo fundraising page. Each day they got closer to their goal. It would take a lot of fifty-dollar and 100-dollar sponsors to cross the finish line, but it was coming.

Ace was competitive by nature, so he set goals. He wanted to be the best of the charity runners. He rightly figured that most of the others were in the same position as him—a few minutes shy of qualifying themselves. So it was a reasonable goal. He even searched the records of previous races to see who his serious challengers would be on this level. He couldn't believe that two of the older charity runners were quite a bit faster than he had been on the Half-Iron. Fehniecair, a man from Germany, was sixty-six and finished a similar race almost two years ago. Circumstances kept him from competing in the Big Race last year, but his previous time was nearly twenty minutes faster than Ace's had been. Then there was Tenderfoot, a forty-eight-year-old woman in the same situation. She qualified two years ago for the Big Race but couldn't make it due to family conflicts. Now she ran for charity. Her previous qualifying time had a fifteen minute advantage over Ace. Ace was motivated. He couldn't win this race or beat everybody, but he would try to be the fastest among the charity runners.

For the next three months his relationship with Charity blossomed. She became his new Saturday riding partner. And then a new foursome began to emerge as Faith and Clay would join with them.

However, for Ace and Charity, biking became the treasured moments of deep conversation. So just for the fun of it, these two made riding in the evenings together a great non-date, date. So it was that two hearts were slowly being knit together.

And to put the cherry on top of this budding relationship, Sundays became a little holy huddle where Charity, Clay, Faith, and Ace sat behind Bruiser and his wife at church.

◌

The months of training had now come to an end. Ace felt ready, and with just two days before the Big Race, it was once again racer registration day, which caused Ace to reminisce. Last year this was only a dream. Last year he volunteered. This year, he was a racer. The swag bag and expo were all to be enjoyed by him; he was a member of the nobility. Then he saw the sign that the FCA breakfast was scheduled for the morning, and Champion was scheduled to speak once again. Ace made a mental note and set his heart to attend. Meanwhile, he continued to wander around the expo, looking for friends and listening to sales pitches on the latest and greatest racing gadgets and apparel.

The day seemed to be getting away from him. When Ace checked his watch, it was 2:22. He smiled and thought of Markist. Ace had put the bumper sticker on the back of his car, so he saw 222 almost every day. As Markist promised, Ace had become sensitized to the number, so it seemed that he saw it everywhere he went. This glance at his watch reminded Ace he was to be about the business of "sharing the love."

Ace made sure to find and thank some friends he made over the last few years. Slider was there—he welcomed Ace and gave him much-needed reassurance. "Ace, you're looking gaunt. I mean you look like a real bad-boy racer. I don't know how you did it because you were always thin, but it looks like you've lost a few pounds and gained a little in the muscle category. You must have followed my advice and stayed away from Momma's brownies. Good to see you, man." They shook hands and Ace moved on, thinking, *Brownies. You can't enjoy them until they are thoroughly baked.* He remembered the illustration from Doc Mentor: trials, like the oven, made for good character. His mind played the tape recording in his head: *So let the trials continue until the character desired is fully formed.* He pondered the possibility...*Could brownies be a part of the spiritual metaphor for athletes?*

Next, Ace saw a friend, none

> ### LIKE A TITLE OF NOBILITY
>
> *When you cross the finish line, your identity changes. It's like the king dubs you a knight, except you become forever an Ironman.*

other than Mr. Reasonable, who was working the first-aid station where they were offering pre-race massages, water, advice, and a training video running on the big screen. It reminded all the runners to properly hydrate during tomorrow's race and be mindful of symptoms to look for if you weren't feeling well, including the remedy for it. Safety, safety, safety: preventative safety was the theme of the first-aid tent.

Ace and Reasonable saw each other at work each week, but the relationship had been redefined. Ace once thought of Reasonable as a great friend. Now he was more of a work colleague, but it was nice to reunite with him in a social context. Reasonable smiled ear to ear as he said, "Look at you, future Ironman! You know you earn that title of nobility. When you cross that finish line, at that moment your identity changes. It's like the king dubs you a knight, except you become 'Ironman Ace.' At least for a day! Enjoy it while it lasts!"

It was a sincere compliment with a tender jab of sarcasm. Because of their previous conversations, Ace knew Reasonable didn't think it was logical to trade a year of training for the glory of a one-day victory, but Ace knew his friend only considered the physical dimension of this race. The glory would indeed only last for a day, but the spiritual dimension is what mattered most. He was truly a different man than he had been a year ago—he had morphed and knew it. Reasonable could sense it as well.

Ace took the moment to thank him profusely. "You know you started all this—you're the one who roped me into volunteering. What was that—three years ago? I suppose I owe it all to you. Without your invitation to volunteer, I suppose I'd still be a bum. I can't thank you enough for helping me get started on the greatest journey ever." The two of them shook hands and Ace continued through the expo tents.

Ace was looking for Buddy. They had not hung out together for Saturday basketball in several weeks. It seemed the relationship had changed and Ace felt like he was the culprit. Lately, he had used his spare time to train and hang out with Charity, so Buddy had somewhat disappeared. Ace had called him the day before to verify their meeting, and he said he would be here, but he saw no sign of Buddy yet.

Ace continued to meander through the expo when he ran into Chairman, who recognized Ace from his picture on the charity application. "Hi, Ace. Allow me to introduce myself. I know you don't know me, but we spoke on the phone over two months ago. I recognize you from the photo you sent. I'm Chairman, from the Big Race charity committee. I trust you got my check in the mail. I got that progress report you sent out. That was very exciting. So can you tell me where you're at in your charity fundraising as of today? That was such a fascinating idea!"

"Well, it turns out that it struck a nerve with a lot of Vietnam veterans, including my dad and a lot of his war buddies, so we've had an amazing response. So far, we've raised exactly $6,832. So we are close to our goal with two days to go. We still need $3,168."

Chairman was so inspired by the progress report he decided to give more, "The Lord has been very good to me this year, so count me in for another $500." Ace stood there dumbfounded for a second before he could express his appreciation. It was clear God was truly providing for this church in miraculous ways.

Later that night, Ace made his blog entry.

The Big Race is almost here. Soon I will be at the starting gate. So let me share a progress report on the fundraising. We've raised $7,332 so far with two days to go. Thanks! That's a miracle in and of itself. Believe it or not, we already made the first installment towards the construction six weeks ago (see the progress report picture attached). I want you to think of it this way: you're not helping me finish the race; you're helping this congregation finish their church building. Now that is cool and something to get excited about!

Wisbit tip: *Faith is discerning what God is doing and then joining Him.*

Wisbit tip: *Two are better than one. If one falls down, he has a friend to help him back up. But woe to him who falls alone.*

Wisbit tip: *You can change a lot in one year. Or you can stay exactly the same. The choice is yours.*

Wisbit tip: *Brownies remind me that life's trials only make you sweeter.*

QUESTIONS FOR SELF-REFLECTION

- Have I ever considered adopting a charity to support with my muscles, my money, and my mind?
- When was the last time I stopped to recognize and celebrate all the progress I have made?
- What signs does God use to communicate to me that He exists, is watching, and cares for me?
- Are you an athlete? Why not make it a goal to run a race and build a church next year?

24

CHAMPION'S A PROPHET

ACE COULD PUSH replay on the FCA breakfast from the previous year, except for one major difference: this year, Ace wasn't Vantex; he was nobility. And he knew many more people. His coaches and a lot of triathletes from the YMCA attended with their families. Ace saw Charity in the distance; she sat next to Remnant, as could be expected (she worked for him) and she saved the opposite seat for Ace as planned the night before.

Before he could make it to his seat, Ace began to connect with friends. It felt like a family reunion—even Doc Mentor had returned. There were plenty of high-fives, hugs, and backslapping to go around.

When he finally got to his table and took a seat, Ace had a surprise waiting for him. Remnant handed him an envelope and said, "I want to be a part of the miracle of building that church in Vietnam. Charity has been your greatest advocate. I assure you it was an easy sell, but you should know you have a winner on your team with Charity. I think everybody at the YMCA knows her and knows what you're doing together."

Charity blushed. Ace smiled, then nodded in agreement and thanked him. Before he could say anything else, the program began. Champion was introduced to a standing ovation once again.

"Who will win tomorrow's race?" Champion began with his raspy old voice, further marked by his slow-tempoed, powerful delivery. "That is the question everyone wants the answer to. I am a prophet and already know who will win tomorrow's race. All 2,000 racers will stand on the beach together ready to hear the starting gun. No staggered start tomorrow, as with the qualifying races. It's the greatest ultra-endurance race of the modern era. So who wins? And how can I claim to really know the answer?"

Champion paused to emphasize his point. "The outcome has already been decided. Tomorrow will only reveal the winner like the lifting of a veil. You see, the race was determined during the period we know as preparation. The winner will be called up on an awards platform. The gold medal, along with the crowning wreath, will be given to the individual who kept their personal integrity when no one else was watching. That individual, in the privacy of their daily routines, carried out personal disciplines. The winner, as Scripture foretold, will be the one who has been 'temperate in all things.' Paul writes: 'Do you not know that in a race all the runners run, but only one receives the prize? You should run in such a way so as to receive the prize, for everyone who is a champion is temperate in all things.'

"There is a lesson for life here you simply must understand. The truly great achievements of life are accomplished by self-discipline. Winning the race tomorrow was accomplished by self-control. The Scriptures tell us that a man with self-control is greater than a man who conquers a city. So how does one gain this power of self-control? Paul writes to Timothy that, 'God has not given us a spirit of timidity, but of power, love and self-control.' The Greek word for power here is *dunamis*, from where we get 'dynamite.' The idea here is that the Holy Spirit is full of divine power to bring about radical transformation. We are talking about major influence directed, governed and motivated by love.

"Look at the story of Adam and Eve and their fall from grace. When they ate from the forbidden tree, one of the effects was that men and women forfeited a large measure of self-control. The gospel of the coming of the kingdom of God with the indwelling power of the Holy Spirit is the power for self-control in the life of the believer. The Spirit of God brings the potential for the full measure of self-control to be manifested through that new life.

"If you heard me speak before, you know I love to preach on the spiritual metaphors for athletes found in the Bible. There you have it—point number one: As a runner must prepare with self-control to be ready for the race, so to the man or woman of faith must also be committed to self-discipline and preparation. The racer disciplines his body; he is careful what he eats, he makes himself work out against his desire to take the easy path. The Christian also uses self-control. He insists on a daily intake of the Scriptures. It's like food for the soul. He commits to righteousness even at the cost of passing on worldly pleasures. This kind of self-control is made possible by none other than the grace of God. You see the metaphor! Anything that's important is rehearsed. The greater the value, the greater the preparation.

"Next is the metaphor of focus. Nothing extraneous is allowed. Paul writes, 'I am not like a man who runs aimlessly, but rather with every step marked with purpose. I run straight for the goal line.'

> ## THE RACE IS WON BEFORE THE EVENT!
>
> *The individual who in the privacy and secrecy of their day-to-day life carried out self-discipline will be revealed on race day and crowned victorious.*

> ## ANY ACTIVITY THAT'S VALUABLE IS REHEARSED.
>
> *90-99% preparation 1-10% execution The greater the importance, the greater the amount of preparation. You must cultivate a heart for preparation.*

"Focus requires the elimination of all extra baggage. Listen to what the writer of Hebrews says: 'Let us lay aside every weight, and the sin which does so easily beset us, and let us run with patience the race that is set before us.' Can you believe how this book is filled with the spiritual metaphor for athletes? What he is saying here is before you run the race, you take off the warm-up suit. In fact, you dress down to a bare minimum. You can't afford to pack anything extra. Every consideration is given to what is necessary and what can be eliminated, for it could mean the difference between winning and losing.

"I know guys who have spent a lot of money to purchase a bike with one thing in mind: the reduction of the number of ounces it weighs. They are fully convinced of this truth—the elimination of every weight that can hinder. So it is with the believer—we are to do a radical inventory of our lives, inspecting every detail, inside and out, to remove sin in all its various forms. We will give an account of every thought, word, deed, attitude and motive. We are instructed not to make room for any of the hidden sins of lust in the heart, removing unforgiveness from our hearts and hatred from our souls.

"Yes, the spiritual metaphor even speaks to the attitude. Let me illustrate: A world-class endurance runner has two fears he must constantly balance to maximize his effort and improve his time. The first fear is that he will expend too much energy at the beginning of the race and not be able to finish. The second fear is that he will finish the race with excess fuel in the tank.[23] The ultimate goal is to cross the finish line at the exact moment his energy expires. Maximum effort released. Nobody wants to wonder after the race is over, *I think I could have done better.* Even though I'm an old man, I can still hear my junior high track coach. He'd position himself about fifty yards in front of the finish line, then he'd scream at me at

---

23   49 Secrets of Power for Living; Chapter 24: "Choose the Narrow Way," page 57-58. Article: "Expend All Energy."

the top of his lungs, 'Kick it in!! Come on, Champion, sprint across the finish line. Run, for God's sake!'

"It didn't matter if I was winning or losing. Coach was there screaming for me to give my last best effort. I can say that in every race I've ever run I have sprinted across the finish line. It's my attempt to leave it all on the track, to run my body to empty and give my best effort. So what is the metaphor saying about attitude here? Do things with your whole heart. As Solomon wrote, 'Whatsoever your hand finds to do, do it with all thy might.'

"The Christian life isn't a sprint, but an endurance race. Plan for a lifetime of serving God. Wisely, give everything you've got to advance his kingdom. Don't burn out, but calculatedly plan to burn on. Halfhearted efforts have no place for the true competitor. Don't finish your life with fuel in your tank, a life of regrets, concluding with, 'I know I could have done more for God.'

"Finally, the metaphor concludes with enjoying the victory. Crowns, glorious crowns!! That's what the Scriptures teach: we race or live for a crown that will never perish, not one of those cheap wreaths that withers with time. Hear what Paul said: 'I have finished my course, I have kept my faith: henceforth there is laid up for me a crown of righteousness, which the Lord, the righteous judge, shall give me at that day.'

"Hey, folks, did you get all that? I started by saying I knew who the winner would be. I knew who would get the crown—namely, the individual who lived a life of self-discipline in the private dimensions of their daily lives.

"The spiritual crown I speak of is available to anyone willing to join the heavenly race. Jesus said, 'Strive to enter in at the straight gate.' The straight gate represents salvation through Jesus Christ. The narrow way represents a life lived by the power of the Spirit, manifesting in self-control in every dimension of a person's life. Think of the narrow way as the narrow lane in which a racer must stay. A winner is focused—he doesn't wander in and out of his lane. He is interested in the shortest route legally possible. When he stays on that path, it leads to a crowning victory." Champion paused to drive home his final point. "The spiritual metaphor is this: you must also come to God through Jesus who is the straight gate and then take great vigilance, focus, and self-control to eliminate all competing affections so you can serve God with your whole heart. That's the narrow path. And it leads to the crown of eternal life. Thank you and God bless you. See you tomorrow morning. Amen!"

CR

Ace was energized by Champion's speech. A deep, satisfying smile crossed his face. With the help of his mentors, Ace had found power to live on the narrow path more each day. It felt good to be reminded of the spiritual metaphor. The pursuit of this was one of the real reasons he had started the race.

Now that the presentation was over, Domestique was making a beeline for Ace. "Good morning, mate. I've got a bit of jolly good news for you. Fancy this, your aqua fin is in my trunk. I picked it up from Dr. Goodfellow's lab late last night. He wasn't sure he'd be able to finish it by race day, but he got it done! And I'd say, he's taking the biscuit on this one."

"Domestique, I thought we agreed to call the whole thing off."

"Oh, I assure you, mate, when you discovered you weren't going to race I called the doctor and canceled the urgency, but when you were awarded a charity spot, I called him back. No promises were made, but he finished it. I'm telling you, this thing is brilliant! It looks like a frog leg. You'll be a new sort of super hero, the amphibious frog man."[24]

Ace was stunned and overwhelmed. "I know I'm supposed to say thanks, but I don't have the money for something like this."

"No problem, mate! He worked the whole thing out with the VA.

---

24   Creation and artistic rendering by Don Smith, Prosthetic Consultant.

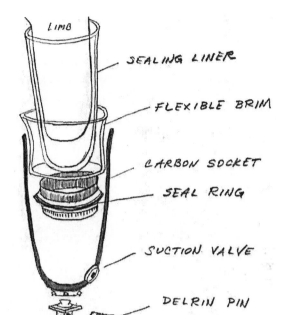

LIMB

SEALING LINER

FLEXIBLE BRIM

CARBON SOCKET

SEAL RING

SUCTION VALVE

DELRIN PIN

FERRIER COUPLER

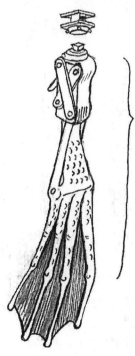

POLYCENTRIC

FROG FIN

He did all the paperwork, and Uncle Sam took care of this one. You are the government-sponsored frog man."

Ace smiled, chuckled, and felt his throat constrict with emotion. You could say that the new frog man had a frog in his throat. "Thank you," was all he could mumble in return.

Domestique suggested, "Come on, let's get out of here and swing by the 'Y' and give this thing a test drive."

Ace looked at him with a twinkle in his eye. "You mean a test *swim*, don't you?"

"Whatever, man!"

Just before bedtime, Ace wrote his last blog post before the race.

We are getting closer day by day. With twenty-four hours to go, we've raised $7,300. Your generosity has greatly encouraged me. Tomorrow I hope to make you proud. If you've never been to the Big Race, come out to the college campus, down by the water, right near the stadium entrance. That's where most of the action is. The race starts at 7:00 A.M. Whether you make it or not, thanks so much for your support throughout this year. I can't say thank you enough.

Late breaking news: I got a specially-designed prosthetic frog leg. Seriously, it arrived today. It's cool—they'll be writing a comic book about me soon: "The Amazing Amphibian Man." Anyway, it should help me kick some butt tomorrow.

P.S. The Wisbit tips today came from Champion's message this morning: The Spiritual Metaphor.

Wisbit tip: *Daily habitual self-discipline is the key to becoming a champion.*

Wisbit tip: *Focus. Do one thing well. Do not allow yourself to become diluted with civilian affairs.*

Wisbit tip: *Races are won during the days of preparation.*

Wisbit tip: *You can tell how important something is by the amount of preparation given to it.*

Wisbit tip: *Crowns. God rewards those who diligently seek Him. He honors those who honor Him.*

QUESTIONS FOR SELF-REFLECTION

- Of all the characters in this story, which do I identify with most? Why?
- Which part of the spiritual athletic metaphor resonates with me?
- If destiny (the winner) is determined by habits (preparation), where are my habits directing me?
- Focus is important in the pursuit of God. What are my biggest distractions moving me off the narrow path? What can be done to either eliminate or minimize these distractions?
- Does the thought of receiving a crown in heaven for faithful service to God on earth motivate me? How so?
- Do I have regrets for a wasted life of halfhearted service toward God? What kind of mid-course correction might be in order for me to finish strong?

25

THE BIG RACE ARRIVES

AT 4:30 A.M. the alarm was going off in Ace's apartment. He set the clock so he'd have to get out of bed to turn it off. Only that meant hopping on one leg while his whole body was still mostly asleep. Ace lost his sense of balance but caught himself on the dresser and slammed the alarm button off with a swat of his hand. It had been a deep sleep and now he was almost annoyed. Morning routine for Ace usually meant a lot of hopping around; his apartment had been modified with a number of holding bars in the most obvious places: bathroom, shower, and wardrobe. When it was time to get dressed, Ace attached his prosthetic leg. Like putting on a sock, he'd put on his gel sleeve, slide his limb into the socket, close the air valve which created suction, securing the leg in place. More often than not, his shoe stayed attached to the leg. Now he was ready to get on the road.

When Ace pulled his car into the university parking lot, the beach area had become a series of temporary tents marking command central for the Big Race. He noticed the car parked opposite him had the same 222 sticker. He wondered if Markist was here, but Markist had already wished him well on his Facebook page and sent regrets he wouldn't be there. He was with his church in Germany on a mission trip, training pastors to make disciples who make disciples. Ace concluded it was somebody with whom Markist interacted. He wondered who it might be.

Ace grabbed his things and went to check in and collect his timing chip before he set up his transition station. That's where he saw Buddy. Last year they were side by side serving the nobility, handing out the timing chips and making sure everyone got the right number. Today, Buddy was at the end of the assembly line, handing out race backpacks with lots of goodies inside—everything but the T-shirts because those had to be earned. They had "Ironman Finisher" printed on them. Only race finishers received the T-shirt.

Buddy handed a backpack to Ace and the two men paused to talk. Ace piped up first, "How ya doin', man? I missed you yesterday, I was looking for you. Good to see you now." They embraced in a man hug and Ace continued. "It seems like our paths haven't crossed much lately."

Buddy was quick to reply. "That's because of two things. First: I got a dog, Goldie; and second: because I got a dog! Which was exactly the chick magnet I hoped she'd be! I met a girl—I'm dating now."

Ace replied with great enthusiasm, "You *are* the man! What's her name? Do I know her?"

"Nope, you don't know her. Her name is Gloria, and she's a good one, for real. She's five-feet ten-inches tall and loves dogs. She's even got me back in church. No kidding! The first date she ever let me take her on was to Sunday service."

"Sweet! You always said you'd dump me when you found a girl! And I was about to apologize to you because I haven't called you lately for the same reason. I got a girl I've been seeing. I mentioned her to you before—Charity from my spin class. And she works at the church, so I'm back in God's house on Sundays as well. And that turns out to be one of the best things that's happened to me."

Buddy stopped him. "Then we'll have to make a double-date—church followed by brunch. We've got to get these girls introduced.

But, seriously, it's great to see you." And then Buddy paused with a smirk on his face as he glanced at Ace from head to toe. "Look at you! YOU are the man! A year ago, we worked this thing together; now you're nobility. You are a freaking Ironman. You look like your old high school days. Man, I'm telling you, you've really slimmed up, tightened up, buffed up, and look great. How did you do it?"

Ace thought a little before replying. "Coaches and mentors, that's how! I got the best coaches in town. They gave me a plan, helped me prepare, and held me accountable. Listen, I decided to chase my dreams, and because I couldn't trust myself to get there on my own, I recruited coaches. I don't know how everybody else got here, but contrary to what many say that this race is for the individual, I can testify that this race is prepared for in community. Coaches help you go further, faster. That's how I'm here today."

Buddy shook his head in disbelief as he declared slowly and dramatically as they parted, "Ace, the man of iron!" Ace's chin buckled as he gave his wiry grin, "I will be an Ironman before the day is over!" Ace waved goodbye as he headed for the transition area to arrange his things.

◌ᴙ

Once his station was systematically laid out and prepared in the most efficient way possible, he removed his running leg by way of the ferrier coupling and placed it in order. The Great Oz was a genius—this removal was quick. Now he grabbed his new prosthetic frog leg and snapped it into place, and with the help of his crutches he navigated to the designated meeting spot at the back of the podium which held the U.S. flag.

The beach was filled with racers lined up wearing bathing caps. Then there were the spectators, the fans, families, and small teams organized in support. Charity was there with a sign she had made promoting their cause: Kingdom Builders Athletic Team, with a byline of Run a Race, Build a Church. It matched his new race day uniform. He was looking officially well put together, and while he was only one racer for the cause this day, he had a team of enthusiastic supporters coming throughout the day.

It seemed to Ace that everybody was here. His coaches were in the race; they would be his competitors. There were also the familiar faces from the previous two races. Now, Ace stood with Charity and Domestique discussing the race strategy, the new frog leg, and what it would mean to navigate in and out of the water and through transition.

Although it was already attached, Ace was still hesitant to use the frog leg. He felt a little uneasy and voiced his concerns. "I feel like I was supposed to learn a lesson from the last two races—namely, never introduce anything new on race day. Nothing but disaster comes of it, and yet here I am doing it again. I fear more zig in my already zigzag propensity."

Domestique offered a suggestion. "Listen, mate, you know the rules. There is no drafting on the bike, but a solid strategy is to draft on the swim. I assure you it's legal and it's smart, and I know you've had trouble swimming straight. What I want you to do is get right behind me. I will literally cut the way. If you stay on my toes, you'll benefit from my wake. I've got a strong kick, so follow my bubbles. I'll take a comfortable wide outside angle on the buoys, and we can avoid the traffic jam. I know the pace you'll need to complete the full 2.4 miles. Here's the plan: I literally want you to stroke into my toes about every minute, so I'll know you're there. I don't want to leave you. If we get separated, pull up and we'll look for each other. Who knows? Perhaps with this frog leg, you'll be cracking and I'll let **you** lead the way."

The two chuckled. Ace was afraid he wouldn't be able to keep up. Domestique was clearly one of the fastest swimmers in this race; he wasn't the swim instructor for nothing.

Ace was concerned, "I don't want to slow you down. You go on without me. I'm a big boy. You know the unspoken rule: every man for himself. This is also your race. Do your best; you've trained for it. I'll be fine."

Domestique's tone was firm and yet remained respectful, "Listen up mate. We swim together. I need to protect my investment. After the swim transition, you're on your own. But during the swim, I insist you stay right behind me. If I'm swimming too fast, touch my toes with two consecutive strokes. There'll be no blasted arguing. That's the way we're doing it!"

Domestique could be forceful as a coach when he needed to be. Beyond his college swim credentials, he was a retired British military SAS soldier (equivalent to American SEAL Team Six). Ace could hear in his voice that he was serious. Ace got out a "Yes, sir." It felt like an order from his commanding officer.

"All right then, frogman, let's own this race." They exchanged a fist bump of agreement.

Charity then reviewed her strategy. "Here's the plan: I'll take care of your crutches, and I'll meet you on the beach at the water exit, help you to transition, and take care of that new frog leg. We don't want that thing lying around.

"Now, let me put my marketing manager hat on and give you some tips. Throughout the day, look for your support team cheering for you. We'll be scattered all over the place. Your part is to acknowledge them. Don't be so focused that you pass them by. These people are your donors. They own stock in you—or at least in your cause. They are funding your church, so show them some love. Wave to them, call out their names as you pass by, and thank them whenever you get a chance."

"If you do this right, Ace, our donations will increase. Right now we are sitting on $7,300. Our goal is $10,000. I realize we will likely get a few donations later on, but today is huge. I'm going to give you more publicity today than your supporters have seen in the last two months. We are going to talk about racing for your Vietnamese church all day. I've got people following you on social media: Facebook, instant message, Instagram, Twitter, and Snapchat. Today you are a celebrity, so make me proud. Now, how about a picture to get things started right with your pretty new leg? Stand right here. Love that sunrise! This is a great opening shot, with the sun just above your head. Hold still and smile," Charity instructed as she snapped a few pictures with her cell phone.

"Yep! I'm posting this with the caption 'Frogman takes on the Big Race to build church in Vietnam. Stay tuned—more to come.'"

Ace obeyed his marketer's orders, but Charity had become more than a marketer over the last several months. He stole the moment from her and said, "That's enough pictures from my marketer, at least for the moment. How about you…" Ace motioned to Domestique, who was nearby, "take a picture of me and my girlfriend." Then he motioned to Charity. "Come on, get over here." She smiled warmly as she sidled up next to him. This was the first time Ace had referred to Charity that way. They put their arms around each other's waists and Domestique instructed, "Say cheese," and snapped their picture.

Ace turned Charity towards himself and gave her a brief but poignant girlfriend squeeze. He looked her in the eye and said "Thanks for everything. No matter what happens today, you've helped to make it the best day of my life. I can never thank you enough."

"My pleasure," Charity replied with an almost giddy smile.

Next to join the small gathering was Bruiser. He had been looking for his star student, but something was off. Bruiser looked very ordinary—no swim cap, goggles or swim suit. He wore casual shorts and a volunteer T-shirt.

Bruiser spoke first. "I heard a rumor…" then hinted with a jerk of his head that Domestique had leaked the info, "that there was a frogman in this year's race." Bruiser stared at Ace's leg and nodded his head with approval. "Nice look! I like that translucent light green color. Very…froggish. I'm glad that mad scientist found a way to benefit humans as well as dolphins. That thing is really cool."

Ace had an observation of his own that needed answering. "So what's up with the volunteer shirt? I thought you were racing! What happened?"

"Since this race is on nationwide news, they wanted someone distinguished, such as myself, to provide the commentary. Since they felt obligated to pay me, I felt obliged to accept. That's what happens to you when you get older—they put you out to pasture. Those of us who are too frail to race get paid to talk about it."

Ace returned Bruiser's sarcasm with a little of his own. "Frail old man that you are, I almost forgot you're almost sixty and your body is all worn out...but it does sound like they went right to the top of the list to get the most qualified commentator. Congratulations! That means one less person for me to finish behind!"

Spinsey and Cheetah joined the growing circle of people. The conversation changed once they were in the presence of a true celebrity—last year's winner. Bruiser and Cheetah had come to know each other through a fraternity of champions which met each year the day before the Big Race.

Bruiser addressed the champ first. "So you're going for back-to-back titles today? You know that hasn't been done for almost twenty-five years, when Steady Eddie got three consecutive titles, with no repeats since then. I think you can do it. You know steady Eddie was an old man at thirty-three, thirty-four, and thirty-five. You got your first at twenty-eight. The future is bright for you. Just be glad I'm not racing today. Otherwise, I'd have to spoil your plans. I don't think there is anyone else here who can beat you."

"Thanks for the encouragement," Cheetah replied. "I heard they turned you into a sports analyst for the day when they found out you were available. I don't know what to say. I was going to tell you I'll be waiting for you at the finish line, but it seems like you'll actually be waiting for me! Just have the camera ready early, because when I break the tape, it's going to be a new course record."

Marshall's voice was heard over the loudspeaker: "Your attention please. Please stand for the national anthem." The American flag was flying high on the beach near the podium. Afterwards, Marshall declared, "Ten minutes to starting time." Then he quickly reviewed the rules and safety precautions.

Capturing the moment, Bruiser suggested they pray, and the small band formed a circle and put their arms around each other's waists. Bruiser then led the group in the Lord's Prayer. When they were finished, everyone said together, "Amen."

When Ace looked up from bowing his head, he saw Marshall walking by. Ace took the opportunity to share his concern about the legality of using his frog leg. Marshall spoke with a bit of surprise, "I didn't expect to see you racing today. What's the story?" Ace replied, "Well, believe it or not, I'm running for charity."

"Sweet! I'm happy for you. It looks like everything worked out in the end."

"Yeah, I suppose so. Anyway, I wanted to make double sure I'm legal. I read the rules, and it sounds like I'm abiding, but it's not completely clear. They don't say much about a situation like this. So, I know it's last second, but I wanted to make sure I was authorized to race with this swim prosthetic. Marshall was amused. "First time I've seen anything like that, but I want you to know I approve it, exclusively for this race. And as the rules indicate for all physically challenged athletes, I give you carte blanche to both give and receive help from anyone in the race and also from any volunteer assistance from without the race. Now get 'er done. Just stay on course." And with that he gave Ace a wink as he continued his walk to the starting gate. He would shortly fire the starting gun shot.

ℭℜ

The tension was mounting at the starting line. The nobility stood, eager for the gun, all 2,000 of them. This was a beach start, which meant the athletes would run into the water to begin the swim.

Among this year's field of competitors were a few notable and unusual runners. Among the elite racers was Speedy G., a new face with great aspirations; and Victor, a long-time pro who had won many triathlons, was taking on the Big City Big Race for the first time.

Up until the singing of the national anthem, Tanga had commanded most of the attention from the press. The gorgeous rising star had reveled in the pre-race limelight. It turned out to be a miniature live-action photo shoot for her. She was happy to oblige.

While Tanga had the attention of the photographers, Nowattie Nowie was clearly the biggest conversation piece among the race analysts. Earlier in the year he had set a new world record for the marathon. This Kenyan distance runner had recently turned his attention to conquer a new frontier: The Big Race Triathlon.

Brian Fieri, last year's runner-up only by a single step, could be

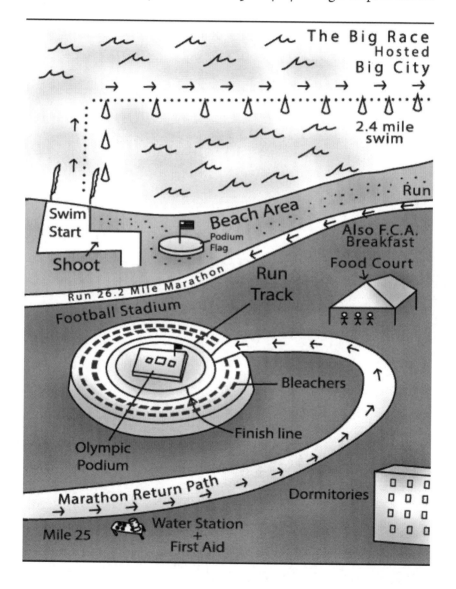

seen standing alone. He looked extremely serious, with a noticeable intensity in his eyes. He promised himself this year would end differently.

To the side of the main throng of swimmers stood Gizmo, who had a few new gadgets to help him towards his goal of a personal record. There was Tenderfoot, whom Ace had sized up as his chief

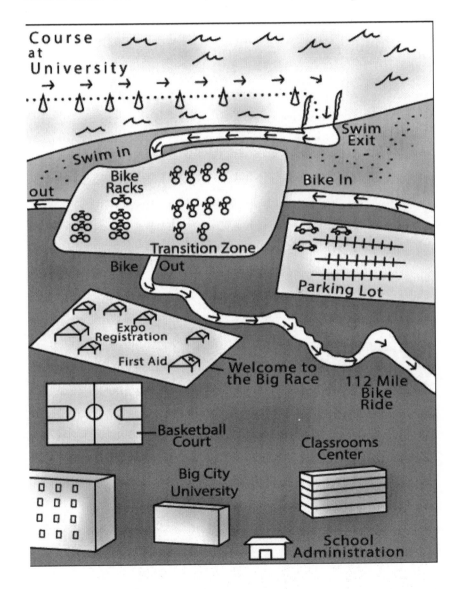

competition among the charity runners. He also saw Fehniecair, the other charity racer that had a better qualifying time than him. Ace wondered how this senior would do.

E.Z., Sloppy Joe, Shorty Cutler, and Walkie Talkie had been recruited by Charity to cheer, wear the team shirts, and support Ace. They stood to the side of the crowd of competitors. They successfully got Ace's attention by waving and holding a sign. Ace took Charity's advice and shouted out to them in recognition. He waved, smiled, and felt energized.

E.Z. was dressed in complete regalia: straw hat and sunglasses completed his stylish island look. The Kingdom Builder T-shirt was worn under his unbuttoned island silk top, with some classy navy shorts and a pair of sandals. He and the rest of the gang were proud of Ace. They began to boast among themselves. E.Z. began by saying, "You know, I taught that young man how to swim."

Sloppy Joe added, "I remember the first day he arrived, greener than green. I got him properly launched into training on a stationary bike."

Walkie-Talkie chimed in. "You know, to finish a race like this, it's all about pacing—not too fast and not too slow. I taught the boy everything I know about planning to go the distance."

The conversation returned to E.Z. "Guys, I think we can all be proud. He is definitely one of us. The 6:30 gang will be well-represented by Ace today." Then they made their way towards Charity and Bruiser, who pulled away from the pressing mob of racers to watch the start.

E.Z. commented to Charity, "Great job helping our boy out, and thanks for inviting us to take the morning shift. I love the design of these T-shirts."

CR

BANG! Another Big Race had begun. Charity gave an encouraging shout. "Let's go Ace, you got this!" She turned to the gang. "We are now officially racing toward *our* finish line. I've got twelve to fourteen hours to finish building our church."

E.Z. asked how close they were to reaching the goal. Charity replied "We still need $2,700 to fully fund the church."

E.Z. said (loud enough for the gang to hear), "I speak for the gang when I say we are each good for another $100." E.Z. was smooth as he committed his buddies. They rolled their eyes but agreed to it. Bruiser chimed in. "Me too."

"You got it." Charity said. "You guys are awesome." Then she roared, "Let's go, Ace!"

Speedy G. had taken great care in planning for this year's Big Race since it was his first. He was a local young man with a big plan. He could swim like a fish.

Speedy G. wanted a little notoriety with this race and had planned carefully how to get it. He pushed his way to the very front of the throng of racers before the gun was fired.

Speedy G. dove into the water ahead of everyone, including Cheetah. He sprinted like there was no tomorrow and led the entire swim. Cheetah couldn't believe it. He was always the fastest at everything. He started the swim in first place last year and never saw another racer until the finish line.

Ace and Domestique took the outer edge around the buoy, avoiding the traffic jam at the turn. Ace kept his head down and his eyes on Domestique's feet. Amazingly, they were among the front of the competition. Ace thought, *This must be like a school of fish swimming in synchronized movement.* While he knew he was swimming faster than ever, he also knew he had a long way to go. This was no short swim—2.4 miles.

Ace began to get his mind in the right place during the swim. Doc's challenge was to occupy his mind with prayer, meditation, and rehearsal of memorized Scripture. Ace had learned to do this during swim practice. Now he went through the alphabet. The first time through, he focused on the names of God. A: Alpha and

Omega, Anointed One, Author and Finisher of his faith, Adoni; B: Beginning and the end...the next time through he thought of the character traits of God. A: awesome, Almighty...B: beautiful...he was lost in pleasant meditation. He was in the zone, and the swim was almost over.

Speedy G. caused Cheetah to swim faster than ever over this distance. It was a grueling pace to start this ultra-endurance race. Yet Cheetah kept Speedy G. in his sights, determined to stay close to him. He didn't know who Speedy G. was, but the longer they swam, the longer he wondered how this man was able to keep up the pace. He thought, *He must be a formidable foe, indeed.* Cheetah never caught the fast swimmer.

Speedy G. accomplished his goal. As planned, his girlfriend Pixie took a photo to prove he had been in the lead at the end of the swim, a one-third winner. He was a hero. Speedy G. was at the front of the greatest race in the world when he left the water. Cheetah was only a minute-and-a-half behind. Speedy G. was gassed. He had spent everything he had sprinting in the swim and had no intention of maintaining this pace on the bike.

Just like that, the rest of the pack began to land beachside. Victor could see Cheetah ahead of him. Shortly after, the first female appeared out of the water. Tanga was known to be a great swimmer and runner. She was faced with the challenge of keeping her lead against a strong field of women she feared could pass her as cyclists, as had been the case in previous races. She felt certain this year would be different.

Domestique and Ace exited the water several minutes later, ahead of almost everyone. They discovered later they were actually 344 and 345, the top twenty percent of all racers at the swim exit. Charity went into action as they left the water. Ace was dizzy and hopping on one leg trying to protect the frog leg. Domestique was under one arm and Charity was under the other. The three of them ran into transition as Ace bounced along, swinging his good leg, hopping between his human crutches. Bruiser furiously snapped pictures as the 6:30 gang cheered.

Charity encouraged Ace: "Awesome job! You are way ahead of schedule, so be careful with your pace because you've got a long way to go. And by the way, we raised $600 during your swim, so we just need $2,100 more. The 6:30 gang pitched in $400, Bruiser sprung for another $100, and that cool picture with your frog leg I posted on Facebook spawned $100 from your great aunt."

Charity talked fast while giving him the update. "Hang in there, you've got ten hours to go." As Ace entered into transition, the sight of Spinsey caught his eye. She was exiting out of transition one and biking away. Ace thought, *I really did swim fast. She is less than three minutes ahead of me.*

At the front of this race was a series of world-class athletes. While Speedy G. had been the first one to mount his bike, Cheetah caught and passed him within the first ten minutes. Others were not far behind. Victor had Cheetah in his sight, and Fieri was only a few seconds behind. Speedy G. tired quickly, dropped the pace, and was passed by packs of bikers with no intention of slowing down. No one knows how much farther Speedy G. rode. He never finished the race. Speedy G. did, however, speed along to his next priority of getting his photos processed in time for his friend's party the next day.

True to his word, Domestique left Ace to fend for himself after he had helped him reach his transition station. He knew Ace didn't want his sympathy or his help. Charity was right there, mostly looking on as Ace removed the frog leg to replace it with his mechanical bike cleat. Although the ferrier coupling helped, overall it was comparatively slow work. Ace, as did most of the athletes, wore a wetsuit. There was just no easy way to get it off with only one leg to stand on. Hopping and sitting slowed him down, while it seemed others zipped through transition more quickly. Even getting on the bike was a challenge. The cleat prosthetic couldn't be attached to the bike until he'd cleared the transition zone.

Ace figured it took him about two minutes longer than everyone else to get through transition one, referred to as T1. At this stage in the race, that meant about fifty people already passed him. However, he took pleasure in finally exiting T1 on his bike, because he saw Tenderfoot and Fehniecair just entering the transition area. He was ahead of his two main competitors by two to three minutes, and the bike was his strength. He was determined that there was no way either of them would catch up on this segment of the race. Ace was on his way to a grueling 112-mile bike ride.

Tenderfoot was a great swimmer and runner. The bike was always the challenging part of the race for her. To her credit, Tenderfoot was in top physical condition; her training had been calculated. She had rehearsed her transition routine to be efficient and effective. She was much faster at this than almost all of her competitors. Her things were laid out in impeccable order and arranged so no motion was lost or repeated. While Ace was passed by nearly fifty athletes during transition, she had passed almost twenty competitors with her focused, skillful navigation through the zone.

Gizmo had a different strategy as he entered T1. He was focused on achieving a new personal record. He was an avid reader, always looking to find any angle to give him an edge. First, there was the personal trainer—form and technique were the keys to increasing speed. Then there was the careful planning of diet and carb-loading for maximum performance. He'd owned seven different bikes over the last ten years. He was constantly on the lookout for anything that could give him a competitive edge. If it was new, given a little bit of press attention and credibility from a winner's endorsement, it had been tried by Gizmo.

Today he was taking special pills that would help keep fluids in him by slowing down the sweating process. The net result: he would reduce his time with fewer stops for hydration.

Shortly after Ace started his bike ride, he discovered those who swam fast were also the ones who biked fast. He wasn't passing anyone. In fact, he was being passed. Ace started counting again. For the first twenty miles, more than 200 cyclists passed him. Ace became discouraged. He had passed no one. He thought he was fast on the bike, but fast is a relative term. He had simply done too well on the swim. He was ahead of many world-class racers simply by following Domestique. Now the world-class cyclists blew by him.

Then Ace saw an amazing sight: a peloton. A group of cyclists had formed into a band of bikers. He wasn't certain if this was something they had conspired to do or if it had just evolved. He saw two of his old riding buddies in the middle of them—Ray Boltz and Jack Rabbit. He looked for Spinsey, but she was not a part of it. Then he remembered she was much farther ahead. Ray Boltz cried out to him as the peloton passed, "Come on, Ace! Join us; why don't you jump on?"

Ace was tired of being passed. He knew the value of riding in the peloton: speed, efficiency, and effectiveness. Others were doing it. Didn't they know there were penalties to be assessed? The rules were clear. This was not a DQ, but a two-minute violation if caught. It wasn't a hard decision. Ace entertained the invitation for about three seconds, but he had learned his lesson. It doesn't matter what others did, and it doesn't even matter if you get caught or not. It was simply a matter of personal integrity.

Ace hollered back, "Not today. Three bike lengths." That's all he could get out, and then they were gone. Ace wanted to go faster, but at mile twenty, he had already settled into his niche twenty-two mile-per-hour average speed. Sometime after the peloton incident, Faith was preparing to edge her way around Ace. First she pulled up behind Ace and began to talk to him. He was glad to see her.

"Hey, Ace! How are you feeling?"

"Well...I wish I was going a little faster, but I'm all right. How are you?"

"Nice day for a bike ride, wouldn't you say? Blue sky, a few clouds, no rain, no wind...it's as good as it gets."

Ace was feeling grateful. "I agree. Just think how much time we've spent training for this. I've got to give some credit to Charity."

"Oh, yeah, she's one of my all-time favorites. She's like a little sister to me. She told me what she's doing for you—the church in Vietnam initiative is brilliant. And since we're talking about it, I must say I love that awesome-looking uniform you're wearing." She read the back of his jersey: 'Kingdom Builders Athletic Team, Race for the Nations.' Nice!"

Ace forgot he was a swimming, biking and running billboard. Faith continued, "How's the fundraising coming? Last I heard you were doing really well: $2,700 or so to finish it."

"As of one hour ago, we were just short $2,100."

"I didn't get a chance to tell Charity yet, but count me in for $200."

Ace smiled and said, "Well, praise God. Thank you."

Then Faith passed in front of Ace, completing the regulation maneuver. She was only going twenty-two-and-a-half miles-per-hour, so Ace was inspired to speed up and keep her in his sight, three lengths behind. They paced together for most of the remainder of the ride.

An hour into the bike race, Gizmo felt the strong need to alleviate the discomfort of a full bladder. As the hours passed, he needed to stop for more than a few bathroom breaks. Not only did Gizmo lose precious time, but his stomach was beginning to feel all twisted up inside. Finally, he got sick, but it didn't make him feel any better.

Gizmo thought, *Those stupid pills—what was I thinking? So I don't sweat, but the exchange rate is with the bladder.* This was not a good trade. Gizmo was feeling too ill to continue. He was done for the day.

26

FOLLOWING FAITH

MEANWHILE, ACE SETTLED into a groove on his bike. He rode heartily following Faith, but didn't draft. He was careful to keep the three-length distance between them. This was going to last several more hours. After hour number two, most people stopped passing him. Eventually, Ace stopped counting and remembered what he was supposed to be doing—redeeming the time. Ace had memorized the entire Sermon on the Mount over the last few months. He had developed a discipline—biking and running had become synonymous with memorizing and rehearsing Scripture. He started with the beginning of the Sermon.... "And seeing the multitudes, he went up into a mountain: and when he was set, his disciples came unto him: And he opened his mouth, and taught them, saying, Blessed are the poor in spirit: for theirs is the kingdom of heaven. Blessed are they that mourn: for they shall be comforted. Blessed are the meek: for they shall inherit the earth."

...and on he went.

Another racer moved to pass Ace and shouted, "Move over to the right!" He scolded Ace as he passed. "Slow riders keep to the right!" Then he cursed under his breath, but loud enough so Ace would hear as he passed by. "#&#* Christians!"

Ace was stunned. He wasn't sure what he had done wrong. He wasn't too far to the left or the right. He was in the middle right side of the path following the path of the biker in front of him. Then he smiled as he quoted the next verse. "Blessed are they which are persecuted for righteousness' sake: for theirs is the kingdom of heaven. Blessed are ye, when men shall revile you, and persecute you, and shall say all manner of evil against you falsely for my sake. Rejoice, and be exceeding glad: for great is your reward in heaven: for so persecuted they the prophets which were before you."

Ace kept smiling. He presumed the man must have read the back of his jersey. He thought perhaps he had just been persecuted for the name of Christ. According to the Scriptures, that meant he was blessed. He was commanded to rejoice at such a moment.

Unbelievable, he thought. The man came by and cursed him right when he was working on that verse in his mind. *God, you are right here in this race with me. You know my every thought, you know right where I am, and you see everything that's happening to me right now.* Ace was awestruck. He couldn't get over the timing, "God, you're right here. Thanks for everything." Then he started giving thanks for everything he could think of for the next fifteen minutes.

Earlier in the race, when Cheetah had passed Speedy G, he went into warp speed. He really was the fastest biker in the field and knew the only way for someone to catch him was on the run. So he was eager to widen the gap and did. Everyone knew that the bike was the critical element: 112 miles—which meant that a half-mile an hour faster than the rest of the field made a big difference over the length of the course.

When Cheetah dismounted his bike, he saw the clock. His time was faster than last year. He was on track for a new world record. He had just had the ride of a lifetime. It was a course record for the bike portion. He was so far ahead that he knew he'd be hard to catch. The distance run wasn't his greatest strength, but Cheetah felt very confident about his chance to win back-to-back world champion titles.

For the next few hours, Cheetah was all alone on the run. He didn't know how far ahead he was, but he knew the competition would be coming eventually. He knew both Fieri and Victor were better distance runners than he was, so he stayed focused as he remembered last year's finish.

Ace hadn't spoken to Faith for more than two hours, but he still chugged along right behind her. She was wearing bib number 888 and Ace thought, *222 times four, there's gotta be a God message in there somewhere.* He thought he was getting a message from God: make disciples who make disciples who make disciples, forever and ever. Now they were within twenty miles of finishing the bike portion, only to have a marathon waiting at the end of the ride. Ace had refocused on the Scriptures and decided to go aloud with his rehearsal, loud enough for Faith to hear. He called out.

"Hey, Faith! Let me give you a little encouragement: 'Don't worry about tomorrow—don't worry about what you're going to eat, what you're going to drink, or even what you're going to wear—for your Heavenly Father knows that you need these things. Consider the birds of the air, they do not plow, they do not plant seed, they do not water, they don't harvest, they don't store in barns, and yet your Heavenly Father feeds them. Remember this: that you are far more valuable to God than the birds. Therefore, don't worry about what you'll eat or wear, but rather seek first the kingdom of heaven and his righteousness and all these things will be added unto you.'"

"Thank you, Ace, you are energizing me. Scripture is food for the soul: man does not live by bread alone, but by every word that proceeds from the mouth of God."

A spontaneous volley of verses followed, with each of them taking turns quoting Scripture. This eventually led to them playing a little game of seesaw, which required less shouting. Ace passed by while quoting a verse, then Faith quickly returned the favor. Back and forth they went, and soon they approached the bike dismount zone.

Charity held a sign with the amount still needed. It said, "Help us fund our church—just $1,900 remaining." The 6:30 gang was gone but they had been replaced by Ace's friends, colleagues, and family members. The small band cheered wildly as Ace came to the bike dismount line. Charity shouted, "You're killing it! You are way ahead of your projected schedule!" She ran beside him. "Way to go! Listen. As you exit this transition to run—you have to stop. We need to pause for a photo op. Remember to love your fans. Trust me, you have a minute or two to spare."

This time in transition (T2) he was a little faster. T1 simply took longer for most athletes. There was no way around it; getting out of a wetsuit was always a wrestling match. But T2 had its challenges for Ace. It meant another change of a prosthetic leg. Now he'd be running with his blade. He discarded his helmet and gloves, wiped the sweat from his face with a towel, and threw down another set of salt tablets with a bottle of Gatorade. He swapped legs, then he was out the exit.

Ace followed his instructions. He found his cheer team, stopped long enough to hug the family and slap a few high-fives with friends, then posed for a photo while holding the sign surrounded by his squad. Ace made the correction, "It's down to just $1,700. I've been riding with and behind Faith for the last few miles, and she said she's in for $200." Charity made the change on her whiteboard before they took the picture, then posted it on the internet to the world.

Time was ticking. Ace said his goodbyes. "I've got to get going. I've got a marathon to run. Just 26.2 miles to go." He turned to leave when Charity said,

> ## TOTAL FUNDING NEEDED
>
> $10,000 *Goal: builds church*
>
> $8,300: *Funded*
>
> $1,700: *Still needed*

"Look for us at the turnaround." Ace hollered back, "I can tell you right now, it's going to be a slower pace than we thought. I'll be lucky if I finish in 5:15. I know we said four hours and thirty minutes, but that's not happening. I am spent more than I thought."

Charity ran beside him trying to finish her thoughts. "That's OK, take it easy. Whatever you do, don't give up. You ought to be gassed, and you're rocking this thing! You're ten minutes ahead on the bike and fifteen minutes ahead on the swim. Listen, don't be discouraged if you need to walk a lot. Everybody walks on this marathon…everybody—even the pros. Take the time you need. See ya in a while." And then Ace was gone.

Earlier in the afternoon, Nowattie Nowie, the current marathon champion of the world, had passed through T2. Having endured the swim and bike, he was ready for his element—the run. He felt strong, and he knew he could catch up with all of them. He felt like a runaway freight train. He began passing the rest of the field, picking them off one by one. Everyone was tired, but the marathon was just beginning. He figured correctly that 200 people were in front of him. But he was the world-record holder in the marathon: two hours, three minutes. He had researched beforehand everyone else's times. The average best among the pros was a miserable 3:45. He figured there was no way the leaders were more than an hour-and-a-half ahead of him. Even if he needed a little extra rest, he'd close the gap. He'd planned his race and things were working out as planned. His sponsor gave him the thumbs-up, and held up a sign as he exited transition: "Leader up ahead by 1:20." Nowattie shook his head in agreement and showed off his pearly white smile.

Throughout the bike and most of the marathon, Victor was in second place, in pursuit of the invisible Cheetah. He didn't know how far ahead Cheetah was; he just knew, ironically, that Cheetah was weak in the distance running. He remembered last year's finish when Fieri caught Cheetah with a hundred yards to go. He didn't win, but he caught up to him. Victor assumed he could catch Cheetah with a mile or a half-mile to go, so he ran hard with that hope. He reasoned he was ahead of Fieri, and if this race was anything like last years, he would be positioned to win.

Ace was dog tired. *When was this race going to come to the end?* He ran, he walked, he meditated, and he allowed himself to enjoy the company of several runners. He would find somebody running his pace, pull up beside them, and engage them in conversation—all the typical introductory questions. A few times, he shared his mission. A few had the courage to ask about his leg. He enjoyed the shocking moment when he declared it was the best thing that ever happened to him. He thanked God for giving him such a testimony. He had a built-in opening to talk about God and why he wasn't bitter. It had become his mark of ownership.

Somewhere in the middle of the run, Tenderfoot slowly passed Ace. As far as Ace could tell, he led all charity runners until that point. She didn't know who Ace was, but he knew her and wasn't going to let this lady pass him without a fight. It occurred to him that he should run with her, get to know her. He picked up the pace a little to match hers and began the conversation. She was easy to talk to.

Ace discovered that Tenderfoot was "super mom." The mother of three teenagers, she had regained some of her life when the oldest got his driver's license a few years ago. Since then, the chauffeur duties were divided. She was running again, a former collegiate cross-country competitor, and now a triathlete with a cause. They exchanged the charities they were running for. Then, Ace found he couldn't keep up with her. He stopped to walk at the water station while she grabbed her water and kept on running. They hollered out a "see ya later" to each other. Ace decided to keep Tenderfoot in his sight. She was ahead of him, but not too far for now. Perhaps he could catch her at the end. Maybe she'd have to walk. He kept her in his sight for a few miles, but after a while, she was gone from view.

Fehniecair, Ace's other charity competitor, had been steady in his pace. Now he was not far behind Ace. He was a man who had no lofty ideas of winning, but he was hoping to be at the top in his age group. His charity app was impressive and inspirational. Today, at age sixty-six, he was the oldest charity racer.

27

AT THE FINISH LINE

VICTOR WAS AN elite athlete; true nobility. He had been in second or third place since the beginning of the Big Race that day. Victor had won several big races in the last few years, but never competed in the Big Race–Big City Triathlon. All eyes were on him. The commentators built him up, wondering how he would do in the Big Race with the best of the best.

Fieri was not far behind; he had his own strategy: he kept Victor in his eyesight throughout the race.

With six miles to go, the course had a long, downhill, zigzag slope, which meant a long straightaway one direction with a switchback turn with a long straightaway the exact opposite direction. It created a nifty way for everyone to get a great look at the whereabouts of their competitors. When Victor entered the top of the sloped straightaway, he laid eyes on his catch. Cheetah could be seen a great distance from him, coming in his direction on the lower end of the switchback.

After several minutes, Victor came to the bottom of the slope. When he looked back he could see Fieri, last year's runner-up, only a quarter-mile behind. From the view at the bottom, Victor could see about a dozen racers who were much further back. But for the first time, he spotted Nowattie Nowie cresting the top of the zigzag.

At mile twenty-one, Nowattie had moved within striking distance of the entire field, especially at the rate he was running. He had the lead female, Tanga, in his sights, and calculated there were fewer than twelve men ahead of him.

At mile twenty-two, Nowattie Nowie first felt the pain in his right calf muscle. He couldn't believe it. Earlier in the race, he had never felt so good. He was off to a great start—feeling strong and enjoying great speed on the bike. Today he was floating. Earlier, during the bike race, he had passed on several of the water stations. He hadn't felt the need; he wasn't thirsty and didn't feel like he was sweating much on the bike. All day, he had felt great, until this moment. This sudden attack seemed so unlikely. It was a nasty, gripping cramp that took him off his feet. He fell to the ground, reeling in pain. Nowattie pulled his toes back to release the spasms. Cramps were almost always the result of insufficient hydration. Nowattie had violated the most fundamental of all the laws of racing. He had missed his fuel intakes at the scheduled times and, hours later, it caught up to him. This knot was crippling and painful. It proved to be race-ending.

At mile twenty-four, one of Victor's sponsors held up a sign that clued him in that he was within striking range. With two miles to go, Cheetah was less than a quarter-mile in front of him.

What a finish it was turning out to be! Thousands of fans were gathered at the finish line inside the stadium. The male front-runners were Cheetah and Victor, with Fieri closing in on the leaders very quickly. The female front-runner was Tanga. She had a commanding lead over all the other women. In fact, she was ahead of everybody, with the exception of twelve men.

For the last two miles, Victor had been gaining on Cheetah. Now, he could see Cheetah fewer than thirty steps ahead. Cheetah made the final turn into the stadium. It was at this point Fieri began losing ground as the others started to accelerate. He could only maintain his pace.

Inside the stadium, thousands of fans were sitting in the bleachers anticipating the final two laps. The last half-mile of this ultra-endurance race was run in front of the grandstands before they crossed the finish line. As Victor took the turn into the stadium, the crowds were already cheering loudly for Cheetah. In the first lap, Victor narrowed the lead. With one lap to go, he was fifteen steps behind Cheetah. Victor was running faster than Cheetah. The crowd could sense that he might catch the leader. The stadium rumbled with excitement.

Victor began his kick early. He stepped up the pace. Now he was only a few steps behind Cheetah. But Cheetah wasn't going down without a fight. He picked up his pace to hold him off, but the finish line was 200 yards away. Victor planned to simply outpower Cheetah for the last 200 yards, so he poured it on. He knew he couldn't afford to be in a foot race with this man for the last forty yards.

Victor finally caught Cheetah and actually nudged by him. Cheetah hung close—only two steps behind him. These two were giving it everything they had. Cheetah had underestimated Victor's kick, and the finish line was approaching quickly. Cheetah wasn't sure if he was going to be able to overtake Victor.

The crowd was amazed. For the second time in history, the race was coming down to a sprint. This 140.6-mile race looked like it would be decided by less than a second. Imagine an endurance race this long being decided by a single step. Such an ending would make a man wonder for the rest of his life: What if…? What if he had trained one more day? What if he had gotten to bed a little earlier? What if he had eaten one fewer bite of spaghetti? What if he had passed a competitor a little sooner at mile fifteen…What if?

Just twenty more yards and all the agony would be over. Cheetah fought back and was now at Victor's side. The crowd roared and a surge of adrenaline powered both athletes. Cheetah quickened his step. Victor poured it on.

In the end, however, there was just no stopping natural talent.

Cheetah was born fast, so his sprint in the end was just enough to pull ahead and cross the finish line a step in front of Victor. It was indeed a new course record. In one moment, there was both groaning and glory. On the other side of the finish line, both men embraced each other and fell into the center of the field to catch their breath on the grass.

Thirty seconds later, Fieri crossed the finish line.

It would be several minutes later before other pro-male competitors entered the stadium and crossed the finish line, each by themselves, separated by various distances.

Less than twenty-five minutes later, Tanga crossed the finish line to a great ovation. She was all alone. The next woman wouldn't cross the finish line for another fifteen minutes. Both she and Cheetah had set new course records today.

The remaining nearly 2,000 competitors crossed the finish line over the next eight-and-a-half hours. The race continued until midnight. There was a seventeen-hour time limit. Anyone who finished after the stroke of midnight received a DNF (Did Not Finish). All who finished in regulation were greeted at the finish line with a cold, wet towel, hat, and T-shirt labeled "Ironman Finisher." They also received a medallion attached to a ribbon, ceremoniously placed over their heads. It was like being knighted, especially when the finish line Vantex team celebrated each finishing racer by exclaiming, "Congratulations! You just finished the Big Race! You're an Ironman!"

While the racing elite finished, the remaining participants were still battling it out. Sheer grit and tenacity comprised the true essence of this race. It was a classic battle of the ages: man against himself. Every step was torture; the weak-minded would never finish. The ill-prepared would fall by the wayside. As Champion had declared, the secret of the self-disciplines was being revealed. Diligence or sloth; broad or narrow way; part of the many, or one of the few.

Just after twilight toward the end of the marathon, something unbelievable happened to Tenderfoot. At mile twenty-four,

Tenderfoot began to experience pain at the bottom of her right foot. She was determined to run through the pain, but her mind raced as she asked herself why this was happening. She had bought a new pair of shoes for the race. She knew better, but since it was the exact same model as the pair she had trained with, there should have been no problem. Maybe it was the new ultra-thin, ultra-light socks she had gotten just for the race. Anyway, it was clear the new combination was the source of irritation now blistering her foot. She was determined—she was so close to finishing.

However, the pain grew absolutely unbearable. Tenderfoot came to a stop at the last water station at mile twenty-five, which meant the next stop was the finish line. She took off her shoe for relief and to assess how much damage had been done. It was ugly; she should have stopped or let up earlier. Her good judgment had been impaired by the proximity of the finish line. Now she had other problems to think about. What should she do next?

Ace was so glad this race was coming to an end. He had been continuously exercising for almost twelve hours. When he saw the water station marked twenty-five, he said, "One more mile." He slowed for a water walk break when he noticed Tenderfoot nursing her foot. Ace recognized instantly exactly what was happening. He remembered his first race and the pain and the feeling of being so helpless. This was a brutal sport. Every man for himself was the unspoken code. A racer wasn't expected to help others with flat tires or blisters. The race had staff for such things. They would supply a Band-aid, some ice/hot salve, salt tablets, a truck with a spare tire, or a truck to take you back as DNF.

For a second, Ace thought, *Oh well, too bad. I guess that means I win the charity champion award after all.* He threw down his water cup as he passed the station and began to run again. Then he stopped. He heard the words of Doc Mentor echoing through his head. "Ace, you've made one giant mistake. You fell in love with racing. You've fallen in love with winning at all costs. You've lost touch with the spiritual metaphor, which is by far greater and more important. Paul the apostle made his point, 'Physical training has value, but that is insignificant when compared to spiritual impact through practical service.'"

The code served a purpose, and winning was important because Paul had also said we run in such a way as to win. But if Ace had learned anything at all, he learned that winning wasn't the only thing. Personal integrity, making sure things are done the right way—honestly, fairly, and in consideration for others, was more important. Christ's whole message could be summarized this way: putting the welfare of others before one's selfish ambition. It was the golden rule: Do unto others as you would have them do unto you.

Ace remembered how much he wanted help in that first race when he had blisters. True, the service station rendered Band-aids, but he needed a shoulder. The last mile of that race was the most painful he had ever endured. Whether he liked it or not, Ace knew Tenderfoot now. They had talked during the race. She was his colleague and a runner with a mission. Ace knew she had the same type of grit he had. She was way too close to finishing, and DNF would not be an option. He imagined her doing exactly what he had done: hobbling up to the finish line, a slow painful last mile.

Ace stopped, then turned around and made the short journey back to join her. As she attached the bandage, he engaged her in a commiserating conversation and insisted on helping her across the finish line. She tried hard to dissuade him, but Ace took on the posture of Domestique and would not accept no for answer. Confidently he convinced her to accept his help. In fact he was certain that he was one of the only athletes who could legally, within the race rules, help her. His PC status actually allowed him to both give and receive help from other racers. Tenderfoot was in no position to argue, and so the two together began their journey to the finish line. It was quite a sight: a man with a prosthetic leg shouldering a woman hobbling on just one leg of her own. It was a strange new twist on a three-legged race.

Many people passed the odd couple. Somewhere in the middle of that last mile, Fehniecair passed them. Ace thought he recognized him and was certain it was him when he saw the sixty-six written on his calf muscle. As he passed, he asked, "Need some help?" It was clear by his accent that he was indeed foreign.

"Thanks for the offer, but we've got this."

Fehniecair commented on the situation. "Young man, that's a practical way to share the love. Good job. You're almost there." Ace wondered if it was more than a coincidence that he used those exact words "to share the love."

They made their way into the stadium hours after the winners had crossed, Tenderfoot still hopping. The stadium was mostly empty, with only a few hundred people still there. However, people had begun to stream back into the stadium for the awards ceremony scheduled to start in forty-five minutes in the center of the field.

At the moment, the crowd was quiet. Then there was recognition from a not-so-small band of Ace's supporters. Charity had mobilized every friend she had from the church—even pastor Chip was there with his wife.

Part of belonging to the Kingdom Builders Athletic team meant running across the finish line with a fiery, Olympic-style bronze torch. It was Charity's job to make sure it was lit. She handed it to Ace for the final lap. It was a symbol of carrying the light of Christ to all nations. It served as a reminder that the light of Christ had been passed from generation to generation, with hope that the final generation would evangelize the whole world by preaching the good news to all nations.

It was an inspirational sight: a man with a prosthetic leg carrying a torch in his right hand, and a woman hopping on one leg beside him. They started to get a lot of attention. Victor was in the stadium in preparation for the awards ceremony and was especially intrigued. Bruiser was standing next to him and knew the story, and quickly shared what it was all about.

Ace lifted his torch up and looked up at the clock as he and

Tenderfoot crossed the finish line together. It was exactly 12:32:22. Ace smiled. There it was again—the final numbers, 222. He had been sharing the love. Now he sensed heaven smiling down on them.

The next few moments were a blur. The volunteers gave them both the full treatment: water, towel, hat, T-shirt, medallion, and the declaration, "Congratulations! You've completed the Big Race. You're an Ironman!" Tenderfoot's husband and three teenagers were there to catch her.

Big six-foot seven-inch Buddy hoisted Ace upon his shoulders as he said, "Reminds me of when we won the state championship!" Ace bantered back, "Oh, yeaaahhh! Sweetness!" And then Ace reflected a little more about Buddy's friendship. "You've been here for me at all the good times of my life. And good times are made better by the people you share them with. Buddy, I can never say thank you enough for being there with me over all these years." Then Ace lifted high the torch. Charity was excited to reveal the donations pledged throughout the day. She looked up and declared "We are now at $8,300. We raised $1,500 today. Good job! Great race!"

Ace replied, "Actually, you did the great job. I did the easy stuff."

Charity was confident that more pledges would come in over the next few days. When pastor Chip heard, he and his wife told Charity they would give a $500 gift to the project. That brought the total to $8,800. Ace was still hoisted up in the air. He wasn't sure where the rest was going to come from, but he knew God was working a miracle. While his body was exhausted, his faith was strong at this moment. He smiled, scrunched up his chin, looked up and shouted to God, "Unbelievable! $2,000 in one day! You never cease to amaze me!" Then he looked at Charity, " I don't know where the rest is coming from, but I feel certain this church will be fully funded before all is said and done. God will provide. The rest will come in some mysterious way that gives Him even greater glory." Then he pumped his torch-bearing hand toward heaven, celebrating both the accomplishment of completing the Big Race and the glorious amount of funds that had been raised.

Just as Buddy let him down off his shoulders, Ace noticed Oz and Scoob for the first time. They were there for the finish, watching from a comfortable distance. They hadn't been invited by Charity, nor did they have any connection with anyone else in Ace's support team. They had come on their own to see Ace fulfill his dream. Oz had a vested interest and wanted to see the bionic amphibious man race for glory. Scoob had been invited by Oz at his prosthetic fitting the day before.

Now Scoob was inspired and offered his hand to Ace. "Congratulations. I needed to see this more than you know. You gave me hope today." Ace returned the greeting with a big smile, then reached his hand out to shake with Oz.

Oz's curiosity needed to be satisfied, so he asked Ace, "So how did the frog leg work out?" Ace replied, "It made me speedy. In a sense, I leapfrogged much closer to the front. I was fast. It worked exceptionally well. You really **are** the Wizard. And unless I'm wrong, you and Dr. Goodfellow put this together for me and finished in record time just for my race. You guys are like angels! I can never say thank you enough."

"Well, I'll speak for the both of us when I tell you it was our pleasure. We get a lot of joy when we see a practical application of our work change a life. It's exciting to see a life retooled to live with exceptional outcomes like yours. When I see you conquer this challenge, which most able-bodied people are unable to achieve, my life has new meaning. Look at you—you're nobility; you're an Ironman!"

28

THE CRIPPLE CROWN

THE AWARDS CEREMONY was set to take place in the middle of the field with an Olympic-style platform and stage. The American flag was raised on the pole. The crowd began to swell into the stadium.

The crowd seemed to be naturally separated into three groups—on the field were mostly the nobility, on the track were the Vantex, and in the bleachers were the friends, family, and fans. Three concentric circles. Bruiser was the Master of Ceremonies. He walked to center stage and prepared to begin.

Spinsey stood proudly front and center stage between Tanga and Cheetah, her two racers. Because she had invested in both of their lives, she felt like the greatest coach of all. Bruiser called for the men to take their places.

Cheetah stood at the top of the platform with Victor at his side in second place, and Fieri on the other side in third place. They each received their medals and were crowned with a green wreath, a true replica of the ancient Greek tradition. In addition, Cheetah received an oversized prize check for $25,000. Tanga then took her turn at the top when the women were called. The women received the same treatment as the men.

Spinsey was bursting with pride over the accomplishments of her two athletes, at least right up until Tanga and Cheetah had their photographs taken together on the platform. Tanga made the most of the photo op and turned it into a spectacle. This was her moment to bask in glory. Her poses were flirtatious and her famous wink worked for her as the cameras were flashing.

Tanga exuded glamour and passion and used Cheetah as an accomplice. She jumped into his arms so he could cradle her as a man would carry his bride across the threshold. Then she gave him a kiss on the cheek. Spinsey's eyes bugged out. Tanga had crossed the line. Like a cat with her claws out, Spinsey's body stiffened. Her eyes flashed lightning and her fists clenched tight. Spinsey did all she could to contain herself. In her heart, she knew this woman was not good for her friend. Exasperated, Spinsey whispered the thoughts inside her head. *Not her, not her! Cheetah, no… That's not the one you want. Anyone but her!*

Bruiser addressed all the participants. "We have come to the defining moment. At this time, I am asking all finishers to turn your medals over. You may be asking yourself what this means. In short, this moment is the equivalent of being at a graduation ceremony where the moment of conferring a degree is made ceremonially complete with the moving of the tassel from one side to the other. Your new identity includes the earned title of Ironman. Congratulations to each and every one of you."

Ace stood with his crowd of supporters in the grandstands. When he turned his medal over, he received a lot of pats on the back. A single tear ran down his face as a lump filled his throat.

Bruiser wasn't done. He made a special recognition to the volunteers and charity runners. He stated at last count, forty-one charity runners had accounted for almost a half-million dollars raised for various noble causes. Ace's team cheered wildly.

Bruiser concluded. "Folks, this race is impacting lives all over the world. And not just the lives of those who are on the receiving end of these charitable dollars. This race literally changes the lives of those who participate. I want to say thank you to all the racers and tell you how much your courage has inspired me today. May God bless you, each and every one. Good night."

Then it was over and the crowd began to dismiss. Doc Mentor had been there for the ceremony in support of Fieri. Now he was about to complete his second mission as he found Ace. "Hey, Ace, congratulations! That is a major accomplishment that you can be very proud of."

Ace responded, "You will be proud to know that this little engine was powered by the Word of God the whole way. Thanks for the tools and the challenge to hide God's Word in my heart. I think I rehearsed the Sermon on the Mount no less than three times. But I wanted to say thank you for all you've done for me, and thanks for contributing to my church."

"How did you do with funding that project?" Doc asked.

"As of this minute, we've raised $8,800."

"Good job! That's a lot of money. I am confident He will supply the balance."

"I agree with you. The rest will surely come. But, Doc, I'm happy and I'm sad all at the same moment. I mean, I'm done. I did it. And now I'm kind of like the dog that caught the car it was chasing. I don't know what to do next!"

"Pay it forward—find someone and coach them, encourage them, set the example. Get actively engaged with mentoring others and change a life. Your big test just became your big testimony. Share your journey. You've got a lot to share. Take the lessons you've learned and pass them along. The things your mentors have taught you—namely Bruiser, Sage, and even the conversations we've shared. That's the curriculum. Help a man get a morning routine, like we shared together. What's next? Open your eyes. God will bring somebody across your path that you can mentor. And when He does, pay it forward."

"OK, I got it. I think God has already brought someone across my path that I could encourage. But I'd feel a lot more confident about paying it forward if I could count on you for some continued coaching to help me know what I'm supposed to be doing."

"It's a deal. Come see me in a couple of weeks, and I'll help you."

∝

The next morning, Ace enjoyed sleeping in until 8:30 A.M., something he hadn't done for the last eleven months. He would have slept longer, but his body was awake. He enjoyed his cereal, Breakfast of Champions, as he checked his newsfeed to see what was trending.

The headline on the sports section intrigued him. It read "Imposters Cross the Line." Then he saw Cheetah's picture with the caption "Cheetah Cheats." Next to Tanga's picture was the caption "Tanga Gets Tangled." He clicked on the link which connected him to an article that revealed that both Cheetah and Tanga had been stripped of their titles late last night when their blood and urine tests had come back positive for substance abuse. The article explained that the governing body of the Global Triathlon Association began using urine and blood testing in 2000. Because of the amazing endurance and ever-increasing course records, it was suspected that many of the pros were under the influence of a performance-enhancing substance.

However, for years it had been impossible to detect the drug Neatofriturium, nicknamed "Neato Frito," which builds endurance by boosting the production of oxygen-rich red blood cells. During the last year, a new test had made this illegal substance easily detectable when checked with a combination of both blood and urine tests. Both Cheetah and Tanga had tested positive for "Neato Frito." The history on this performance-enhancing drug revealed that it was engineered by a chemistry student at a prestigious state university just before the turn of the new millennium. The thing that made it so clever was what the designer later called "the cloaking device," which made it undetectable, until now, when other chemists finally found a way to trace it.

The news article stated that this year truly would go down as "the year of the cheaters."

Ace stopped reading and thought, *This could have been me. This was me! All my life, all I wanted to do was win at any cost.* This morning, Ace had his integrity. This year's race may be forever remembered as the year of the cheaters, but for Ace it would be remembered as the year that the hypocrite that he'd been had been transformed.

Ace remembered the story Sage had shared with him about the Bible character Jacob and that the meaning of his name was best translated "sly." Sly-Jacob! That rascal had his leg dislocated as a constant reminder that he belonged to God, that his strength came from God, and his victories came from God's strength and not his own.

Ace thought about Cheetah with a bit of compassion and empathy. *Yep, that's me, God's rascal. Except for the grace of God, there go I,* and he said a quick prayer. "Lord, thank you for what you've done in my life. I know I'm not what I ought to be, but thanks to you, I'm not the man I used to be. Lord, keep me in the palm of your hand. I'm no better than they are. I'm prone to wander, Lord. I know it. I feel it." Then he paused with a lump in his throat before he continued in broken tones, "OK, God, I get it. The gift of my leg is my constant reminder that I belong to you, my strength is in you. Thank you for everything. And, yes, thank you for this leg. I suppose without it, we wouldn't even be talking right now.

"And, Lord, have mercy on Tanga and Cheetah, even as you had mercy on me. Make yourself known to them. Use me, Lord, as it pleases you, to make me a channel of your love and truth. Amen."

Then the phone rang. It was Charity, who wanted to share a bit of additional news. First, they caught up with each other on the late-breaking news. Both were clear on the updated outcome, but Charity had something else to share. "Actually, I just got off the phone with Bruiser. He definitely knows about the whole fiasco. That guy is on all kinds of committees. I tell you, once they found out he wasn't going to race this year, they started asking him to run this whole thing. Anyway, he was there till late last night trying to clean the whole thing up. You know, reputation management, damage control for the image of the Big Race."

Charity concluded in exasperation, "It's enough already, Ace. I don't want to talk about it anymore. The reason I called is we got our last thousand for our church from Victor! It turns out that whenever Victor wins a race, he makes a $1,000 gift to one of the charity runner's organizations. Late last night when he discovered he was the winner after all, he told Bruiser he wanted to give to your cause. Bruiser said he saw you carrying the torch across the finish line. Apparently, Bruiser gave him an earful about what our charity is all about. Soooo...Bruiser called me because he knew I was your project manager. He wanted me to be the bearer of good news. We're done! The church is **completely** paid for. So all praise to God. It's like you said: 'God will provide!' Now He's done it!"

Ace was curious. "OK, I'm happy *and* puzzled. I thought we needed $1,200. What about the remaining $200?"

"That would be me. I wasn't going to ask others to give without giving something myself. This is a great investment. I want to be a shareholder. This is a noble cause worthy of making a little sacrifice for." Charity then concluded with a smile in her voice. "It's an honor for me to give the last $200."

Ace was stunned. He knew what this meant because he knew what a true sacrifice this would be for her—$200 was a big stretch. This was like the widow woman in the Bible who gave her last two mites. The widow gave all she had. Charity worked two jobs to keep up with her bills. He figured (rightly) that she had no extra to give.

Ace was choked up as he began to thank her. "Charity, everyone else gave out of their abundance. I know this is a sacrifice for you. You've given your time and now your money. I'm sitting here smiling and halfway crying with tears of joy because of you. You've gotta be the best thing that's ever happened to me. There is no way I could have done this without you. You got this project done! You got it across the finish line! You are amazing! All I can do is thank God for you!"

Charity was quick to deflect the praise, "God did it, not me."

Ace was still filled with so much emotion that his voice quivered as he continued, "Yes, but I feel so blessed right now. You've gotta see the irony in this: I feel like HE has taken 'this rascal' and made me a 'prince' through the gift of a missing leg. Why? To insure I'd stay humble and to keep me usable.

"Think of the insanity of God, showing off by taking the weak and making them strong. Taking the poor in spirit and making them mighty. Showering the humble with His power. And right now I get it! He has given me the privilege of wearing the cripple's crown! This is my life, His strength being made perfect in my weakness."

Ace glanced toward heaven and prayed spontaneously and sincerely. "Father, thank you for this missing leg and all the good it's brought to my life. All glory and praise to you. Amen!"

This is the conclusion of the Parable of the Ironman.

GOD'S GREATER GLORY:

Routinely showing off His power to an unbelieving world by choosing the least likely candidates to do the impossible. For God has chosen the foolish things of the world to confound the wise; and God has chosen the weak things of the world to confound the things which are mighty; and the humble things of the world, and things which are despised; this is what God has chosen; this is true and he has even chosen things which are not, to bring to nothing things that are: Why? That all the glory should go to God and not man. For it is written; He that will boast, let him boast in the Lord.

Cf. 1 Corinthians 1:27-31

Wisbit tip: *You can transform your weak spot to your sweet spot with a dramatic change in perspective, view your every "thorn" as a blessing.*

Wisbit tip: *Your pain has a purpose. A wise man uses pain as a signal to draw closer to God and is comforted. A fool, in his pain, turns away from God and becomes bitter.*

QUESTIONS FOR SELF-REFLECTION

- Could it be possible that if I belong to God, that tragic events in my life, even evil opposition, are allowed for a greater good? Is there any evidence in my life that I believe this is true.
- What's the difference between suffering, trials, and weakness?
- Can you think of other bible verses or stories that illustrate the point God uses suffering/weakness/trials for his greater glory?
- What is a proper response to suffering? Do you agree or disagree with Sage's proposal to rejoice in such situations? See Romans 8:28, Genesis 50:20, James 1:2-4.

The end.

C&   For clarity on the cast, see
the Character Sketches
in the Appendix.

Dak Ruong Church
Vietnam

Built in honor of Robert "Rusty" Eastwood
to fulfill his desire to bring the gospel to the land he had
once bombed

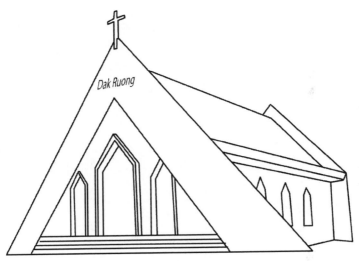

Made possible through *International Cooperating Ministries*
www.icm.org

Partnership with

**KINGDOM
BUILDERS
ATHLETIC TEAM**

Please visit the websites

www.kingdombuildersathleticteam.com

A PRAYER TO GIVE YOUR LIFE TO GOD:

Heavenly Father, I believe God became a man, the Lord Jesus Christ. I believe I've ignored and rejected your righteous ways, even your previous offers of friendship. But now, I want to be re-united as friends. The way I've acted, I don't deserve to be accepted by you. I admit I can't get back to you on my own. I can't ever make restitution. Now, I believe that Christ's death on the cross paid the complete price of redemption. I owed a debt I could not pay and He paid a debt, my debt, He did not owe. I choose to trust in Christ for the forgiveness of my sins. I chose to repent. I acknowledge you as Lord. I will no longer live for myself, but from now on I ask you to help me live for you and your will. I trust completely in your mercy and love. Father, write my name in the book of life, adopt me into your family, and send your Holy Spirit to come and live in me. Give me new life that I might be born again. Thank you for hearing my prayer. In Jesus name, Amen.

RESOURCES

GREAT WITH GOD

A ministry committed to global discipleship. Our Vision: We make abiding disciples of Jesus Christ who make abiding disciples of Jesus Christ. The 222 Principle. We train every mentor to be a catalyst for spiritual growth, empowering others through personal example, tools, and resources to become mighty in spirit and equip them to pay it forward.

Find more at:
www.GreatWithGod.com or get the iPhone app.

ICM

International Cooperating Ministries (ICM) is a nonprofit ministry with a compelling vision: A healthy church within walking distance of everyone in the world.

For more information, visit www.icm.org or call 1-800-999-3892.

KINGDOM BUILDERS ATHLETIC TEAM (KBAT)

Run a Race–Build a Church!

Find more at:
www.KingdomBuildersAthleticTeam.com

APPENDIX

The man to whom this book is dedicated:
Dr. James Pitzer Gills

DR. GILLS IS a deep man of Christian faith. He is authentic; he lives what he believes. I admire him as do most who know him well. He has indeed set the bar high, especially when it comes to excellence, innovation, frugality, generosity, and abundance of fruitfulness. In my eyes, he is simply among the most productive men who have ever walked the earth. He is easy to esteem, as he is the only man I know who is so exceptionally accomplished in the multiple fields of business, medicine, athletics, family, writing, and also great in faith. He was named Amateur Athlete of the Year for 1991, and is the only man on the planet to complete six Double-Ironmans before the turn of the millennium. At his age of seventy-eight, I caught him performing his usual habit (of thirty-five years) of riding his bike to work.

As a businessman, he was elected Entrepreneur of the Year for the State of Florida in 1990. Medically, he was awarded the prestigious Innovator's Award by his colleagues in the American Society of Cataract and Refractive Surgeons in 1996. As an ophthalmologist, Dr. Gills has performed more cataract surgeries than anyone else in the world. He loves to pay forward his physician success with support in medical relief as he has helped to build hospitals around the world.

He has also been a prolific author of books on spiritual topics for many years. His books include: *Exceeding Gratitude for the Creator's Plan; Believe and Rejoice; Overcoming Spiritual Blindness; Resting in His Redemption; God's Prescription for Healing;* and *Discovering the Joy of Catalytic Giving for Christ.* His Christian books have a printing of over nine million and have been distributed to more than 2,000 jails and prisons.

Dr. Gills is married to Heather "Peaches," the virtuous woman listed in Proverbs 31, a woman of prayer. He admits that choosing Heather was his greatest accomplishment and that everything he has accomplished was made possible by her loyalty and support. They have been married over fifty years. Together they have two exceptional adult children (Shea and Pit) who now stand upon their parents' shoulders and proudly move the family legacy of advancing the cause of Christianity around the world. Together they glory in their seven grandchildren.

I'm sure that sounds like a lot already. But it's almost impossible to be that productive with your time and not make a lot of money. Perhaps his most inspirational aspiration is his desire to die broke. That's right! He doesn't like to talk about it, but he is the consummate philanthropist. He loves to give. It's his spiritual gift, coming alongside of worthy, efficient, and effective ministries to lift them up and spur them on. So among all of his accomplishments, he loves to endorse and financially support International Cooperating Ministries (ICM).

Dr. Gills was attracted to ICM by his love for the gospel-leverage it produces. He loves to tell others that he has seen ICM give a 100 to one match for its donors over a twenty-year period. He has come to the conviction that he wants his giving to ICM (for the discipling of all nations) to become his "Magnus Opus" of his already impactful career. He has a legacy goal to see 5,000 more churches brought into existence (ICM has 8,000 church buildings world wide as of 2018).

Now, Dr. Gills loves giving to build churches in over ninety nations and says that ICM is the best leverage in the Kingdom. His personal vision statement, described in his recent book Catalytic Giving, is to get the anointed word of God into the souls of men and mentor them to maturity; and Dr. Gills says no one does this better than Dois Rosser, founder of ICM.

If you're interested in learning more about the ministry ICM, I invite you to visit the website ICM.org.

CHARACTER SKETCHES

Ace: <u>A</u>ugustin <u>C</u>hristopher <u>E</u>astwood. Ace is a common nickname for an exceptional athlete who has a knack for winning. Ace, the naturally great athlete who excels in all sports competition. Augustin means "the majestic." Christopher is symbolic of Christian. Eastwood is simply the toughest name I could think of to make the acronym A.C.E.," so he is named after Clint Eastwood, a famous Hollywood actor, one of the original tough guys of the 1960's and 70's. When you combine all that, you have the majestic Christian tough guy, exceptional athlete. Our star and lead character, "Ace." His character is transformed from halting bitterness by following the coach's prescription to a fruitful disciple.

Mara: Means bitter. Ace's fiancée who dumps him as she becomes bitter about the loss of his leg.

Felicia Taylor: This is an onomatopoeia. If you compress these two words it sounds like facilitator. She is the facilitator of the grief care group. Represents Christian counselors who are committed to helping people recover from trauma.

Chaplain: Christian clergy on assignment in the military who was wounded in battle. Empathetically tries to help Ace see a greater purpose to his suffering, but Ace isn't ready to listen just yet.

Watson: The investigator. Named after the sidekick to Sherlock Holmes. Discerning, keen alertness to small details. He is not willing to let shallow answers rob us of the truth. He keeps digging.

Mr. Reasonable: Real name is Jake Reed. Reed is also a tool of measurement. Reasonable; calculating cost benefit analysis. Only sees the physical dimension and completely misses the Spiritual

Athletic Metaphor. He never joins the team. He has no eyes to see and no ears to hear the gospel. Thus, he misses his opportunity to enter the kingdom and his opportunity is snatched away before it began.

Buddy Bonanno: Buddy, as in best friend of Ace. And Bonanno, as in my best friend, Reggie Bonanno. He represents an unconditional, long-term support system.

Titan: Big, exceptionally tall. Basketball center and triathlon volunteer. Represents all athletes who offer dignity to their opponents and honors them as esteemed rivals. How you play the game is more important than the outcome.

Shoveele: Shover. Shoves Ace to impede his scoring drive to the basket. Represents all those willing to commit a hurtful purposeful foul to insure winning. Represents all athletes who choose to physically fight their opponents, rather than honor them as esteemed colleagues.

Champion: Proven winner. This character is a cross between two great mentors: Dr. Jim Gills (eight-four years) and Dois Rosser who is ninety-seven years old at the writing of this book. Both are going long and finishing strong. Both are committed to making disciples worldwide. Champion represents all coaches who both live and preach the Spiritual Athletic Metaphor.

Doc Mentor: Is intentionally modeled after my admired mentor, Dr. James P. Gills, who is truly one of the world's greatest endurance athletes of our era and also a world-renowned eye surgeon. He represents a master mentor and is the voice of wisdom and spiritual growth. The mentor who models his message of abiding and surrender. See appendix to learn more about "Doc."

Remnant ben Yahuda: Faithful and loyal to the end. Enduring. In this context, remaining true to the original vision of the YMCA. In a general sense he represents all those who faithfully endure. Also reminds of the faithful remnant of the Jewish people. Their purpose, as we heard later from pastor Chip, was to be a source of blessing to all the other nations. Represents all Christians and Jews who have remained faithful to God's purposes throughout the generations.

Charity: She represents a life of genuine love, hospitality and service. Others before herself, she is more concerned in helping others succeed than her own self-promotion. She works at the church as the care director and is modeled intentionally after my wife, Sherrie. She represents the virtuous woman of Proverbs 31, the real PBJ, "pink and black jewel," a woman who is both feminine and yet strong.

Spinsey: Spin instructor, living the Christian life with a wrong set of priorities, literally spinning to keep control. She represents people who have a good work ethic as their top value. Slightly off center, she loves racing first and God is a much lower priority.

Bruiser Le Truce: The bruised one, a Christ figure. He gives his life away (his race spot) so that Ace may find life. He represents the voice of accountability and truth. Uncompromising disciple of the Spiritual Athletic Metaphor. Unyielding commitment to reading and obeying the guide book (Bible).

Domestique: The swim coach from Britain. Domestique is the title of a type of bike racer, who goes before to prepare the way. In the Tour de France, the Domestique team member will take the lead to break the wind, while his teammates benefit as they draft behind. The Domestique usually does not win, but sacrifices his strength so another team member will win. He represents another type of Christ figure, and athletes who are willing to play a primary role, but receive secondary credit. Similar to Charity in that he is more concerned with helping others succeed than self-promotion.

Tanga Bravo: Is the seductress star triathlete. Tanga gets tangled in her pursuit to win. Represents all those who become unfruitful because their love for God is choked out by the cares of the world and the lure of wealth. She is willing to win at any cost, even if it means breaking the rules. God is not impressed with the win or the loss but how you played the game. Nor is he impressed with the amount of gold someone accumulates. His scoreboard is measured in honesty and integrity.

E. Z.: Another onomatopoeia. It sounds like easy. His is the voice of a little exercise could be good for you, but don't sweat it; too much energy expended could be bad for you. The philosophy of the island lifestyle: "Don't worry, be happy." Represents the Christian whose primary goal is pain avoidance, rather than obeying the command: if any man will come after me, let him deny himself, take up his cross daily, and follow me.

Walkie Talkie: He is his name. He represents the workout profile of those who show up at the gym and do more talking than exercise. Represents the all-talk Christian. Faith without works is dead.

Shorty Cuttler: Represents the get-in-shape-quick marketing lie. They sell a hollow way to physical fitness by promising a little effort will do a lot of transformation. Represents those Christians who will not pursue holiness because the cost is too high. So they rely on cheap grace, planning that God will forgive them regardless of their sinful choices. They are willingly self-deceived.

Sloppy Joe: This is an athlete who also happens to be carrying around a lot of extra weight in the gut. Represents the philosophy that you think you can get fit by paying attention to working out but not to your diet. It takes both. Just the opposite of Walkie Talkie. He represents the Christian who doesn't read the Scriptures and yet thinks serving alone is the answer. Works without faith is also dead.

Bobo: Simply formed from the initials of the meaning of his character. Blink On Blink Off. His physical training is marked by seasons of commitment followed by seasons of distraction. Even noble good things can become a distraction. He represents the proverb: good things become obstacles to the better things. The Christian with divided interests. In a spiritual sense, he keeps coming back to the Lord, but his lack of continuous self control, his lack of conviction with godly habits renders him ineffective for kingdom impact.

Faith: Represents the voice of mature Christian faith. She speaks Scripture and she is strengthened by Scripture. She sees by faith what could be and then pursues it. For those paying attention to the cover art, you see the number 888, which is Faith's race-bib number. The number 888 is the numeric value of the name of God, Jehovah, in Hebrew and also for Jesus in the Greek.[25] So the idea is not just Faith, but following faith in the great I am, God Almighty. A character in the distance, a character to be followed, Faith.

Vanna Teia Fair: This is the glamorous life. Representing the illusion that outward appearance is what's important. If you look good, you are good. If you look good you will be accepted. Represents those Christians who allow the cares of the world and the deceitfulness of riches to choke out their fruitfulness. Also honoring with this name one of the inspirations of this book, *Pilgrim's Progress*. The character is named after the famed location in the story, Vanity Fair.

Vintage: An older athlete wearing bib number 144, a biblical number in the book of Revelation, symbolizing the remnant of God who are faithful to the end. The voice of a stinging reminder that God's standards are to be kept holy.

---

25   The Sacred Code by David Teuling. Adding the Greek letters of the name "Jesus" combine to 888.

Slider: Represents the life of one who is willing to make small compromises. A lifetime of small compromises will lead to being unfit to compete (have impact) in the work of sharing the gospel. Represents those Christians who allow the lust of the flesh and friendship with the world to choke out their fruitfulness. Symbolizes Christians who, through compromise, are no longer salty and are therefore no longer *effective*.

Markist: The voice of multiplication. Trumpeting the sound that we need to make disciples who will be able to make disciples. Pay it forward. Introduces the 222 principle. His bib number is 153, which is a tip-off that he is himself a "Theomatician." This is a group of scientific Christian mystics who look for evidence of God's design in the universe and most particularly try to prove the inspiration of the Scriptures through adding and multiplying the numeric value of words.

Deuce Aaron, aka "Double A:" The deacon at the wrong church who also is a personal private athletic trainer. He represents all false teachers who come into the flock of God as wolves in sheep's clothing. They may hide behind titles such as Christian, coach, deacon, elder, pastor, or priest. But Jesus gave this warning: beware of false teachers which come to you in sheep's clothing but inwardly they are like ravenous wolves. You will know them by their fruit. A hint was given as this man comes from the First Church of the Angel of Light (1 Corinthians 11:3). Satan is known himself as an angel of light. He is a liar, a deceiver, a wearer of disguises. He is crooked in all his ways. The fruit of hypocrisy is the chief characteristic of this character. He says one thing but does another.

Marshall: The triathlon race course director and official enforcer of the rules; in that sense he represents God our lawgiver and judge. Somebody's got to be in charge, and that would be Marshall.

Goldie: The golden retriever dog. The ultimate chick magnet. Inspired by my son's dog, Bronson! Here is the formula: take a dog for a walk; make new friends.

Gloria: Tall woman of God. Solves the elusive girlfriend dilemma for the tall Buddy Bonanno. Good things come to those who wait and those who seek.

Fehniecair (feh'-niece-air): Onomatopoeia. Sounds like "finisher" or "finish air." At sixty-six, he represents those who kept the faith, and remained faithful over a lifetime of service. He finishes well. The unknown Christian from Germany who has a car with a 222 sticker on the bumper.

Nowatta Nowie: Another onomatopoeia. Sounds like "no water now." He represents the life of a Christian who fails to care for the regular intake for spiritual nourishment. Things are going well at the beginning, but the fuel needful for the journey is neglected, which results in a race-halting muscle cramp. He represents the person who has shallow roots in faith. They failed to feed their faith and when unexpected difficulty comes they are ill prepared to stand and thus they fall away from the faith. Don't neglect to fuel your soul with daily Scripture reading and weekly worship.

Brian Fieri: Fieri means faithful. He is a faithful disciple of Doc Mentor. Back-to-back silver medals in The Big Race. He followed the coach's prescription and it has paid off royally.

Gizmo: As in someone who is always into the next gadget or latest trending idea. Represents those who seek success in new and novel ideas, and all short-cut philosophies, instead of in the word of God. All too often the church is looking for better methods. God is looking for better men.

Cheetah: Nickname of Chet Wildman who is the fastest triathlete in the world. Also named after the fastest animal on the planet. However, his name has a double meaning and could be listed as Cheater. His last name "Wildman" hints at the problem. He represents all rebels who want to write their own rules. He actually thinks he is above the rules. Pride comes before the fall.

Victor: His name reminds us of Victory. He is the real winner. He represents the disciple who follows the voice of the Holy Spirit as his coach and follows the prescribed plan and thus wins a gold medal. He understands the joy and responsibility of giving. He regularly takes a portion of his earnings to advance the cause of Christ. A clear channel of God's resources will be given more resources. He who is faithful in little will be faithful with much.

Speedy G.: Represents the quick starter who has not counted the cost and is unable to finish the race as it gets longer and harder. A little difficulty and change in the course and they are out. Represents those who have a shallow faith with no deep roots of commitment; these fair-weather disciples fade away when the going gets tough.

Scoob: The Shaggy look-alike from the Scooby-Doo cartoon series. Simply a guy who is lost and living life by accident and because of past trauma, he is without purpose. But Scoob seems to get right in the middle of the action whether he wants to or not. His curiosity is peaked and he is inspired to action. Look for Scoob to make a return in the sequel *Irontorch*.

The Great Oz: Don Osbourne, sometimes affectionately called "the Wiz." This is a creative genius. He represents the ministry of equipping. For any great team, there is an equipment manager and a team doctor/trainer. He serves to make others great by creating resources so they can succeed. He also happens to be a real person who is a very good friend of mine. Don Smith, (Osbourne), "Oz," served as the prosthetic counsel for this book and the prosthetic artist.

Chip Heard Jr.: Another onomatopoeia. Sounds like Chippard or Shepherd junior. Our preacher who is rightly identified as the Junior Shepherd as Christ is the Chief Shepherd. He has two hidden strengths. He pastors a church called the House of Prayer, which is in alignment with Jesus' declaration, "My house shall be called a house of prayer for all nations." Is your church known as being great in prayer? Few are. Use the *Great with God Pocket Guide* to learn how to pray with greater fervency. He preaches the unchanging purpose of God, which is to make disciples of all nations. This is the voice and message of a real mentor, full-time missions mobilizer, Bob Sjogren.

Sage: His name means old wise one, ancient wisdom. Wisdom gathered through a lifetime of experience. He represents the voice of understanding life's purpose through identity and destiny and also the purpose of pain. Sage is modeled after a real man, Dick Woodward, who became a quadriplegic later in life. They say your pain will either make you bitter or better. Dick was bedfast for twenty years, and his pain drove him to greater intimacy with Christ and also to a personal intensive study on understanding the purpose of suffering. He eventually wrote his discoveries in the book *30 Biblical Reasons Why God's People Suffer.*

Lauwiel ("Peaches"): This character is in honor of a dear friend, Heather Gills, wife of the book's honoree, Dr. Gills. She is best known as "Peaches" to her grandchildren. Her character represents loyalty by all who faithfully endure life's challenges.

Chairman: He is his name and in charge of the charity racers' committee. He is obviously the right guy for the job. He represents those who are committed to righteousness and yet flexible enough to receive a creative solution. He lives his life in harmony with his task, as he extravagantly contributes twice to help fund Ace's Vietnam church.

Wendy: Member of the peloton. Her name gives you the impression she can ride like the wind.

Jack Rabbit and **Ray Boltz:** Members of the peloton. Their names give you the impression they can ride very fast. In the end, the idea of going fast becomes more important to them than honoring the rules of the race.

YMCA: Represents a place of making disciples, and therefore symbolizes the American church in a general sense. It is filled with great diversity and led by a remnant of faithful pastors (coaches).

Fresh Start at Grace Baptist Church: Represents a place of recovery for broken people, and therefore symbolizes all healthy evangelical churches that offer practical help to the least, the last, and the lost. While Ace, the character, is not certain about the validity of the program, it's this writers intent to praise all such programs recognizing the vital role they often play in providing a process for the recovery of spiritual and emotional health.

House of Prayer: Represents all healthy churches whose *focus* is worldwide discipleship and the purposeful cultivation of personal intimacy with God for their members.

Pixie is her name: photographer.

Trailblazer: A physically challenged amputee who inspired Ace as a predecessor who competed and finished The Big Race. Whom will your life inspire? Do the unthinkable by faith and become an inspiration to others. With God nothing shall be impossible.

Resilience: Part of the peloton, the voice of encouragement. Every failure is simply a stepping stone to success. The incurable optimist, who turns every adversity into an advantage.

Clay: Younger brother of Charity. So named because he is a moldable triathlete. A great candidate to be discipled by Ace in the exciting sequel, *Irontorch*. A fun novel where the adventures of Ace continue. (In such a novel we might see Ace take a shot at the Paralympics). How fun would that be?

REFERENCES

49 Secrets of Power for Living. Published by the Institute of Basic Life Principles, Oak Brook, IL, 2ND printing 2009, P. 57-58.

Achieving True Success: How to Build Character as a Family. Samuel Smiles, *The Destiny Chart*, Published by International Association of Character Cities, Oklahoma City, OK, 2000, P. 7.

Advanced Seminar Textbook. Copyright 1986, Institute in Basic Life Principles Inc., Printed February 2000, 10TH printing, Oak Brook, IL., P. 49-83.

Gills, James P. *Resting in His Redemption: The Basis of Prayer and the Christian Life*. Charisma House, Lake Mary, FL, 2011.

Gills, James P. *Temple Maintenance: Excellence with Love*. Creation House Press, Lake Mary, FL, 1989.

Kelly, Matthew. *The Rhythm of Life: Living Every Day With Passion and Purpose*. Beacon Publishing, 2004.

Kendall, R.T. *The Thorn in the Flesh: Hope for All Who Struggle with Impossible Conditions*. Charisma House, Lake Mary, FL, 2004.

Koning, Otto. *The Pineapple Story Series*, 1997 Lecture: "The Weapon of Rejoicing." Published by IBLP.

Maxwell, John C. *The 21 Irrefutable Laws of Leadership: Follow Them and People Will Follow You*. 1998. Published in Nashville, Tennessee by Thomas Nelson.

Morley, Patrick, David Delk, and Brett Clemmer. *No Man Left Behind: How to Build and Sustain a Thriving Disciple-Making Ministry for Every Man in Your Church*. Moody Publishers, Chicago, 2006.

Sjogren, Bob. *Unveiled at Last: Discover God's Hidden Message from Genesis to Revelation.* YWAM *Publishing, Seattle, WA, 1992.*

Sjogren, Bob. *Lecture:* "The State of the World 2018."

Smith, Dan. *Profile of an Ironman. Contribution from Lifesport, Senior Coach Dan Smith, Training Peaks, Oct. 2015.*

Teuling, David. *The Sacred Code. Artesian Books, Muskegon, MI, 1993.*

USA Triathlon Commonly Violated Rules and Penalties. Published 2018.

USCWM. Map published 1985 and distributed 2018. Modified and adapted for storyline enhancement.

Wilkinson, Bruce. *The Secrets of the Vine: Breaking Through to Abundance. Multnomah Publishers, Sisters, Oregon, 2001, P. 91-95.*

Wolf, Tom and Pam. *Finding Your God Given Sweet Spot. Xulon Press, 2011, P. 108-120.*

Woodward, Dick. *30 Biblical Reasons Why God's People Suffer: A Month of Devotional for Hurting Hearts.* 2ND *edition 2007. A special publication of International Cooperating Ministries, 1901 N. Armistead Ave., Hampton, VA, 23666.*

ACKNOWLEDGMENTS

CONTRIBUTING MENTORS

To all my mentors listed below: Thank you for taking an interest in me. Your thoughts have molded my life and are found throughout this book. In many ways, I have tried to follow you as you follow Christ. I watch you, I listen between the lines, I think deeply about your comments, I learn from your example and your life stories. Thank you. My life is richer because of you. I consider you contributing authors.

Master Mentors

Dub and Mary Sue Leatherwood (parents), Dr. James and Heather Gills, Dr. David Mayer, Dana Hardee, Matthew Hartsfield, Dois Rosser Jim Clarke, Luke Lloyd, Earl Chantlos, Tom and Pam Wolf.

Teaching Mentors:

Dick Woodward: Your life story was one of the chief contributors of this very book. Your teachings have shaped my life greatly over the last decade. It was a great pleasure to have known you.

Bill Gothard, Bruce Wilkinson.

The Champion Mentors:

Bill Scaar, Coach Benny Carter, Steve Gray, Joe Sherrod, Dave Troutman, Bob Sjogren, Rick Leatherwood, Sam Lombardo, John Nill.

Author Mentors:

Paul Bunyan, Bill Hybels, Otto Koning, Don Richardson, E. M. Bounds,

David Dewitt, Matthew Kelly, Ralph Winter, Gordon McDonald, Henry Blackaby, Oral Roberts, John Piper, R. T. Kendall, Paul of Tarsus.

Barnabas Mentors:

These are my partners, colleagues, friends, and family. I dare not list all their names here for fear of overlooking someone (except my wife) because of a lifetime of contributors. Thank you all. It is a joy doing life together with you. Iron sharpens iron.

Sherrie Leatherwood: You are the most talented, alert, diligent, insightful, and loyal wife ever. Thank you for the virtuous woman you are. You are a true source of grace to me. You reach me by your example. I love you.

Ghost Writer Mentor:

The Lord Jesus Christ in the person of the Holy Spirit.

*Disclaimer: To all my mentors: If you heard one of my characters saying something that sounded a lot like you, it's because it **was** you! I don't claim to have had many original thoughts; just about everything was inspired by one of you as the original source. Thanks for pouring into me so I could pay it forward in the form of this book. To God be the glory.

---

೧෨   For further explanation defining the types of mentors, refer to *The Mentor's Mantle: Best Practices of the Master Mentor*, coming publication of Robert Leatherwood.

36065585R00186

Made in the USA
Lexington, KY
10 April 2019